THE
SHADOW ROADS

THE
SHADOW ROADS

Book Three of the Swans' War

SEAN RUSSELL

An Imprint of HarperCollinsPublishers

THE SHADOW ROADS. Copyright © 2004 by Sean Russell. All rights reserved. Printed in the United States of America. No part of this book may be used or reproduced in any manner whatsoever without written permission except in the case of brief quotations embodied in critical articles and reviews. For information address HarperCollins Publishers Inc., 10 East 53rd Street, New York, NY 10022.

HarperCollins books may be purchased for educational, business, or sales promotional use. For information please write: Special Markets Department, HarperCollins Publishers Inc., 10 East 53rd Street, New York, NY 10022.

EOS is a federally registered trademark of HarperCollins Publishers Inc.

ISBN 0-380-97491-6

This book is dedicated to

Sean Stewart and Neal Stephenson;

artists, craftsmen, friends

Acknowledgments

As usual, there are people to thank: my editors Diana Gill and Tim Holman; my wonderful agent, Howard Morhaim; my wife, Karen, and her family, June, Nori, Don, Lorraine, Michael, and Carlos, who have been a source of tremendous support and assistance during a trying year.

THE
SHADOW ROADS

Prologue

What Went Before

The children of the sorcerer Wyrr did not die, but dwelt for an age in the river as "nagar"; ghostly spirits. The Knights of the Vow were formed to stop the children of Wyrr from ever finding their way back to the land of the living, but members of the brotherhood were seduced by promises of power and long life, and they hid away "smeagh"—arcane objects that could allow the children of Wyrr to return one day. By this means Wyrr's two sons and his daughter made bargains with mortals and appeared again among the living.

Wyrr's children, powerful sorcerers, had fought among themselves for a thousand years, and when they reappeared in the land between the mountains their hatred was undiminished, and they took up their feud again. Thus it was that Lady Elise Wills and a traveler named Alaan became the enemies of a knight known as Hafydd, who had contrived to start a war among the principal families of the land between the mountains so that he might come to power in the ensuing turmoil.

Unable to destroy Hafydd, Alaan lured him into the hidden

lands—into the Stillwater—a vast swamp that Alaan believed only
he could escape. But Alaan's plans went awry when he was
wounded by one of Hafydd's guards, and his wound festered in the
foul waters of the swamp. Alaan would have been caught and killed,
but he was rescued by a stranger accompanied by an army of
crows. This man, Rabal Crowheart, showed him a ruin where
Alaan found a chamber containing a great enchantment—the spell
that separated the land between the mountains from the hidden
lands, and the land of the living from the kingdom of the dead.
Alaan recognized then that the enchantment had begun to decay.

Learning that Alaan was wounded and pursued by Hafydd,
Elise Wills found the wanderer who could draw maps into the hidden lands and forced him to make her a map leading to the Stillwater. She, the Valemen, and Alaan's friend Pwyll, set off, hoping
to save Alaan. They didn't know that map maker, Kai, had also sent
a legendary warrior into the swamp—a near giant named Orlem
Slighthand.

While he lay in delirium from his corrupted wound, Alaan was
approached by an ancient man-at-arms offering him a gem he
claimed had been left for a child of Wyrr, by Wyrr's brother, Aillyn.
Fearing it was a smeagh that would bring Aillyn back into the
world, Alaan refused it, but Hafydd was not so wary and took the
gem, thinking it was a stone of legend that had once belonged to
the great sorcerer Tusival.

A running battle was fought through the wetlands, both between Elise and Hafydd, and between strange creatures whom
Crowheart claimed were the servants of Death. In the end the companies met at the mouth of a tunnel that led out of the Stillwater.
Here they fought a desperate battle, in which the magic Elise summoned almost destroyed them all—but the survivors found themselves again in the land between the mountains, many swept into
the River Wyrr, which seemed to have destinations for them—
though they were destinations none would have chosen.

One

The disk of light stretched and wavered, flowing left then right. *The moon,* he thought. *That is the moon. . . . But who am I?*

Dust mote stars spun slowly in the black. Light began to grow, and he slipped down into the cool, dark depths. He could feel the others here, their numbers beyond counting. Slowly they made their way toward the breathing sea, some so weak they were barely there, others. . . . Others were as strong and clear as the risen sun.

But what are their names? Have none of them names?

Once he had been a traveler. Of that he was almost certain. A traveler whose journeys had become legend.

Once he had gone into a great swamp and battled Death himself.

The bright light faded, and he rose again, floating up toward the waning moon, the faint stars. Something swam by, pale and flowing.

A fish, he thought. But it was not. It was a man, blue-pale, like the belly of a fish, eyes like moon shells. For a moment it paused and gazed at him, sadly.

Who are you? he tried to say, but no words would form.

And then he was alone. He felt himself rising again, the wavering moon growing—so close. His face broke the surface, moonlight clinging to him, running out of his hair, his eyes. He took a breath. And then another.

"But who am I?" he whispered.

"Sainth?"

He looked around, but saw nothing.

"Sainth?" The voice came from a shadow on the water, black as a starless sky.

"Sainth . . . ?" he said. "Is that who I am?"

"It is who you were," the voice said.

"And who are you?"

"I am the past. Perhaps not even that, but only a shadow of the past."

"I think you are a dream. This is all a dream."

"You are on the River Wyrr, where things are not as they should be."

A shard of memory knifed into his thoughts. "Death . . . Death pursued me!"

"His servants, perhaps. Death does not venture beyond the gates of his dark kingdom . . . yet."

"But why were his servants abroad in forms that could be seen?"

This brought a moment of silence, and he felt a breeze touch his face and sigh through the trees along the shore.

"They have not yet appeared so in the land between the mountains, but only in the *hidden lands,* as they are called: the kingdom of Aillyn, of old. Tusival's great spell fails, and the wall that surrounds Death's kingdom is falling. His servants clamber through the breach. They are preparing the way for their master to follow . . . as was foreseen long ago."

"But how can this be? Death cannot leave his kingdom."

"Aillyn . . . Aillyn meddled with his father's spell. He used it to sunder his lands from his brother's. Fear and jealousy and madness have led to this."

The man who had been Sainth felt himself sinking again, sinking beneath the weight of these words. He laid his head back in the waters, blinking at the stars. Each breath he drew sounded loud in his ears. The waters were neither warm nor cool. A soft current spun him slowly.

"*Sainth,*" he whispered, listening for resonance.

Yes, he had memories of one called Sainth. But there were other memories, as well.

Death's servants had stalked him through a drowned forest. Death's servants!

For a moment, he closed his eyes, blotting out the slowly spinning stars. A man, almost hidden in a cloud of screeching crows, surfaced from memory.

Crowheart!

"*Sainth*?" came the oddly hissing voice again.

"I am not he."

"Then who are you?"

A light flickered behind closed eyes. "*Alaan.* . . . I am Alaan!"

"*Perhaps,*" the voice said, almost sadly. "*Perhaps you are—in part. But you were Sainth once, and you have Sainth's duties to perform. Do not forget. You cannot shirk them.*"

The man who believed he was Alaan opened his eyes. "What? What are you saying? What duties?"

But in answer he heard only the soft murmuring of the river.

He floated on, the currents of memories filling him, spinning him this way, then that. How dreamlike some of them seemed, shrouded in mist, or washed out in the brightest light. Some were lost in darkness. Rabal Crowheart he remembered, and Orlem Slighthand. But surely these memories were confused, for Slighthand had served the sorcerer named Sainth, whereas Crowheart was a memory of this life—of Alaan's.

But the currents all seemed to flow together, like two rivers joining to form a new waterway. New, but made up of the tributaries.

Perhaps I should have a new name, the man thought—neither Alaan nor Sainth. But no, Alaan would do. Alaan would do for this life, however long it proved to be.

Waving arms and legs, he turned himself so that his head lifted clear of the water, and he searched the darkness. The Wynnd was broad here, but he could make out a line of trees, poplars, swaying gently in a soft breeze, moonlight shimmering off their leaves.

He set out for the shore, his strength seeming to grow with each stroke. A light, appeared among the trees. It was unlike the cold light of the stars, for this was orange-yellow and warm. *Fire.*

The man who had once been Sainth slowed his pace as he neared the shore. He could see other fires now. It was an encampment, he thought. And then a strand of music wafted out over the water and wove itself into the night sounds.

Fáel. He had found an encampment of black wanderers.

For a moment he hovered out of sight, silent in the slowly moving waters. On the embankment some Fáel men were watering horses in the dark. They must have just returned from somewhere. He could hear their muffled voices as they spoke softly. The horses splashed in the shallows beneath the low embankment, drinking, then lifting their great heads to peer into the night. Their white faces appeared to glow palely in the moonlight. He wondered if they sensed him here, in the dark.

"Nann is distressed," one of the Fáel said. "I have seen it in her face. And Tuath . . . Tuath has not been out of her tent in two days. Nor has her needle stopped in all that time. A vision has possessed her, they say."

Alaan could hear the uneasiness in the men's voices. Even among the Fáel the vision weavers— for certainly that is who they were speaking of—were viewed with a mixture of awe and loathing. Too often their visions were of dark events, calamities pending. Yet such visions had allowed the Fáel to escape or at least mitigate such disasters many times. Thus the weavers were tolerated, even treated with some respect, but they were also feared and shunned—outcasts among the outcast.

"The one with no legs . . . he has unsettled Nann as much as any. As much as that small boy who makes speech with his hands. I don't like what goes on. We should have been gone from this place days ago. Why we remain is a mystery to me. War is gathering, has begun already if the rumors are true. We should flee—west or south—as fast as our horses will bear us."

"Nann is not foolish. She is wise and cautious, Deeken. Bear with her yet awhile. There might be more for the Fáel to do than simply fly."

"We'll not be involving ourselves in the wars of the Renné and the Wills—the wars of men. Our people have taken oaths."

"Long ago, Deeken. Long ago. Nothing is as it once was. Up, you!" he said, clucking at the horse whose lead he held. The two men turned the massive beasts and led them back up the bank, into the firelit camp.

Alaan gazed into the darkness along the shore. Among the shadows there were bowmen watching the river. He could sense them.

For some time he waited, patient as the river, holding his position near to the bank. And then he slipped ashore, silent as a serpent. He was in the central open area before anyone noticed him.

A group seated beneath lanterns stared at him, gape-mouthed. A determined-looking Fáel woman rose and was about to sound the alarm when Alaan noticed a legless man seated in one of the bent-willow chairs. Alaan stopped, as surprised to see this ghost as they were to see him.

"Kilydd?" he said.

The man only stared at him, his mouth opening and closing soundlessly, like a fish gasping for water.

"Go back," the man managed finally, his voice a frightened whisper. "Go back into the river where you belong."

Two

The shaft of an arrow, jaggedly broken off, protruded from the links of mail, a bit of wine-dark blood drying on the polished wood and staining the armor. Hafydd cursed. It had been one of those meddlers from the north who'd shot him—which he would not forget.

He cleaned the shaft with a fold of his cloak, then took hold of the wood. Pain coursed through his shoulder, far worse than when the arrow had entered. For a moment he closed his eyes and let the pain wash through him, like a wave of fire. He focused his mind on the feel of the shaft in his fingers. In a single, slow motion, he drew the arrow out, then doubled over, gasping. He tried to press a fold of his robe against the wound, but the arrowhead was caught up in his mail and stymied his efforts. The world began to spin, and he fought to keep his balance and push back the blackness at the edge of his vision. Nausea shook him, and he broke out in an unhealthy sweat.

After a moment, the pain subsided enough that he could sit up and examine the wound, half-hidden beneath his armor and the padded shirt beneath.

It appeared worse than he expected—the foul Stillwater corrupted it, no doubt. He would have to bathe it in the River Wyrr. That would heal almost any hurt he might have. He covered the wound, ignoring the ache. Rising to his feet unsteadily, he set out into the wood in search of the river, which he sensed was nearby.

Less than an hour later he saw the Wynnd sparkling through the trees. He drank from the waters, and sat for a moment on the grass, exhausted—unnaturally exhausted. With great effort and pain he managed to pull his mail shirt over his head and bathed his wound in river water. Almost immediately, the pain receded, as though it had been driven deep, almost beyond feeling—almost.

He set off, again, along the bank, where a narrow footpath had worn away the covering of green. The breeze was redolent with the scent of pine trees and the musky river. And then a tang of smoke reached him.

Hafydd was not beyond caution when it was deemed necessary. He was, after all, without his guards and not wearing a shirt of mail. And though he could press back an army with his spells, he was ever vulnerable to an arrow, as recent events had shown.

Creeping through the underwood, he pulled aside the thin-limbed bushes and peered through the leaves. Flames crackled, and he heard voices speaking softly. People crouched around a cooking fire—a woman, a man, a child—eating from crude bowls. Beyond them, angled up the bank, an old skiff lay burdened with their baggage, oar blades pressing down the summer grasses.

Hafydd watched them warily for a moment. Watched the woman clean their dishes in the river while the man doused the fire and the child picked a few huckleberries from low bushes bordering the path. As he searched among the branches, the child sang quietly to himself, his plain, freckled face bobbing among the summer-green leaves.

To a man who had seen so many conflicts, they looked like refugees to him—a family displaced by war. By their dress, likely people of little or no wealth, no property, certainly. Tenant farmers.

He decided they would likely not want to help him, a grim-looking man-at-arms, obviously wounded, likely on the run.

Hafydd drew his dark blade and stepped out into the open, grabbing the boy child by the scruff of his neck with his bad arm. If the boy struggled, he would easily break free, so weakened was this arm and so painful even this small movement.

"I want only passage across the river," Hafydd said. "Nothing more. Bear me over, and I will set your child free. Refuse, and I will kill you all and row myself."

The father had stepped forward, but stopped when he realized what he faced—a trained man-at-arms bearing a blade, his manner deadly.

"Don't hurt him," the father pleaded, his voice breaking, hands up in supplication. "Leave him, and I'll bear you across. You need not fear."

"He will accompany us," the knight said. "I'll release him upon the other shore, and you may go where you will."

The frightened father nodded. His wife, white-faced and near to tears, had begun to tremble, so that Hafydd wondered if she would collapse. The knight pushed the boy forward as his father stooped to retrieve his oars.

Caibre's long life of battle had brought Hafydd memories and skills he had never dreamed of. Almost before the father knew it himself, Hafydd could see that the man intended to strike him with the oar. And when he did, the knight easily stepped aside, pushing the boy down roughly and putting a foot on his chest, the point of his blade to the boy's heart.

"And I had intended you no harm. Yet this is how you repay me!"

The woman did fall on the ground, then, or perhaps threw herself forward on her knees. She was sobbing uncontrollably, her entreaties almost lost beneath the tears coursing down her cheeks. Her hair fell out of its ribbon and clung to her wet face.

"Don't . . . ," she cried. "Don't hurt him! 'Twas a foolish thing my husband did. Foolish! I'll row you across myself and offer you no harm."

Hafydd stopped, his sword poised over the heart of the boy, who was too terrified even to cry. If he'd had both his arms, he would have considered killing them all and rowing himself, but he was one-armed for the moment, and the Wynnd was broad.

Before the father could move, Hafydd struck him across the side of the face with the flat of his sword, a vicious blow that drove the man to his knees. Upon his face two thin, parallel lines of blood appeared, and the man swayed, dazed.

"Get up, boy," Hafydd said. "You will sit in the stern with me."

The woman strained to push the boat down the bank, but she managed and scrambled into the bow with the oars. Hafydd put the boy before him on the pile of baggage and took the stern seat, sword in hand.

"Row," he said.

They set out into the river, the slow current taking hold of them. The woman put her back into her work, pulling at the sweeps with obvious familiarity. She was pale and shaken, her hair breaking loose from a braid and shivering in the wind. The boy sat still as stone, his hands covering his eyes.

"There be patrols upon the eastern shore," the woman panted. "The river is watched."

"And why is that?" Hafydd asked. She was obviously trying to ingratiate herself with him, fearing for her child.

"The war," she said, clearly surprised. "The Prince of Innes invaded the Isle of Battle. That is what put us on the river. But we've heard now that the Renné drove him back over the canal, with the loss of many."

Hafydd sat back a little in his seat. That fool Innes wouldn't go to war without him? Would he?

"Is this a rumor, or do you know it for truth?"

" 'Tis no rumor. We left the Isle as soon as the Prince crossed the canal. The roads were choked with people fleeing. We could have sold our skiff a dozen times, but we used it ourselves, to keep safe our child."

Hafydd cursed under his breath. He left Innes alone for a few days and what did he do? Attacked the Renné—*and lost!*

The eastern shore was steep and falling away, trees leaning dangerously, their roots exposed. Hafydd had the woman row south a little, for they were north of the Isle of Battle, she said. Shortly, the bank sloped down, and there they found a patrol of men-at-arms in purple and black—men serving the Prince of Innes.

Hafydd hailed them, and they recognized him. The woman put the boat ashore, silent now, looking warily at the men-at-arms, then guardedly at Hafydd. The knight stepped ashore, tossing his shirt of mail down on the grass.

"I must bathe in the river," he said. "And then I will take a horse. Two of you will accompany me."

The captain of the patrol bowed his head, not arguing.

Hafydd looked back over his shoulder at the mother and child. "And these two . . ." He paused. "Kill them."

There was a second's stunned silence, then one of the men drew a sword and stepped forward. The woman threw herself over her son, where she lay sobbing as the sword was raised.

"No, let them go," Hafydd said, unsure why. Unsure of the odd feeling in his heart. "He is only a boy. Death will find him soon enough."

He was cast down upon cold stone in a place of faint twilight. The creature, the servant of Death, fled into the night, its cry echoing nightmarishly. The claws of Death's servant had poisoned him, he was certain, for he could barely move his limbs, and lay on the stone waiting for Death to come breathe him.

To his right, gray waters lay mercury still, to his left, a shadowy cliff. To his shame Beldor sobbed, sobbed like a child now that his time had come. But he sobbed half from frustration, for he had been about to send Toren to this very place when Samul had interfered; and then the servant of Death had swept him up into the sky. He could only hope that the foul creatures would find Toren, too.

The stone beneath him began to tremble, and a terrible grinding noise assaulted his ears. Above him, the cliff shook, then appeared to move.

Death's gate!

He tried to move, to crawl away, but at the same time he could not tear his eyes away. Here it was, life's great mystery. What lay beyond? No one ever returned to tell. And now, he would know.

The grinding of the gate seemed to continue for hours, a dark stain spreading out from its base. Beldor had managed to wiggle a few inches, and there he stopped, exhausted, his sobs reduced to whimpering.

How vain all of his pursuits seemed at that moment, all of his absurd pride, his boasts, his petty triumphs. He lay there trembling in fear, like every ignorant peasant, his Renné pride reduced to whimpers.

From beyond the gate he heard scuttling and muttered words he could not understand. For a moment he closed his eyes, suddenly unable to bear the sight of Death.

Silence. But he could feel a presence—a cold, like opening an icehouse door. When he could bear the suspense no more, he looked.

A shadow loomed over him, black as a well by night. Not even a shimmer of surface, only fathomless darkness.

"So, we meet at last, Lord Death," Beld whispered, his mouth dry and thick as paste.

"You flatter yourself, Beldor Renné," a voice hissed. "Death barely noticed your passing—nor did life. But perhaps you will yet gain a chance to leave your mark. To do something to affect the larger flow of events." The voice paused, and Beldor felt himself being regarded, weighed. He struggled and managed to gain his knees, where he gasped for breath, his head bowed because he had not the strength to lift it.

"You might be of some small service, yet," the dark voice hissed. "I am the Hand of Death, and I will give you an errand, Beldor Renné. If you manage it, you will be returned to the kingdom of the living for your natural span of years—though likely a sword will see you here much sooner. What say you, Lord of the Renn ? A second life is granted to few."

"Yes, whatever you ask," Beldor gasped, "I will do."

"Then you will deliver this to the knight known as Eremon, councilor to the Prince of Innes."

"Hafydd," Beldor whispered.

"So he was once called. You will tell him that Wyrr was laid to rest beneath the Moon's Mirror."

An object appeared from the shadow and was thrust into Beld's hands. It was hard-edged and bound in soft leather, warm as a woman's skin. A book.

"H-How do I proceed from here?" Beld stammered.

"Like this," the shadow whispered.

From above a dark form fell through the twilight, and Beld was snatched up in the claws of Death's servant. He closed his eyes and clung to the book as though it were a shield that protected his life.

Hafydd leaned back in his chair, staring gravely at the book. Beldor Renné stood by, watching, glad to have the cursed book out of his possession. Just holding it had filled him with fever and dread.

Hafydd put a hand to his temple, the other arm immobilized in a sling. "Have you any idea what you bore into this world, Beldor Renné?"

"It is a book, Sir Eremon. I know nothing more."

"You did not open it?"

"I did not. To be honest, I was afraid to."

"And for good reason," Hafydd observed, still staring down at the open pages. "You could not have read it anyway, for it is written in a language that has not been spoken in a thousand years. It is a long, very elaborate spell. One that, to my knowledge, has only been performed once in all of history—to catastrophic results." Hafydd leaned forward and with great care turned the page, for a moment taking in the text. Beld thought the knight looked paler since he'd opened the book, as though the blood had drained from his face.

There was a ruckus in the hall outside, and the door was thrown upon. In strode the Prince of Innes, followed by two of Hafydd's black guards.

"Tell your guards that when I wish to see you, they do not stand in my way!" the Prince demanded. He was shaking with anger.

Beldor had only ever seen the man at tournaments, but he despised his arrogance. Coupled with the man's obvious dullness of mind, it was an enraging combination. The Prince glanced at him with disdain.

"What is it you want?" Hafydd asked, as though he were being annoyed by a child.

"I want to know if Lord A'denné is a traitor. How we shall prosecute our war, now? What your spies have learned of our enemies' intentions. . . ." This seemed to exhaust his list of questions for the moment.

"Of course A'denné is a traitor. Have him killed—or tortured. Whichever will give you the most satisfaction."

This took the Prince aback. "Should you not speak with him first?"

Hafydd went back to gazing at the dreadful book. "I don't need to."

Innes tilted his head toward Beld. "And what of this one? He is a Renné . . . here, where he can do great damage."

"Lord Beldor?" Hafydd said, still engrossed in the page. "The Prince doubts your loyalty. Take my sword out of its scabbard."

Beld took two steps and pulled Hafydd's sword from the scabbard that hung from the back of a chair.

"Now kill the Prince with it," Hafydd said.

Beld turned on the shocked nobleman, wondering if his own pleasure showed. The Prince dodged the first cut, but Beld did not miss the second time, catching the nobleman at the base of the neck and cutting diagonally down until the blade lodged in the ribs. The Prince fell and twitched terribly for a moment, before he lay still in a growing pool of red.

Hafydd looked up at one of the guards standing just inside the door. "Find a retainer of the late prince and bring him up here. We'll kill him and tell anyone who cares that he was the assassin."

Hafydd closed the book, picked it up somewhat gingerly as he rose. "Leave the sword," he said to Beld, "and come with me."

They walked out into a hallway and in a moment entered Hafydd's rooms. Hafydd took a seat in a chair but left Beld standing. The book he laid on a small table and, from within the folds of his cloak, took out a green gem on a gold chain. He held this up so that it sparkled in the light, like a shard of the river in sunlight.

"Tell me the message again," Hafydd said.

Beldor closed his eyes a moment, and slipped back into the nightmare. " *'Wyrr was laid to rest beneath the Moon's Mirror.'* That is all." He opened his eyes to the light and filled his lungs with air.

"And those were the Hand's exact words?"

"Yes. I'm quite sure. The few moments I spent before . . . that place are burned into my memory. I fear I shall never forget them, waking or sleeping."

"No, you shall not. Call in one of my guards."

Beld opened the door, and one of the silent guards came quietly in, his presence reminding Beld of the Death's gate, for reasons he could not quite explain.

"Send out word. The legless man who goes about in a barrow— Kai, he calls himself now. He must be found and brought to me immediately—unharmed." The guard bowed and turned toward the door. "And one more thing. Find all the local midwives. I require the corpse of a stillborn child." Hafydd nodded, and the man left.

"Prepare yourself for a journey, Lord Beldor," Hafydd said. "I think we shall take Lord A'denné with us as well."

"The traitor?"

"Yes, I like to have one of my enemies in my company—like a whetstone, it keeps me sharp."

"What of the war, Sir Eremon?"

Hafydd looked up from the gem, which spun slowly on its chain. "It is of no concern to either you or me. Let Menwyn Wills fight it if he wants. Let him lose. It matters not at all. We've made bargains with the darkness, Beldor Renné. There is no going back."

Three

The raft spun slowly in the current, tracing a wandering path down the broad river. Upon either bank lay woods of oak, pine, and beech, with poplars raising their tall flags along the shore. Dusk crept out from the shadows beneath the western bank and ran like ink over the still waters. No one among the somber company knew where they were, not even the well-traveled Theason. Only Cynddl and Tam remained awake, watching the shores, quiet in their own thoughts.

"Have you ever known the Wynnd to be so . . . empty?" Tam asked.

Cynddl shook his head. "No, but I think we're on the Wynnd and not one of its hidden branches, all the same." He raised a hand and pointed. Some distance to the south, smoke candled above the trees on the western shore. "A village," the story finder said. "We might even reach it before dark."

As they drew nearer the smoke, a small boat appeared out of the bank's shadow and shaped its course directly for the raft.

"Someone has taken notice of us," Tam said. "We best wake the others."

He gave Fynnol's shoulder a shake, and the little Valeman stirred, looking around, confused. Cynddl woke the others, all of them exhausted and disreputable-looking, their clothes in ruins from their ordeal in the Stillwater and near drowning in the tunnels. Somehow, Prince Michael appeared the worst for his experience—perhaps because his clothes had been so very fine to begin with. Baore sat up and rubbed sleep from his eyes, then plunged his head into the river, emerging with water running from hair and eyes, his scant beard dripping.

Theason stood and surveyed the river carefully, then pointed. "That is the island that marks the mouth of the Westbrook," he said, and turned to face the others. "Theason doesn't know how he will tell your people that he failed, Cynddl." The little traveler shook his head forlornly.

The boat, containing three men, caught up with them easily, but these were not fishermen, as Tam expected. They were men-at-arms in Renné blue. Two of them held bows with arrows nocked. They were not wearing armor—that was almost the first thing that Tam noticed—to his surprise. But then wearing armor in a small boat on the river would have its own dangers: small boats could overturn.

"And where might the river be taking you?" one of the archers asked. He was a big man, with massive hands easily bending his bow. Beads of sweat streamed down shiny cheeks.

"We go to Westbrook," Prince Michael said. "Why do you care?"

"Because there is a war, though perhaps you lot are too stupid to have noticed."

"A war?" Michael raised both hands to his forehead as though he'd been struck by a sudden pain.

"Yes, we've driven the Prince of Innes from the Isle of Battle." He gestured with his arrow. "I'll have your names and your home villages." He seemed to notice Cynddl for the first time. "You . . . you're Fáel."

Cynddl nodded.

"How came you to be traveling with this lot?"

"Good fortune smiled upon me," the story finder said. "I have no home village, but my name is Cynddl from the Stega. You needn't fear. My friends are all from the far north, the Wildlands, and have no side in the wars of the south."

"Is that so?" the man wondered. "You've no weapons?"

Tam's sword was lying on the raft, hidden by the bodies stretched out.

"None," Tam said quickly.

The man squinted at them. "And you've no belongings?"

"We had belongings," Prince Michael offered, "but they were lost to the river farther north."

The man's eyes narrowed shrewdly. "And have you silver?"

The occupants of the raft all looked at each other. "The little we possessed went into the river," Fynnol said.

The man laughed. "Well, at least you've paid for your passage. The river will let you go now. Pass on."

The river sentries pulled back to the shore, and the occupants of the raft took up the crude paddles Baore had fashioned for them, using their only substantial edged tool—Tam's grandfather's sword, which he had given to the enterprise reluctantly.

The ungainly raft lumbered toward the shore, the fragrance of Fáel cooking on the breeze and the graceful curves of their tents visible through the trees. Near the low embankment, upon a round rock like the back of a turtle, crouched a small boy. He stared into the waters and rocked gently back and forth. No adult seemed to be near, and the child could hardly have been more than four.

"He does not look like one of your people," Tam said to Cynddl.

"He's not," the story finder concurred.

"But we know that child!" Fynnol said. "Is that not Eber's son—Llya?"

"He does look a bit like him," Baore said, breaking his silence for the first time in many hours.

Cynddl hailed the archers in the Fáel tongue, and they lowered their bows, calling back to him with relief and joy. Tam could hear the call spread back up into the camp, and though he didn't understand the Fáel language, the name Cynddl could not be missed.

The raft took the soft bottom and came to a stop, turning slowly, still pulled by the current. Tam and the others followed Cynddl ashore, but Prince Michael came reluctantly.

"You do not looked pleased to be here, Michael," Tam said.

"I have been here before." He looked at Tam oddly, a crease appearing between his eyebrows. "I came to deliver a warning . . . from Elise Wills. She had been aided by some young men from the north, and she feared for their safety. They traveled in company with a Fáel named Cynddl. And here we all are together."

"We received your warning, and we did heed it—in degree. And look, we're all alive." Tam gave a small bow. "So I thank you."

Prince Michael bobbed his head.

The small boy, who had been perched on the rock, had fallen in beside them, almost running to keep pace. He stared up at Baore as though he were a great wonder, making Tam smile despite his exhaustion and the events of the last few days.

The elder named Nann appeared, and beside her, in his long robes, stood Eber son of Eiresit. His son ran and took hold of his father's leg, peering out from behind the volume of robes.

"You are all safe!" Nann said with feeling. Her eyes closed to creases, and a small tear appeared. "Theason! You found them!"

"Theason found them, yes," the small man said, not meeting her eye, "but he failed you, good Nann." He met her gaze with difficulty, his own eyes glistening. "Alaan did not escape the Stillwater with his life."

"But Alaan lives," Nann said. "He came out of the river just after dawn, looking like a nagar. But rest and food have restored him."

Theason's eyes glittered. "Thank the river," the little man said. "Thank the river."

Four

They sat in bent-willow chairs beneath the spreading branches of a massive beech. Colored lanterns cast light upon the somber gathering of Fáel and men. Tam still felt fatigue deep in the core of his body, a slight buzzing in his exhausted mind. They had eaten, but there had been no time for sleep before they were called to a council of elders. The lighthearted Fáel were somber that night: Cynddl, Nann, and several others. The outsiders were battered and tired looking: the Vale-men, an unnaturally pale Alaan, Theason, Prince Michael—and to everyone's surprise and relief— Rabal Crowheart, who had wandered into camp an hour before. Even the camp itself was subdued, the murmur of voices and the crackle of fires being all that was heard. There was no music or laughter, as though the appearance of the strangers had brought grief into the wanderers' joyous world.

When everyone had settled, Nann nodded to Tuath. The vision weaver held a large, covered hoop, her white hair and skin, and pale ice-blue eyes stood out here among the dark-colored Fáel, as though she were of some other race—a people that lived among the ice and snows of the distant north.

Tam thought Tuath was reluctant as she removed the cover of her embroidery hoop, revealing her vision. Tam, and everyone else, recoiled at the sight. The light exposed a partially completed creature, with ivory chest and belly like a snake, skin faintly scaled and somewhat blue, a serpent's tail, and, upon its four-fingered hands, dark claws. No hair could be seen upon this thing, and its face was malevolently demonlike—though Tam would have to admit that it was also quite human. It was muscled like an animal of the wild, lean and hard.

"What is that!?" Cynddl demanded, sounding like a man who'd had the breath knocked from him. Tam could see the story finder's eyes flick to the thing, then away, as though he couldn't bear to gaze at it too long.

"I don't know," Tuath answered, pale lips curling back in revulsion for what she'd created. "We were hoping that Alaan might tell us."

Alaan stared at this terrible portrait and seemed suddenly more ashen, his lips tinged with blue, as though a nagar lay just beneath the surface.

"Alaan . . . ?" Nann prompted.

The traveler took a deep breath and leaned back in his chair. "A soul eater," he whispered, then closed his eyes. "A monster. Only one has ever walked the surface of the earth, created by a sorcerer from a spell given to him by Death—or so the tales say."

"Why has this thing appeared to Tuath now?" Cynddl asked. He slouched in his chair, and though he had eaten and bathed and wore fresh clothes, water had not washed away his fatigue, nor had his clothes covered it.

"Because one will appear, I would imagine," Alaan said. "Isn't that what a vision weaver does—sees things that might be?"

Tuath nodded, uncertainly, Tam thought. "It might already exist," she said softly.

"Hafydd has made a bargain with Death," Fynnol said, surprising everyone. "I-I saw it . . . in the tunnels. Hafydd found me and held a sword to my throat, trying to find out what I knew about Elise Wills and her allies." He looked around at the others defensively. "Samul Renné appeared, and Hafydd spoke to him as though they were allies. I thought it was all up for me, but a shadow appeared. . . . Not really a shadow but a darkness that seemed to press back the light. Out of this darkness came a voice claiming to be the Hand of Death. Even Hafydd fell to his knees before it. The shadow offered Hafydd a bargain. He could live for many lives of men if he would deliver two sorcerers to him."

"Sianon and Sainth," Alaan said.

But Fynnol shook his head. "Wyrr and Aillyn," the little Valeman said, causing Alaan to become very still and alert.

"These two are already dead—if they ever lived at all," one of the Fáel elders said.

"That is not quite true," said Eber son of Eiresit. "They sleep, but they are not dead."

"Nor are they alive," Alaan answered. "Not in any way that we understand." The traveler stared down at the ground a moment, his manner stiff and grave. "Let me tell you a tale. A very ancient tale that even the story finders do not know." He pressed the fingers of his hands together and touched them to his dark-bearded chin. "It began with a swan, a black swan who became known as Meer, and a sorcerer who was called Tusival. 'Tusival First Born,' he was sometimes called. Like many creatures of that distant age, time had little sway over them, and they lived on and on, year after uncounted year.

"But one day Meer was wounded by hunters and only just managed to escape. Luck was with her, however, for Tusival found her and nursed her back to health. Ever after, the swan stayed near the sorcerer, watching him.

"One night, Death came to Meer out of a rainstorm. *'I see you watching Tusival,'* Death whispered, *'Tusival who saved you from me. But you are a creature of the water and air, and he is a man and a sorcerer. You shall never know him as you are. But I can offer the gift you desire. I can make you a human—as beautiful as you are now. But by night you will become a swan again—an evenswan.'*

" *'You have come to tempt me, but I know you, Death,'* Meer said. *'What is the price you will ask for this?'*

" 'Your children will be born from a clutch of eggs—those hatched by day will take human form, like their father, those born by night will be evenswans, as their mother will be.' Death paused, staring at her from his dark cloud. 'And they will all be mortal, coming at last into my kingdom, where they will serve me.'

" 'Aiye! You are cruel and heartless!' Meer lamented. 'I will not give my children to you. No, they will live as I do, untouched by age.'

"Death retreated then, a hissing whisper reaching her. 'We shall see.'

"And Meer continued to watch Tusival, something stirring within her that she did not understand. In time, Death came to her again. And again he offered to grant her deepest desire. 'You shall know the love of men,' he whispered. 'You shall know the depths of it and bear you children out of that love.' But again Meer refused him, though not so quickly.

"Finally, Death came to her, saying her mortal children would live many spans of common men, and finally she agreed, for her love for Tusival was great, and the yearning she felt had become a torment.

"By moonlight Death performed his magic, and where the swan had been a woman swam in the waters, her mass of black hair afloat on the surface. She walked out onto the bank, and Death could not bear it. He who was heartless and cold was bewitched by the sight of her, heartbreakingly beautiful as she was. He poured out his heart to her, saying that he had never felt such passion stirring within before. That he was like a man awakened after a lifetime of sleep.

" 'And what would become of our children?' Meer asked. 'They would come to me,' Death said. 'You would all come to me and dwell in my kingdom.'

"And Meer spurned him then, saying, 'You shall have them soon enough.' She went then to Tusival, who lost his heart to her, for he had never known a woman so captivating, and yet, despite her dark beauty, he felt he knew her.

"Soon she was with child, and it was then that she told Tusival who she was and of her bargain with Death, and Tusival cursed Death and vowed to thwart him or to have revenge upon him.

"Three eggs the evenswan laid, and watched over them in both her forms. *'Those born by day shall take human form,'* Death had said. *'Those born by night shall be as their mother.'*

"Two eggs hatched before sunset—boy children, both—but the third was hatched by night, and from that egg came a dark-feathered swan, a changeling who, by morning, became a girl child, as human as her brothers. But the joy of the parents was tempered by their bitterness, for one child was a changeling, and all three would be mortal.

"But Death had not done with them, yet. Spurned by Meer, his wound festered in his dark kingdom. One night he ranged out into the kingdom of the living, and, finding the swan child, Sianon, aswim on the river, he drew her down into the waters to drown and carried her back to his kingdom. But others had seen this act of treachery and told Tusival, who wept bitterly.

"Saying that Death had broken his word, Tusival vowed that he would have his daughter back. Twice he led armies to the gate of Death's kingdom, but both times his army broke upon that cold stone. Bitter and angry, the sorcerer swore that Death would never have his sons, whom he named Wyrr and Aillyn. To this end a great spell was made to wall Death into his kingdom, and Death never again walked beyond the borders of his dark land." Alaan looked up at the others. "When he had made his great spell, Tusival collapsed from the effort, saying, *'There . . . never again will Death set foot in the kingdom of the living, nor see its light nor feel the warmth of humankind.'* But an old man, Tusival's servant in the arcane arts, was touched with the sight, and he was troubled and stared off into the dark distance. *'No,'* said the old man, *'Death will escape in time, and when he does the kingdom of the living will fall.'*"

There was silence among the Fáel elders and their guests. They shared glances, despairing and brief. The whole camp had fallen quiet, so that only the river could be heard, whispering as it wandered south toward the sea.

Nann leaned forward, her chair creaking. A skein of hair had escaped a tight braid and stood out from one side of her face, adding to the appearance of fear. "Cynddl told us that servants of Death were abroad in the hidden lands, snatching living men into the darkness." She paused as though to catch her breath. "Has it begun already? Has Death escaped into our world?"

Alaan was drawn back to the conversation from some distant place. He gave his handsome head a little shake. "No, Nann, not yet, but there is some breach in the spell that isolates the kingdom of Death from the kingdom of the living. There can be no other explanation. The spell is breaking down or Death has learned to defeat it. If Tuath's vision is true, Death will have a sorcerer create a soul eater, almost certainly to destroy Aillyn and Wyrr. How a soul eater can destroy Wyrr, who joined his spirit to the river, I don't understand."

Llya sat forward in his father's lap and began to move his hands.

"What is it?" Nann asked nervously. "What does the child say?"

"He says that *'he knows where Wyrr sleeps,'*" Eber answered, his voice soft and filled with sadness.

"Who knows?" one of the elders asked.

"Death knows," Alaan said, gazing thoughtfully at the child. "And now Hafydd will know as well."

"Why does this matter if Aillyn and Wyrr passed from this world an age ago?"

Alaan rubbed his fingers to his brow. "If it matters to Death, there is a reason. Only Aillyn and Wyrr might have the knowledge to restore the spell that walls Death into his shadow kingdom." He looked over at Eber. "Does Llya speak to Wyrr, good Eber?"

Eber shook his head. "Llya hears only the mutterings of the sleeper. Bits of dream and nightmare, nothing more." The man drew his son closer, within the circle of his arms, as though he would protect him.

Llya must have understood the question, for he began to move his hands. Eber watched a moment, then translated. "He says the sleeper does not hear. He is like Llya, in this."

The gathering was silent a moment as everyone was drawn into their own thoughts.

"Where does Wyrr sleep?" Cynddl asked.

"I don't know," Alaan replied. He looked to Llya, but the boy shook his head.

"Then there is only one person who might answer that," Alaan said, "if she still lives." He rose to his feet. "I have rested long enough." He bobbed his head to Nann in a small bow. "I must make a journey now, before Hafydd can unleash the soul eater—a dangerous journey."

"But what can this thing do?" Tam asked. He pointed a finger at Tuath's disturbing creation. "If it seeks sorcerers who have long passed from this world, why should we fear it?"

"Death has not sent this thing after Aillyn and Wyrr for no reason. He means to escape his prison and tear down the world we know." Alaan drew himself up, and Tam could sense his resolve. "You don't understand the danger. Only once before was a soul eater created, and it slew the great Tusival and dragged his carcass back through Death's gate. This thing is monstrous. As pitiless as a viper. It is a bringer of death. If I can't stop it, if I can't find the places where Wyrr and Aillyn have been laid to rest, then it will have them, and there will be no hope of repairing the spell that walls Death into his kingdom."

"But how can Wyrr and Aillyn be any threat to Death?" Cynddl asked.

"I don't know," Alaan said, and he looked thoughtfully at Llya. "Keep that child safe at all costs. I will be gone at least a fortnight. Perhaps longer."

"Will you go alone?" Crowheart asked, speaking for the first time that night.

"It will be a dangerous journey," Alaan said. "The most perilous I have undertaken, but I will ask no one to accompany me, for I won't have their fates on my conscience."

"I will go, all the same," Rabal said with finality. He sat back in his chair, as at ease as a man who'd just volunteered to walk to town.

"I'll go," Cynddl offered. "You'll need an archer if the way is so perilous."

"I'll bring my bow as well," Tam said. "There is no going north for me now, not with what I've learned." He turned and looked at his fellow Valemen. "I'm sorry, but there is no choice for me."

"Well, I won't be left behind because I'm the only one with common sense," Fynnol said, but his manner belied his words. He looked haunted and frightened.

"I'll stay here," Baore said, "for I have offered my service to Lady Elise Wills."

Prince Michael stood. "If they will have me, I will go with Alaan and the others."

"I would gladly take you, Prince Michael," Alaan said. "But if you truly oppose Hafydd, then your knowledge will be needed by the Renné. You must stay and offer your service to Lord Toren, or whoever commands the Renné forces."

"Against my own father . . . ?" the Prince said softly.

"He has allied himself with Hafydd," Alaan answered. "How can you choose otherwise?"

The Prince nodded and hung his head.

"We must go into Westbrook, this night," Alaan said, clapping his hands together. "We'll need to find almost everything for our journey—horses, weapons. I leave at first light."

Five

She felt as though she were being torn in two.

"I'm as divided as my appearance," Llyn whispered.

The night air required a light shawl, and she drew this close around her where she sat, hunched as she would never normally be. Her thoughts jumped between two men—both of whom were gone—missing. Yet they were ever present in her thoughts.

If only one were to return, she could stop feeling so divided. At this thought, which had appeared not for the first time, she shook her head.

This was all ridiculous. Toren did not feel toward her they way she did toward him. He did not have the feelings for her that Carral did. How foolish she was being!

Her head knew this. But feelings were not wise. That was the sad truth of them. Feelings made fools of the wisest, even the eldest. They did not care if you were noble or if you were an uneducated costermonger. All were treated the same—fools in their turn.

And yet her feelings for Carral were not feigned. They, too, were strong. And he felt the same, and even more so—she could sense it.

Unlike Toren, he would never see her face, never look upon her with horror, as did all who saw her. No, all of her thoughts and feelings for Toren were foolish, utterly misplaced. She had no doubt of this.

Then why could she not put Toren out of her mind? Out of her heart?

"You sit up late, my lady," a familiar voice said.

Her breath caught. "Have you not injured me enough, Alaan?"

"More than I ever meant to. No apology will suffice for what I have done." He was in the dark, some dozen feet away. She, too, was in the shadow of a tree, hidden even from starlight.

"Then why are you here?"

"To offer my humble apologies, even though they will mean nothing."

"I do not accept them," she said firmly. "Begone."

But he did not go. She could sense him there, lurking in the darkness.

"What is it you want of me, rogue?"

He shifted from foot to foot. "There is a man here in Castle Renné—he is called Kai—"

"Yes, the man in the barrow. I have heard all about him."

"You can't begin to know Kai's story. His life has been longer than any mortal man's. Had you heard that?"

"I had not. . . . How would you know this?"

"Because my memories, Lady Llyn, stretch back to times forgotten. To times when the Kingdom of Ayr was a wildland, a vast forest we called Tol Yosel—the River Lands. The forbears of the Renné and the Wills were hunters, or fishers of the great river— later called the Wyrr, after my father."

She tugged her shawl closer, as a chill seemed to wash through her heart. "You frighten me, rogue," she said. "Tell me no more. I do not wish to know why you have come. Leave me in peace."

"Peace is no more. We are at war." He took a few steps across the walkway, gravel scuffing beneath his feet. His voice seemed to have aged; though melodious yet, it was heavy and world-weary. "You know that Hafydd is a sorcerer."

"I know that *you* are a sorcerer!" she said angrily.

He did not respond right away, and when he did his voice was quiet, conciliatory. "Kai cannot fall into the hands of our enemies. Hafydd cannot find him. It is of the utmost importance."

"Why?"

"You would not believe me if I told you."

"You do not think me intelligent enough to understand?"

"I think you too intelligent, Lady Llyn. That is why you wouldn't believe me."

"You are a flatterer and a rogue. Where is it you go now?" Llyn asked, not sure why.

"I have a task to complete, and then I go to war, I think."

He stood still a moment, as though expecting her to speak.

"Luck to you then, Alaan," she said, feeling confused and weak, unable to maintain even feelings of anger.

"Luck to us all, Lady Llyn." But he did not go. She could hear him breathing, almost, she imagined, hear the beating of his heart. "May I offer an observation?"

"Of what?" she asked apprehensively. He had never asked for permission to speak his mind before.

"Of Lady Llyn."

"You may not!"

She imagined the shadow gave a slight bow and turned away again, taking a few purposeful strides.

"What is it?" she called out. "What is it you would say?"

He stopped, farther off, now. For a maddening moment he said nothing. Llyn felt herself lean forward, holding her breath, her heart racing.

"You shall regret this choice you've made, Lady Llyn. I will tell you this—when you stand before Death's gate you will wish you had lived, for it is a place of regrets." He hesitated, then said very quietly, "You will wish you had lived."

And he was gone.

For a moment she sat utterly still, unable to rise, as though the wind had been knocked from her. And then she was striding toward the stairs. She snatched up a lantern that stood there and went quickly down the path Alaan had taken. He was not to be found. But then she stopped. There, beyond the doveplum tree was a narrow cleft in the in the shrubbery that she knew had never been there before. She stared into this dark void, the light dancing as her hand trembled. There was a path into her garden! She almost felt an urge to walk down it, to see where it led. But she only stood and stared, her arm quickly tiring as she held the lantern aloft.

In a moment she turned and hurried away, breaking into a run. She dashed up the stairs and slammed the door behind her, almost dropping the lantern to the door.

"Your grace?" came the voice of her maid of the bedchamber. "Is something wrong? Your grace is as pale as a cloud."

"Call a guard. Quickly!"

Two guards came, at the run, and Llyn's servant led them down into the garden.

"It is just here," Llyn called from a shadow, as the guards approached the place where the path had opened. The two guards stumbled into the bushes, breaking branches and trampling the flowers. Llyn drew nearer and watched them go, their lantern growing smaller and dimmer, as though they walked off into a wood. And then it disappeared altogether, though there was a wall not three yards away.

It was some hours later when the two guards returned, looking flustered and out of sorts. They had followed the path into the wood for some distance, but when they tried to retrace their steps they could not. Instead, they found themselves several furlongs away, near the river—and they had not walked a tenth that distance they were certain.

In the garden the path could no longer be found.

Llyn shut herself up in her room and bolted the doors, looking around as though the walls might open up, or a man appear out of thin air. That night she did not go to bed but sat up, awake, feeling as though she were being torn apart, like everyone in Castle Renné could walk unannounced into her little kingdom.

For many hours she paced, forth and back, like an animal in a cage. Finally, she stopped before the window where her reflection floated, faint and ghostly, against the night. She turned her face so that only the good side could be seen, peering out of the corner of her eye.

Half a beauty, she thought.

Very slowly she turned her head, seeing the teeth clench and the lips turn down, bracing herself. The ruined landscape of her face appeared; the eye with its lid greatly burned away, the bubbled skin across her cheek, red and coarse. Even her lips were reduced to thin red lines, as though someone had made her mouth with the haphazard slash of a dull knife.

She realized the thing floating in the dark glass looked like a creature out of nightmare. "You will have no pity from me," she whispered to the creature and a tear rolled down its ruined cheek.

Six

They did not wait for morning but set out by the light of the waning moon, which lit the road faintly and made monsters of tree stumps and spies of every bush. Above them, a small flight of crows swarmed from tree to tree like a wayward breeze. Alaan set a good pace, as though the shattered moon was bright as the morning sun, and the night passed with hardly a word between them. Many times they dismounted and led their horses through shadow, and twice Alaan used a flint to light one of the torches he carried. The smell of burning pitch assailed Tam's nostrils, but a small province of light spread around them. Beyond this, the kingdom of night lay hidden.

"The land between the mountains is behind us now," Alaan said quietly, "but we mustn't relax our guard. Once I've opened a pathway it remains open for some time. We could be followed."

Tam had not asked where they were going, assuming it was into the hidden lands, and any destination there would mean nothing to him, but as their horses trotted along the dark road the Valeman pressed his mount forward, drawing up beside Alaan.

"Where is it we go, Alaan?" he asked. "What place could be more perilous than the places we have been?"

Alaan did not answer right away, but kept his gaze fixed on the dark ribbon of road. "We go into the borderlands of Death's kingdom, Tam. A place from which only one man has returned."

"Who? Who returned from Death's kingdom?"

"No one who passes through the gate returns, but I went once into the borderlands. We will try our luck again." He glanced up at Tam, his face ashen in the moonlight. "I will tell you honestly, Tam— Death will not suffer our presence there. He will send his servants to find us."

Tam let his horse drop back, falling in behind Alaan. He found himself wishing that he'd never left the Vale of Lakes, that he was there still in the late-summer light, walking through the ripening grain or drawing water from the spring that murmured the names of newborn children—or so it was said. Anywhere but following Alaan to this place he had named.

They carried on by torchlight, stumbling over rock and root, until faint light began to devour the shadows, and the stars overhead snuffed out, one by one. By a small lake, Alaan stopped to water the horses and let everyone rest. Cynddl kindled fire, and they made a meal as the morning spread west across the world.

Alaan had produced enough gold that night to buy them horses and tack, arms and supplies. No one asked where this wealth had come from. Nann had given them new bows, and Tam decided to try his, stringing it for the first time. Light reflected off the polished grain of the yaka wood, as he nocked an arrow and drew back the string. The sound of an arrow hissed over the grass, followed by a sharp *thwack* as it lodged in the bark of an old butternut.

"You won't get that one out Tam," Cynddl said. "The grain will be too tight and old."

"I took care not to shoot it that hard. How is your new bow, Cynddl?"

In a moment there was an archery contest under way, with everyone but Alaan and Crowheart involved. Tam noticed that Alaan watched over them without a hint of a smile, his eyes darting often to the tree line, then along the shore of the lake.

He is a wary traveler, Tam thought. And we should take a lesson from that.

Cynddl was the best archer that day, though only slightly better than Tam. Fynnol came third, but did not seem to mind, as the competition was very stiff, and he had acquitted himself well.

"Time to go," Alaan announced, as Fynnol proposed a rematch.

Their horses had been grazing nearby, and were soon saddled and packed again. As Tam tightened the girth strap on his horse, Fynnol and Cynddl came near.

"So what did Alaan say last night?" Fynnol asked quietly. "Did you ask him where we go?" He stroked the nose of his horse, which he had positioned to shield their conversation from Rabal and Alaan.

Tam lengthened one of his stirrups, the worn leather warm and supple in the sun. He realized he did not want to be the bearer of this news. "We go into the borderlands of Death's kingdom, Fynnol."

Fynnol blinked several times. "But no one returns from Death's kingdom."

"Alaan said we will not pass through the gate—and that he made a journey there . . . once." Tam hesitated. "Dangerous, but not more so than other places we've been." He tried to smile reassuringly, but neither of his companions appeared to be reassured.

By the time they set off around the lake and up the slope into a shady wood, the morning was advancing. Beyond, Tam thought he could make out hills, all but obscured by haze.

A whole morning's toil was needed to break out of the trees. The wood began to thin, then turn to scattered pines and firs. Weather-worn rocks broke through the surface, here and there, like the backs of ancient whales. And then the tree line was behind them.

They were on the side of a low, rounded mountain, the world spreading out below.

For a moment, they all stopped to let the horses catch their breath. They had traversed the slope back and forth, not attacking it directly, but even so, the climb had been difficult. An empty wind blew at this elevation, and the only sound was the occasional call of a distant crow.

"Well, Tam," Fynnol said, breaking the silence, "we set out to trade for horses and look! Did you ever expect to own ones as fine as these? And they were free."

"Oh, I think you've paid dearly for your horses," Alaan observed.

"Let's hope the price will not be more than we can afford," Fynnol answered quickly.

On the shoulder of the mountain, crows seemed to be the only animals. A few were always near at hand, but many more could be seen at a distance, perched on the branches of stunted pines or dotting stacks of lichen-yellowed rocks.

Prince Michael had told Tam that his company had been attacked by an army of crows in the Stillwater, and he'd displayed the scars on his face and hands to prove it. Tam looked over at Crowheart sitting on his horse, staring out over the lands below. The horses all seemed to perk up their ears when Crowheart was near, as though they listened for him to speak. He had a way with animals, that was certain, speaking to them quietly, calming them with a touch of the hand. Tam only hoped that he had control of his crow army, for their bills looked fearsome.

A dark bird lit on the branch of a fire bush. Tam caught the movement out of the corner of his eye and thought at first it was another crow. But the nearby crows all took to wing, crying out in alarm. And then Tam heard, *whist, whist.*

The little bird hissed loudly, but it didn't seem to be scolding any of them, for it looked pointedly out over the distant lowlands.

Cynddl's hand shot up. "There!"

Far below, by the small lake where they'd rested, a dozen riders traversed the open meadow. Fynnol cursed, but Alaan sat impassively on his horse, his eyes fixed on the riders.

"I feared as much," he said grimly. "Hafydd has many spies. Some must have been watching the Fáel encampment." He stared for a moment more, then turned his horse but paused before pushing on. "They would catch up with us, *now*," he said looking over his shoulder. "There are greater dangers in these lands than Hafydd's spies. Beyond this mountain is a wide valley that we *must* traverse. There is no way around it. I'd hoped to wait and cross it at first light, but we may be forced to travel by darkness now. Keep your weapons to hand." He spurred his horse and set off up the slope.

The whist leapt into the air, circling up, until it became a black speck in the sky—a fragment of night lodged in the blue.

They hurried on, pressing their tired horses up the mountainside where cliffs, broken and jagged, loomed over them. Tam glanced up from guiding his horse over the uneven terrain. There was, no doubt, a way among these, or Alaan wouldn't be leading them on, still he didn't like their situation. He twisted a bit in his saddle, the leather creaking in complaint. The riders were just disappearing into the trees below, having rounded the lake.

Tam felt a sudden familiar tightening in his stomach. Memories of the black guards pursuing them down the Wynnd, of the fight at the ford at Willowwand, of the night Baore was struck by an arrow beneath the north bridge. He pulled a drinking skin from his saddle to put a little moisture back in his mouth, suddenly dry as sand. And what was this Alaan was saying about the valley beyond?

The base of the cliff was a jumble of broken rock, some pieces larger than barns. Alaan led them among these, never once having to double back. Tam wondered if he'd been here before, or if this was his arcane sense that found paths where other men couldn't. Alaan never said that he created paths but always that he "found" them. As though they were there all along but hidden from others.

They were forced to dismount and lead their horses over a field of stone, but only Alaan's sorrel and the dark bay Crowheart rode went along willingly. Twice Crowheart turned and spoke to Fynnol's horse when it balked, and then the gelding followed docilely.

They picked their way among house-sized boulders, crows gathering now in numbers on the tops and on ledges. The crying of the birds in the hollow wind added a sense of urgency, and Tam hurried on, feeling a prickling on the back of his neck, as though the men behind were gaining—within arrow range.

Don't be a fool, he told himself, *they will take some time to climb that hill, even if they don't spare their horses, as we did, and go straight up.*

He wondered who these men were. Certainly it was Alaan they were following. Did they know he was a sorcerer? Surely they must. Did this not intimidate them at all, or had Hafydd taught them ways to deal with Alaan?

Of course Tam still had no idea of what these children of Wyrr were capable. Hafydd had revealed himself a little in the Stillwater, but Alaan was still a mystery. He could travel paths no one had ever seen into lands unknown. He was a formidable swordsman and far stronger than he appeared, Tam was sure. But could he match Hafydd's control of fire? Or Elise's apparent command of water? Tam hoped there was more to Alaan than he'd revealed so far. They would have need of all the arcane knowledge they could find to fight Hafydd, he was sure of that.

Almost at the base of the cliff, Fynnol called out to Alaan, pointing up. There, silhouetted against a quickly clouding sky, stood a man. Tam blinked once, and when he opened his eyes, the man was gone. Alaan cursed, but went on, offering no explanation.

Tam felt his anxiety increase dramatically. Who had that been atop the cliff? Alaan did not seem pleased, whoever it was. Tam loosened his sword in its scabbard and pressed on, his eye flitting over the landscape as though the very rocks threatened them.

Their efforts brought them to the foot of a narrow draw that wound up through a deep cleft in the broken cliff. A game path clawed up the steep draw, meandering from one side to the other, and Alaan urged his horse up this.

"Tam," the traveler called, looking back once, his face disturbingly apprehensive. "Give your horse to someone. Take a bow and follow behind. We need a rear guard."

Tam took a bow and quiver and gave the reins of his horse to Crowheart, who was already leading his own mount and a packhorse. Rabal made a quick string of his charges and set off after Alaan, Fynnol close behind. Cynddl took his own bow and quiver from his saddle and placed himself just ahead of Tam, where he kept looking back warily. Tam could see sweat on the story finder's brow, his gray hair plastered tight to his forehead.

"If you see any movement, Tam, I have my bow ready."

"I'm just as worried about men ahead of us, or overhead," Tam said, glancing up. "Certainly the riders who follow are two hours behind us."

"I don't think so," the story finder said, puffing as they climbed. "Alaan made sure that we traversed back and forth across the face of the hill, saving our mounts, but these men saw us and will come straight on. Their horses will be tired, and perhaps they will be too, after they've led much of the way on foot, but they are likely not far behind now."

"Then hurry on, Cynddl," Tam said, "I've seen enough of Hafydd's guards to last me a lifetime."

Tam glanced up, wondering, unable to suppress a feeling that rocks or arrows would come raining down on them at any moment.

Before they reached the crest the first man appeared behind. He was horseless and carrying a bared blade that glittered in the sun. Tam called to Cynddl and heard the word pass up the line to Alaan. They pressed on more quickly, all of them gasping for breath now, unable to speak. Tam stumbled, trying to look back and forward at the same time. He bloodied his knee, but pulled himself up and hobbled on.

Another man appeared below, a bow in his hand. Above him

Tam could hear the panting horses, hooves clattering over frost-shattered stone.

Another archer appeared and let an arrow fly.

"They're shooting at us!" Tam called up, watching the high arc of the arrow. It plummeted down toward them but well wide, having been caught by a breeze above the walls of the draw.

"Shoot back," Alaan called, hardly able to spare the breath.

Tam stopped and took aim. He was shooting downhill, which was never easy. He might waste an arrow to find the range. He drew back the string, finding the bow stiffer than his last. The arrow flew down the draw, the Fáel bow every bit as good as its reputation.

The men at the bottom scattered as Tam's arrow passed among them, but he thought no one was hit. He could see heads rising up above stones and shrubs. That might slow them a little.

Tam turned and hurried to catch up with his companions. Cynddl had given his horse to Fynnol and came back to join Tam, bow in hand, his young-old face drawn tight with concern, gray hair plastered to his sweating brow.

"Shall we make a stand here for a while and let the others reach the crest?" Tam wondered. He gazed down the draw, where there was movement among the stones.

"Alaan says to keep them back but not to fall behind." Cynddl pulled back his arrow and let it fly, then quickly nocked another. "Alaan's attention appears to be drawn up, in the direction we're going, as though the threat from below is not the real concern."

Tam glanced at the story finder, then back down the draw. "That's not what I wanted to hear."

"Well, perhaps I'm wrong," Cynddl said. "Let us hope so."

The two scrambled up the draw, their eyes darting back and forth between the path and the men below. Tam tripped again and had to catch himself with a hand. Nothing was broken but an arrow, and he quickly had another from his quiver.

The draw narrowed around them, gray-brown ramparts of stone jutting up to either side. The path was no longer straight, but curved and turned back and forth, as though cut by a meandering river. Horses and men bobbed up the path, the sound of shod hooves echoing off the walls.

Alaan stopped, and called down, "Tam? Cynddl? Can you stop them at the bottom of the narrows for a time?" He took two deep breaths. "Hold them back as best you can, but try to keep yourself out of sight, so they don't know if you're there or not. The moment they think you're gone, they'll rush up the slope."

"Go on," Tam called. "Leave these men to us."

Tam and Cynddl hid themselves as best they could at the bottom of the narrow section, stepping out every minute or so to loose an arrow at the figures below. Tam could see them running between boulders, hiding themselves for a moment, then dashing to the next place of safety. There was little chance that they would be hit at this distance, but Tam and Cynddl were excellent archers and kept their pursuers fearful, for they never missed by much.

Cynddl leaned out from behind the stone wall, gazing down the draw. His whole manner was catlike, Tam thought, poised to pounce or run. The story finder dressed as he had when they traveled down the river—in Fáel clothing, though the colors were mute—greens and browns.

He stepped out into the opening, sent an arrow hissing down the draw, then jumped back behind the wall of stone.

"How long do you think we should stay here?" Tam wondered.

Cynddl glanced up the narrow path between towering stone walls. "I don't know. How long would it take them to reach the crest?"

Tam shrugged. He sent an arrow down the draw, narrowly missing a man who dived behind a pile of stone. "We've almost reached a juncture here. If these men get any closer, we'll start hitting them." Tam glanced up the cleft behind. "They'll almost certainly try to rush us, or we'll pick them off one at a time."

"Yes, that makes sense," Cynddl said. "Once they've worked their way up to that little stand of pines, we should turn and run."

Tam was surprised at how patient they were, considering that the men making their way up the draw certainly meant to kill them. When they left the Vale he would never have expected that, in a short while, he would be so composed under attack. But since leaving the Vale his life had been in danger more times than he cared to count. Passing through the crucible had changed him.

Crows, perched on narrow ledges above, began to caw and flutter their wings.

Fynnol appeared, running. "Come up now, as quick as you can." He didn't await an answer, but turned and dashed back up the way he'd come.

"Your cousin had a sword in hand," Cynddl observed.

Tam nodded. Both he and the story finder stepped out into the opening and fired at men leaping behind rocks and bushes. Without a word, they turned and sped up the draw. The slope was steep, and they were soon gasping for breath, forcing themselves to go on. The walls of the cut snaked up, then suddenly opened. Tam glanced up and saw the others not far off, the crest hovering just above them. They appeared to be waiting, though their attention was focused upward, and all bore arms.

When Tam finally caught up with the others they barely glanced his way, keeping their gazes on the crest. A massive man stood there, as large as Orlem, an enormous bow in his hands. Another, just as large, walked up beside him, bearing a staff that looked like it had once been the trunk of a substantial tree. The two near giants stared down on the smaller men below, their faces set and hard.

"My eyes are playing tricks?" Tam said, barely able to gather his breath.

"No, they're the Dubrell: Orlem's people," Alaan said softly.

"There are more like Slighthand?"

"There is only one Slighthand, but this is the race from which he sprang."

"What do they want?" Cynddl asked. "We're about to have Hafydd's spies on our backs."

"Yes, we're caught between the hammer and the anvil. The Dubrell want us to go back, but we cannot. I'd hoped to cross their lands before they became aware of us. They don't look kindly on outsiders."

"That isn't particularly comforting," Fynnol whispered, rocking from one foot to the other, an arrow drawn and ready to shoot. "If we stay here, we're going to be fighting a company with more than double our number. Can you not speak with these giants?"

"They don't speak with outsiders. They just drive them off."

Fynnol kept glancing nervously down the draw. Around them a small army of agitated crows cawed, their dark eyes glittering in the dull light.

The giants above wore roughly woven cloaks of gray, and leggings bound with leather thongs. Their hair and beards were earthy brown and long, faces turned to leather by wind and sun. There was so little expression in those faces that Tam thought they looked like statues.

Crowheart pointed to the left. "Can we move the horses there, behind those rocks? Archers will kill them all in a moment if we don't do something to protect them."

Alaan continued to stare at the giants above. "Move them slowly. Don't meet the eyes of the men above and do nothing they might take as threatening."

"If we can get into the cover of some rocks here," Tam said, "we might drive Hafydd's guards back. We have the advantage of our position."

"Which was my plan," Alaan said, "before the Dubrell appeared. If only we'd brought Orlem . . ."

The crows began a raucous chorus, bouncing up and down where they perched on rocks and stunted trees. At the narrowing of the draw, the birds on ledges bent down and scolded something below.

"They're coming," Alaan said. "Everyone turn around slowly."

The traveler nocked an arrow as he faced the men appearing down the rise.

Alaan let fly at the first men erupting from the fissure in the stone. He missed by a handbreadth, his arrow shattering on the stone. The men dropped down but still came on. Some of them bore round shields, and the others collected behind them. The angle of the ground made the shields doubly effective, for they hid more of the man than they would on level ground. Tam and the others poured arrows down the draw, but these were less effective than they should have been. If they could have used their horses, they would soon have been away, but the giants at their backs held them fast.

"There are only two of the big men," Fynnol whispered to Alaan. "Perhaps we should rush them?"

"No, they have allies you've not yet seen."

"Then we're about to engage Hafydd's men at close quarters," Cynddl said, "and there are still ten of them and only five of us."

Crows began to fall on the men, battering them with their wings, stabbing at their eyes with sharp beaks. The company faltered but did not stop.

Tam cast his bow aside and drew his blade. Here was a fight he did not relish, even more so as their backs were vulnerable to these hostile giants.

Something gray hurtled past Tam, followed by another. He was knocked aside, and when he scrambled up, a pack of wolves was swarming over the men coming up the draw. The men fell back, trying to defend themselves with swords and shields. But there were twenty wolves, large and fearless, snapping and snarling as they dove at the men from all directions, even as the crows fell on them out of the sky. The wolves clamped onto limbs with their great fangs and refused to be dislodged.

"Don't fire any arrows!" Alaan warned, as Fynnol raised his bow. "These wolves belong to the Dubrell."

Crowheart and Cynddl went to the suddenly skittish horses.

They might never have seen wolves before, but they knew a threat when they met one. Tam saw that Crowheart quickly calmed them. They almost seemed to gather behind him, as though he were their protector.

Hafydd's men were as disciplined as Tam expected. They didn't break and run, but formed a tight circle, back-to-back, and made their way down the draw, fending off the marauding wolves as best they could. The men were much bitten and torn by the time they reached the bottom of the draw, and though they bared their teeth and shouted at the wolves, Tam could see how frightened they were.

The sound of the wolves snarling and howling echoed up the narrow draw, then silence. The wolves reappeared, padding back toward Tam and the others, their heads held low. They eyed the strangers and growled, baring bloody fangs. Some were wounded or bloodied from their battle, and Tam thought he had seldom seen a sight so frightening. The hair rose on the back of his neck. He lifted his sword.

"Offer no harm to these animals unless they attack," Alaan cautioned. "They're all but sacred to the Dubrell; as valued than their own children."

But Alaan's hope that they would not be forced to fight was clearly vain. The wolves came directly toward them, their eyes unwavering and filled with malice. Their growling and snarling grew louder as they drew near.

When only a few paces off, Crowheart walked out, putting himself between the wolves and his companions. His sword was back in its sheath, and his posture indicated a man at ease—not one who feared he might be torn apart in a moment. Softly he spoke to the pack, and the wolves raised their heads, perking up their ears as though they'd met a friend. They circled about the outlandish figure, sniffing him, then licking his hands. All the while he kept speaking to them in a soft warm voice, the words too quiet for Tam to make out.

Slowly Tam turned his head to find the giants above him conversing in whispers. One of them called out, and the wolves reluctantly tore themselves away from Crowheart. They loped up to their masters, where they circled about, wagging their gray tails like dogs.

Rabal's crow army washed out of the cleft in the rocks, rising up like a blot on the clouds. A few of the black birds detached themselves from the vanguard and flew to Crowheart, landing on his shoulder and outstretched wrist. There they cawed defiantly and preened themselves with nervous movements.

Tam tried to calm his breathing. The wolves, with their bloody muzzles, suddenly seemed like pets, when a moment before they'd been tearing into the flesh of armed men. Several of the wolves were wounded and limping. The giants crouched down and examined the hurts, their faces grave and filled with concern. One of the giants stood and performed a head count. He set off down the draw, Tam and the others making way for him.

He stalked down the slope, his great arms swinging like tree branches in a gale. In a moment he was crouched over something on the ground. He bore up a bundle of gray fur, carrying the wounded animal up the draw.

He passed the strangers without even a glance. The wolf he bore was panting too quickly, and bleeding from a wound in its side.

The giant turned at the top of the draw, where all the wolves gathered around him. He looked back at Alaan and his companions, his manner angry and grief-filled and fierce.

"Go back," he said in a strange accent. "You cannot pass through these lands. Go back while you still live."

"I can heal their animal," Crowheart whispered to Alaan.

Alaan stepped forward, his manner respectful but not cowed. "We have not come here to bring you trouble," Alaan said. "And we are deeply sorry for any that we have brought. But Crowheart can heal your wolf, for he has this gift, given to him long ago by a sorcerer."

Rabal glanced at Alaan as though he were about to protest, but he kept his peace.

The grieving giant laid his wounded animal upon the sparse brown grass and spoke with his companion, their voices so deep they seemed to rumble up from some tunnel into the earth.

"Who are you?" one of the giants asked, his voice drum deep.

He addressed Crowheart, but it was Alaan who answered. "He is a healer," Alaan said. "Rabal Crowheart is his name."

The larger of the Dubrell crouched, stroking his dying wolf. He peered at Alaan a moment.

"We know you," the giant said, long, deep vowels tumbling slowly out of a cavernous chest. "The whist is your servant."

"Jac is no man's servant, but he follows me all the same."

"He is a bird of ill omen and not welcome here." The giant glanced over at Crowheart, whose minions still preened themselves upon his outstretched arm. "But if the crow keeper can heal Arddu, we will be in your debt." He turned and spoke with his companion in what, Tam realized, was not so much a different language as an almost impenetrable accent.

"Bring your horses," the giant said. "It is not far."

The giant took up the wounded beast and led the way down the mountain. Only one carried a sword—a blade as great as Orlem's— the other wore a long knife on his belt. Tam guessed that men this large did not worry much about enemies.

The Dubrell set a pace that the men found difficult to follow, and they were soon back in the saddle, pressing their horses on, for the great stride of the giants ate up the furlongs. Presently they were down among the trees again, the forest growing more dense.

"Look," Cynddl said, his eyes turned up to the trees that towered overhead, their boles a dozen feet broad. "These are spruce— but unlike any I have seen before. Giant spruce!" And then he stopped as a vista opened up before him: a broad valley, hazy and green, at its center a turquoise lake. The story finder pointed. "It is the forest cloud: the alollynda tree!"

Above the fabric of green, stood the round crowns of several trees that seemed to float over the surrounding forest. They were spring-green against the dark color of the conifers.

"There must be twenty of them!" Cynddl said. "There can't be a stand so large in all the land between the mountains."

Tam did not quite understand the status of the alollynda among the Fáel. Certainly it was not a sacred tree, as the silveroak had once been to men, but the wanderers prized it above all others. Its wood was coveted for fáellutes and other musical instruments. Even the smallest, most simple object made of alollynda was accorded the highest value among the Fáel. Aliel had told Tam that when an alollynda was cut down wandering companies of Fáel would gather and spend days preparing for the event. Three alollynda saplings would be planted according to ancient teachings, though fewer and fewer of these had survived over the years. No one knew why. The alollynda had all but disappeared from the land between the mountains, only a few still standing in the most remote places, or on slopes where they could never be felled without being dashed to splinters.

The giants stopped often to look at the ground, reading animal prints, Tam guessed. They did not speak much, but kept their heads up, their eyes darting here and there, aware of all that transpired around them.

"Who are these people?" Tam asked Alaan, as they rode near each other.

Alaan glanced at the massive men who led them, then seemed to decide that it was all right to speak. "The Dubrell are the remains of a race that prospered long ago, though even at their height their numbers were not large. There are only two areas I know of where they still dwell; unfortunately, one of these lies on the shortest path to the place we're going. I'd hoped we might slip through before they were aware of us. They're not a warlike people, but are suspicious of outsiders, whom they encounter very infrequently. We are thought to be bringers of bad luck—you heard what they said about my whist."

"You have been here before," Tam said.

"Yes. Once. I explored the route we follow now, thinking that I might come this way one day. They were not so lucky then—to catch me in a draw with enemies at my back . I eluded them. Apparently they haven't forgotten, however." Alaan glanced thoughtfully down the slope to the giants making their way through the widely spaced trees. His handsome face was thinner now, pale and slightly aged, though his dark beard was still neatly trimmed, his traveler's clothes a little too well tailored.

Alaan went on. "Orlem told me that he wandered up onto a mountain—centuries ago—because he'd heard a story that other Dubrell had disappeared there; Dubrell who knew the ways of the wildlands and the mountains. He went searching to see what had become of them, but instead found himself wandering in strange lands, much as happened to you on the River Wynnd. He walked into the beginnings of a war in the land between the mountains. A company of armed men, beating the countryside for conscripts, came across him, and he was taken into the army against his will. But his size and strength, as well as his unexpected talent for war, brought him to the attention of Caibre, whom he served for many years—before he fell under the spell of Sianon." Alaan glanced back at Tam, who had been staring at him, as though he could come to some understanding of this enigma who called himself Alaan.

"But Orlem became your friend," Tam said.

"He was the friend of Sainth, not Alaan."

The sun sank behind the mountain, and a long shadow washed down the slope, catching them like a returning tide. Dusk flooded among the trees, and they were soon squinting into the shadows, trying to see their way. But as the giant had said, it was not far.

What Tam first thought was a cliff turned out to be a stone wall, and set into it, a large gate. One of the giants whistled an odd pattern and overhead was heard the scraping of wood on stone. A square of light appeared high up in the wall, and a few moments later they heard a deep thud inside, and one of the massive doors cracked open. The giant pulled it wide so that it screeched on its hinges. The wolf pack bid their masters good-bye, and disappeared into the night. Inside, a dark courtyard could be seen, lit only by a single lantern, a candle burning within.

"There is room for your horses in our stable," the giant said. "If some of you will follow me. The healer should go with Wolfson."

Alaan and Rabal followed Wolfson up a stone stairway, leaving their companions to tend the horses.

The giant took the candle lantern off its hook and led them into the stable, which was occupied by a few large draft horses. The companions soon had their own horses stripped of saddles and gear, rubbed down, and fed and watered. Tam thought that their horses would not likely see such comfortable housing again until they returned to the land between the mountains. After a fortnight in the wilds, such a stable might look like a comfortable inn to him and his companions as well.

"Come with me, now," the giant said, waving at the door. "I am Stonehand."

"I'm Tam, and this is my cousin, Fynnol, and our friend Cynddl, who is a story finder."

The giant appraised Cynddl with his large, surprisingly kindly eyes.

"We will take our supper soon," Stonehand said. "If your friend can heal Arddu, then you shall share our meal."

"And if he can't?" Fynnol asked quickly.

"That is not for me to decide."

They went up the stairs and through a tall door made of oak planks thicker than Tam's hand was broad. A small entry hall opened up before them, the woodwork rough but the feel of the place homey. They shed their mail and boots there, leaning weapons against a wall. After a hard day of travel and the excitement and fear of their contest with Hafydd's guards, the smell of cooking food lifted Tam's spirits.

Light spilled out of a door onto the plank floor, polished from years of use. Stonehand led them through the door, and inside they found a good-sized chamber, well lit by candles and a fire in an imposing hearth. Cool mountain air flooded in the windows, for even in summer the nights were chill at this elevation. A few pieces of rustic furniture, of a size that made Tam feel like a child again, were spread randomly about the room, and to one side stood a long, high table, with benches to either side.

A rough blanket had been spread before the fire and on this lay the wounded wolf, panting, mouth lolled open and wet with drool. Crowheart, Alaan, and the other giant knelt over it, Crowheart washing the wound with a damp cloth.

"He will live," Rabal reassured the giant, who was obviously much affected by the beast's suffering. "He will not be well for a few days, but he will live."

"The blade sank into his gut," the giant said. "How can he live?"

"He will live," Alaan said. "If Rabal says he will be healed, he will be healed."

The giant looked up at him. "Then he must be a sorcerer's pupil, for Arddu's blood loss alone would do for most animals."

"Luck has smiled upon you today, for Crowheart was nearby," Alaan said.

"Luck . . . ?" the giant said disdainfully. "If not for you, Arddu would not have been wounded, for those men were your enemies, not ours."

Alaan didn't answer, for surely the giant was right, Tam thought.

Stonehand stood looking on, bent just a little to gaze down on the injured beast, the lines of his face deep with concern.

Crowheart began to sing or chant softly over the injured animal. He stroked the slick fur around the wound and scratched gently behind the wolf's ears. The words he sang could not be made out, but their meaning could almost be grasped, though no quite.

Tam had a moment to observe their hosts. They were like to Orlem Slighthand in size—Baore might have almost reached Stonehand's shoulder. Certainly they would be more than double Tam's weight, and Tam was not a small man. Their bodies were thick and muscled, and a little round about the middle. They appeared to have been rather crudely carved compared to someone like Fynnol, who was slight of waist and wiry as a weasel. Their faces were half-hidden by beards, and thick hair flowed down to their shoulders. Although he would guess there was little vanity among these giants, their hair was clean, and their clothes, though worn and mended expertly here and there, had been recently laundered.

"I will be here all this night," Crowheart said. "Break your fast and leave me to my duties."

Reluctantly, the giants gave way to Crowheart. Stonehand went to the hearth and took the lid from a blackened iron pot that hung from a hook. His companion retrieved bowls and plates from a cupboard and set the table. In a moment they were all seated, eating a thick stew and chunks of dense bread. Stonehand rose to shut the windows, for the room was rapidly cooling.

The sound of howling wolves came to them through the glass, distant and eerie.

"Will you set a guard this night?"

"The pack will stand guard. The men who chased you today would be foolish to come here, but if they do, we'll know."

The giants could have easily been brothers, but it turned out they weren't. It seemed they were reluctant to speak with the strangers, but every time they looked over at Crowheart and found their wolf still alive, their reticence softened a little.

"Are you the only two living here?" Alaan asked. "It seems a large keep."

"There is a third here this night. He might show himself by and by," Stonehand said. "Others kept to the mountain this day to hold the strangers at bay. We're here for four full moons to watch the north pass." He gestured with a hand. "It is quiet duty, but needed all the same."

"There is some threat from the lands to the north?" Alaan continued.

The Dubrell glanced at each other, then Wolfson answered.

"You're the first in many a year. 'Tis the to the south that our lands are threatened."

Stonehand glared at him, and Wolfson fell silent, applying himself to his stew without looking up.

A door opened then, and an old man came in. If anything he was taller than the two giants present, even though he stooped a little under the weight of his years. White beard and hair made a great contrast to his sun-stained face and troubled blue eyes.

The old man stopped short when he saw the strangers gathered at the table, then his gaze took in Crowheart sitting by the injured wolf. Immediately he crossed to the animal, and Wolfson rose and went to where the old man crouched, stroking the wolf's head.

Wolfson began speaking in their strangely accented language, of which Tam understood only a few words. It occurred to him then that if these giants were isolated enough to have developed such a thick accent, how did they learn to speak the common tongue as it was spoken in the land between the mountains?

The old man muttered a few words, then raised his eyes from the wolf to stare at Crowheart. After a moment, he got stiffly to his feet and walked over to the table. Stonehand stood up as the old man approached, his manner respectful. Alaan quickly followed suit, and the others did the same.

"This is Uamon, who dwells in this place," Wolfson said, and introduced the strangers, forgetting no one's name.

"Sit," the old man said. "Eat while your dinner is hot."

Wolfson brought Uamon food and drink and seated him at the table's head.

Fynnol glanced over at Tam and raised an eyebrow, but Tam didn't know who or what this old man was either.

The Dubrell had a few more words, then Uamon spoke.

"Where is it you travel?" he asked in a smoky voice.

"South," Alaan said, though Tam sensed he was reluctant to be their spokesman.

"South?" Uamon said. "Better you went some other way."

There was an awkward silence.

"Our route lies south," Alaan said firmly.

Uamon dipped a spoon into his bowl, raising it to blow gently on a steaming chunk of lamb. He had a gentle aspect, this old giant, but there was also a sorrow about him, Tam thought.

"Our people have trouble to the south," Uamon said. "It is my duty to ask what would take you there?"

"I seek someone who lives beyond your lands."

Again Uamon sipped at his stew. "Beyond our borders you will find dark lands. Shadow lands. My people don't go there willingly. Of those few who have, only one returned."

"We all have our duties," Alaan said. "Ours lead us south. If you will let us pass, we shall bother you no more."

"I suppose if a man goes seeking Death, one cannot stop him, for Death can be found anywhere—even within this room." He glanced over at the wolf, who moaned quietly by the fire. "But what of your companions? Do they understand where it is you go?"

"We have met Death's servants before," Fynnol said. "Once you have faced them, there is nothing left that will frighten you."

"Do not be so sure of that. My people have long stood vigil over our southern border. Beasts have been seen there that were the stuff of nightmare." He shivered visibly. "What duties could take you to Death's kingdom, I wonder?"

Alaan's reluctance to answer was obvious, but clearly he felt there was no choice. They must have free passage from the Dubrell. "We will not go there—not to the gate. Only into the borderlands."

"Ah. *Only* into the borderlands," Uamon said softly. Still he concentrated on his food, not looking at Alaan. "I fear you do not understand what it is you do. Where it is you go."

"I have been to the borderlands before," Alaan said.

Uamon's head lifted, his troubled blue eyes coming to rest on Alaan. "What do you seek there, if it is not Death?"

"I seek . . . knowledge."

"Better to sit at the feet of a wise man."

"No wise man is foolish enough to have learned what I wish to know," Alaan said, his voice growing testy. "Is it not enough that we are men of good character, and that we mean no harm to your people? There are other races with their own struggles, their own troubles. We seek only to bring aid to our own people."

Uamon gazed at Alaan a moment, while the other giants shifted uncomfortably on their benches. They did not think Alaan should speak to their elder so.

"It is not enough," Uamon said. "I must be assured that your duties will not bring greater suffering to my own people—for this could be done without it being your purpose. The lands to the south are a great mystery."

Before Alaan could answer, a deep rumbling was heard. Tam felt suddenly disoriented, as though he were falling. His soup slopped over onto the table, and he felt himself thrown violently back, then forward. And then it was calm, only a spray of sparks from the logs shifting in the fire.

"They happen more often now," Stonehand said, looking not at all surprised. "The earth is restless."

"No," Alaan said. "A great spell is unraveling. A spell that walled Death into his kingdom and held two great lands apart. The earth tremors will grow worse. Even the mountains might not stand against them, and in the end Death will be released and overrun the world of the living."

Uamon's spoon stopped as it traveled to his mouth, and his hand trembled visibly. He glanced over at Crowheart, then back to Alaan. "How do you know this?"

"Because I saw the chamber where the spell was made. I didn't realize what it was then, but now I know. The spell is decaying, and I seek the help of someone who might know how it could be repaired."

"You know too much of sorcery," Uamon said quickly.

"I don't know enough," Alaan answered. "Will you let us pass through your lands?"

Uamon stirred his spoon through his soup. "I will consider it," he said, then rose from the table, disturbed by what he had learned. Stonehand and Wolfson lurched to their feet as the old man rose, and the others did the same. Uamon crossed the room without looking back, closing the door softly behind him.

The companions stared at the closed door for a moment, then turned back to their food. An awkward silence settled over the room, broken only by Crowheart humming over the injured wolf.

Tam, Fynnol, Cynddl, and Alaan were led to a long barracks, where a dozen beds lined up against one wall. Stonehand had slipped away and lit a fire in the hearth here, but the room was still cool and damp. The beds were made for the Dubrell and seemed almost comically large to the companions, especially as they were each made for one man.

Cynddl lay down on top of his bed, staring up at the ceiling. "I shall need a growth spurt before I fit this bed."

"Yes," Fynnol said, "I've heard of having large shoes to fill, but I hate to think what having a large bed to fill might mean."

Cynddl laughed, always appreciative of a quick wit. "We might comfort ourselves that they're single beds," he offered.

Alaan climbed into one of the massive chairs by the hearth in the room's center.

"What do you make of these giants?" Cynddl asked him. The story finder rose and went to stand with his arm resting on the back of the second chair. "Given that the hidden lands have seemed almost empty of people, I'm surprised at how suspicious they are. Who could they possibly be fighting against?"

Alaan glanced up at the Fáel, and then back at the wavering flames. "I'm not sure, Cynddl, but they fear things that come from the south. The Kingdom of Death is not distant. If the spell that walls Death in is failing, then they no doubt have reason to be fearful and suspicious. The Dubrell are tied to the lands hereabouts and will not easily be driven off, but what exactly is going on I cannot say. It was such a long time ago that Orlem dwelt here. Much has changed. You should all sleep. We're safe here, and you might not have that luxury again for some time."

Tam lay awake for a time, even after the candles had been blown out. He finally drifted off as Alaan left his chair by the fire and sought his own bed.

He didn't know how much time had passed, or what woke him, but he found himself aware in the darkness. The fire had burned down to embers, and a faint light of stars or moon illuminated the window. The even breathing of the others reassured him a little: no one else had been wakened. But then he heard a horse nicker.

He was at the window in an instant, staring down into the court-yard below. At first he thought their horses were being taken, then he realized that riders were dismounting—perhaps a dozen of them, it was hard to tell in the faint light. He could see one of the giants holding a lantern aloft and armed men going purposefully about their business.

And they *were* men, for they didn't reach the giant's shoulder. Some led horses into the stables, and others went silently to a door in the lower part of the building.

"What is it?" Alaan asked, propping himself up in bed.

"A company of riders," Tam said, pulling on breeches and drawing his dagger from its sheath.

Alaan rolled out of his bed onto his feet, silent as a stone. He was at the window instantly, hands resting on the ledge.

"Have the Dubrell betrayed us?" Tam whispered.

"Perhaps. Wake the others."

They barricaded the door into the room with the massive chairs, and all waited silently. Their weapons had been left in the entry below, out of courtesy, and all they had were daggers and the fireplace poker.

"What of Crowheart?" Cynddl asked.

"Stay quiet and listen," Alaan said. But there was nothing to be heard.

Alaan lit a candle, and they pulled the chairs away from the door. In the hallway they found no one.

Alaan balanced on the balls of his feet, his every attention concentrated on listening. "Tam?" he whispered. "Come with me. You two stay here and open the door to no one until we return. If you are threatened, you might have to go out the window."

Alaan held the candle high as they made their way along the hall and down the steps, the treads set at almost double the height of the steps Tam was accustomed to.

The large chamber where they had dined was empty but for Crowheart, who sat cross-legged by the prostrate wolf. The healer made no sounds, but stayed perfectly still, his eyes closed.

"Rabal?" Tam whispered. "Rabal . . . ?"

"Leave him," Alaan said. "He is in a healing trance and should not be roused unless we're threatened."

In the entry they found their weapons still leaning against the wall. Alaan sheathed his dagger and straightened up, for he had been half-crouched, like a man about to do battle.

"Whoever these men are, I think they're no threat to us."

Tam was reassured by the sight of their weapons, which had clearly not been disturbed.

"But what goes on here?" Tam whispered. "Who are they?"

Alaan shook his head. "I don't know, Tam. The Dubrell have secrets, that is certain."

Alaan opened the door and looked out. The courtyard was empty, lit only by the last sliver of moon, the ancient light of the stars. He led the way out into the cool night and down the giant stairs. In the courtyard they found barely a sign that the riders had been there. And then Tam saw a faint gleam on the cobbles and bent to retrieve a small object.

"What is it?" Alaan whispered.

"I don't know. It's too dark to tell."

Alaan looked into the dark stable, but there was little to be seen there without light, and they hadn't brought a candle lantern. They were up the cold stairs and inside in a moment.

By the fire, Crowheart sat unmoving. Tam paused for a moment in the doorway. He could see the even rise and fall of the wolf's chest, and he was certain it slept peacefully. Whatever magic Crow-heart was performing seemed to be working.

They slipped up the stairs, and the others let them back into their barracks, where it seemed warm after the cold of the courtyard. Cynddl and Fynnol looked anxiously at their companions as they returned.

"Who are these men?" Cynddl whispered. "What do they want here?"

"I don't know," Alaan answered, shaking his head. He went and warmed his hands by the fire. "Clearly they are friends or allies of the Dubrell."

"I didn't know that men traveled through the hidden lands except by accident," Fynnol said. He dropped to his knees before the fire, which had been built up again in their absence. Tam could see that his cousin was unsettled, wakened from sleep to find himself threatened.

"There are a few who can find their way here, Fynnol," Alaan said. "Crowheart is one. But for the most part, what you say is true."

Tam remembered the small object he had found and fished it from a pocket. He moved to the hearth so that the light shone upon it.

"So, what is that, Tam?" Alaan asked.

"It appears to be a small broach. Oak leaves, I think."

He passed it to Cynddl, who knew more of trees and plants than the rest of them combined.

Cynddl turned it over in the firelight. "It's a fan of silveroak leaves." He looked up at Alaan. "Didn't you tell us, the night we met by Telanon Bridge, that a fan of silveroak leaves was the token of the Knights of the Vow?"

Alaan held out his hand. He examined the silver ornament carefully, turning it over in his hand several times.

"That is the token of the Knights," he said at last. He looked up at the others, his face dark with concern or confusion. "Did these men wear the gray robes, Tam?"

"No, they were all differently dressed. Nor was their armor made to a pattern." Tam tried to call up a picture of what he'd seen of the men in the courtyard. "Some wore surcoats, and others did not. I saw no devices upon the shields, nor did they bear standards."

"That is strange," Fynnol said thoughtfully. "In a battle it is easy to kill your own men if they're not clearly marked."

"Yes," Alaan said, "if you're fighting men."

Seven

*H*e *went about in a barrow.* Beatrice Renné could not get that
thought out of her mind. He looked a bit like a hog as well; round
and soft of flesh, his pate bald, and skin of pinkish hue. But he had
saved the life of Lord Carral Wills, and for that she would allow a
man in a barrow into her hall, and treat him with all the goodwill
such a deed deserved.

"It is a story that will surely be made into song," Beatrice said.
"Certainly it shall. How you found each other, then managed to get
off the Isle without being discovered either by the men of Innes or
the many searchers that Kel sent out. . . . It is almost miraculous."

She thought Lord Carral looked rather improved by this unexpected expedition across country. A healthy color suffused his
face, and he appeared to have been somewhat strengthened by his
ordeal. Certainly his carriage was more erect. Perhaps it had
merely taken his mind away from the loss of his daughter, and
that would not be a bad thing. She herself had struggled much
with the loss of her nephew, Arden—and his part in the plot
against Toren had only made it harder. Though, of course, he had

acted honorably in the end. It was a small comfort, but she clung to it all the same.

The evening was warm, but they sat by the cold hearth—there were many things that one did not discuss by open windows, after all, no matter how close the night. Lord Carral was dressed in Fáel clothing, and she thought it became him in some way, though of course he did not have the night-black hair or the dusky, silken skin.

She glanced at his companion again and had to cover her revulsion with a gracious smile. "I cannot begin to tell you how grateful I am, good Kai. Anything we might do to repay, you have only to ask. . . ."

The legless man smiled at her in return—not an entirely appalling smile, she thought.

Carral shifted in his chair, clearly a little uncomfortable.

"There is a greater tale to tell," the minstrel said. "But I don't know how we should even begin, for it is such a fantastic story. . . ." He paused, a hand rising to his forehead, which he massaged gently. "We have spoken, Lady Beatrice, about this man—the 'ghost' who came to me in Braidon Castle."

"This is the man, Alaan. The sorcerer?"

"Yes, though it seems the name Alaan is not quite correct either. You see, he made a bargain with a nagar."

"A river spirit?" Lady Beatrice asked. She kept her face completely neutral at this news. She was prepared to listen to any kind of story from Carral Wills at that moment, so happy was she to see him safe.

"I don't know if that would completely describe this particular nagar, for this nagar had once been the son of a great sorcerer named Wyrr, from whom came the river's ancient name."

Lady Beatrice felt herself nod, willing Lord Carral to go on. "And what, exactly, do you mean, 'he made a bargain'?"

"I don't know quite how to describe it, or if I even understand it. In return for power and knowledge he allowed this spirit . . . to enter him in some way."

"You mean he is possessed by it?"

"That is not precisely true, if you don't mind me saying so," the legless man interjected. "It is a bargain. The man gives part of his life to the nagar, the nagar's memories and some portion of its personality become part of the man."

"It sounds horrifying!" she said, with some feeling.

Kai nodded agreement to this sentiment.

"So he is not really Alaan, but some conjoining of these two souls—Alaan and . . ."

"Sainth." Carral said. "The youngest son of Wyrr."

"But have the children of Wyrr not been dead for centuries? The stories are very old and not widely believed."

"A thousand years Sainth has been gone," Kai said, "but not dead. His father sustained him in the river."

"But the father, Wyrr, did he not die in some even more distant age?" Lady Beatrice wondered why she was asking such questions. This sounded like the stuff of old ballads.

"He did not die," Kai said quickly. "He went into the river— joined his spirit to it in ways we cannot understand. Ever since he has dwelt in the waters, sleeping, perhaps, but not dead."

"Then this Sainth is risen again?"

"In a way. Certainly he no longer dwells in the river."

Lady Beatrice nodded, though she did not really understand.

"Sainth, the youngest son of Wyrr, was given a gift by his father— the ability to travel paths no others could find."

"Yes," Beatrice said. "I remember some of the old songs. Was there not some terrible price for this?"

"He could never find a place that brought him comfort," Kai said, "a woman whom he thought beautiful enough. There might always be some fairer place, a woman more lovely. His siblings were equally cursed, though they chose to be great warriors—the brother wanting to be obeyed out of fear and the sister to be loved and served by all she met. These two fought after Wyrr went into the river, and the One Kingdom was broken. Eventually the eldest son, Caibre, murdered his brother through treachery and made war on his sister. Those two died when they brought the tower of Sianon down on top of them."

"And this knight Hafydd, whom we apparently spared, has made a bargain also. That is what's happened, is it not?" Lady Beatrice was a little surprised to hear herself say this, but it suddenly seemed apparent. How else did Hafydd come back from the dead?

"Yes. That's what we believe," Kai answered. He shifted in his barrow, which was softened now with fine cushions the Fáel had given him. "He's made a bargain with Caibre. It can be no other."

"There seems to be no end of disturbing news," Lady Beatrice said.

"And there is more." Carral joined both hands upon the head of his cane. He seemed to stare blankly through Lady Beatrice, giving her an odd feeling that she was not there—that her existence was so fleeting it was hardly noticed. "Sainth had companions. Men who traveled with him for long periods—many lives of men, in some cases. The sorcerers were untouched by Death, or by his ally Time, and those who served them lived very long lives—longer than even the sorcerers likely expected." He paused a moment. The only sound, a candle fluttering. A sprinkle of black dust floated down from the chimney and settled on the iron dogs in the hearth. "Kilydd was such a man, a companion of Sainth. And beyond all expectations, he still lives."

"Now, Lord Carral," Lady Beatrice said. "How can you be sure of this?"

"Because I have met him, and I have met another as well. A man named Orlem Slighthand, who was celebrated in many songs. And *he* cannot be mistaken for any other."

Lady Beatrice sat back in her chair, shaken by Carral's confidence. "There have long been rumors that Sir Eremon was a sorcerer, or had some knowledge of things arcane. And then we began to hear that he was Hafydd, who had once been our ally but who turned against us and was left for dead on a battlefield—a fate of his own making. But now, these things you tell me. . . . I fear what you might tell me next. These men who were once companions of Sainth; are they a danger to us?"

"No," Carral said firmly. "They might in truth be our allies, and welcome they would be." Without turning his head or making any kind of gesture, he said, "Kai, who saved my life upon the Isle of Battle, was once known as Kilydd, Lady Beatrice."

A lifetime of training in the social graces would not allow her to laugh, or even to look surprised, but how had this legless man made such a fool of Lord Carral? Was he really so grateful for being rescued? Perhaps he was.

"You do not believe me, Lady Beatrice," Carral said, not disguising the disappointment in his voice.

She had forgotten how sensitive he was. His blindness did not seem to be any hindrance when it came to judging the reactions and feelings of others. He had divined her reaction from her slight pause.

"I don't blame you. I should not have believed it myself, but for things that happened while Kai and I made our way across the Isle of Battle. Like his master of long ago, Kai has the ability to travel paths that others cannot find. It was by this skill that we avoided capture by the Prince's men. And we stopped at the dwelling place of . . . Is there another in the room with us?" he asked suddenly.

"The three of us," Lady Beatrice said. "Why?"

A little trickle of soot tinkled on the grating, and Lady Beatrice was on her feet of an instant, crossing the carpet as silently as she could. In the hallway outside stood a guard, and she gestured for him to be silent, leading him back into the room. All the while she continued talking in the most natural tone of voice as if not a thing were amiss, and Carral followed her lead, continuing his story.

At the hearth she pointed up into the blackness, and by gestures made the guard, who was not quick on the uptake, understand her meaning. Removing his sword from its scabbard, he bent and shuffled into the tall hearth, twisting awkwardly to look up. A knife glanced off his helmet and clattered down onto the stone. The guard bellowed and thrust up into the chimney. A second later a small, utterly black figure tumbled down in a rain of soot, the guard holding him by the ankle.

The soot-covered spy snatched up the knife and drove it into his assailant's leg. In a flash he was up the chimney, the guard crumpling to the floor, crimson flowing from his wound.

The noise brought others running into the chamber, among them Fondor Renné.

"He's gone up the chimney!" Lady Beatrice yelled.

The smallest and youngest of the guards threw off his helm and scabbard and wriggled up the chimney himself, black dust raining down into the hearth.

Fondor ran for the door. "Onto the roof!" he bellowed.

"A healer!" Lady Beatrice called, running out into the hallway. "We must have a healer!"

She came back in and, taking off her scarf, tried to staunch the guard's wound where it bled around the dagger blade.

"Are you unhurt?—Lord Carral? Good Kai?" she said, glancing up from her efforts.

Neither of them had taken any harm.

Guards and servants came rushing in, relieving Lady Beatrice of her charge. They bore the man out, a manservant pressing on the wound.

Lady Beatrice caught sight of herself in a glass, blood spattered over her moss-green gown, her hands crimson. A servant brought her a washbasin, and she quickly cleaned her hands, drying them on an offered towel. A glass of brandy was pressed into her hands, and she drained half of it in a most unladylike manner. Her hand trembled so that she spilled the amber liquid as she drank.

"It seems assassins are always in our halls when you are present, Lord Carral" she said.

"That was no assassin," Kai offered. He sat in his refurbished barrow, for the Fáel had rebuilt it with the finest woods, beautifully carved and polished. He was, apparently, untroubled by what he'd witnessed, though Lady Beatrice did see him conceal a dagger within the folds of his clothing. "He was spying. Listening to your conversation, which I would guess he'd done before."

This assertion brought Lady Beatrice up short. A bell struck the hour somewhere in the castle's depths.

"My, it has grown late," Lady Beatrice said, though she really wanted to speak with Fondor. It had never occurred to her that a spy would lurk in the chimney! Rising to her feet, she smiled graciously at her guests, only just remembering that Lord Carral could not see. "We will have to continue this conversation on the morrow," Lady Beatrice said. "Lord Carral, your room awaits you." She rang a bell to call in the servants. "And good Kai. I hope you will feel welcome among us. I've had rooms prepared, near to Lord Carral's. Only tell us what you need. . . ."

"I thank you, Lady Beatrice, but I will go back to the Fáel this night. I wish to speak with Alaan before he disappears again."

Lady Beatrice hesitated.

"I will have two guards take you in a cart." She glanced at the sooty hearth. "I feel suddenly that Westbrook is not so safe a place."

In the long hallway that led to the various guest apartments, Carral was stopped by a woman.

"Lord Carral?"

Carral knew the voice immediately: one of Llyn's servants. "Yes?"

"Lady Llyn has sent me to inquire . . . after your well-being."

"I should like nothing better than to convey this small news in person, but the hour is so late."

"I don't think her ladyship would mind, sir. She is awake, so concerned have we all been since you were lost."

He arrived dressed like a Fáel, and for some reason this jarred Llyn. So anxious was she to see him, but the man who descended the stair into her garden seemed a stranger, dressed in his exotic

Fáel clothing. No doubt his travails had changed his mind on many things, given him a new view of his plans, his future. She felt almost certain that he had come to tell her that he had been in the grip of a brief madness. That his feelings for her had been overstated, caused by the terrible loneliness he felt at his daughter's passing.

He used a light cane to feel the steps as he descended, then he swept it across the gravel path, finding the stone border and following it. For a moment, she stood watching, afraid to speak.

"Llyn?" he called softly.

"I am here," she said, her voice emerging as a whisper. He hadn't used her title, and this gave her hope.

He stopped a few paces away, and still she felt rooted to the spot. Neither spoke. Only the little stream that whispered among her flowers voiced its feelings, but Llyn did not understand these, either.

"I suppose I am a fool for it," Carral said, trying to control the emotion in his voice, "but as I made my way across the Isle of Battle, I kept thinking that I must survive to have the gift of your company again."

Lynn felt her eyes close, and a tear slipped down her cheek. "It was a fair thought," she whispered. "I believed you had been lost, and I alternately mourned you and cursed your stubbornness for insisting on accompanying the army. But here you are safe"—her voice all but disappeared—"and I have no words for what I'm feeling."

He came forward a pace, and she put her arms around his neck, burying her face in the crook beneath his chin. She closed her eyes and felt the warmth of him, the strange scent of his Fáel clothing.

His hand came up and stroked the undamaged side of her face, brushing back strands of her hair. Llyn felt as though she were lifted on a rising wind of emotion, soaring up and up, free of life's gravity. Was this what love felt like?

She heard a door, then hurried steps on the gravel path. Neither moved to separate themselves until a soft voice of one of the servants came out of the shadow by the wall.

"Your grace," said one of Llyn's servants. "Do pardon my intrusion. It's Lord Toren . . ."

Llyn held her breath.

"He's returned, ma'am."

Without warning, Llyn began to sob, a storm of feelings surging and whirling inside of her.

Eight

Stars and a swaying lantern on a pole did little to press back the night. The waning moon, barely a sliver, hid its feeble light behind a cloud, and the trees loomed over the road like malevolent giants. With each revolution of the wheels the axle squeaked, like a whimper of resignation.

Kai rode in the back of the cart, upon the pillows from his barrow. The cart jounced and staggered over the uneven road, the single horse snorting and shaking its harness in protest at being taken from its stall so late. Kai held on as best he could as he was thrown this way then that.

The two guards sat upon the high seat, one smoking a pipe, which Kai was certain he was not allowed on duty.

"Not too much farther," the smoker said, then drew on his pipe, releasing, with some satisfaction, a cloud of smoke into the night.

They had crossed the bridge over the Westbrook and turned now to follow along its bank, the squeak of the cart wheels blending in with the songs of the crickets and tree frogs.

Kai had to admit that he was in misery. Having seen the proud

Renné in their castle, he was more aware than usual of his own circumstances. He who had once been great among the great, had been the lover of Sianon, now a landless vagabond—a man who went about in a barrow. He needed to make his tea of blood lily, for the ghost pain was strong that night. How had his long life come to such a pass?

A torch was lit on the road before them, and from it another. Kai tried to boost himself up to see past the two guards. Probably men with an oxen and dray delivering barrels to Westbrook. Who else was abroad at such an hour?

But there was no dray, and the men blocked the road, others quickly surrounding the cart and its surprised occupants. In the flickering torchlight Kai could see the dull gleam of steel.

They had adjourned to a room without a hearth. A room seldom used but for summer, for it had little to recommend it—not even a charming view. But it seemed a very safe room in which to speak, in light of what had happened that night.

"Then this man Kai is everything Lord Carral claimed?" Lady Beatrice looked over at Toren.

Dease had gone off to his rooms to find a bath and sleep, but Toren had too much to tell and had quickly bathed and changed. He ate while they talked—which would have been unspeakably rude under any other circumstances. Lady Beatrice, however, was prepared to forgive him anything that night. She thought he looked the worse for his journey, thinner, almost gaunt, and deeply fatigued. She could see that in his eyes. But once she had heard his story, the look in his eye took on different meaning.

She was still in a state of disbelief. Carral's ravings about Kai seemed positively sane after the things she heard from Toren.

"Yes," Toren said, sipping his wine, "all that and more."

Lady Beatrice shook her head. "I received a note from Lady Llyn not half an hour ago. She implored me to do everything in my

power to keep Kai safe. I have no idea why, or even how she knew
he was here."

Toren stopped eating. "I have always found Llyn's opinions to
be worth listening to."

"I agree. Unfortunately, I let Kai go back to the Fáel encampment before I heard from Llyn. At least I had the foresight to send
guards with him."

Toren relaxed visibly. "A company of guards should keep him
from harm."

Lady Beatrice pressed her eyes closed. "I sent only two men in
a cart."

Toren turned to Fondor. "Can you send out a small company
of men-at-arms to accompany Kai?"

"Too late," Lady Beatrice said. "They left sometime ago."

She reached out and squeezed Toren's wrist as though to reas-
sure herself he was really there. Tears welled up in her eyes, but she
managed not to weep.

"This close to Westbrook," she said, "certainly he will be safe."

Toren nodded and turned back to his meal.

"And where is Elise Wills, now?" Lady Beatrice asked.

"I don't know. We were, most of us, separated in the cave. She
could be anywhere."

"She could truly be dead, this time."

"It is possible."

"Then what shall I tell Lord Carral? His daughter did not die in
the Westbrook, as we thought. But she might now have truly
drowned in another place. A distant place that can only be reached
if one has a magical map."

"He must be told the truth," Toren said, "no matter how difficult it is to accept."

"I suppose." It was clear to Lady Beatrice that she would be the
bearer of that truth. Although Toren had shouldered the responsibilities of his inheritance, there were certain duties he shunned.
Lord Carral would be left to her, which was, perhaps, as it should
be. But either Toren or Dease would have to speak with Lord Car-

ral eventually. He would want to hear this news at first hand. He would, she realized, want to know why his daughter had let him think she was dead—had let him go through the torture. What pain this would cause him!

"But Hafydd, or whoever he is now, was not seen to survive this place. . . . What did you call it?"

"The Stillwater." Toren moved in his chair, stretching a little as though he were in pain. He wore a deep red jacket with silveroak leaf clasps, the white of his linen shirt at his wrists and neck hardly paler than his face. He applied himself to his wine, then refilled the glass himself, for they had sent all the servants out. "But Hafydd will have survived."

"We should have lopped off his head upon the field at Harrowdown, when we had the chance," Fondor said.

Lady Beatrice did not hide her reaction to this statement, and Fondor looked suitably contrite.

Lady Beatrice took up her own glass, which appeared to be emptying at an alarming rate. Her poor mind could not grasp all that was being said. It was enough that Hafydd still lived and that he had made a bargain with a sorcerer long dead, but all that Toren now told her! Servants of Death appearing and dragging Beldor off into the night, Elise Wills alive and in thrall to some sorcerer who should have been dead a thousand years ago. And now Toren claimed that this legless man, Kai, really had been a servant of a son of Wyrr. A man without possessions, who went about in a barrow!

"I will want to speak with Kel, as soon as possible." Toren paused, his fork suspended halfway to his mouth. "I still don't believe the Prince of Innes would start this war without his precious counselor present."

"And a lucky thing for us that he did," Fondor said. "I've had reports from Kel. It was a close-run battle. If Vast had not arrived when he did . . ."

"Vast shall be suitably rewarded," Toren said, and the fork continued its journey.

"Yes," Lady Beatrice said. "He shall."

A knock at the door was followed by a guard. "News, Lady Beatrice," the man said.

"Yes, what is it?"

"Highwaymen have fallen on your guest of earlier this evening."

Lady Beatrice felt herself sway. "What do you say?"

"The two guards were found dead in the road just beyond the first bridge. The cart was taken. No sign of the crippled man they accompanied."

Fondor and Toren looked at each other an instant, then were both on their feet and running out the door.

Nine

Lord Kel Renné rode along the crest of a low hill, gazing out over the Isle of Battle, the shimmering curve of the canal in the distance and smoke from the pyre where they had burned the fallen still hazing the view.

Tuwar Estenford sat upon his horse near at hand, and he too stared out over the canal and to the lands beyond. "There is an army there, my lord," he said firmly. The old man shifted in his saddle, trying to relieve the pain in a leg that had been gone now many decades. *Ghost pain*, he called it, in his ghost limb.

Kel saw the old warrior wince.

"Yes, but what will Innes do with that army? That is what I wonder?"

"It is what he is wondering as well," Estenford said. "He is not a smart man. He would not have considered the possibility of losing the Isle. Contingency plans would not have been in place. Now he would like to find something that will allow him to save face. Some small thing, for he has not a large enough force to cross the Wynnd—not yet. But if he could manage some small deed here—

kill a few of our men on patrol, or cross the canal in one place and take a few hostages. That is what we must be on guard for."

"Lord Kel?" One of his lieutenants motioned to the grassy, southern hillside. A rider was galloping up the slope, his horse in a lather.

"A messenger from the Duke of Vast."

"So I see," Kel turned away from the view out over the canal, taking one last look, as though he might catch a glimpse of an army hiding in the wood.

The rider, hardly more than a boy, was himself out of breath when he arrived on the hilltop. His mount heaved beneath him like a bellows. The boy, blue-eyed and lightly bearded, banged a hand to his chest in salute. "I come from the Duke of Vast with a message for Lord Kel Renné," he said, rather needlessly, Kel thought.

"Yes, yes. Let me see it."

Estenford intercepted the letter, keeping himself and his horse between Kel and the messenger. Kel could see by the tenseness in the old man's carriage that he was ready to kill this young messenger in an instant if need be. The assassination of Kel Renné would do quite nicely as a face-saving act for the Prince of Innes, and Tuwar would give his life before he would let that happen.

Kel rode a few paces off with Tuwar in tow and broke the letter's seal. Inside he found a sheaf of papers, the first written in Vast's nearly illegible hand.

> *My Lord Kel:*
>
> *A company of my men-at-arms apprehended Lord Carl A'denné attempting to cross the canal to the Isle. This in itself should, of course, cause no alarm, but my men observed Lord Carl try to rid himself of some papers as he was found. These were fished from the canal at some risk. When brought to my attention I quickly perceived they were documents copied from my personal correspondence, some of which was of a sensitive nature regarding our preparations for war with the Prince of Innes. It seems that*

young Carl was playing us for fools, and was, all along, a loyal ally of Innes. I confronted him with these papers, which I have included with this message for your perusal, and I must say, his answer was less than satisfactory. I deemed it wise to keep him secure until I could consult with you, but to my shame, he has escaped. I'm sure he will try to make his way over the canal again, so all of your troops should be alerted to this. I have men out searching for him now. With luck I will have him again before this letter reaches you.

Your servant,
Vast

Folded in with the letter Kel found some sheets of paper, wrinkled, and water-stained. They were all in the same hand and were copies of letters from various Renné to the Duke of Vast and from Vast to Toren and Lady Beatrice. Kel leafed through them, skimming over the contents, finding little of real import. Still, they had been copied by Carl A'denné, and there could be no other explanation for this than that he was a spy for Innes, pretending he had changed sides—he and his father. Kel felt a little twinge of disappointment.

"What is it, sir?" Tuwar asked.

Kel handed him the bundle of letters without explanation. The old soldier read through them slowly. After a moment, he looked up, eyes wrinkled to slits. "This is the same boy who saved your life?"

"The very one."

Tuwar glanced down at the letters again. "I find this very odd. Certainly there was nothing to be gained by keeping you alive."

"So one would think. Tell me, Tuwar, why would Carl A'denné be in possession of letters he had copied from Vast as he crossed back over into our territory? That seems a rather foolish thing for such a clever young man to do."

"It does, sir, but I have seen wiser men make worse blunders."

"I suppose."

"I'll alert the men to be on the look out for Carl A'denné." Tuwar turned and gestured for one of his escorts.

"Tuwar . . . ," Kel said.

"Sir?"

"If you find him," Kel said so that no others might hear, "be sure he is brought to me unharmed, if at all possible."

Tuwar regarded his young commander a moment, his head tilted to one side, but he asked no questions. "As you say, Lord Kel."

Ten

Adiffuse, misty light spread over the eastern horizon, where the stars wallowed, then went under. Tam was awake, feeding the fire, when Alaan returned to the room.

"The wolf seems to have survived the night," Alaan said, "though Crowheart looks the worse for it. He says he will be able to ride today, but I don't think he will last the distance I had planned." Alaan began gathering up his belongings and packing them for the day's ride.

"You think the Dubrell will grant us passage then?" Fynnol asked.

Alaan tightened saddlebag buckles. "I don't know, but we must cross their lands all the same."

Fynnol stopped his packing and stared at Alaan, not liking what he heard.

"Have you learned anything of the riders?" Tam wondered.

"Not a thing. I dropped the broach you found back on the cobbles. I hope they'll find it. None of the Dubrell were about, nor were the riders. There are more mysteries here than answers."

"It is a place with many stories," Cynddl said. He leaned against one of the giant chairs, his arms crossed as though he were cold. His manner was subdued and his gaze lost in the flickering of the flames. "As can be seen by the size of the keep, many Dubrell dwelt here, though long ago now. This is a crossroads of sorts, but not of the usual kind. It is a crossroads between the land between the mountains and the hidden lands. Armies have passed through here, and fugitives, brigands, and sorcerers. War has come upon the Dubrell without warning from men with whom they had no quarrel. Many a farmstead has been burned, many a village.

"But this is the giants' home, and they will not leave it. They have a love for this land that is told in their stories and songs. Borenfall—Heaven's Doorstep—they call it." Cynddl closed his eyes. "They built this keep to watch over the north pass, by which we arrived yesterday. Beyond the gates you will find mounds where the dead have been burned and buried; both Dubrell and men. Last night, as I lay awake, I saw the battles fought here, the giants almost always outnumbered. They are not warlike by nature, but when they are angered . . .

"There was once a race of men who lived several days' ride to the north. They were warlike and merciless. They preyed upon the Dubrell, raiding their villages and putting everyone to the sword— or so the giants believed. One winter night a young man, hardly more than a boy, stumbled into a village of the Dubrell. He claimed his name was Raindel and that he had escaped from the land to the north, where the men held many Dubrell captive, keeping them as slaves. The giants were forced to do the most menial work, even pulling the plow, for the men said that horses were too valuable for such work. The boy had crossed the north pass in winter, and was frostbitten and fevered and near to death. The Dubrell who looked upon him went into a silent rage. More of their kind were gathered from all across the valley, and in the dead of winter they forced their way through the deep snows of the north pass. The first village of men they found at night and fell upon the unsuspecting inhabitants, putting everyone to the sword, burning all the buildings.

There they found a few of their kind living in squalor, little better than animals." Cynddl paused a moment, rubbing his brow so that Tam could not see his eyes. "And so it went, village after village. Even the keeps of the men were not proof against the rage of the giants, who felled great trees and, using them for battering rams, shattered the strongest gates.

"The last men met the Dubrell on a winter field, their land in flames all around. They brought forward all the Dubrell who remained in the land and gave them into the keeping of the invaders. Chests of gold and other valuables were given as well. 'Leave the few of us who remain in peace, and we will never raid your lands again, and never again will we keep your people for our slaves.' But the Dubrell were not satisfied. Many wanted the blood of this last army as well. A great argument ensued and finally they reached an agreement. 'Leave these lands this day, and we will spare you. Ride beyond the Shattered Mountain, and settle there. Any of your kind still dwelling here on the morrow will pay the price for what you have done to our people.' "

The men knew that many would die in such a march, but all would die before the wrath of the Dubrell, so they gathered their remaining people and made what preparations they could to travel north. They passed into a winter storm and were never heard of again.

Cynddl went to his bed and began packing his belongings, looking at no one, his face tired and pale. The others left him in peace and packed silently for a time. When the door opened and Stonehand appeared, they all started.

"Uamon would speak with you," the giant said. "Come, break your fast."

In the large room they found the wolf sleeping peacefully, Rabal in a heap beside him, snoring softly.

"He is happier with beasts than men," Uamon said. The old giant rose as they entered and motioned them to the table, where he sat alone. A warm mash of grain was ladled from a steaming iron pot.

"Have you an answer for us, Uamon?" Alaan asked. "There is little time for what we must do."

"Time chases all of us," Uamon said. "But I have duties to the Dubrell that cannot be ignored. I know you not, Alaan, but that you have come from afar where few men travel. Enemies followed you—evil men, perhaps. And you go now to the south into lands of mist and fear. This concerns the Dubrell, for our southern border is threatened by strange beasts that appear only on the darkest nights. Our people there fall victim to sickness and despair. Some have gone mad. Shall I send strangers there? Strangers who know something of magic?" He drank from a steaming cup. "You seek knowledge you say. A noble endeavor. A spell decays, you tell us, and soon the world will be overrun." He fixed his troubled blue eyes on Alaan. "If we did not struggle against dark creatures, I would not believe you." His gaze wandered to the sleeping wolf. "But perhaps you have been sent to aid us, to deliver us, for in the long war against the night we are losing." His eyes seemed to glisten a little, but then he returned his attention to Alaan. "If you will take Wolfson with you, I will grant you leave to cross our lands."

Alaan drew in a long breath and placed his fingertips together. "To the southern border of your own lands—I have no objection to his accompanying us—but there he must return."

Uamon nodded. "Agreed."

Alaan looked over at Tam, not hiding his misgivings. He turned his gaze back to the giant. "Wolfson must understand—I will not tolerate his interfering in my duties."

Uamon did not look away. "Nor will Wolfson tolerate your endangering our people." The two stared a moment more, then both looked away. The rest of the meal was eaten in silence.

The outsiders were soon carrying their bags and weapons down into the courtyard. Tam wanted to ask about the men who had arrived so late at night, but followed Alaan's example and said nothing.

Wolfson had their mounts saddled and waiting in the courtyard. The great gate creaked open, and Stonehand waved to them from the top of the wall. Wolfson did not ride—it would have taken a Fáel horse to bear his weight—but Tam remembered that his stride was long. On his back the giant carried a pack, and in his hand a staff. A sword swung at his side, and from his pack hung a massive iron helm. They filed out, Wolfson waving to Stonehand.

Off to their right, in the shadows of the trees, Tam saw movement.

"Wolves," Crowheart said. "But do not be concerned, you are with me." He glanced over at the giant who plodded along beside him. "And I'm sure Wolfson would not let us come to harm."

Tam nodded. Not that armed men should normally fear wolves—but he had seen what the pack had done to Hafydd's spies the previous day.

The path led down into the trees, the birds all around singing of morning. The grass was damp with dew, and the air still mountain-cool. Tam looked back once where a hole in the trees opened up, and there on the wall of the keep he thought he saw another standing beside Stonehand—someone who did not reach the giant's shoulder.

"So who were those men who came last night?" Tam called to Alaan. "The Dubrell did everything they could to keep us from knowing they were there."

"So they did," Alaan answered. He slowed his horse a little so that Tam caught up.

"What did you mean when you said they would only need surcoats if they were fighting men?" Tam asked, a little afraid of the answer.

Alaan did not respond immediately. They rode on through the pure mountain morning, the light playing down through the trees. "You heard Uamon talking about a threat to the south. I don't think the Dubrell are frightened of men, somehow. Their numbers are small, but they are formidable warriors. I have seen what Slight-hand could do—how he could turn the tide of a battle all by himself. No, the giants are fighting something else. And these men who came last night, these men who carry the token of the Knights of the Vow, they are the Dubrell's allies. That is what I think. I have seen battle-hardened men-at-arms many times, and these men were so hardened. But I somehow doubt that Lord Toren's friend, A'brgail, knows of their existence."

"It's as though the past has come back to haunt us," Tam said.

"Yes," Alaan answered. "One would think time would be a more effective barrier, but it has not proven so."

As they rode down into the green valley below, Tam could see ribbons of smoke spiraling up above the trees, but no villages or buildings could he find. On the lake's west shore he could see fields of irregular shapes, one spotted with the dark forms of cattle, but there were no other signs of men—or Dubrell.

They made reasonable time, and despite the urgency of Alaan's commission, the company did not seem to hurry. It was as though the threat that lurked to the south paralyzed them a little, slowing their pace.

Tam found himself taking pleasure in the day, in the flight of birds or in the patterns made by sunlight falling on the forest floor. He could see why the Dubrell loved their valley, and it was some time before he remarked its great similarity to the Vale of Lakes. Though of course the Vale had many more fields and small villages and roads. This valley hardly appeared to be inhabited at all.

When Tam pointed this out to Alaan, the traveler answered, "The valley stretches far to the west, where there are villages and much farming. That's why I chose to come by the north pass. I thought we might slip through without being noticed, but luck did not favor us."

They rode that day through the valley, which appeared to be a place of peace and quiet beauty. Fynnol, however, didn't look at peace; nor did he seem to notice the beauty around him. When Tam commented on the similarity between this valley and their own, Fynnol barely raised his head to look but only nodded and fell back to brooding.

Cynddl was equally quiet and troubled, though Tam suspected it had little to do with any events of that day or even anxiety about the future. He had seen his friend look this way before—the stories of this place disturbed him, and there was no place where he could hide from them. Tam had come to realize that the life of a story finder was not enviable. For every story that rose from the ground like a gift, there were many that rose like cadavers, disturbing and best left unknown. The stories of men were too often stories of war and treachery, greed and revenge. Cynddl had once told him that stories of love did not linger and last the way stories of hatred or violence did—as though the intensity of the emotions sustained the stories over time. Tam wanted to believe that love would be stronger than hatred, but it appeared not to be so.

Wolfson drifted apart from them as they traveled, and now and then Tam would catch a glimpse of him striding beneath the trees, a wolf or two gamboling about his heels.

And to think, Tam found himself ruminating, they had set out to travel a fortnight on the river to buy horses upon which to ride home. That had been their idea of an adventure—the adventure of a lifetime! He suspected that if he lived to tell his story in the Vale, none would believe him. No, that was not true: his grandfather would believe.

Evening brought them to the base of a wooded hill that stood out from the terrain around like a massive burial mound. They filled their drinking skins from a spring that Wolfson knew.

"It is a good place to camp," the giant said, crouching before the spring. The water splashed out of a cleft in the rock and fell into a diminutive pool, bordered by large, flat stones, no doubt placed there by Wolfson's people. Darkness was perhaps an hour off, and already the mountains were casting long shadows over the green valley. "There is a often a cool wind from the north at night. Air sweeping down off the mountains."

"We will make our camp on the hilltop," Alaan said, waving a hand up the slope.

"But the hilltop will offer little protection from the wind," Wolfson argued.

"No, but it will offer protection from other things."

Wolfson stood, rocking from one foot to the other. "My people don't go up on this hill. It is a cursed place."

"We will chance superstition," Alaan said, and led his horse toward the wooded slope.

It was almost sunset as they crested the mound. There were fewer trees there, and the vantage offered unobstructed views to all points of the compass. To the north, rugged mountains and the long valley winding off to the west. They looked down on the forest from the hill, and into the large meadows that interrupted the green carpet of trees. Cynddl began pointing and naming species of trees by the differing shades of green.

Already a cool breeze flowed down from the mountaintops, and the companions all found cloaks from their packs. Wolfson looked accusingly at Alaan, but the traveler did not seem to notice, or if he did, care. As the others unsaddled horses and collected firewood, Alaan stood staring off to the north, his face grim. One of Wolfson's small pack of wolves came into camp then, and it took up a place next to Alaan, sitting and staring out over the forest as though it too looked for something.

"What is it, Alaan?" Tam said quietly. He had positioned himself so that Alaan was between him and the wolf.

"No fire," Alaan said. "We will stand watches tonight."

"Are we so close to Death's kingdom?"

"Yes and no. Our task is too important to risk by complacency." He turned away and fetched his bow from his saddle, then walked once around the hill, examining the lay of the land, gazing off into the south for a while, where the dark clouds of a storm hung low, obscuring the landscape.

Alaan returned to the others. "If we make camp over here," he said, pointing to the south, "there is a rock outcropping that will give us some shelter."

In a few moments they had established themselves in the lee of a small rock face, out of the worst of the cool wind.

"We might start a fire here after dark," Alaan said, looking at the lay of the land. They were in a natural hollow, now, which would likely hide their fire from anyone below. Smoke, of course, would not be hidden, but by dark in this breeze it would be quickly swept away and hard to see on such a black night.

"Who is it Alaan fears?" Fynnol asked Tam, as darkness fell. Tam could not see his cousin, but he could hear the concern in his voice.

"I don't know," Tam said, "but he is watching the north."

Indeed, the traveler had posted himself in the brunt of the breeze and sat, hunched against the wind, staring toward the mountains. Stars appeared, but the moon had not yet risen, and the forest spread out as dark as the ocean.

Upon the hilltop, the trees bent and creaked to the wind, branches flailing the darkness. Leaves and pine needles whirled by, and the wind whistled eerily from all around.

"Well, it is a good night for a ghost story," Fynnol said as he used a flint to fire some tinder. "Cynddl, certainly you must know a good ghost story? Something that will creep into our dreams and wake us all at the slightest noise."

"I know too many stories that will do that," the Fáel said, "but I think tonight is a night for a different kind of tale." Cynddl shifted himself, warming his legs by the fire, for the wind bore the cold of the mountains. "This is an old story of the Dubrell, one that Wolfson must know. The kingdom to the south has always loomed over the valley of the giants, like a dark, shadowing mountain. Even in more peaceful times the people of this valley lived uneasily in that shadow. It ruined their sleep and troubled their waking hours. For some it was like a dark place in the mind. A dark place of fear that never went away even beneath the midday sun. There were no monstrosities escaping the southern kingdom then, only the whisperings of Death's servants. To most these whisperings were no more than chill breezes, disturbing one's sleep. But to others there were words in such breezes—words and promises. A group of Dubrell heard these promises and heeded them. Secretly their numbers grew—"

"This is a lie!" exploded Wolfson. "None of my people ever had dealings with the southern kingdom!" The giant had risen to his feet and glared down at Cynddl, pointing a massive finger at the story finder. His other hand went to the hilt of his sword.

"The stories I find are true," Cynddl said evenly, "whether you believe them or not. I apologize if this story disturbs you."

"I won't listen to lies!" the giant said, and stormed off into the night.

Everyone was silent a moment, uncertain what to do, then Crowheart said, "I would hear the rest of this story."

"So would I," Fynnol agreed.

Alaan, who had come to stand just at the firelight's edge, nodded.

Cynddl composed himself again, his eyes losing focus as he looked within to that place where stories were found. "Secretly their numbers grew," he said again, "and they began to whisper among themselves, whisper of overthrowing the leaders of their people and making bargains with the kingdom to the south, so they would not have to live in fear. On a moonless night they came here, where a tower stood—Thollingkep it was called. By deception they had the gate opened, and slipped within. . . ."

Tam was no longer staring into the fire, but into the darkness. He realized that Wolfson stood not far off, listening.

"A terrible fight ensued, but the Dubrell of Thollingkep were murdered—man, woman . . . , child. A war broke out among the giant folk, a long war that finally saw the defeat of the traitors— those who had listened to the whispers. That is why the Dubrell don't come here now. It is a cursed place they say—a haunted place."

Wolfson appeared out of the darkness. "How did you know the name of this hill?" he asked, his voice quiet now.

"Cynddl is a Fáel story finder," Alaan said. "He can hear the stories of a place. What he says is true. There is no lying to a story finder."

Wolfson stared at Cynddl a moment.

"That is not the story I've heard," the giant said. "The elders say that Death sent a plague through the eastern parts of our land, and it swept the children away. He sent emissaries to the elders of these lands, then, and promised to return the children if they would make war on their brethren. As a token of his goodwill he sent a child—a single child who had died, now returned to the living. In their sorrow the fathers took up arms against their own people."

Cynddl shook his head. "That is not the story I have found here."

"Death lets no one go who has passed through the gate," Alaan said. "No one. I'm sorry."

Wolfson hung his head a moment. His hand dropped from the hilt of his sword.

A deep blaring note, like a distant horn, came to them then, carried on the wind. Tam barely noted it, but Wolfson pulled himself up, turning his head slowly, listening, completely alert.

"Did you hear that?" the giant whispered. The faltering firelight played across his bearded face, now suddenly strained and grim.

"I thought I heard something," Fynnol said, looking up at the giant in apprehension. "What made such a sound?"

"A horn," the giant whispered, still turning his head, seeking sounds on the wind. "There! Again! Did you hear that?"

Tam heard.

Wolfson grabbed his axe.

"Shall we douse the fire?" Cynddl asked.

"No. Build it up!" the giant said as he strode toward a stand of saplings. "And find more firewood."

He began to hack the saplings down and lop off the branches. Alaan took up their own axe and went to the giant's aid, not even stopping to ask questions.

"Here," Wolfson said, tossing a sapling to Alaan. "We must have spears. Sharpen that and harden it in the fire. Iron tips are what we need, but this will have to do."

"What's out there?" Fynnol asked. He stood looking on, almost bouncing with fear.

"Perhaps it isn't us they're after," Wolfson said, still chopping branches away. "We might hope." And he said no more.

Tam strung his bow and found all his arrows before searching for more firewood. The wind continued to howl through the trees, and, overhead, clouds buried the stars. Firelight grew as they heaped on dry branches, lighting the sentinel trees, coloring the apprehensive faces of his companions a dull orange.

Tam threw another armful of twisted branches on the fire and wiped away the sweat from his forehead and eyes. The call of the horn was heard again, but this time closer, the sound making the hair on his neck stand up. Wolfson's pack surged into camp, their own hackles erect. They were fretting and growling, howling sporadically. They gathered about their master but kept their eyes on the darkness to the north, their teeth bared.

Tam stood by the fire, his bow in hand, one of Wolfson's makeshift spears planted in the earth. They all arrayed themselves with their backs to the fire, Wolfson in the center, Cynddl, Tam, and Fynnol close to him, Alaan and Crowheart to the outside.

A different sound was carried on the wind now—the sound of breaking branches, of something crashing through the trees. The wolves began snarling and yapping at the darkness. Overhead the crows screeched and fluttered from branch to branch.

Whatever crashed through the wood stopped just at the shoreline where light met the sea of darkness. Wolfson took up a dead fir branch, all its needles turned to brown. He thrust it in the fire, then held it up flaring and crackling. Whatever lay beyond the firelight hesitated but did not retreat.

The horn sounded again, this time very near, and there was a sudden stamping in the darkness, then out of it shot some darkskinned creature, the height of a pony. It went straight for Wolfson, who tossed his brand at its face and stepped forward, driving his spear into its neck.

A boar, Tam realized, but huge and grotesque. Wolfson sprang out of the way of the tusks, and the beast charged into the fire. Tam leapt aside as burning logs were thrown every which way.

More creatures thundered out of the trees, some larger than the first. Wolves leapt at their legs from behind, and they kicked and threw their heads, but kept coming, snouts down, aiming to gore the men. Crows fell upon one, tearing at its eyes so that it veered aside and stopped, trying to shake off its tiny attackers. Crowheart stepped forward and calmly cut its throat with a sword.

Tam was struck from behind as he drove his makeshift spear into the shoulder of the largest of the creatures. He was thrown down on the ground and only saved himself from being trampled by rolling nimbly to one side.

"Go up!" Alaan shouted, pointing at the pinnacle of stone that leaned over the camp.

Fynnol was already scrambling up, tearing moss away from the rock in his efforts. Tam swept up his bow and quiver and tried to follow. The giant boars seemed to be everywhere, charging in all directions, chasing after wolves, trying to shake off the attacking crows. Though Tam didn't know who had fallen, he went bounding up the rocks hand over hand, his bow and quiver thrown quickly over a shoulder and threatening to get in his way and cause a fall.

Fynnol reached down and grabbed the first thing that came to hand—Tam's hair—and pulled him up onto the small summit. A boar tried to follow, snapping at Tam's heels, but Fynnol put an arrow in its snout, and it fell away, squealing.

A moment later they pulled Cynddl onto the peak and the three sent a rain of arrows down into the creatures that ran amok below. Fire had spread everywhere, catching in the dry grasses and in the dead branches of trees. The scene was chaos, with Wolfson in the middle, surrounded by his wolves, charging this way and that. Rabal's crow army lit upon the faces of the beasts, but Crowheart was nowhere to be seen.

"There must be twenty of them!" Fynnol shouted.

Rabal and Alaan appeared from behind, climbing onto the crowded summit. They began calling to Wolfson. "Come up! Come up!" though Tam didn't know where the giant would stand.

The largest of the beasts threw himself at the little hill of stone, and the men hacked and thrust with their swords. The pig would have thrown them all off but a rock rolled beneath its feet, and it slid down, landing on its side, where the pack fell upon it.

Wolfson came clambering up the slope then, and the archers tried to drive off the beast that chased him. The giant clung to the stone just below them, there being no room for him on the crest. He held on to the stone with one hand and brandished his sword with the other. Below, among the patches of flame, the enraged boars gathered, snuffling and squealing, arrows bristling from their faces and flanks. Shadows wavered across the ground and trees, and here and there fires flared up as some dry bush or grasses were touched by flame.

"They're going to charge us," Wolfson said, he looked behind. They were little more than a dozen feet above the giant creatures, and to their backs the ground was even closer as the slope of the hill rose up. "I think we have no choice but to run into the trees. Down the slope there are some great oaks and maples. We might climb up and be out of their reach. They will be gone by sun-up, if we can stay alive that long."

The wind whipped the giant's hair and beard, and blew bits of flaming vegetation past their faces. They all stood, gasping for breath, sweat running freely down faces turned the colors of sunset by the firelight. Alaan had blood running down his arm and covering his hand, though he didn't seem to notice.

A crashing in the forest behind caused them all to jump.

"They are behind us now, too," Alaan said, hefting his sword.

"They're going to charge!" Wolfson warned, and certainly the beasts did seem to have worked up their rage, squealing and pawing at the ground. Tam could see them in the orange light of the spreading fire. The eye did not admit their size—the largest the height of horses, but twice a horse's bulk. Lethal-looking tusks protruded from their snouts, and their small eyes glittered madly in the flickering light.

The wind blew fiercely across the hill, whipping the men's clothes and hair. It moaned through the trees, tossing branches and fanning the growing flames. A horn sounded, echoing down the wind. Wolfson braced himself for the assault, which he would meet first.

The squealing reached a frightening crescendo, and the terrible beasts charged in a mass.

Out of the trees, at that very moment, plunged riders.

"Hafydd's spies!" Fynnol cried, pointing.

"Into the trees!" Alaan shouted.

Tam turned to run, but more of the creatures loomed out of the dark. He fired an arrow, then another. The dark mass did not falter but charged through the underwood directly for them.

"Jump!" Cynddl cried, and they all threw themselves from the small summit.

Tam crashed through some sparse bushes and scrambled to his feet, ignoring the scratches and cuts. His bow was gone, so he yanked his sword from its scabbard and crouched low, ready to fight man or beast. From his place in the shadows he stared into the small clearing, and there, lit by burning trees and patches of grass, he saw a battle, between mounted men and these creatures, out of someone's nightmare. The horses wore trappings that protected them from being gored, and the men seemed to know their business, as though they'd fought such beasts before.

To Tam's surprise, Wolfson leapt down from his perch and waded into the battle, calling out to the men, who answered him with words Tam did not know. Alaan ran out of the shadows to guard the giant's back, and they leapt upon any animal thrown down by the riders, hacking at its throat or cruelly taking out its eyes.

The remaining creatures crashed into the dark wood, the sounds of their progress loud over the howl of the wind. They were gone.

The riders dismounted and immediately began beating out the flames with their cloaks. Wolfson took up the ruins of someone's bedding and did the same, flailing at the burning grass, coughing from the smoke. Tam sheathed his sword and followed the giant's example, choking and covering his mouth. But the flames fought back, refusing to be beaten, consuming all the fuel left by a dry summer.

Tam wondered if the whole hill would catch fire, perhaps even spreading down into the valley, when a drop of cool rain splattered on his forehead and ran down into his eye. In a moment it was raining hard, and the fire was failing. One of the strangers made an effort to keep flames in the fire pit, and by this frail light Tam and the others gathered their trampled belongings, some of which had been spread far beyond the small circle of light.

"I don't know what use a boar would have with my spare breeches," Fynnol said, "but clearly one of these foul beasts made off with them." He was rooting about in the bushes on the edge of the darkness. "That's probably why they attacked—not a stitch to wear among the lot of them."

The men who had come to their rescue were obviously the men from the giants' keep, the men the Dubrell had gone to such pains to hide. The strangers kept glancing at Alaan and the others, their gazes filled with questions.

Two of the giant boars lay dead not far from the fire, and Tam could see them now. They were gray-skinned, short-legged, and armed with tusks like daggers.

"Shall we spit one and roast it?" Fynnol asked, coming up beside Tam, who stood staring at one of the monsters.

"You won't want to eat them," one of the riders said, his accent not so thick as the giants'. "The meat is foul and will give you the belly torment. Some people it's killed."

Tam turned away from the beast and came back to the fire, cool rain streaming down his face and neck, soaking his clothing. On the edge of the small clearing, Wolfson was speaking with the man Tam guessed was the leader of the riders. Their impenetrable accent kept Tam from understanding their words, but it was clear they were arguing, and the man was red-faced with anger.

Some riders had posted themselves as guards around the camp's perimeter, but the others gathered with the outlanders around the fire. The downpour had slowed to light drizzle so that the drying power of the fire was just greater than the rain's ability to make them wet. There was no other conversation in the camp, and no one would look at the giant and the angry rider, but all ears strained to pick up what was being said above the drumming rain and the harshly moaning wind.

With a final shouted word, the rider turned and stalked directly to the fire. He took a seat on an empty saddle, which had obviously been set out for him, and stared a moment at the flames. Tam thought the man was trying to calm himself.

Wolfson did not move, but watched the men seated around the fire, his face filled with concern.

The captain of the riders looked up from the flames. "So you have come from the land beyond," he said evenly.

Alaan nodded, glancing once at Wolfson, who stood in the dark and rain, alone. A wolf trotted up and licked the giant's hand, as though it sensed his need for comfort.

"From the land of men . . . ?" the rider said.

"Yes," Alaan admitted, "from the land of men."

This caused a stir among the riders, who glanced one to the other, as though Alaan had confirmed something miraculous.

"Our ancestors came from the land of men," the rider said. "Eight generations my people have dwelt here, in Borenfall. Orlem Slighthand led my ancestors here to aid the Dubrell, and we have been here ever since."

"Slighthand!" Alaan said, surprised. Tam could see the traveler in the firelight, rain like dewdrops on his beard, running down his face like tears. His eyes darted from one rider to the next as though he were weighing them—weighing the truth of this last statement.

Slighthand!

"You know of Slighthand?" the captain asked.

"I know of Slighthand," Alaan agreed. "Why did he bring your people here? Were you mercenaries?"

The captain of the riders shared a glance with the man beside him. "We were members of a knightly order that Orlem Slighthand had founded with another named Kilydd. Orlem had become lost in the land of men, where he met a sorcerer who gave him the power to travel hidden lands. The Dubrell were besieged by men from the south, and Orlem brought my people to aid the Dubrell, whose enemy was cunning and ruthless. We have dwelt here since, on lands the Dubrell granted us." He pointed. "Not far to the east. Orlem Slighthand promised that we would one day return to the lands of men."

"It is a only a story," Wolfson said, coming and standing over the men seated by the fire—looming over them.

Tam realized then that the giants had been hiding his company from the riders—not the other way around.

"But you are Knights of the Vow," Fynnol said. "Isn't that true?"

The riders all stared at this new voice, but none of them answered.

"We found a token of the Knights of the Vow in the courtyard," Alaan explained. "A small broach made in the form of a fan of silveroak leaves. It is the token of a knightly order in the lands of men."

The riders shifted in their seats, not meeting Alaan's gaze.

"Don't speak of this matter, if you'd rather not," Alaan said. "How many of your people are there?"

"Six thousand," the captain said. "Two thousand are men-at-arms."

"Would you leave us now," Wolfson cried, "in our greatest need?"

"Eight generations we have given to your struggle!" the captain spat out. "We would go to the land of men, where there is peace."

Alaan sat back and ran a hand through his wet hair. "The same enemy threatens our lands. The same war spreads everywhere. I know nothing of your accord with the Dubrell, but it appears to me that your part in the war is to fight here. When the war is over, I will come and lead you back to the land of men, or I will send another to do so."

Wolfson turned away, as though a sudden pain coursed through him.

The captain of the riders rose up from his saddle to stand before Alaan. "This war does not end," he said firmly. "We could
come with you now."

Alaan shook his head. "I travel south, into the borderlands of
the shadow kingdom—"

"You will not return from that place," the rider said, distressed.
"It is the place of nightmares, of unspeakable horrors." He waved
a hand at the giant boar that lay two dozen feet away. "These are
the least of the monsters that come from the south. The Hand of
Death will steal the life from you. You will lead no one back to the
land of men, for you will be drawn into the darkness."

Alaan shrugged. "I have traveled into the borderlands of
Death's kingdom once before. I returned unharmed. I see no reason why I shouldn't do so again."

"The borderlands were quiet then," Wolfson interjected. "The
threat was small. Now monstrosities appear on dark nights. And
new monstrosities far too often. My people die defending our borders." He gestured to the captain. "Nathron's people die."

"Even so, that is where I must go. The safety of all our peoples
depends on it." He stood and looked the captain of the Knights in
the eye. "I will return for you. Or send another. I swear."

Eleven

They lay in the long grass, trying not to breathe. Lord Carl looked over at Jamm, his battered face turning slowly crimson. With ribs that were either broken or badly bruised, thanks to the ministrations of the Duke of Vast, Jamm could hardly keep his breathing quiet. Carl was terrified that the thief would cough and give them away, for he had coughed much the night before.

A dozen feet off, a small company of men-at-arms had stopped to water their horses. They wore the livery of the House of Vast and were, almost certainly, searching for Carl and Jamm.

The dawn had only just broken, the coarse grass slick with dew, the ground beneath them a cushion of moss. They had slept here for a few short hours, Jamm unable to continue. Their stolen mount had been abandoned in the night, set loose in a field with some other horses in hopes that she would not be discovered for some hours yet.

We should have cut her throat and left her in a wood, Carl thought, somewhere she wouldn't be found for a day or two. If she were found that day, Vast would know where to send his men-at-arms. Escape would be nearly impossible with Jamm so injured. What a beating he had taken!

But even so, the little thief's instincts remained intact. He reasoned that the Duke would assume they would go to Kel Renné. Best to do something unexpected, that was the rule Jamm lived by—do the unexpected. So they set out for the river, hoping to cross over and make their way to Westbrook. The Isle was large enough that Vast could not keep it all under his eye at once. And Jamm was clever enough to keep them out of sight for some time yet, unless luck turned on them—which it might at any moment if the little man coughed.

"They won't have gone this far," one of the men-at-arms said firmly. He had a deep voice, thick and heavy like the rumble of distant thunder. "That little thief couldn't go more than half a league, even on horseback. We saw to that."

The others laughed.

Carl saw Jamm bury his mouth in the sleeve of his jacket.

Don't cough, Carl willed him. *Don't cough . . .*

"Who's this, then?" one of the others asked.

Carl heard the men all rise to their feet, swords slipping from scabbards.

"Ah," the deep-voiced one said, " 'tis only some Renné, hoping to find the last few men of Innes to hone their blades on."

Carl dared not look at his guide, fearing what he would see.

The Duke's men greeted the Renné.

"So what game has Carl A'denné been playing?" one of the newcomers asked.

Carl could hear the stir of excitement among the horses being watered as the other horses appeared. The grass stirred over him in the breeze, and a wren scolded. He felt like it was only a matter of time, perhaps only a moment, before they were discovered. Jamm could not run, and how far would Carl get, chased by mounted men? He closed his eyes and tried to calm his heart. It was over. They had only this last moment of freedom.

"Seems he was spying for the Prince of Innes, or so we surmise. But he must have been playing both sides. He came over the canal the other night with a little thief guiding him. Someone knew the thief by name, and Vast soon had the story from him. A'denné and his thieving friend slipped away by night, a sure sign of his guilt, I say."

"Well," the Renné said, "we'll soon have the story from A'denné himself."

"Not if we find him first," the Duke's man growled. His company all laughed.

"We've been ordered to bring him to Lord Kel alive," the Renné said.

"We've been promised a reward to bring back his head and leave his body for the crows," the man of Innes answered. There was silence for a moment, and Jamm coughed.

He'd muffled the sound as best he could, but not well enough.

"What was that?" one of the men asked.

Carl heard blades being drawn, followed by footsteps through the long grass.

Jamm looked at him, eyes wide. He knew he couldn't run. Would the men of Innes kill them before the Renné could intercede?

Suddenly something shot through the grass.

"There!" someone yelled.

Carl rose to his hands and knees, prepared to fight or run.

A small pig flew out of the grass onto the road, and the men of Innes took after it. Swords flashed, and the pig squealed and screamed. The little animal dodged this way and that, as the men flailed away at it, finally landing a blow and spraying them with blood. The pig still ran, and a second blow brought it down, but it was up again, struggling forward on three legs. It only went a few feet before one of the shouting men raised a sword over his head, two-handed, and finished the little animal. The men were all laughing and pointing at the swordsmen who'd missed.

A wind sprang up then, combing through the grass. Carl and Jam went crawling off, the sound of their progress lost in the wind and the cruel hissing of the fields.

Twelve

Dease noted each of his visits to Lady Llyn Renné in the back of a book. He did this so that he could not lie to himself about the frequency of their talks. There were reasons of decorum that would justify this scrupulous accounting—you simply didn't visit a lady too often unless you were betrothed. But that wasn't really his concern: he didn't want to appear foolish before Llyn. Everyone in the castle knew that she loved Toren. It was Dease's fondest hope that she would one day see the futility of her feelings for Toren, then Dease might woo and win her affections.

But now he had heard another rumor; while he was away, Llyn had often been visited by Lord Carral Wills, and she had allowed him into her garden and met with him face-to-face.

A feeling like falling came over him, and he could not help but shut his eyes. The darkness brought no comfort. Unlike Dease, Lord Carral was blind. The minstrel could never look upon Llyn's scarred face. She did not know that the people who loved her cared not at all about her appearance, no matter how terrible she thought it herself.

Dease didn't care, that was certain. The longing to be in her presence, to be near to her, was at times unbearable. He would lie awake nights thinking of nothing else. He dreamed of Llyn, of seeing her face for the first time. In some dreams she was hideous beyond bearing—and he would run away, down long endless hallways. In other dreams her beauty was dazzling. Sometimes he dreamed that he traveled far, and against great odds, found a cure for her burns, and carried it back to her.

But these were dreams. In real life, he kept count of how often he visited so he should not appear too foolish—like an infatuated boy.

A maid curtsied him out onto the balcony, where he stood, gazing over the walled garden. By day, he had never seen it. By night it was a mysterious place, filled with shadows and unrecognizable shapes in shades of gray. Lavender was the scent of the place, and a small tinkle of running water was its voice. That, and the sighs and whispers of the trees.

Dease gazed down into the shadows, starlight glinting off the water of a small pool. He struggled with the feelings inside of him, as he always did in this place.

"Ah, Lord Dease," came Llyn's lovely voice. It stabbed into him like a blade—then the pain dissolved into an ache.

"Lady Llyn," Dease said softly.

"I cannot tell you how happy I was to hear that you'd returned."

"And that Toren had returned with me, no doubt."

A small hesitation. "Yes . . . I was happy to hear of Toren's return, as well."

Movement caught his eye. She was there, beneath the thin foliage of a lace maple. Her famous blond hair caught his eye, and he remembered the scent of it—that night they'd danced, she in costume and carefully masked.

He shut his eyes a moment and breathed in the scent of lavender.

"Lord Carral is a guest of Castle Renné, I've been told?"

"Yes," she said, her voice soft and tentative. "He has become our ally, as you've no doubt heard."

"So I understand." Dease read much into her voice, into the pauses, the little inflections, the warmth with which she said a name. Later he would revisit each little nuance, wondering what they meant. Pondering them over and over, until he had made so many interpretations of her words that he would finally lose all sense of what she might have truly meant.

"There are rumors all around the castle that you traveled to some distant place and saw magic performed. . . ."

"We did not appear to travel far—a few days' journey—but we were in strange lands all the same. It all seems like a dream, now—or a nightmare."

"And did you meet a rogue there who called himself Alaan?"

Dease was taken aback by this. "Has someone told you of our journey already?"

"No one has. But you did meet such a man?"

Dease moved his hand on the smooth railing, gazing down into the dark, trying to make sense of this new interest. "Well, I would not say I met him. He was ill nearly unto death and hardly able to mutter a few words most of the time, let alone carry on a conversation."

"Then Toren did save him?"

"No more than a number of other people. We all fought Hafydd, who sought this Alaan to murder him."

"How utterly strange," Llyn's voice drifted up from beneath the canopy of leaves. A moment she was silent, the soft whispering of the wind in the branches, like some languorous speech, too slow for man to comprehend. But then, Dease thought, the trees had so many years to live, why should they hurry like short-lived humans?

"And Samuel and Beldor; did you ever find them?"

"Yes. Toren granted them immunity, as long as they never again set foot on Renné lands."

She seemed to consider this a moment. "It is like Toren to be compassionate, but not at the cost of justice. What transpired, I wonder, to lead him to make such a decision?"

"It was very simple, really: we needed Samul and Beld to fight Hafydd and his . . . supporters."

"Ah," Llyn said. "The Renné have made many such alliances in our history. Some for good. Some for ill."

He could almost feel her staring up at him through the leaves, and he was suddenly uncomfortable, almost embarrassed.

"What became of Samul and Beld?"

"No one knows. It is something of a miracle that Toren and I survived and found each other. Many, I fear, were lost, including Samul and Beld, which would be for the better, in many ways."

"I suppose it would, though I would dearly like to know what they were thinking, trying to murder Toren." He saw her thick cascade of hair shake in the starlight.

"Beld did not need to think; he hated Toren completely. Samul . . . ? Well, who ever knew what Samul was thinking?"

"I did not know him well," Llyn said, "but it would seem to be true. He was a hidden man. I wonder how many people came away from conversations under the impression that Samul agreed with them, when he did not at all? There was never any truth to him. Nothing revealed. I wonder what made him so?"

The question did not seem to really be addressed to Dease, but he tried to answer it all the same.

"I don't know, Cousin," Dease said. "He was always thus. Even when we were children, or so I think now."

"I shall have to hear the story of your adventure in its entirety sometime. I am delighted to see you have returned unharmed. And the blow to your head that you suffered trying to save Toren?"

"It is healed. The headaches gone"—he raised his hands, and smiled—"as if by magic."

"There is some good news, I'm glad to hear."

There was the quick crunch and scatter of gravel as someone trotted along the path.

"Your grace?" a maid said softly.

"What is it, Anna?"

"A company of men-at-arms has just arrived with a man they found wandering in a wood. He is said to be Lord Samul Renné."

Dease closed his eyes, leaning his weight against the railing.

Suddenly his head throbbed, and the fatigue that had beset him seemed to cast its net over him again, dragging him down. He thought he might begin to sob and went quickly from the balcony, collapsing into one of the chairs in the small drawing room.

Would he never be shut of Samul and Beld? Could they not die or flee? As long as they remained alive he would know no peace. The truth would come out one day,

Llyn's words came back to him then. *There was never any truth in him.*

She should have been speaking of me, Dease realized.

He turned to look back out toward the garden but caught sight of his own dark reflection in the glass of the opened door. How shadowed his eyes were. How contrived the look of his face. He was becoming more like Samul each day, a hidden man. A man in whom there was no truth. And how would he ever change that now?

Thirteen

There were a few cells hidden away beneath Castle Renné, though nothing like the "dungeons" one read of in stories. Dease made his way down the uneven stairs by the light of a lantern, careful with his footing. The stone treads were crudely made, uneven and broken in places—easy enough to lose one's footing and stumble. He wiped away a cobweb that netted his face, then ran a hand over his hair to search for spiders.

He came into a passageway, its vaulted stone ceiling lost in smoky shadows. The air there was cool with a dank odor of newly turned soil. A guard at the end of the passage rose quickly from the box he'd been lounging on, clearly worried that Dease would upbraid him for lazing on the job. Dease, however, could not have cared less.

"Lord Samul," Dease said.

The man bowed nervously. "This way, your grace." He lifted a lantern from a hook set into the wall and led down a short side passage. Before a door with a tiny, barred window he stopped.

"That will be all," Dease said, and the guard waddled off.

Inside the cell a candle flickered, offering dull illumination to a cot, a small desk, and a single, straight-backed chair.

"Samul?"

A form rose from the cot, tossing back a blanket. "Dease?" Samul appeared in the candlelight, rising stiffly. He crossed the few paces to the ironbound door.

"I'm glad to see you alive, Cousin," Samul said, keeping his voice low.

"And you, Cousin," Dease answered. "But what folly brought you here to Castle Renné? You must know that Toren will keep his word."

"I was washed out of the Stillwater into a little tributary of the Wynnd. I didn't know at first where I was."

Dease hung his lantern up on a hook by the door. It drove back only the worst of the shadows. The effect of this was to give to Samul's face a cast of distress that was certainly not there. None of Samul's emotions ever showed on his face—which had led many to speculate that he had no feelings.

"I might have slipped quietly away, but when I heard war had broken out I knew I had to return to warn Toren. You will hardly believe me, but Hafydd has made a bargain with Death."

"We know," Dease answered. "One of the northerners, Fynnol, saw . . . you in league with Hafydd. Or so the Fáel say."

Samul's hands came up and curled around the bars. "No, Dease! I had no choice but to pretend to serve Hafydd. It was Beld who made a bargain with Hafydd, not I. In the Stillwater Hafydd approached me alone and offered me a place of prominence in his court when he overran the land between the mountains. He spoke very seductively about all that I could have and achieve, and gave me a small leather case, which he said contained an egg. I was to open the case and break the egg just before Alaan led us out of the Stillwater. Out of range of Hafydd's influence I came to my senses. But when I went to destroy the egg Beld found me and snatched the egg from my hand, and broke it open. A wasp, flew out—I swear it is the truth—and Hafydd then believed that it was I who had signaled him. But it was Beld." He stopped to take a breath and collect his thoughts. "I saved Toren from Beld. Has he forgotten that?"

"I'm sure he hasn't. You also tried to murder him. He hasn't forgotten that either."

"And what of you, Dease? Have you forgotten your part?"

Dease looked around quickly, wondering how far voices carried down these passages. "I've not forgotten, Cousin," he whispered. "That is why I'm here. I'll try to intercede with Toren for you—and with Lady Beatrice as well. But they will never trust you. Be sure of that. If I cannot sway them, I will get you out of here somehow." He glanced back down the hall. "This guard is fond of his drink. I shall slip him enough brandy to put him to sleep if I must."

They fell silent then, the two conspirators. The lantern guttered and went out, leaving Dease in near darkness, only the frail light of Samul's candle pushing back a thousandth part of the darkness. Dease glanced quickly around and he realized *he* could be in the cell, and the little window through which he could see Samul's faint silhouette his only view of the outside.

He reached up and clasped Samul's hand, which still held the bar. "Is there anything you need?"

Samul laughed. "In such luxurious surroundings what could any man want? A new pallet and bedding would not be out of order. Candles. A book to read. Ink and paper. I will soon go mad down here if I have nothing to occupy my hours."

"I'll see to your needs, Samul. As soon as I can." Dease reached up and took his lantern down from its hook, feeling the warmth still rising from it even though the flame had vanished. He turned away, leaving his cousin's haunted face framed in the barred window.

"Dease?" Samul called before Dease had gone a dozen paces.

"Yes?"

"And a cloak of wool. It is damp and chill down here. A man can never get warm."

"I'll find you one," Dease said.

He lit his lamp again from the guard's and carried on down the passage, the small, barred windows of empty cells gazing at him reproachfully as he left.

Fourteen

Elise and A'brgail supported each other as they fought through the final yards of bramble and into the failing sunlight. A'brgail glanced quickly behind. The day was all but gone, the western sky awash in molten cloud.

"He's no longer near," Elise said calmly. Her gaze appeared to rest upon some distant place, far out of his view.

A'brgail was humbled by her strength. He leaned an arm on her thin girlish shoulders, but she did not falter or even seem to notice. Her slight frame was stronger than his—stronger than any man's, he expected. If not for Elise he would never have survived the flooded cavern. But surviving that took all his strength, and he couldn't have walked another furlong without her. He shook his head. Elise stood erect still, though her golden hair was tangled, her clothing so torn to ruins that it was barely decent. Where she had been battered against the stone walls in the maze of tunnels, her skin was darkly bruised and scraped raw. She lowered A'brgail to a fallen trunk and sat down on a little hillock opposite.

"Are we in the hidden lands, yet?" the knight asked. "I've seen no landmark I recognize. No village or road. Not even a dirt track that might lead us . . . somewhere. We must not yet have found our way back into the land between the mountains."

"We're back to our own lands," Elise said, her voice far away. "Though where we are I cannot say. Lost. . . ." She said this last word wistfully. Then to herself, *Lost.*

A'brgail regarded her with what he realized was pity—this thing he had once vowed to destroy. This abomination, who appeared to be a troubled young woman, sad beyond measure. "Are you well, my lady?" he asked softly.

"No, Sir Gilbert," she said, shaking her head, her gaze fixed on the open fields. "I have not been well since I sold my soul to a monster."

"You don't seem much like a monster," he answered, to his surprise.

"No? I fear it will show in time." She looked down at her hands, turning them over as though not sure they were hers. "I have her memories, her sensibility and feelings, struggling against my own, against my nature. Sianon was without remorse, without affection. Her lovers were too numerous to name, and she loved none of them. Her own children went into battle to gain her love, and when they died she did not mourn. It was the price of her gift—all loved her, but she cared for no one. That is not true; she loved one man— her own brother, Sainth, who has made a bargain with Alaan."

"My brother," A'brgail said softly.

Elise did look up at him then, a crease appearing between her eyebrows, as though she tried to look inside him.

"It is a tangle of relations," she said, running her hand absent-mindedly over her torn breeches.

"But you are not Sianon," A'brgail insisted. "Alaan swears that he is not controlled by Sainth, and in truth, he does not seem greatly changed, though I have been loath to admit it until now."

"But Alaan and Sainth are not so different. Sianon . . . she is my opposite in almost every way. And I have already given in, once, to her . . . appetites." She played with a frayed edge on her torn breeches. "A part of me did it only for pleasure, as a man might go to a brothel"—she closed her eyes, cheeks burning—"but the part of me that is . . . me—I was not so callous. My heart was . . . touched. It will sound naive, but I swear I felt it open—like a blossom." She closed her eyes, as though to staunch the tears.

A'brgail found himself wanting to comfort her, though he feared it was the spell that surrounded Sianon that made everyone want to please her, to win her favor, but he couldn't help himself. "Don't be ashamed of having womanly feelings," he said. "Better to have a broken heart than no heart at all."

"Easily said," Elise answered, opening her eyes and blinking rapidly. She wiped a dirty sleeve across her cheeks. "But thank you all the same." She stood. "We must go on. I need to know where we are and how far it is back to Westbrook."

"Not far," said a voice.

Elise spun around to find a Fáel standing a few yards off, a sword in hand.

"Archers have their arrows trained on your hearts," the man said. "You would be wise not to move."

"And who are you?" Elise asked, trying to keep the pride of Sianon in check.

"I am Brendl," the Fáel answered. "And you would appear to be beggars, by your dress, but I suspect that is far from the truth."

A'brgail realized that other men lurked in the shadows of the trees as the dusk settled around them.

"I'm Elise Wills, and this is Gilbert A'brgail, a knight whose deeds, if they were known, would win him great renown."

"Elise Wills drowned in the Westbrook," Brendl said, "or so it is said."

"I did go into the Westbrook, to escape a man who calls himself Sir Eremon, but I did not drown, as you can see."

The Fáel nodded, a little bow of acknowledgment. "You are very much alive, but whether or not you are Elise Wills . . . that is for others to judge. Come with me."

"And where will you take us?"

"Not far," he said. Other Fáel appeared out of the wood then, all uncharacteristically well armed.

Elise glanced at A'brgail and nodded, to his relief. He could not have put up any resistance. He barely managed to gain his feet without help. A Fáel came to his aid, and he made his way through the shadows beneath the trees, with Elise supporting him on one side and a black wanderer on the other.

In a few moments they broke out of the trees into the quickly failing light.

Brendl raised a hand and pointed. "There. The tower cities of my people."

A'brgail pulled himself upright and gazed down the hillside into the dark shadow of the undulating blue hills. There was water there—a small lake, perhaps—dark as steel in the spreading twilight. And then he saw them; the three worn stone towers—raised by the hand of nature—extending like misshapen fingers from the smooth water. Upon their crests the cities of the Fáel—Aland-or, Fylan-or, and Naismoran.

"How in the world have we come here? It is far from where we began."

"Leagues," Elise said.

They made their way down the hillside. A rubble wall protected a sloping pasture, and they clambered noisily over loose stone and down into the soft grass. Sheep appeared to float in the twilight: small, dim clouds upon the heath.

It was a long walk down the hill, darkness growing about them. The final furlong passed beneath the stars. A cool breeze sprang up from the north, and in his exhausted state, A'brgail began to feel chill. A flint road appeared before them, a pale gray ribbon winding down toward the darkened lake.

Atop the towers, lights appeared, much closer now, and the knight could see that the buildings stretched for some distance down the tower's sides, the structures clinging there by what means he could not guess. At the road's end they came to a ferry dock, a broad, flat barge rising and falling almost imperceptibly between stone pillars. Two tall Fáel stepped out of the shadow of a small blockhouse. One came forward, a hand laid lightly on the hilt of his sword. The other stood back, an arrow knocked, the curving yaka wood bow gleaming in the starlight. Brendl went forward and spoke to them quietly in the language of their people.

A moment later he returned to the outsiders. "Come, we will cross to Aland-or. The elders will decide what to do with you."

"Is it against some Fáel law to walk abroad by night?" Elise asked stubbornly.

A'brgail thought that Brendl looked a bit embarrassed. "We have received disturbing news from our people who travel the land between the mountains. There are rumors that the Renné and the Wills are about to go to war, if they have not done so already." He waved a hand to a good-sized boat.

A'brgail needed help to climb aboard, but they were soon crossing the flat water, six men at the oars, another half dozen guarding the strangers, though A'brgail thought they were going out of their way to offer no threat. The oars disturbed the stars, wavering all around them, and sent them spinning away in their wake. A'brgail pulled his tattered robe close against the cool breeze and dampness of the lake, but Elise seemed unaffected. Just to sit was a relief. A'brgail felt the weakness of his limbs as he slumped on the thwart, unable to sit upright.

Each stroke of the oars sent the boat surging forward, the bow rising a little, black water rippling by. Like most of the inhabitants of the land between the mountains, A'brgail had spent some time in boats. The Wynnd and its tributaries were the main roads of the land, after all. He might not know a good boat to look at it, but to ride in one was a different thing. This boat rode the waters lightly, tracked straight and true, and did not bob or roll about. He ran his fingers along the gunwale, the planking; all was smooth and fair, the scantlings surprisingly fine.

Overhead, nighthawks cried. A fish shot into the air, splashing immediately back into its element. Was the surface invisible by night, he wondered? Did fish fly out into the air unwittingly?

As I am doing myself, he thought. For he seemed to be in a world not his own, confused, gasping for breath.

The woman beside him was an abomination. A grand master of his order had been burned alive for doing what she had done. Bargains with nagar always went awry. But even so, he could not help but feel pity for her. He had seen the agony she was in, clearly, but an hour before. She was paying the price for what she'd done. He hoped that she would be the only one to pay. He also hoped that Lady Elise would never give rein to the thing within her, for Sianon was a heartless monster. A woman who lived for war and felt no remorse for the lives it cost. Yet, Sianon was also their only hope—she and Alaan. Hafydd could not be defeated without them.

The tower of Aland-or loomed out of the darkness, and a small stone wharf appeared at its base. They clambered out onto the steps. Brendl went quickly up to the guards and spoke low. A'brgail found himself staring at them, wondering if any small movement or look would betray what was being said or indicate their intentions. The guards only turned to regard them solemnly.

"This man does not speak your language," Brendl said, "but he will take you up into the city. I will send you on without guards if you give your word to cause no trouble."

"What choice have we?" Elise asked, bristling a little. "But yes, we will give our word."

Brendl bowed to them once, then climbed nimbly back into the boat. In a moment he was lost in the dark, only the quick rhythmic splash of the oars marking his progress.

At an unseen signal from the guards, ropes began singing through blocks somewhere high above. A large woven basket appeared out of the dark, landing with a gentle thump on the stone. Their guide opened a small gate in the basket's side and motioned for Elise and A'brgail to step inside. In a moment the three of them were rising smoothly through the air, the dark, star-speckled lake spreading out below.

A soft breeze found them as they rose, and A'brgail had the feeling that they had taken their leave of the world and were in flight, floating up like a hawk on a rising breeze. He glanced over at Elise, barely discernible in the faint light. She stood with a hand on the narrow rail, gazing out over the still waters. How careworn she looked. Her youthful face overcome by the concerns of someone much older.

But how old would Sianon be, he wondered?

A'brgail also wondered what thoughts were preying on her mind, for she was an enigma to him—he who had not much experience of women, let alone a woman who had made a bargain with a nagar.

The basket slowed, then settled into a wooden structure, a small plank floor opening up around them, dark wooden beams, carved with birds in flight, curving overhead. Lanterns cast their inconstant golden light there, and A'brgail saw that the structure was elegant and lightly built, which no doubt it would need to be, for it was cantilevered out over the edge of a cliff.

Their guide spoke with the Fáel who served there, and one of them turned to the strangers, and said haltingly, "I will take you to a place where you will wait. Please follow me."

He led them out of the door, not bothering with a lantern. They passed along a narrow walkway, smoothly paved with stone. The city of the Fáel opened up before them, lit here and there by lanterns hanging over doorways. The walkways were not broad; three men might lie head to toe and span the one they were in. Upon each side stood buildings, some shops, others apparently residences. They did not exceed three floors, there at least, their doors brightly painted, deep stone walls topped by plastered and half-timbered gables, all crowned by steeply pitched slate roofs. Everywhere he looked the famed craftsmanship of Fáel could be seen: a bench carved with flowers, windows intricately leaded and some of stained glass.

The city had a certain organization and harmony; at the same time as it appeared to have developed in some random manner. Down a set of finely made stairs their guide led them. Around a bend, a small park opened up before them, a pond in its center.

There couples walked, and elders took their leisure on benches. A troupe of musicians played on a small pram that drifted aimlessly over the waters.

A'brgail saw Elise hesitate. He could almost feel her desire to linger in this place, to listen to the music—some part of her was the daughter of Lord Carral Wills, after all. The Fáel admired him greatly, and that could be said of few men.

Their guide stooped, and a hushed conversation ensued with a white-haired man, who then hurried off. The guide motioned them on. Another flight of stairs led them down, but this was on the edge of the tower, for it looked out over the world. A few clouds, smooth and still, hung in the brightly starred sky. The waning moon would rise in an hour or two. A'brgail wondered if he would be able to stay awake that long. He had never known such exhaustion.

They were led through a pair of large doors made of yaka wood, the planks wider than any A'brgail had ever seen, or even heard of. Inside was a long chamber with windows opening out to the world beyond.

"You are in the Chamber of the Rising Moon," their guide said. His look was suddenly solicitous. "Is it true you are the daughter of Lord Carral Wills?"

"It is true, yes."

"But we had heard you died in an accident."

"It was no accident, and I did not die," Elise said, a great weariness coming into her voice.

The man made a small bow and backed away quickly. "I will send you water for washing, and food and drink. The elders will come shortly. You have arrived unexpectedly, and they must be found and decisions made about who will attend you."

They were left alone in the room, which was both elegant and spare, the decorations understated and strange to A'brgail's eye, for the artistic sensibilities of the Fáel were different from the other peoples of the land between the mountains. Columns were narrow at their base and spread as they rose, seeming to whirl up to the curving beams overhead. Opposite the long bank of windows that looked out toward the east, tapestries hung over the stone walls, their colors rich and deep.

"They must curtain these windows to protect the tapestries from the morning sun," he said, thinking aloud, but Elise barely acknowledged that he had spoken.

Even the scenes in the tapestries seemed strange to him, filled with disturbing images, completely unlike the tapestries he knew that depicted legends of courtly love or famous battles.

Elise, it seemed, sensed his bewilderment.

"Vision weavers!" she said, as though it were an answer to a question. She glanced over at A'brgail, and his face must have registered his confusion. "These are the work of vision weavers. That is why they look like dreams or nightmares."

For a moment more she gazed at the strange images, then slumped into a chair and stared out listlessly toward the eastern horizon. A'brgail followed her example, finding the chair soft and welcoming.

A few moments later he was wakened by the sound of doors opening. Two young men and a young woman hurried in, bearing trays: water for them to wash themselves and platters of steaming food. A'brgail didn't know which he needed more, but decided that it would only be polite to first wash himself as best he could.

Elise did not wait to be asked, but plunged her face into a basin like an old campaigner. If the Fáel were surprised by this, they did not show it. Their dark faces remained masks of politeness. A'brgail was impressed by how far the goodwill toward Carral Wills would stretch.

A'brgail retched terribly, bile welling up and burning his throat. Hands seemed to be supporting him while another struck him gently on the back.

"I think he's done," a voice said.

The knight tried to open his eyes, but the world was reeling, and he closed them again. He was lowered to the floor, where he lay still a moment, his position awkward. His hands seemed to be restrained, as did his feet.

"Be wary. If she does the same, we'll have to cut the gag off."

A'brgail was not sure how long he lay still, or even if he was conscious the whole time; but when he opened his eyes again the world seemed to have stopped spinning, though his vision was blurred.

"What's happened to me?" he asked.

No one answered a moment, then a woman's voice was heard. "You've eaten something that didn't agree with you."

"Why are my hands bound?"

"Because of the company you keep."

A'brgail twisted around, trying to see the source of the voice, but his eyes came to rest upon Elise, who appeared to be chained to a stake, a gag tied over her mouth, and a pyre at her feet. Fáel men stood by with flickering torches. Even with his vision blurred, A'brgail could see that they were frightened. No, they were terrified.

"You're making a mistake," he said, trying to muster his energy.

"It was not our people who made this mistake," the woman said. She came and crouched down before him.

"She wakes!" a man said quickly.

The woman reached out and touched A'brgail's brow, as though she tested him for fever. "We will deal with you by and by," she said gently.

Elise was given some time to recover, and when she had done so, A'brgail watched her struggle against the chains, veins standing out on her neck.

"I don't think even *you* will break such chains," the woman said. "I am Adalla. This is Idath," she said, indicating an older man. "And Tannis."

A young woman nodded. Adalla regarded Elise a moment, her manner determined, but there was kindness in her face. A'brgail would not have wanted her judging him—she had an air of disinterest about her that suggested leniency was not something she indulged.

"I will remove your gag," she said, "but be warned—if you begin to mutter or speak words we don't recognize, these men will set the pyre aflame and you, and the thing you bear, will be turned to ash. Do you understand?"

Elise nodded.

Adalla signaled, and the young woman named Tannis removed her gag.

"This is not the usual Fáel hospitality," Elise said darkly.

"For which we will make no apology," Adalla said, pacing back and forth before Elise. "We know who you are and what you've done." She nodded to the young woman. "Tannis is an accomplished vision weaver. She foresaw a woman making a bargain with Sianon, just as she and her sister saw the return of Sainth and Caibre." She turned and retraced her steps, hands behind her back, head bent as though she watched every step she took. "But then, as often happens, her visions became unclear. Tannis saw Elise Wills becoming the defender of the peoples in the land between the mountains. She also had a vision of Elise Wills falling, her shadow taking up the sword against us, carving out a kingdom of her own, and making war—perpetual, brutal war." She stopped pacing and stood gazing at Elise. "Two visions. One will be true. One will not. If we set you free, will Elise Wills fight to defend us, or will the shadow inside you triumph and plunge the land between the mountains into a century of war?"

Elise closed her eyes. "I don't know," she whispered.

"Lady Elise," the woman said with feeling. "That answer will not gain you your life."

"Lady Elise will never give in to Sianon," A'brgail called out. "I am sure of it."

Adalla answered without looking at him. "Men would give their lives to gain Sianon's favor. We can't trust your word, man-at-arms."

"But I have traveled with her, watched her risk her life for others—a thing Sianon would never do."

"I will gag you if I must," Adella threatened, and the Knight fell silent, frustration and anger boiling up inside him.

"Perhaps you should burn me," Elise said, meeting Adalla's eye. "I didn't know when I made this bargain what it would mean. What it would mean to have her memories. . . . Sianon traded her heart for the love and utter devotion of those around her—"

"But have you done the same, traded away your heart?"

Elise's eyes closed again, and tears appeared, trembling among her lashes like a drop of rain in a spider's web. "All I know is that I feel as though I did these things, sacrificed my loved ones without remorse, sent legions to their deaths. She once had a meal interrupted by the news that one of her armies had been destroyed—to the last man. She finished her supper, then spent the night with a lover, as though nothing had happened. I am sinking beneath the weight of these memories, of my own remorse and self-loathing. I am living a nightmare. Death might release me. I might welcome his cold embrace." Elise broke down then and began to sob, tears flowing freely down her cheeks.

"Set her free," Tannis said gently.

Adalla turned to the young vision weaver. "Have you not been listening?"

"To every word. She will never give in to the monster she bears. She would die first. Set her free. That is my judgment."

Adalla turned to the silent man who accompanied them, Idath.

"Tannis is right, I think. Sianon would never have urged us to take her life. Lady Elise will win this battle against the creature inside. She is clearly the daughter of Carral Wills, giving no quarter to the darkness."

Adalla nodded to one of the guards who stood nearby, and he began releasing Elise's chains. Another guard cut A'brgail's bonds, but he could not rise for loss of feeling in his legs and was forced to lie a few moments more.

Elise stepped free of the chains and down from the pyre, chaffing her wrists. "Would you have burned me?" she asked, confronting Adalla.

Adalla did not blanch. "Yes, though I would have regretted it all the rest of my days."

Elise and the Fáel elder stood gazing at each other a moment, then Elise stepped forward and embraced her, as though she were a lost loved one. "I hope you have done the right thing," she whispered. "I pray you have."

Fifteen

By morning the sun threw aside the covering of cloud and emerged full and round and filled with warmth. The birds sang songs to its grandeur and the high, green valley of the Dubrell sparkled with the night's rain. Beneath the sun the travelers began to dry, and by midmorning their spirits had lifted after the events of the previous night.

"There are no end of secrets here, it seems," Fynnol said, as they stopped to let their horses drink from a rain-swollen stream.

Tam thought his cousin looked less haunted that day. It seemed to him that Fynnol had begun to think Death had singled him out and sought him relentlessly. But he had escaped the darkness again and now slouched in the sunlight beside the little creek. He almost looked at peace, as though he'd passed through the Lion's Maw again, and the river that stretched out ahead was slow and calm.

Cynddl stood on the shore, his horse stretching its head down into the cool waters. Gray-haired and pale, Cynddl looked like an outsider dressed in Fáel clothing. He also looked much older than his thirty-some years—older than when Tam had met him near

Telanon Bridge in the far north, that was certain. The story finder stared into the waters, his face grim and his manner distant. Who knew what stories he found in such places? It seemed anywhere men had made their dwellings tales of war and treachery abounded. And men lived here, in this land of the giants. Mcn led here by Orlem Slighthand eight generations past: Knights of the Vow, it seemed. And now they wanted to return to the land of their ancestors. If they only knew what a place of strife that was!

"How far is it now to the border?" Fynnol asked. He rose to his feet and walked up the stream a few paces, bending to drink from cupped hands, the clear water dripping through his fingers.

"We will come to the edge of our lands tomorrow evening," Wolfson answered. "Beyond that we do not travel." The giant knelt on a rock at the stream's edge, as though someone so large could not easily bend down. "Where has the healer gone?" he asked. "Where is Crowheart? We should stay close together. Thcsc lands are no longer safe."

"He went into the wood," Alaan said. "Leave him be. He is protected by his guardian crows."

A sudden furious cawing brought Alaan to his feet.

"Quiet!" he ordered.

The sound of a horse cantering sounded through the wood, and Alaan had a sword in hand. A moment later a rider appeared. He was the youngest of the men-at-arms who had found them the night before. His horse made a dash for the stream, and the young man sawed at the reins to turn it away. Winning the short struggle, he then almost tumbled off the horse from apparent exhaustion. Wolfson took the animal by its bridle.

Cynddl steadied the young man, who looked ready to drop.

"Don't let my horse drink too much," the rider gasped.

Indeed the horse was slick with sweat, wild-eyed and dancing back and forth. Crowheart came out of the trees and immediately took the horse from Wolfson, leading it in a slow circle, letting it drink a little, then walking it again. Almost immediately the beast grew calm and docile.

The young rider had collapsed at the stream's edge and drunk his fill. He sat back, his legs stretched out, hands out behind to offer support. His face was red, and he still gasped for breath.

Wolfson crouched beside him. "I fear to ask the reason you have ridden your horse to exhaustion, Wil. What has happened?"

"Men forced their way through the north pass. The men who were pursuing the strangers." He glanced up at Alaan. "They had knowledge of the arcane. That's how they drove the sentries back." He stopped to catch his breath, as though a few words had taken it all away. "My company are hunting them now, but there must be a sorcerer among them—"

"Hafydd!" Tam said.

Alaan shook his head. "He has matters more important."

The giant had crouched by the rider, but he jumped up now. "We should go back and help the Knights," he said, taking up his pack and swinging it in an arc over his shoulder. It thumped into place, and he groped behind for the other strap.

"We won't go back," Alaan said, and Wolfson turned on him, glaring down at the much smaller man. But Alaan did not blanch. "We won't go back," he said again. "Our task lies to the south."

"But what of the riders?" Wolfson argued, still staring down at Alaan.

Tam knew that he would have been intimidated under such a stare.

"You go, if you must," Alaan said, "but I can't afford to feel compassion for these riders. Not now. You don't know what's at stake." Alaan spoke to the others. "We must ride." But then he turned back to the young man, who still sprawled on the ground. "I thank you for your warning, Wil, but I can't help you now. My war is with the southern kingdom and its allies in all lands."

Alaan put a foot in a stirrup and swung up into the saddle. The boy had gained his feet by then, and taken the reins of his horse from Crowheart. He watched as the strangers crossed the stream and faded among the trees.

"Come back for us!" he called, as they disappeared from his sight. "Do not forget us."

For a moment Wolfson stood, one foot in the stream, the other on the shore, then he waded quickly through the water and pulled himself up onto the far bank. Tam saw him look back once at the young rider, who stood holding his horse, watching the men go. And then the boy was lost to sight, and Wolfson came striding up behind, his face red.

A crow touched Tam's face with the tip of a wing as it sailed by, then landed on its master's shoulder. Crowheart reached up and stroked its dark neck, and Tam was sure the bird closed its eyes in pleasure.

Tam glanced behind again. They forced their way into the wood without conversation, pressing their mounts at speed. Tam could feel the tension in the company. Hafydd's minions hunted them again. For him and Fynnol and their Fáel friend this was a return of the nightmare. They had been lucky to survive their journey down the River Wynnd, ignorant as they were then. They hadn't even known why they were being hunted.

The trees opened up, and they rode through tall grass, the tufts waving in the breeze, tapping the horses on their flanks. Tam found himself behind Crowheart.

"Rabal?" he said. "Why have you come on this journey?"

What he had wanted to say was, *Why do you risk your life?* but this had seemed impertinent.

Crowheart lifted his shoulder and brushed the crow off. It took to the air with a soft, cawing complaint. Rabal turned to look at Tam, his black eyes peering out from behind the sea of dark hair, the bushy brows, the beard that grew high up his cheeks. "I come for the same reason as you, Tam," he said, "to find out who I am." Crowheart spurred his horse and rode ahead.

Tam had tried to answer, to say, *But I know who I am,* but no words had come.

"Keep up, now," came Wolfson's voice from behind, and Tam pressed his horse on.

The giant had taken up this rear position, watching behind for the men who had forced the north pass. His great staff thumped the ground at each step, resounding like a falling log. Tam had taken to listening, trying to find any noise of pursuing horses above the sound of their own mounts.

The sky appeared to thicken, a thin gray paste spreading over the high vault, uniform and oppressive. Wind came from the north, giving voice to the lands around. High overhead, eagles soared against the gray. Occasionally Tam would see wolves trotting through the trees or the long grass. Twice they came upon herds of cattle being moved by a pair of giants. The cattle seemed to pay no heed to the wolves, to Tam's surprise. The giants stared at the strangers and waved at Wolfson, who stopped to warn them of the riders—or so Tam assumed.

An hour before sunset Alaan stopped them and built a fire among the trees on the crest of a hill. It was a good place to camp—easily defended—but when Tam went to unsaddle his horse Alaan stopped him.

"We won't camp here," he said.

They built the fire up, raising a berm of dark earth around it to stop its spread. When this was done, Alaan led them on into the gathering gloom. They made camp in almost total darkness sometime later. No fire was kindled there, and they ate a cold supper of bread and smoked meat. Alaan picked the places for each man to make his bed—a small depression in the ground, the shadow of a bush—so that none was easy to see in the darkness. Watches were chosen, and Tam drew the first, which he would stand with Crowheart. How they would know the time to call the next watch Tam did not know, for the stars couldn't be seen.

"If we have fortune on our side, the men hunting us will find the fire and wait until it has burned low before they approach. That is what any wise man would do—wait until it is very late before they attack. By then it will be very hard to follow our tracks."

Alaan had again brought them to a hilltop for the night, though this one was much larger—not a mound like the last had been. To the north there would be a clear view in daylight, though it was nothing but a sea of darkness that night.

Tam strung his bow and put his quiver where he could easily put his hand on it. He and Crowheart settled themselves on the ground in a place where they could both look to the north and watch over their companions—had there been any light!

"I can see nothing," Tam whispered.

"We shall have to trust to our ears this night," Crowheart answered. "But don't make enemies out of the wind sound, or the creaking of a tree."

Easily said, Tam thought, but he knew that when one listened hard enough every sound became a threat. Instead he found himself fighting to keep his eyes open and slipping into near dreams, his mind wandering to fanciful things. Crowheart began to snore softly. Tam reached out and put a hand on Rabal's arm, the leather of his jacket cool in the night—but Crowheart did not stir.

Tam stood and gave his head a shake, moving his arms and shoulders to work the kinks out. The clouds had thinned, he realized, and hazy stars began to surface. A faint landscape began to appear: areas of darkness and dull gray. Tam could hardly tell what might be hillside or wood.

And then he thought he saw a light flicker. Tam rubbed his eyes and looked again. It wasn't a firefly.

"Rabal!" he whispered, shaking the man's shoulder. Finally, he tugged on his beard, and Crowheart stirred. "There is a light below."

Crowheart scrambled up. Tam could barely see him in the dark, looming to the right—larger and more solid than Tam, like a mound of shadow. "I see nothing," Crowheart said, after a moment.

"No, it was there. I'm sure of it." Tam searched the darkness, trying to find the flickering light; but after a moment he was no longer sure where in the massive darkness he had seen it.

For a long while they stood, staring into the night. Crowheart began to shift from one foot to the other. Even Tam started to wonder if it had only been his imagination. And then it flickered again.

"There! Do you see?"

"A torch," Rabal said softly. "I'll wake Alaan."

"No need," came a voice from behind. "Not with all the noise you two are making."

Alaan came and stood to the other side of Tam. The flame would flicker into existence for the briefest second, then disappear again for a long moments.

"I think Rabal is right—it's a torch. And whoever carries it is following our track. They might be giants, or the Knights who are their allies, but I think we should assume they are allies of Hafydd." Alaan stopped as the light appeared again for an instant. "They're not so far off. Can you wake the others, Rabal?"

"What shall we do?" Tam asked. "Shall we saddle the horses?"

Alaan was very still in the darkness, staring out over the valley below. "No, best to meet them here. The wind is in the north, so the smell of our horses will not reach them. We'll go down the hillside a little . . . and prepare a surprise for them."

Tam heard his companions stirring as Rabal found each of them in the dark. They pulled on boots and took up their weapons—weapons that had been set out where they would come easily to hand.

Fynnol appeared at Tam's elbow, the Valeman recognizable in the dark by his size—the smallest of them. He shifted about, unable to keep still.

"How many are there?" Fynnol whispered.

"I don't know. No more than we saw chasing us."

Fynnol nocked an arrow, though clearly whoever bore the torch was still far beyond range of their bows. "But was that rider right? Is there a sorcerer among them? Could it be Hafydd?"

"Alaan doesn't think it likely. Nor do I. Hafydd wasn't among them when they pursued us to the north pass. He couldn't have found his way into the hidden lands alone. He hasn't that gift."

"I hope you're right," Fynnol said, his voice squeezing out of a dry mouth.

Cynddl came and instinctively stood beside Fynnol so that the little Valeman had a friend to either side. Tam could sense Wolfson in the dark, standing still as a mountain.

"We'll let them come partway up this slope," Alaan said. "There is a little break in the trees. Do you see? That patch of gray not far below?"

Tam was not absolutely certain that he did. He glanced up at the sky, where the stars stood out, cool and bright. Even starlight would help.

"Quiet now," Alaan whispered. "We don't want them to know we're here."

Tam nocked an arrow and pulled back against the bowstring, getting the feel of it. His own mouth went dry, and his breath came in short, quick gasps. It did not matter that he had been in such situations before, he still felt fear wash through him like a cold wave.

The torch appeared, flickering dull orange. Black, bitter smoke drifted up to them. Tam thought he could make out shadows moving in the dull light—men and horses. A thought occurred to Tam.

"How do we know these aren't the knights who came to our aid?" he whispered to Alaan.

Before the traveler could answer, a horse nickered down the draw, and one of their own mounts answered.

The shadows below stopped, then scurried into hiding. The torch was doused.

"Does that answer your question?" Alaan said softly. "They will try to come upon us with stealth, maybe work their way around to the east or west."

"To the west lie bluffs," Wolfson whispered in his deep tones. "Some might climb them by day, but not by night. If they find their way to the east, the hill will channel them up a little draw. Some of us could await them there."

"We are a small enough company as it is without dividing our numbers further," Alaan said, and Tam could hear the concern in his voice.

"Then we will await them here," the giant said, "where they may come at their leisure."

"How far to this draw?" Alaan asked.

"Only a little distance," the giant said. "Less than a stone's throw."

Alaan was quiet a moment, and Tam could almost feel him weighing the different options. "Here," he said, "help me with this stone."

Tam could just make out the dark forms of Alaan and Wolfson bending over a large boulder. They broke it free of the ground and sent it trundling down the slope, the sound of shattering branches following as it went. Curses were heard below as men scurried to get clear of the boulder bearing down on them out of the darkness.

"Go back!" Alaan called. "Go back while you still live!" Then quietly to the others he said, "There. Now there is no doubt what they face. They will not be such damn fools as to come up this way. Fynnol, stay here with Rabal and watch. Shout if you need us. Everyone else follow Wolfson. We shall see this draw."

The stars shone a meager light down beneath the trees, and the men stumbled over rocks and roots as they followed Wolfson's great shadow through the wood. Tam started as the giant's small pack of wolves appeared out of the night, gamboling around their master. But then they must have caught the scent of the men below, and they slunk along silently, growling low.

"Here," Wolfson whispered.

Tam could see little—shadows overlaid by shadows—and all shapes seemed strange. The ground under his feet was soft with grass and mosses, and a wind whispered up the hillside, carrying the scent of pine and spruce, the fecund floor of the forest. An area of greater darkness yawed open like the mouth of the wood. Perhaps this was Wolfson's draw.

"But I can see nothing," Cynddl complained.

"My wolves will warn us of their approach," the giant said, "if we don't hear them stumbling and gasping up the draw."

Tam crouched, an arrow ready. He tried to quiet his breathing so that he might hear the slightest sound. The leaves battered together, and a hollow breeze hissed through the wood. An owl hooted three times, and far off he heard a wolf howl.

And then the sound of a rock rolling, thumping over other stones, before coming to rest. A muttered curse.

Tam pulled back his bowstring a little, feeling it bite into his calloused fingers. A smell stung his nostrils—like metal being forged.

He heard the others sniffing the air. A dull light seemed to seep up from among the underwood below. Faintly, trees and bushes were illuminated. He drew his bowstring back, aiming down the narrow draw. Certainly someone would appear with a torch . . . but what he saw did not seem to be torchlight.

A dim, glowing snake of silver wound around the roots a half dozen paces below. And then another. It seemed to branch and flow upward, like molten metal.

"Quicksilver!" Alaan cursed. "Up into the trees!" He turned and in three steps had thrown himself up into the crook of an oak. He did not stop there but scrambled frantically higher, shaking the branches as he went.

Tam stood for a moment, entranced, as the quicksilver wove in and out among the rocks and roots, it branched and swirled and joined again.

Cynddl grabbed Tam's arm and pulled him nearly off balance.

"Do as Alaan says!" the story finder hissed.

Even giant Wolfson dragged himself up into a tree. Tam and Cynddl followed suit, just as a snake of quicksilver seemed to dart at Tam's boot. It went after the wolves then, who watched it, mystified. It touched the paw of one and the wolf leapt back, howling in pain. The pack was off then, tearing into the dark, snakes of silver coiling through the wood after them.

Men came pounding up the draw, swords at the ready. Tam saw they were careful not to step on the strands of silver that twisted around their feet.

An arrow flashed, and one man staggered, plunging a hand into the quicksilver trying to balance. He screamed like he'd thrust his hand into molten iron. Up he leapt, but it was too late. The quicksilver spread up his arm, and he danced in a circle, screaming.

Tam shot the man coldly in the throat, and he fell back, tumbling slowly over and over down the long slope.

It was over in a trice. Arrows shot out of the trees, and the dozen men were quickly driven back. Scrambling to avoid arrows, men stepped into the quicksilver, and the wood echoed with their screams.

The cold heat of the quicksilver soon dissipated, and Alaan swung down from his branch, boots thumping onto the forest floor.

"Quickly!" he whispered, "before they regroup. We must be gone!"

Tam stumbled off into the darkness after the traveler, glancing back every few feet, fearing that a silent tendril of quicksilver chased him. That it would coil around his leg and drag him down, screaming.

Sixteen

Jamm was not healing. His cough had grown worse, and he labored terribly to breathe. The heat of his fever could be felt at a distance, and his face was an unnatural orange-crimson.

He's going to die. That's what Carl thought. The little thief was going to cough himself to death or simply drown in the fluids gurgling and bubbling in his fouled lungs.

Carl watched helplessly as Jamm endured another spasm of coughing, bent double on the hard ground. They had found a spring concealed in a grove of willows that stood like an island in fields of ripening oats. It was not a good place to hide during the daylight hours, for if anyone approached, there was nowhere for them to go but into the wheatfield, but Jamm could not go a step farther. Carl tried to keep watch all around, but it was difficult, for the fields were small and bordered by thick hedgerows and trees. It would not be difficult for a company of armed men to approach, unseen until it was too late.

They were hungry, too. No amount of springwater would fill the void in Carl's stomach. He found himself eyeing the green oats and wondering if he could eat them and if they would provide sustenance. Carl's stomach growled loudly.

The day, Carl noted for the first time, was very fine. Just past high summer, warm but with a breeze from the west. If not for the hedgerows, they would have been surrounded by an undulating sea of soft green. A few errant clouds sailed slowly across the blue, casting small islands of shade on the lands below.

Carl heard someone talking, then the squeak of an axle, the hollow thumping of hooves. Jamm stopped coughing then and perked up, listening.

"Someone comes!" he said, and tried to suppress a cough.

Carl bent to try to lift his guide but the little man was bent by another spasm of coughing.

"Go!" Jamm managed, gasping. "Leave me."

Carl looked over his shoulder. He could still hear the sound of someone approaching—a voice . . . muttering.

"I'll help you up, Jamm. We'll lie in the grainfield until they're gone. Come."

But Jamm succumbed to his coughing—almost retching, the attack was so violent. Before Carl could decide what to do, a man appeared, coming up a path through the willows. He was leading a small horse that drew behind it a battered old cart. Seeing Carl, he raised a hand and waved, then took off his straw hat and wiped his forehead with a shirtsleeve. Carl waved tentatively back. He glanced down at his red-faced companion, who was surely not fit to be moved.

The stranger bore a load of rough-sawn oak in short lengths. A box of tools perched on top, mallet handles and spokeshaves protruding. The man brought the horse to a stop and stood staring from Jamm to Carl.

"Help me get him into the back of the cart," the man said. "My wife is a healer."

Jamm didn't protest as he was loaded aboard, but Carl thought he felt light as a child, as though his flesh were melting away. The man filled a wooden bucket and let his horse drink, then led them down from the willow grove. He seemed to take a circuitous route, and paused once behind a shielding hedge while some farm laborers passed in the distance.

" 'Tis a terrible sickness your friend has," the man said, shaking his head.

"Yes," Carl agreed.

"Has he had it long?"

"Just over a day."

The man took off his hat and wiped his brow again, his face creased and troubled. Carl guessed he was a man coming to the end of his fifth decade, his hair thinning, manner quiet and thoughtful. His skin was stained by hours in the sun, and his hands were large-knuckled and calloused, his forearms thick. He was a tradesman, clearly. A woodworker of some kind.

Carl had the feeling that the man was not quiet just because he was in the company of strangers, but that he spoke little to others—despite the muttering Carl had heard. Complaining, it had sounded like. The complaints of an aggrieved man. Even so their benefactor did not offer his name, nor did he ask Carl's or any other question that Carl would have expected under such circumstances.

It was nearly evening when they arrived at the man's home. His wife came out the door to greet him—she was delicate and sad-eyed, frail with disappointment. Her fair hair was graying—ashes and snow—and her hands were thin-boned and worn from work.

"Man's sick," the stranger pronounced, and his wife hurried around to the back of the cart.

She took one look at Jamm, and said, "Bear him in, Thon. We'll put him in the back room. No—in the attic over the woodshed."

Carl and Thon carried Jamm up a narrow stair to a white-washed room beneath the eaves. His limp form was laid on a bed, where he was instantly seized by another fit of coughing.

The woman put a hand to Jamm's forehead, then lightly touched the dark bruises and cuts on his face. Gently she peeled his shirt away from his sweating torso to reveal more bruises.

"Who beat him like this?" she said softly.

Carl looked warily from man to woman. They would turn them over to the Renné in an instant once it was learned who they were—or worse, to Vast.

"Soldiers," Carl said. "Drunken soldiers."

The woman turned to her husband. "I will need cold water from the well and cloths. We must bring his fever down. Boil waterwillow bark in my small pan."

The man went off, his boots almost silent on the stairs.

"Open the window, would you?" she said. "A breeze will help. Poor man. His ribs are cracked or broken, and bile has collected in his lungs."

Thon returned with a bucket of well water and cloths. The woman soaked a cloth and gently bathed all of Jamm's wounds and bruises. One cloth she folded neatly and laid across his forehead, a single large towel was soaked and laid over his torso. The window opposite was opened, and a breeze swirled softly through the room.

"We don't know how to thank you," Carl said, as the husband retreated down the stairs again. "We were just traveling across the Isle when the soldiers found us."

"We know who you are," the woman said, gently washing Jamm's neck. She didn't look up as she said this, but perched on the bed's edge, her face serious and sad. "You needn't fear anything from us. We won't give you away to the Renné or their cursed allies."

But she did not say his name, nor offer her own.

Carl lowered himself stiffly into a straight-backed chair. The rush seat felt like the softest down cushion.

"Go downstairs," the woman said. "My husband will get you some supper and warm water to wash in. You needn't fear for your friend. He is safe. We have common cause, you and I. We will keep you from harm if we can."

Carl was not sure what purpose would be served by sitting at Jamm's bedside, so he dragged himself up and went down the steep stair, leaning heavily against the wall. He was so drained by their

ordeal that he could have lain down on the stairs and gone to sleep.
These people might plan to turn them in for the reward, but at that
moment he did not care. Let him just have some food and rest.

Thon knelt before the hearth, stirring a small pot. A large iron
kettle hung from a hook over the flames, the scent of herbs and
lamb permeating the air. The room, though not unpleasant, was
modest. A hearth, a table and chairs, some once-elegant furniture,
now covered in cheap fabrics. A bureau, a bookcase, half-full, a
footstool. A sideboard held a set of very fine dishes, though they
were chipped and faded. Newly made candles hung by their wicks
from a beam, and the sun made swimming squares of light as it filtered through thick, nearly opaque glass.

Thon stopped his stirring and ladled stew into a bowl for Carl.
He took a seat at the table. The spoon he was given was silver and
monogrammed with the letter L. Eating in silence, he continued to
regard the room. Two portraits hung on the end wall; one of a corpulent nobleman, the other of the same man and his family—wife
and seven children. Carl glanced at the man stirring a pot over the
hearth. There was indeed some resemblance in the high brow, the
dissatisfied mouth.

Thon's wife came lightly down the stairs and favored Carl with
a wan smile, then went to the hearth, straining the waterwillow bark
into a cup. She disappeared up the stairs again.

Thon wiped his hands on a square of cotton and crossed toward
the door.

"Must see to the horse," he said, and was gone. Carl heard the
hollow clatter of wood being piled, then the squeak of the axle. In
a few moments Thon returned. He washed his hands and face in
warm water, then ladled himself some stew. He placed a half loaf of
bread on a board on the table, along with a much-sharpened knife.
With fresh butter it was a great treat.

Thon's wife descended the stair again, washed her hands, and
joined them at the table, where dutiful Thon brought her food and
cutlery.

"He's sleeping, now," she said. "He needs that more than food.

It is a wonder he's alive—a beating like that! He won't be fit to travel for a few days, but then we'll arrange to get you back to the eastern shore, into the protection of Lord Menwyn or the Prince of Innes." She bobbed her head toward Lord Carl. "We are not alone, here," she went on. "There are others of us who suffered under the Renné." She let her gaze come to rest on her silent husband. "Our families were stripped of their property and positions when the Renné invaded. And we're reduced to this. . . ." She waved a hand at the room around her. "We thought all our hopes had been answered when Lord Menwyn Wills and the Prince of Innes crossed the canal—but we were betrayed. Some traitor had alerted the Renné and they came with an army to drive Lord Menwyn away! How I hope that spy is found and his head—"

A silent rebuke from her husband stopped her. "Excuse my outburst, but both our families have suffered greatly these many years. We have a right to our bitterness."

"We haven't done so badly," Thon said mildly, as he buttered a piece of bread. "Many lives are worse than ours. We've not been blessed with children. That is my only regret."

"If you aspire to nothing, you will achieve nothing," the woman snapped.

Thon did not look at her. "Want little, and you shall have all you need," he answered softly.

His wife glowered at him, then returned to her meal, perhaps unwilling to pursue this argument before a guest. But Carl sensed it was an old feud. He glanced at the paintings on the wall. It occurred to him that the dissatisfied nobleman in the painting was *her* forbear, not Thon's.

Under the ministrations of Lady Languile, as she preferred to be called, Jamm recovered quickly. Carl was frightened the entire time he was there and kept cautioning husband and wife to say nothing to anyone—not even to their confederates who were also loyal to the Wills. There was nothing he feared more than word getting back to the Prince of Innes that Carl A'denné was alive on the Isle of Battle. How would Lady Languile feel to know that the cursed traitor of the invasion was sleeping beneath her eaves, and she was hiding him from the very man who would take his life—the Duke of Vast.

From outside they could hear the sharp sound of Thon's spoke-shave as he fashioned a wheel. The man worked tirelessly and without complaint. Carl was beginning to think he felt some joy in his occupation.

"What will we do when I am well enough to travel?" Jamm whispered. Carl had pulled the straight-backed chair close to Jamm's bed. A warm breeze hissed in the leaves outside, and sunlight dappled the floor and wall.

"I don't know," Carl answered quietly. "We'll have to slip away and hope that nothing comes of it. After all, who are they going to go to? The Renné? They are supporters of the Wills. I worry a little about their confederates—whomever they might be."

"Let us hope that they will simply be mystified when they find us gone. The trouble will be getting away from Lady Languile. She is never far afield, it seems."

"True. We might have to go out by night, though how we will get down that rickety old stairway, I don't know."

"We'll go out the window," Jamm said. "Leave it to me. In a few days. I'm almost well enough to travel. We owe these people that. I'm sure I would've perished without—"

The sounds of a horse cut off Jamm's speech. Carl jumped up and, standing well back from the window, looked out. Through the leaves he could see a wagon driven by two men entering the quad-rangle made up of Thon's house and outbuildings.

"Who is it?"

"Two men in a wagon. Local people I would guess."

Thon put down his tools and strode out to greet the visitors, shaking hands with each in turn.

Carl went closer to the window, hoping to hear what was said. The whispering of the wind in the leaves made it hard to distinguish the men's words.

"They've been hereabout, Thon," one of the men said, "looking into people's houses, offering a reward. A considerable reward. Someone'll get wind of them here and turn them in, sure."

"I don't let them outside the house by day, Hain."

"Someone'll see them in a window, then. Or the Duke's men will come upon you unexpected and find them in your house. Then it will be you and them going headless."

"I'll take any risk to rid this island of the Renné."

"You're a brave man, Thon. None of us doubt that. But still, they're at risk here, and so are you. We can move them, one stage at a time. It's all arranged. Day after tomorrow we'll have them in a boat on the river and upstream to the eastern shore. That's safest for you and them, and you know it."

"I'll have to ask the missus if he's well enough to travel."

"Tell her he won't have to take a step. It's all arranged. If you give us some hay to cover them with, they'll be safe as houses. Here, give me a hand to unload this oak. It's got a few knots you'll have to cut around, but the grain is tight as any you'll see."

Carl looked over at Jamm. "Shall we go out the back window and run for it?"

Jamm shook his head. "I'm not well enough to travel on foot—not yet." Despair appeared in his eyes. "You could, though."

"I'm not leaving you behind."

"You're a fool, Carl A'denné . . . a loyal fool."

When Thon came for them, Jamm could not descend the stair unaided. His fever was gone, and the rasping in his lungs greatly diminished, but he was not well.

"He's not ready for this journey," Thon's wife argued. "He needs more time to recover."

"We can't afford to keep him here any longer. Hain's right. 'Tis only a matter of time until they're found here."

Against the healer's protests Jamm was lifted onto a bed of hay in the back of the cart. Carl took his place beside him, and the two of them were covered in hay, the dried grasses rustling and settling over them. A golden light filtered down through the hay, and Carl could almost make out Jamm through the crumpled stems. The cart set off, jouncing down the lane to the road, the hay moving and swishing around them as it settled. The sun beat down on the covering of hay and soon had Carl sweating, the heat almost unbearable. When they passed beneath the shade of a long row of trees Carl heaved a sigh.

The two men who bore them on sat talking of the small doings of the Isle, hardly touching on the recent attempted invasion by the Prince of Innes. They discussed the personalities of horses and children as though they were of equal interest. The progress of various crops were examined, varieties of apples debated, and the beauty of various young women carefully weighed.

"People coming. Be still," one of the men said.

A greeting was heard and a conversation engaged in. Unfortunately they had drawn up in a patch of sun, and Carl's head began to ache from the heat. The conversation, about nothing in particular, went on at horrific length, or so it seemed. Carl was almost at the point of sitting up and demanding they at least be moved to the shade if they must talk the afternoon away.

But finally the axle started to squeak again, and the slow, sure trod of the horses' hooves began along the dusty road.

"May I speak?" Carl whispered.

"All clear now," the driver said.

"We are baking back here."

"There's an inn not far off. We'll stop there for a jar of ale and get you something to drink, as well."

"Can you leave us in the shade?" Carl asked.

"Aye. That we can."

The inn seemed infinitely far off, but then Carl fell asleep and lost track of the time. He awakened as the cart rolled to a stop, and Jamm poked him in the ribs.

"Shh," the little man cautioned.

There were voices around them now, conversation and laughter. A stableboy brought water for the horse and was instructed to leave horse and cart in the shade, which thankfully he did. Carl lay so still he became stiff and sore from lack of movement: couldn't have the hay pile writhing around.

The inn seemed uncommonly busy, but then Carl remembered hearing the men say that people who'd fled at the first signs of war were returning now that the invading army had been driven back. People were rushing back to protect their property and see to crops and gardens.

After what seemed like hours, familiar voices approached, and the two men climbed up onto the box.

"Walk on," the driver ordered, and gave the reins a shake.

The cart trundled out of the yard and onto the road again. A hill presented itself, and Carl could hear the horse straining and heaving to reach the top. Once there the cart stopped.

"I think you can safely sit up now," the driver said.

Carl pushed himself up, brushing the hay away from his hair and pulling all that stuck from sweat to his face. He blew hay dust out of his nose and rubbed his eyes. The driver and his companion, two slow-moving men in their fifties, smiled at their state.

One handed Carl a jar of ale. "Here, this will help a little, I'd guess."

Hills on the Isle of Battle were not large, but Carl guessed this might be the highest point on the island. The fields and woods spread out all around, their irregular shapes making a crazy, random pattern. That a land of such apparent peace and rustic beauty had become a place of fear for him stuck Carl as entirely wrong. He almost drained the jar of ale in one go, then leaned back against the plank that made up the cart's side. The sun was blocked by ancient elms, their lofty boughs reaching up into the air.

"Two hours more," the driver said. "Then you can rest a few hours. Without a moon we can't move so easily by night, for a lantern might attract the attention of the companies of men-at-arms and other soldiers who are still about on the island. Hey up! Here comes someone over the crest." The driver sent the horse on. Carl and Jamm slid back down beneath their quilt of hay, the cool breeze a pleasant memory.

Greetings were exchanged with the other party, distances questioned, weather dissected, the steepness of the hill cursed. A jest was told, everyone laughed, and they set off again. The road down snaked back and forth across the face of the hill, descending in a gradual but steady slope. Most of the way was shaded by a small wood, for which Tam was grateful.

"Men-at-arms," the driver hissed.

A moment later the familiar sounds of a company of riders permeated the hay: the creak of leather, the snorting of horses. Carl tried to lie still, not even to breathe. The cart rumbled off the road onto soft grass and came to a halt.

"You've not seen two young men hereabout, have you? Strangers. One a nobleman's son, the other a thief."

"We've not, Captain," the driver answered, "but I hope we do. The missus thinks we could find some use for the reward."

Some of the riders chuckled.

"Anything in the back other than hay?"

"Just hay, Captain."

"And where are you taking it?"

"Up to Toll's Hill. Traded some oak for two piglets due from a fall litter. This bit of hay is a down payment like—a show of good faith."

"Well if it's just hay . . ." the rider said.

"Aye! Careful with that sword!"

A blade hissed down through the hay not three inches in front of Carl's face. The point dug into the boards on the cart's floor. The rider drew his sword out, and Carl closed his eyes wondering if it would strike him next.

"Worried for your hay, are you old man?"

"You just . . . frightened me, that's all."

"I'll do more than frighten you if you start telling me what I can do and not do."

"I apologize, Captain—most humbly."

"Be on your way then."

The cart rolled on. Carl could hear the riders set off, then the sounds of their passing were lost in the rumble and squeak of the cart's progress.

"Are you both unharmed?" the driver asked after a while.

"Cut the space between us," Carl said.

"We can be thankful for that. Men of that cursed Duke of Vast," the driver spat out.

If they'd only known that cursed Duke of Vast was secretly in league with the Prince of Innes and their precious Menwyn Wills. It was clear none of them had ever met Menwyn—or perhaps it wouldn't matter. His character was of no consequence—it was the promise that he stood for that counted. The unspoken promise.

A few hours later the cart came to a stop.

"You can come out now," the driver said.

With some difficulty Carl raised himself up, brushing away the hay. They were in a barn, large doors open to the fading day. Pools of shadow gathered beneath the trees outside. Carl thought he might plunge into one and hang there suspended, like a swimmer— let the coolness wash into him.

He climbed stiffly down from the cart and helped Jamm do the same. His muscles almost cried out as he stretched them, then walked back and forth the width of the barn. The smell of cattle and pigs assailed his nostrils, and the milking cows chewed hay, staring unconcernedly at him, flies buzzing about their glistening noses.

"I'm afraid you'll have to spend the night in the loft," the driver said. "I'll bring supper out to you later." He opened the top of a wooden barrel. "There's clean water in here from the well." He looked in. "Though not as much as there should be—that lazy son of mine! Drink what you want. Take a bucket and wash off the hay dust." He looked around at his barn as though he'd not bothered to do so in many a year. "It's not much of an inn, but you'll be safe here this night, I think."

"It is more than we should expect," Carl said. "You've taken great risk bringing us here, and that shall not be forgotten. I think Lord Menwyn himself might hear of it one day."

The man glanced at his cousin, the two of them suppressing smiles of satisfaction. "Well, we've done only a small part. You've a distance to go yet."

Jamm had collapsed onto a milking stool and leaned back against the rough planks of a stall.

"Jamm! You don't look well at all."

"All that heat. . . . Not good for my fever."

Carl went to the water barrel and filled the wooden dipper that hung there. He gave Carl a drink and poured the rest of the cool water over the small man's head. Twice more he did the same, and Jamm began to revive a little. He even tried to smile.

"Supper!" the driver said, and he disappeared toward the house while his cousin took a fork and emptied the cart of its hay, then led the horse away.

"Well, we've come this far," Tam said, "wherever 'here' is."

"Toll's Hill, or so our driver told the riders."

"If he wasn't lying. They were very careful not to speak each other's names—harder to do over the course of a day than one might think."

"Did you notice they never spoke our names either? Wouldn't it be a jest if they'd mistaken us for someone else!" Wrinkles appeared at the corners of the thief's eyes.

"I don't think there's much chance of that. Certainly the description the captain offered fit us well: a nobleman's son and a thief."

Jamm nodded and looked away sadly, and Carl immediately felt badly. Jamm had been a loyal guide, risking everything to get Carl across the canal . . . and into the hands of the Duke of Vast.

"Jamm—I'm sorry. I don't think you're a thief," Carl said.

Jamm absentmindedly put a finger in a hole in his breeches. "I am a thief," he said softly. "I've been one all my life. 'Once a thief,' they say, and it's true. Once you've been branded a thief no other life is open to you." He glanced up at Carl. "We'd best get some sleep. It might be a long day tomorrow."

Before they could fall asleep, a meal was carried out to them, as well as blankets for their beds. The hayloft made a soft mattress, and they fell asleep to the cooing of pigeons that lived in the barn's upper reaches. A bit of starlight found its way through windows and the gaps between the ancient boards, offering dull illumination to the geometry of the barn—beams and posts, braces and rafters. A bit of rain fell during the night, spattering down on the roof. A lonely sound, Carl thought.

Sometime late in the night Carl was jarred from a harsh dream by desperate fluttering and wings beating against wood.

"What is it?" Carl mumbled.

"An owl," Jamm whispered. "Got into the barn through some hole. He's feasting on pigeons."

Carl slept poorly after that and woke to a skiff of downy feathers upon the hay. A few whirled up in a small breeze and went spinning down from the loft through thin shafts of sunlight that leaked between the boards. He sat up and found their gray blankets spattered with down and crimson.

"Is it time?" Jamm mumbled, still half-asleep.

"Time for what?" Carl asked.

"To meet the executioner," Jamm whispered, then his eyes sprang open, and he saw Carl, and he began to weep.

Seventeen

They carried him across the river in the stern of a boat, his barrow turned upside down in the bow. On the floorboards, Ufrra lay tied and gagged. Four manned the sweeps, which had been silenced by rags so that they did not beat against the tholepins. There was no conversation, just the odd whispered word, almost lost in the language of rain spattering down on the surface of the moving river.

Kai considered throwing himself over the side, into the dark water. He'd been there before—when his legs had been cut off by Caibre. The river had saved him then, though he was not so sure it would do so now. He had been Sainth's companion, that day so long ago—now he was no one. A crippled man who went about in a barrow. A man with no possessions and no home. Only loyal Ufrra to tend him. Ufrra, who was even more lost than he, more dispossessed.

A torch appeared through the rain and darkness. The man at the tiller pointed. "There!" he said. "We can let her go downcurrent a little."

*   *   *

He was a corpulent, bald man in a barrow. The task of wheeling him was perhaps beneath the black-clad guards, so they had allowed an empty-eyed mute to bring the man into the tent. Beldor Renné wondered what made this castoff of so much interest to Hafydd.

The sorcerer, as Beld now thought of Hafydd, sat in a camp chair, his feet stretched out before him. A thin, frightened boy polished his boots. On a table at his side, a walnut box contained the book Beld had borne from the shadow gate. Hafydd never let it out of his sight.

After the "assassination" of the Prince of Innes, Hafydd had moved out here into the field and quietly assumed control of the army. Even if Menwyn Wills suspected Hafydd of ordering the Prince's death—and he would be a fool not to—there was nothing he could do about it. The family of the Prince of Innes were without an heir, as Prince Michael had not only joined with their enemies, but was now almost certainly dead. The Wills had always had less power in their alliance with Innes, but now they effectively had no power at all, as Hafydd had cowed the leaders of the army.

And now this legless man had been found and brought to Hafydd, for what purpose Beld could not imagine.

Hafydd looked up from the boy polishing his boots. "Who would have thought that you could survive an entire age. . . ."

The legless man did not look particularly cowed by Hafydd, as everyone else was. He answered as though there was nothing odd in the situation. "Yes, when Caibre had me thrown into the river the odds did not seem to favor me."

"How did you survive?"

The legless man shrugged. "I believe that water spirits rescued me, but I am told that this is merely a trick of my own mind."

Hafydd contemplated this a moment, rubbing fingers absent-mindedly over his bearded chin. "Many unexplained events have occurred on the River Wynnd—though this must be one of the

strangest." Hafydd propped his other boot up so the boy could pol-
ish it. "That was long ago—an age—and you have had your revenge by living all the while that Caibre slept." Hafydd fixed his
gaze on the legless man—the gaze that reduced hardened men-at-
arms to frightened children. "Now I have need of your skills. You
will take me into the hidden lands, Kilydd, or I will take away the
seed that you require for your pain."

"You would be surprised how long I can endure that pain," the
legless man said.

"That pain, perhaps, but I have other agonies I can minister,
other wounds that I might open." He looked over at Beldor. "Put
your blade to this child's throat."

Beldor scooped up the bewildered child before he understood
what had been said. Beld held him easily, pinning his arms, and put
a sharp dagger against the soft skin of his throat. The boy stopped
struggling.

"An innocent child, Kilydd, but Lord Beldor does not care,"
and then to Beld, "do you?"

Beldor shook his head and smiled. He watched the legless man
and wondered what he would do. Would he surrender because of
this threat to a child who meant nothing to him?

Kilydd shook his head. "Let the boy go, Hafydd. I will take you
where you ask."

"No, I won't let him go. He will come with us . . . as a reminder
to you. I seek a place called the Moon's Mirror. How long will it
take to travel there?"

"How can you be sure I know where it is?"

Hafydd came to his feet. A tall, proud man, he towered over the
creature in the barrow. "Because this boy's life depends on it, as
does yours."

The legless man considered a moment. "I traveled there once,
long ago, with Sainth," Kilydd said. "It is not a short trip—five days
more or less—and we'll require a boat at the end."

"Could a wagon make the journey?"

The legless man thought a moment. "Perhaps, but not easily."

"We need a cart to take you, we will manage a small boat, as well." He turned and noticed Beld, still holding his dagger to the frightened boy's throat. "Let him go, Lord Beldor. He lives—for now."

A boat was loaded across the back of a wagon, into which went most of their provisions. Kai did not know what arrangements Hafydd made for the army, but he took only a small company— twenty guards, a herdsman, and a handful of servants, and Lord A'denné, who remained silent and aloof from everyone. All were on horseback but for Kai and two others, who rode in the wagon at the fore of the column. For some hours they traveled along a road, going south, but then Kai directed them into a small lane that wound up a wooded hill. A stream coursed beneath the trees, and they crossed it several times as they passed back and forth. At the hill's crest they looked out over a wooded land, no farms or hills in sight. The guards whispered among themselves, but Hafydd did not seem surprised to find the land utterly different than it should have been.

The cart track had disappeared not far back, but the wood was not dense—maple, beech, oaks, elm. The underwood was sparse, and they found a way for their wagon among the trees. Kai guided them unerringly, and Hafydd pressed them to make better speed.

The day was fine, sunlight tumbling down through the boughs and trembling upon the forest floor. Several times they stopped to take down some small trees to let the wagon pass, but for the most part they went forward, if not quickly, at least not as slowly as Kai expected. The boy, who had had the misfortune to be blacking Hafydd's boots when Kai arrived, rode between Kai and the driver, silent, sullen, frightened. Every now and then he would look around at the unfamiliar landscape as though measuring his chances of escape, but always he would find them too small or he would lose his nerve.

Twice streams had to be crossed, but the fords were passable. At dusk a large meadow opened up before them, almost a prairie, and they made their camp in the trees on the edge of the flowing grass. A fire was quickly kindled from deadwood, and the servants began making camp and preparing a supper.

The man Hafydd called Kilydd, but who called himself Kai, was tended by a mute servant named Ufrra, a strange creature, strongly built but oddly gentle. He laid fragrant bed of cedar boughs for his master, covering it with threadbare bedding. A tea he then prepared, which seemed to bring relief from some pain, for Kai's face had been twisted in silent agony for some hours.

Beld watched in interest, still wondering who this man was. He was leading them into the "hidden lands," but that was really all Beld knew. And Hafydd had said something about the man being alive all these years. But how ancient did that make him?

The bootblack, whose name was Stillman—Stil, for short—had gravitated into Kai's circle. The legless man spoke kindly to him, and the boy took to aiding the mute servant. Beld watched as he helped Ufrra lift Kai from his barrow and deposit him on his bedding. There was not much protection that a legless man could offer this waif, but perhaps the boy didn't know that. Kai was the only man in the company who did not seem to fear Hafydd, and he had saved the boy's life once. Perhaps that was enough. As Beld well knew, one made alliances where one could. Perhaps the boy sensed that Kai was softhearted—softhearted among a company who would murder a baby if ordered to. He looked around at the dark-clad guards going quietly about their business—almost as mute as Kai's servant. There was not a shred of humanity among them, the nobleman was certain.

Kai noticed Beldor's gaze fixed on him.

"Is there something you wish to say to me, Lord Beldor?"

"Hafydd will kill the boy as soon as he has what he wants. He'll kill you too."

"No, he won't kill me. He might have need to travel the hidden lands yet, and I am one of the few who can lead him there.

What of you, Lord Beldor? What is it you offer him that no one else can? Maybe it is you he has no need of." Kai looked up, "Ah, Lord A'denné. . . . Is there something I might do for you?"

"I have been ordered to lay my bed here, beside Sir Eremon's other captives."

"An enemy of Hafydd's is a friend of mine," Kai said, and turned to Beld. "Be sure to report that to your master, it might curry you some small favor."

"You know I won't harm a cripple," Beld said. "So how much courage does it take to be insolent to me?"

"Oh, Kilydd is more courageous than you can imagine, Lord Beldor."

Beld turned to find Hafydd standing behind him.

"He once was attacked in a tower by six assassins. He might have escaped—I'm almost sure he could have—but what glory would that have gained him? No, he killed them all in a few hours. My best-trained assassins. One would have easily killed . . . well, you, Lord Beldor." Hafydd turned his intimidating gaze on Kai. "No, you mustn't underestimate Kai. He is not afraid of you because he would almost certainly kill you in a fight—as long as he kept the dagger he conceals in his clothes. But I will tell you this, Kai. If you are leading me astray, or roundabout, I will kill the boy, then your servant, then Lord A'denné. Their lives are dependent upon you."

"I shouldn't worry to much about mine," Lord A'denné said evenly. "My life is forfeit no matter what."

Hafydd stared at Lord A'denné who tried to meet his gaze, but after a minute he looked away.

"Lord Beldor," Hafydd said. "Come to my tent."

Hafydd was the only man in camp who did not sleep out under the stars, though Beld knew it was not because he was soft. His pallet was laid out in a small pavilion, and before it sat a folding chair of clever design and a trunk that doubled as a desk. A pair of candle lanterns provided the light, and a guard at every outside corner the security.

Hafydd took the chair, where he put his fingertips together and tapped them against his bearded chin. "If I were you, I would keep my distance from Kai, who is something of a sorcerer and a more dangerous man than any imagine."

Beld gave a half bow, wondering if he had broken some unknown code or law. Did sorcerers bear respect for one another, even when enemies, the way that men-at-arms did?

Hafydd reached into his cloak and took out a stone on a gold chain. "Do you know what this is?"

"It appears to be an emerald," Beld said, "though I have never seen one so large."

Hafydd held it up so that it spun slowly in the light. "It might be an emerald, in truth—or might have been, once. But it is something quite remarkable now. It seems to be a conscience, or something very like one. I'm not quite sure how it came into my hands, though I believe it must have been arranged by my brother—Caibre's brother, Sainth; the man we know as Alaan, my whist. Fortunately, I recognized its purpose before it had the effect Alaan hoped." He held the chain out to Beld. "I want you to keep it safe. Wear it around your neck. I want to observe its effect on you. See what happens to a man who grows a conscience."

Beld hesitated, wondering if he were being played for a fool.

"Take it. It won't harm you. Many believe a conscience is a necessary part of a man's personality. Let us see if it will win, or if your true nature can resist it." He leaned forward and dangled the chain on his fingers, the green stone still turning slowly.

Beld reached out and took it reluctantly. He did not like things arcane. The cursed book had made his skin crawl. Now this.

"Put it over your head, Lord Beld. Wear it at all times. Tell me if you have any feelings of regret or remorse. I will have you kill Lord A'denné in a few days, and we will observe the effect that has on you." The knight gave him a tight-lipped smile. "Good night, Lord Beldor. Sleep well."

⋆   ⋆   ⋆

Beldor found his bedding laid out not far from the others who had been abducted, within the same circle of guards and isolated by other men-at-arms from Hafydd's tent. Beld realized he was not trusted any more than Kai or Lord A'denné. He had tried to murder his cousin for appeasing the Wills, then offered his services to the Wills when his plot had failed. Who would trust him now? Certainly the Hand of Death had entrusted him to carry the book to Hafydd, and to serve him, but then what fool would betray the Hand of Death?

Kai had been right. He glanced over at Lord A'denné, who sat talking to the bootblack, Stil. The nobleman would be dead in a few days. Likely he knew it. Kai would be kept alive as long as he was useful. The bootblack . . . he was so inconsequential that his life could slip away at any moment. Hafydd might feed him to a dog.

And here he sat, on Death's doorstep, with these others. He reached up and pressed the hard jewel inside his cloak against his breastbone. Why had Hafydd given it to him? What did he mean it was a "conscience"? A man could not grow a conscience if he had not been born with one. That was a truth. Beld regretted none of his actions—oh, he regretted not killing Toren when he'd had the chance. It was the weakness of other men that they took action, then felt regret and remorse afterward. Beld lived with the consequences of his deeds. He did not weep and tear his hair and allow guilt to torture him. That was for weaklings and fools. Men like Dease and Arden. Men who hadn't the stomach to live with their own choices.

He stopped pulling off his boots. And here's where his choices had led him—to the camp of Hafydd, where he was expendable. Where Hafydd hung a bespelled jewel around his neck to observe the effect.

But I was offered reprieve before Death's gate. What choice had I?

None; that was the truth. Anyone would have chosen as he did—not to go into the timeless night.

Beld lay down, gazing up at the great sea of darkness bejeweled by a haze of stars. Something at the edge of his vision caught his attention, and he turned to find the bootblack staring at him, his look utterly cold and filled with hatred. Beld did not think he would sleep well that night.

Eighteen

The eyes of the blind shed tears. That capacity remained when all went dark. That is what Dease thought as he sat with Lord Carral Wills.

They perched in a high, round window in Castle Renné, light, shattered by the stained glass, scattered all around and over their hands and faces. The scene depicted in the stained glass was the fall of Cooling Keep and the destruction of the Knights of the Vow—though the Knights had survived—as had too many other things from the past.

Lord Carral held a delicate hand to his forehead, and a splash of blue spread over the skin. Blue tears streaked his face, but he did not sob; nor did his shoulders shake.

"I'm sorry, Lord Carral," Dease said softly.

"No, it is good news you bring. My only child, my Elise, alive." His shoulders began to shake, and he kept his face partially hidden with his fine-boned hand. "But why did she let me think she was dead?"

Dease did not know how to answer. In truth he had no idea why she had done so. Certainly he could manufacture some possible explanations, and would if need be, but he really did not know.

"I'm sure Lady Elise had her reasons," Dease said.

Carral straightened a little and turned his body away, as though ashamed of this show of emotion—though somehow Dease suspected he was not.

"Has this thing taken her over completely?"

"The nagar? She claimed it had not. I don't know your daughter, so it was difficult for me to gauge, but those who did know her did not react as though she were in any way . . . strange."

"Thank the river for that," Carral said. "Is she alive now, I wonder?"

"Many of us survived the flooding of the tunnels, and as she had already survived the river, I'm sure she is unharmed." Dease was not at all sure, but he hoped his doubts could not be heard.

Carral did not exhibit the normal gestures of sighted men. He did not nod or shake his head, he seldom smiled or frowned. His habitually blank expression was enigmatic—until he wept.

"Then perhaps she will reappear soon. We might hope."

"We do hope. Let it be sooner rather than later."

Carral wiped away the tears on his face with the flat of his hand, as though he had just become aware of them. Sunlight threw the images of Cooling Keep down upon the floor and across Lord Carral's back. Flames danced in his hair. Very stiffly he rose. Down his back Knights tumbled to their deaths.

He did not turn to face Dease but fixed his pale eyes on the dim hallway that opened up before him. His shadow loomed over the fall of Cooling Keep.

"When you saw her . . . Lord Dease, was she . . ." He swallowed, his throat apple bobbing. "Did she seem well? Unharmed?"

"She appeared to be perfectly well. Healthier than either you or I."

Carral tried to smile in response, took a step, then stopped. "Thank you for taking the time to speak with me, Lord Dease. I know how busy you are at this time."

"I wish I could do more. I wish I could summon your daughter up with a spell, but alas, I am no sorcerer."

"You have that to be thankful for, Lord Dease. That and much else." Lord Carral set off, his steps small, like a frail old man, suddenly. Dease watched him the length of the hall. As Lord Carral walked farther from the window he faded into shadow, Dease's eyes being adjusted to the bright light falling through the stained glass. In a moment he faded entirely, like a man walking into fog. Only the slow tap of his cane upon the marble floor could be heard, like the ticking of a distant clock.

Nineteen

Carl helped Jamm into the boat, lowering him onto the stern thwart. The thief lost his balance and his boots thudded heavily on the floorboards.

"Shh," one of the boatmen cautioned.

It was dark, the smallest sliver of a waning moon sailing among an archipelago of cloud. The two boatmen were nervous, fidgeting, constantly searching the darkness with their eyes. The man—almost a boy—who had brought them there, Carl on foot and Jamm on a pony, whispered good luck, and set off, wanting to get as far from the fugitives as he could.

"Climb in now, your grace," one of the watermen said.

Carl took his place in the bow, and the two strangers, little more than shadows in the darkness, slid the boat down the mud bank and into the River Wynnd. They both clambered nimbly aboard, and the boat bobbed on the river, finding its equilibrium. Carl did not much like boats. They always seemed tippy and unstable to him, the surface upon which they rode moving and treacherous.

"Don't be worried, your grace," the nearest waterman said. He must have sensed Carl's anxiety. "My brother and I have spent our lives on the water," the man whispered. "You'll not get a toe wet on this little voyage."

And with that the two men shipped their oars and dug the blades into the dark river.

They pushed off toward midstream, the low, treed banks ragged shadows in the distance. Over them the stars and shred of moon glittered in a great arc. The men rowed silently, having silenced their oars with rags. Only the dipping of the blades could be heard, the drops of water dripping as the oar was lifted clear of the surface.

Carl looked over at the western shore. A fire burned there—Renné guards, perhaps. They would watch the river by night in case the Prince of Innes tried to cross the river in force. Carl wondered what had happened to his father. He should never have stayed. Carl knew in his heart that it was a mistake, but his father would not be talked out of it. Stubbornness was a family trait.

Even though the current would be less near the bank, the watermen were afraid to stay close lest they be discovered by Renné patrols watching the Isle's shore. Jamm was all but invisible in the stern, likely curled up in a ball, still not well after his ordeal. If not for the four days spent in the house of the healer, Carl was sure he would have died. But they had moved him too soon. Jamm was no longer recovering. Oh, he wasn't getting worse, but neither was he getting well. This could not go on. Carl had to get the little man somewhere where he could rest.

"I judge we've come far enough," the waterman said to his brother, and they began turning in toward the eastern shore.

Carl did not like what he was about to do. He slipped his dagger from its sheath and leaning forward encircled the forward rower's head with one arm, putting the edge of his dagger against the soft part of his neck.

"Row to the western shore, now," he said evenly and clearly, "or I'll cut your brother's throat."

"What . . . ?" the other waterman swore, turning in his seat.

"He has a knife to my throat, Brother . . . ," Carl's captive breathed. "Please do as he says."

The oarsman turned them in a circle and sent them toward the west.

"So, how is it you're a traitor, Lord Carl, when the Duke of Vast has ordered his men to kill you on sight?"

"It is a long, complicated story, my friend," Carl said. "If you knew what scum Innes and Menwyn Wills, were you wouldn't be so keen to support their war. Row on and make no noise. I don't want to do harm to your brother."

"But there is one other question I have for you," the man asked softly. "Can ye swim?"

And with that the two brothers threw themselves to one side. The boat rolled, slewed, and suddenly went over, throwing them all into the river. Without thinking, Carl had let his man go, not wanting to cut the man's throat, despite all his threats.

"Jamm!" he called, as he surfaced.

"There he is, Brother," the older of the waterman said. "Sink him."

"He might have his dagger, yet," the other answered. "Slide me an oar."

Carl went under, surfacing on the boat's other side. "Jamm," he whispered again, but there was no answer.

He took hold of the submerged gunwale, the slick planks of the boat glistening dully in the faint light.

"Where's he gone?" one of the watermen asked.

"Under, I'd guess. Thought he probably couldn't swim. He was too nervous when he climbed aboard."

Carl felt a little turbulence near his leg. He recoiled, but then reached under the boat. Someone was under there, clinging to a thwart. Carl ducked under and came up in utter darkness, but there was air to breathe.

"Jamm?" he whispered so softly he barely heard it himself.

"Here," came the equally soft reply.

"Hold your breath," Carl said, "we have to go under."

In the darkness he found his guide clinging to the thwart,

breathing too quickly. He waited until he heard a quick gasp, then took the little man down. They surfaced a few feet away, and Carl swept an arm under Jamm's and across his chest. Something hard knocked against his shoulder, and Tam realized he had an oar. With some difficulty, for he was working one-handed, he slid the oar under Jamm's other arm. It was not much, but it would provide some buoyancy.

Slowly Carl took them toward the western shore. They heard the soft whispers of the watermen for a while, heard them struggling to right their craft and bail the water out.

"Will we make it?" Jamm whispered.

"Yes. Trust me. Kick your feet a little if you can—up and down. That's it. Lie back. I will keep your head above water."

Toren Renné was a contradiction to the eye, Carl thought, for he was both grim and fair. His youthful good looks, upright posture, and wheat-colored hair were at odds with the hard set of his mouth, the suspicion in his clear blue eyes.

"But he is a thief. Why would I take his word over the word of the Duke of Vast, our ally for all of my life?" Toren watched Carl closely, weighing his response.

"Because Jamm is telling the truth, and Vast is lying. I can tell you no more than that."

"But Vast came to our aid on the Isle of Battle when he clearly could have thrown in his lot with the Prince of Innes. It seems a strange thing for a man to do if he was secretly allied with Innes."

"It does, though I meant to do the same—fight against the Renné so that the Prince would think me loyal, and I could still spy for you. As your cousin Kel will tell you, I saved his life at great risk to my own. That is what brought me here. Someone saw me save Kel and reported it to the Prince. The rest I have told you."

Toren looked over at his mother, Lady Beatrice. Carl could not help but hope this noblewoman would intervene on his behalf.

Lady Beatrice favored her son with a tight, sad smile, a dip of her graying curls.

The room was summer-warm, afternoon, a small breeze rustling the curtains and pressing against the cut flowers in a vase on a low table. Two guards stood behind Carl, ready to restrain him if necessary, but his hands and feet were not bound, which he took to be a good sign. Bits of black debris kept tinkling in the fire grate and, from up the chimney, men could be heard working.

"I have nothing to gain in coming to you," Carl said. "If Vast caught me, as you say he claimed, with stolen letters, I would certainly have returned to the Prince of Innes. But I will assure you, it is death for me to cross the river. The Prince will see me dead the moment I'm found. And if not for a stroke of luck, Vast would have finished me on the Isle."

"There is a truth I can verify," Toren said. "Kel reports that Vast's men were told to kill you on sight, which I take as being somewhat strange. Anyone would want to question a spy if given the chance."

"Whatever you decide for me, Lord Toren, beware of Vast. He is in league with the Prince of Innes. There is no doubt of it."

"Yes, but the Prince of Innes is no longer alive, so I don't know what that will do to Vast's alleged alliance."

"The Prince is dead?"

Toren nodded, his curls bobbing. "Assassinated by one of his own guards, it is said."

"Hafydd!" Carl pronounced.

"That hated name," Lady Beatrice said, making small fists on the arm of her chair. "Why do you blame him?"

Carl felt his shoulders shrug. "It can be no other."

"It is not much of a reason you offer, but nonetheless, I agree." Toren shifted in his chair. His gaze seemed to focus high on the opposite wall, and his face was troubled and unhappy. "We will have to consider this matter carefully. Until then I'm sorry, but we will have to confine you to a cell."

Carl bowed his head. "I can survive a cell, but Jamm needs a

healer. He almost died on the Isle. I fear a damp cell would bring
back his fever and coughing."

"We will look out for your friend," Lady Beatrice said.

Toren nodded to the guards, and they led him out.

"I don't know what we should do with him, Mother. He accuses
one of our oldest, most loyal allies of treachery, yet it was Vast who
came to our aid on the Isle of Battle. There is only really one thing
that gives me any doubts. Vast ordered Lord Carl killed on sight.
Strange."

"Vast is a passionate man."

"Yes, but he is not foolish. Certainly he would have wanted to
question Lord Carl."

"I am more influenced by the utter lack of guile in Lord Carl.
Everything he said had the ring of truth." Lady Beatrice sat back
in her chair and closed her eyes a moment.

Toren felt his heart go out to her. Her life was so difficult.

"Yes, but that would mean that Vast is our enemy. Vast . . ."

Twenty

The cells smelled of mold, damp stone, and candle smoke. Toren took the lantern from the guard and hung it on a rusted hook.

"Dease?" came a voice from within the cell.

"No, Cousin, it is I."

Samul's face, paler than Toren remembered, appeared in the barred frame of the small window. "Toren. No doubt my reputation for hospitality has drawn you."

"Yes, that was it," Toren said.

Samul gazed at him a moment, saying nothing. Samul's thoughts were always hidden, and here, in the shadows, Toren could not hope to read his cousin's face. Rage might lurk behind those eyes, but Toren would never know. After all, Samul had plotted to murder him, and Toren had not guessed it.

"What brought you back, Cousin?" Toren asked. "You agreed never to return to Renné lands. Have you forgotten our bargain?"

"Have you forgotten that I saved you from Beld?"

Toren paused. "I remember that you tried to murder me, Samul."

Samul took a step back, almost disappearing into the gloom

of his cell. His voice echoed a little against the hard walls. "Yes, but then you were betraying us to the Wills—all your vain attempts to make peace. If you'd listened to me, you'd be ready for the war you are fighting now. You were wrong, Toren, and I was right."

"Yes, in some ways you were right, but when I disagree with a member of my family I don't try to murder him."

"And how many lives will be lost because you were pursuing an impossible peace with an intractable enemy? Your death would have saved lives."

Toren shook his head sadly. There would be an undeniable logic to Samul's argument. Beld might have tried to murder him from hatred, but not Samul. He would only have done it out of conviction.

"I cannot trust you, Samul Renné," Toren said softly. "You shouldn't have come here."

He could hear Samul's breathing—exasperated.

"I was spewed out of a little hole in the earth into a shallow stream," Samul said disdainfully. "A patrol found me as I made my way to the river. I had no idea where I was. Certainly, nothing would have induced me to set foot on Renné lands, for our bargain was still sharp in my mind."

Samul appeared at the window again, the shadows of the bars drawing dark streaks upon his face. "Coming here was an accident, Toren. I swear it."

Toren nodded. He did not really doubt it. Samul was too smart to have returned to Renné lands.

"What will I do with you now, Samul?" Toren said. "I swore that if you returned to Renné lands, you would pay for your plot against me. What will I do with you now?"

"Can you not let me go?" Samul whispered.

Toren paused a moment, sadness settling upon him like a weight. "If you were me, is that what you would do?"

"No," Samul said. Toren could see him shake his head. "No. It's not what I would do."

Their silence filled the dank chambers. The guard coughed at his post. Toren could hear Samul breathing raggedly, wondering if he had just pronounced his own death sentence.

"You could let me escape. I would disappear, Toren. You would never hear my name again."

Toren did not answer. It was the easy decision—and leaders could not always take the easy way. What message would Samul's release send? That Toren Renné was so softhearted that he could not even execute his own assassins!

"I can't let you go, Samul. You know that."

"Then why have you come here?"

"I don't know. To find out why you were here. To tell you my-self what will be done."

"And what will be done?"

"You shall meet the executioner, and I shall weep for your loss, for the love I feel for you."

Toren turned and started down the passageway between the narrow cells. He had not gone five paces when Samul called out.

"You might cut off my head, but I am still loyal to my family, despite all that you might think. I will give you this one last gift, Toren Renné: another matter where I am right and you are wrong. I have been speaking with Lord Carl across the corridor. Vast is a traitor. Carl A'denné is telling the truth. Vast will betray us."

Toren stopped only an instant. "Vast will not betray us," he said, and went on.

At the top of the stairs he met Dease, who hurried down a corridor bearing a paper, folded and sealed.

"A Fáel brought this," Dease said. "It is from A'brgail."

Toren broke the seal and opened the letter, walking a few paces into the light of a lantern.

> *Lord Toren:*
> *I have just arrived at the Fáel encampment where the*
> *Westbrook meets the Wynnd. Elise Wills is here, and much*

is afoot. I think I will be off this night, and would like the honor of your counsel before I set out.

Your servant,
Gilbert A'brgail

Toren looked up to find Dease watching him closely.

"Will you have a horse readied for me, Cousin? I will ride to the Fáel encampment within the hour."

"I will have guards ready to accompany you as well."

Toren nodded. "Do you know where I might find Fondor?"

"In his rooms, why?"

"I must arrange an execution." Toren set off down the passage.

He found Fondor in the company of Lady Beatrice, both seated by a cold hearth, now barred with steel against chimney sweep spies. Toren looked at the letter again. It was from Kel—intelligence from his many spies.

"But why would Hafydd go off now? We are at war."

Fondor shrugged. "I don't pretend to know the mind of that blackguard. Kel says that the army and the allies of the late Prince of Innes are unhappy, restless. They resent Hafydd, and now that he is gone they see a chance to take control of the army again."

"It sounds like wishful thinking to me," Toren retorted. He looked down at the letter again. "If A'denné has gone off with Hafydd, then his son, Carl, is either mistaken about his father's loyalties, or he is lying. And this legless man—"

"Kai, whom we had here beneath our roof and whom we let fall into Hafydd's hands," Toren's mother said. She put a hand to her brow a moment and gave her head a quick shake.

"And this about Beldor . . . ," Toren said. "Beldor was snatched up by one of Death's servants. If the rest of this letter is as truthful as that, how reliable can it be?"

Fondor looked at Lady Beatrice as though he worried Toren was raving. "Kel thinks this news is reliable," Fondor said, "and Kel is not often mistaken."

"Yes," Toren said softly. "Yes. You're right. Kel is not often wrong." He stood up and walked to the window, looking out at the final light of day, the growing shadows. "I will go out to the Fáel encampment and speak with A'brgail and Lady Elise," he said.

"And I will see to the execution," Fondor said. "I hope you're right about this, Toren."

"So do I, Cousin."

Fondor made a quick bow to his aunt and went out, his boots echoing down the passage outside. Toren listened to them fade before he turned to find his mother regarding him. He often thought she must have been very beautiful in her youth, and her poise and grace were undiminished by time. But her face was so careworn now. It made him sad to see it. The burden of his father in his tower was great. It would almost be better if the man died, instead of coming back to sanity every now and then—like a man coming back to life, then dying only to be reborn. One could never quite stop grieving—or hoping.

"Yes?" Toren said after a moment.

"There is one other matter I think you must attend to," she said.

"Only one?"

"One that matters. You need to visit Llyn"—she took a deep breath—"and make her realize that her hopes for you are vain."

Toren began to protest, but then realized that his mother would not listen to this, now. When she had set her mind to a thing, there was no denying it.

"But Llyn has so . . . little," he said weakly.

"Lord Carral loves her," Lady Beatrice said.

"But he is a Wills."

"Then let her become a Wills!" his mother snapped. "It matters not. She deserves more than her books and her garden. You know she does."

Toren nodded. "When I return from the Fáel."

His mother nodded, her face softening. She even favored him with a small smile.

Twenty-one

Toren stared at the embroidery hoop Tuath held up to the lanternlight. For a moment he closed his eyes and felt the slight soothing this brought.

Tuath flipped the cloth covering back on her work of horror.

Immediately, Toren lifted his wineglass, feeling the wine, dry and slightly bitter, on his tongue. "There is no news to lift the heart," he said, lowering the glass. "Monsters abroad and sorcerers reborn, our land about to be overrun." He looked around the group—Fáel and men. "I feel I have fallen into a tale of old, a tale of heroes—but I don't feel that I measure up to the heroes of stories."

"We have not been tested, yet," A'brgail said softly.

Lady Elise sat upon a Fáel chair, pillows and rich coverings around her, yet she was still dressed in men's cast-off clothing, mended and worn. Her gaze was far away, and Toren felt sympathy for her. This was certainly a time to test her, a girl who had likely thought that life would consist of little more than marriage and the vain conspiracies of her family.

One of the young men from the wildlands hovered a few paces behind her, and the giant, Orlem Slighthand, sat in a chair to her right, as though that was his rightful place. A white-bearded old man named Eber was seated next to them in the circle, and beside him three Fáel elders whose names he had already forgotten. Gilbert A'brgail sat, with two of his gray-robed Knights standing behind his chair, two-handed swords drawn but point down on the trampled grass.

The snow woman returned to her seat, placing her embroidery hoop beside her. Toren found it difficult not to stare at her. Her beauty was cold and otherworldly, but beguiling.

"Alaan will try to find his way to this place," Elise said. "This place where Wyrr sleeps."

"And where is that?" Toren asked.

"I wish I knew," Elise said.

A small boy, who had been standing on the edge of the conversation, slunk into the circle of light and crawled into the old man's lap. He began to move his hands strangely.

"What does he say, Eber?" one of the Fáel elders whispered.

Eber nodded as the boy stopped. "Llya says that he can lead us to the waiting isle, now. That is where Hafydd will go to make his soul eater."

The Fáel elder shivered visibly, and everyone present seemed completely distressed.

"Who is this child?" Toren asked.

"He is Eber's son," the vision weaver said. "Llya hears the voice of the river."

"Our river? The Wynnd?"

Tuath nodded. "Though I would not call it ours," she said. "The great sorcerer Wyrr joined his spirit to the river. That is the voice that Llya hears."

Toren looked back at the small boy, who seemed almost repellent to him.

The boy began to move his hands. "The voice in the river is . . . *murky*," the father translated. "Its words are muddled, confused, almost riddles, but Llya says it will lead him to the waiting isle, now. There is no time to be lost. Hafydd will go there and perform his outrage. The lands will be overrun." The child leapt off his father's lap, moving his hands wildly. "Boats, he says. We must have boats and leave this night." The old man swept the boy back up into his lap, holding him close, pinning his arms. Tears streamed down his cheeks and into his white beard—crystals upon snow.

Boats were found that night, and they were on the river at first light, bows parting a low mist that swirled in their wake. Toren took to a boat with A'brgail, Dease, and six men-at-arms, half the number Renné, the others Knights of the Vow. They also brought Theason, for none of them were experienced watermen; nor did they know the hidden lands. Ahead, Toren could see Elise, standing in the stern of her craft, Baore and Slighthand at the oars with another small company of men-at-arms in gray or Renné blue. The old man, Eber, sat in the bow, Llya by his side. How reluctantly the man had agreed to let his son lead them.

The day was overcast, but windless. Along both shores poplars and willows stood above the low fog. Toren looked over to the east, wondering if the enemy would see them and whether they would send boats to intercept.

"Too foggy on the eastern shore for us to be noticed," A'brgail said. He was looking at Toren and reading his thoughts, apparently.

"I'm sure you're right." Toren sat down on a thwart. "Are we mad, do you think? Shouldn't we be staying here and fighting enemies we know exist?"

A'brgail shook his head. "You were in the Stillwater, Lord Toren. You know this war is not about the Renné and the Wills—not anymore."

Toren closed his eyes at mention of the Stillwater. "It seems like a nightmare, now," he said, "not something that really happened—that really *could* have happened." He had not even returned to Castle Renné that night—there had not been time, or so he told himself. There was a part of him that thought perhaps he was avoiding the talk he had promised to have with Lady Llyn—the talk he had promised his mother. He had sent a note to Lady Beatrice explaining briefly what he had learned and where he went, but even so, he did not expect her to understand.

Overhead a gull circled, its cry echoing over mist-laden waters. Men strained at their oars. Toren rose to catch sight of the other boat. Only Elise could be seen, standing wrapped in a dark Fáel cloak, the mist swirling about her waist.

"Fondor and Kel can fight a war," A'brgail said. "You needn't worry. You left them a good design. Put that out of your mind. We travel to the real war, now. I only hope Alaan will find us."

"You were cursing him before, your half brother."

The knight nodded solemnly, his manner pensive. "I do not condone what he did, but it is too late to concern ourselves with that now. We must stop Hafydd by whatever means. I will worry about Alaan then—if any of us survive."

Within the hour high cliffs rose to either side of the river, though Toren knew full well that there were no such cliffs below the Westbrook—not for many leagues at least. The mist persisted late into the morning and a light drizzle fell, making the floorboards and thwarts shiny and slick. Toren had his oarsmen keep close to the other boat, for in this fog and poor light they could easily be separated. Without Llya to guide them he didn't know what might happen. They could be lost in the hidden lands forever.

The cliffs seemed to close in on them, cutting off much of the faint gray light. The stone was dark with rain and streaked with slick streams. Pressed into this narrow space, the river flowed more quickly, sweeping the boats along. The oarsmen were glad of the rest, and Theason, who had been hunching silently in the bow, scrambled aft to take the tiller with apparent confidence.

"Do you know this place, good Theason?" A'brgail asked, raising his voice to be heard over the river.

The little traveler shook his head. He sat straight at the helm, his face serious, but his eyes seemed to dance, looking here and there, as though he had just returned to a home from which he'd long been parted. The rest of the company were anxious, wondering where this unnatural child led them, worried that the speeding river would become dangerous. Toren found himself imagining rapids, towering waterfalls.

But the river did not change, though it snaked through the gorge at good speed. Toren wished they were on horseback, for he was a masterful horseman. Boats, though he had traveled in them many times, were not to his liking. Unlike many, he could swim, so he didn't fear the water itself. It was just that the river was unpredictable, worse than the maddest horse. It could suck you down into its depths and never let you up.

He glanced again at Elise, who remained standing in the stern of her boat even though the river swept them along at speed. She was of the water, now, while he was of the land. A difference much greater than that between Renné and Wills.

Along the base of the cliff, low gravel beaches appeared, and the river began to broaden a little. Toren's boat drew nearer the other, and he could make out the faces of the seated men, who all seemed to be drowning in a mist. He gazed out ahead, where Elise watched, and there in a thinning patch, thought he saw something white, almost human. A face gazing back at them, then a movement of the arm as though beckoning them on, before it disappeared into the swirl.

At dusk they drew the boats up on a bar of gravel and made a camp. Toren was glad to find solid ground beneath him and stood gazing at the gorge.

"I hope we don't have to climb up there," he said to A'brgail.

The knight was opening a bag, but stopped and stared at the cliffs. Ferns and even small trees grew on ledges and out of cracks—bits of green scratched on the monolithic gray, like isolated words scattered over a page.

"Only a spider might climb that," A'brgail said. "If we can't pass through by boat, we'll die here."

"A comforting thought, Gilbert."

The knight went back to his task, and Toren walked a few paces down the bar to the very tip, the gravel curving back behind him toward the cliff. The mist, which had persisted all day, continued to swirl ever so slowly over the waters, shadow turning it dark.

Elise, still dressed in her long cloak, stood twenty paces away on the far side of the bar. She was staring fixedly at some point downriver, and Toren crossed over to see what it was that so fascinated her. She heard his boots grinding through the gravel and gave her head a shake.

"What is it you see?" Toren asked.

A sad, quick smile touched her lips. "I see a river leading I know not where. I fear there will be branches, and I will be forced to choose—my choices will mean that some will live, while others will die."

"It is ever so for those born to power, my lady."

"I was not born to this power," she said bitterly. "It was forced upon me by Hafydd, though he did not know it."

"Everything he touches is harmed."

She nodded.

"Your father knows you're alive, now," Toren said.

"You told him—"

"Lady Beatrice told him. She thought she must."

Elise nodded; her blond curls were gathered into a knot behind her head, only a few managing to escape, and these bobbed with her every movement. Something caught her eye, Toren could see, and he looked out over the water, where something dark moved.

"A black swan," Elise said, realizing that he'd seen. "A symbol of the House of Tusival and his heirs."

"But they have been gone from this land for hundreds of years."

"We are no longer in your land, Lord Toren."

"Perhaps it is an omen?"

"Of what, I wonder," Elise mused.

Toren turned and looked at her. She was pretty, though not beautiful, he thought. Her face was a bit too long, and thin, her nose inelegant, yet she had a presence, a calmness that touched him. The air of sadness about her was thicker than the mist, and it was not feigned or imagined. Tragedy haunted this young woman. He almost wanted to move away, as though it might strike any who were close, but at the same time he wanted to put his arms around her and offer comfort.

Poor Lord Carral, he thought, as if the man did not have enough sorrows to bear.

"Do not be concerned, Lord Toren," she said, perhaps sensing his unease, "I am flesh and blood, as filled with feelings as any." She turned and met his eye. "I am just . . . filled with centuries of memories, of a life rich and too recklessly lived. Only vaguely do I remember the river, all the long years she slept there. The life of Elise Wills—my life—seems hardly a flicker to me now—a life briefer than a winter morning. And yet that is the life I long for. To have it back—my foolish cousins, my hateful aunts. I would choose it all if I could."

Toren nodded as though he understood, though he didn't, and he was profoundly aware of it. He felt suddenly small and very human speaking to this woman.

Another smile appeared on Elise's face. "Do you know, I once thought that we should marry and do away with our families' foolish feud."

"Perhaps we should."

Elise shook her few escaped curls, her smile disappearing. "No. Elise Wills you might have condescended to marry to achieve peace . . . but this creature who stands before you now . . . She is a monster."

"You are no monster."

"Oh, I am. You can't imagine the things that Sianon did. And these are my memories now, my past. No, Lord Toren, you are wise to be repelled by me."

"I do not find you repellent."

Elise smiled wickedly. "Oh, don't you? Then perhaps we should consider marriage." She saw the change of his face and laughed. Her hand touched his arm. "Don't worry, Lord Toren, you are safe from me. I don't know how, but I lost what heart I have to a boy from the wildlands."

Toren looked over at the big Valeman who was bent over the kindling fire, fanning it with a handful of green leaves.

"No, not poor Baore." She turned her gaze on the Valeman as well. "I don't know what I'll do with him. Perhaps you might take him into your service? I fear he is in danger with me. Everyone is in danger with me."

She turned and walked away along the very edge of the gravel, little hands of water lapping up at her feet.

Dinner was somber, the strangeness of the place affecting everyone. The men-at-arms were uneasy and kept their distance from Eber, Llya, and Elise. They must have seen the swimmer as well, Toren thought, and knew full well this gorge wasn't on the river below the Westbrook. Toren had warned the men before they set out that they might travel into strange lands by arcane means, but they clearly hadn't believed a word. They were honest men, but the arcane frightened them—and for good reason, Toren thought. He was not at ease himself in this place. Only Theason found the journey to his taste, drinking in the sights, his eyes glittering. The quiet little traveler had come alive that day, and now busied himself about the encampment like a man newly in love. He examined the few plants supported by the gravel as though they were treasures, and even climbed some distance up a cliff to fetch down a flower—all in near darkness.

Two fires had been built, one for the men-at-arms, where the Renné mingled with A'brgail's somber Knights, and another for everyone else. The Knights of the Vow kept glancing at Orlem Slighthand, who sat still and silent across from Toren. He seemed a legend come to life, to Toren, massive and powerful, wielding a two-handed sword as though it were made for one. Too many things seemed to be emerging from the past, Toren thought, not all as welcome as Slighthand.

Eber came back out of the darkness, having put his son to rest a short distance away. As he settled onto a log, firelight flickered on Eber's long, pale beard, so that it looked like his face was surrounded by flame.

"Your son sleeps, good Eber?" A'brgail asked.

The old man shrugged. "I hope he will." He glanced up into the dark. "This place is so strange. I should never have consented to bring him on this journey. It is not for children."

"My guards will protect him, good Eber," Toren said soothingly. "I have sworn it."

"Why would they protect him?" the old man snapped. "They are frightened of him. He disturbs them . . ."

"He unsettles you, Eber," Elise said, "but you would give your life to protect his."

Eber was taken aback by this, but he did not gainsay it. "I am his father. I love him above all else." The old man then rose in agitation and disappeared into the darkness.

The river hurried by, muttering. Everyone was silent.

"Who is Eber son of Eiresit?" Toren asked softly. "You know him, Theason?"

The little man lifted his hands in a helpless gesture. "I met him on the river, many years ago now, where he makes his home at Speaking Stone. He was kind to me, welcoming me into his house, sharing much of his lore of healing herbs. He speaks little of his past. His wife died, and memories are painful to him. When I met him I thought he was a little . . . mad—living by the river, trying to understand its secret speech. And now his son hears it, and Eber wishes he had never listened, that he had never made his home by the Wyrr at all." Theason shook his head sadly. "Eber son of Eiresit, and Llya son of Eber, are like seers—only they hear voices from the past, echoes, words, fragments of sentences. The small boy who cannot speak is the tongue of the river. You are all troubled by him, but I think him the most miraculous thing I have ever encountered. I would give my life to preserve his. He gives voice to the ancient river. What is more wondrous than that?"

"Eber son of Eiresit is more than he seems," Elise said quietly, then she rose and went into the darkness, leaving them all listening to the babble of the river.

They set guards, not for fear of men—for who could find them in this place?—but for fear of the darkness. Toren knew that not a night would fall for the rest of his life without memories of the creatures that had come for them in the Stillwater. Lying there beneath the open sky, he felt vulnerable, small. The strange river muttered, so that even Toren found himself listening for words. Occasionally the call of a night bird echoed eerily.

Toren rolled and sighed for several long hours before oblivion found him. He didn't know how long he'd slept but he woke to a hand on his shoulder and someone requesting quiet.

"Come," A'brgail said, "but be silent."

Toren rolled out of his blankets and, barefoot, followed A'brgail. The mist had cleared away, and a sliver of moon hung almost directly overhead, casting a faint light. The knight led him down to the edge of the water, where the small pebbles cast up by the river made less noise beneath their feet. Twenty paces on he saw a figure crouched by the water, with another standing nearby, like a sentinel. In the water, a few feet before these two, a pale creature of mist and moonlight. Toren could see its eyes, like moons. Elise—for certainly it was no other—appeared to be speaking, but Toren could not parse her speech from that of the river.

The creature slipped beneath the surface, like the moon going down into the sea, and Elise rose, staring down into the waters a moment. Orlem stood silently by, his large shadow still as the towering cliffs. Elise turned and started down the beach toward A'brgail and Toren, who had not a moment to slip away.

"Wake everyone," she said as she passed. "We have rested enough. Hafydd makes all speed."

Twenty-two

Menwyn Wills did not like waiting in the dark. His guards—and he had brought plenty of them—lit only a single lantern, and it threw barely any light at all. The moon was a crescent so thin it hung like an arc of silver wire in the star-scattered black. Shifting from foot to foot, Menwyn flattened the tall, dew-slick grass. The scent of the river touched his nostrils, and the air was damp and almost cool on this warm summer night. A few feet away the river slipped by, silent as a serpent.

Menwyn reached down and slid an inch of his sword from its sheath, assuring himself that it would slip free if he needed it. Of course, he hadn't used a blade in many years, not since he had given up the tournaments, but he trusted that the training of his youth had not abandoned him altogether. Tonight would not be a good night to find that assumption wrong.

"My lord," one of his guards whispered.

Alerted, Menwyn stopped shifting and stood perfectly still. For a moment he heard nothing, then a small splash sounded along the bank, as though an oar had entered the water. The dark bulk of a boat appeared almost before them.

"My lord?" came a voice from the river.

"Yes, Vast, is that you?"

"Do not speak my name. Voices travel far over the river."

"Come ashore then."

The boat hissed up onto the grassy bank, and Vast stepped quickly over the side. The lantern was brought forward and lifted up where the light fell upon the faces of the two men. Vast pulled up the hood of this cloak.

"Best take that away," he whispered.

The Duke reached out and clasped Menwyn's hand, taking his elbow with the other.

"Is it true, then?" Vast whispered. "The Prince of Innes is dead?"

"Yes. Assassinated by one of his own guards we're told; but no one believes it."

"Hafydd murdered him," Vast stated.

"Hafydd or one of his cursed guards." Menwyn felt the heat of anger course through him. "There is even a rumor that it was Beldor Renné," he whispered.

Two folding stools were set out for the noblemen, and they sat down by the riverbank, their guards around them at a respectful distance. Menwyn did not really think this was a trap. Vast was not likely to risk his own life in this way—not that he wasn't a brave man, but he wasn't foolish either. He had no way of knowing how many of Menwyn's guards lurked in the darkness—surely he knew it was more than a few.

"Innes was a fool to strike any kind of bargain with that sorcerer," Vast said softly.

"He was bespelled, that is what I think. His own son tried to warn him, but he wouldn't listen. I'm sure Hafydd killed the son as well, for Prince Michael went off with Hafydd and didn't return."

Vast shifted on his stool. A guard brought them each a glass of wine, and they toasted. Menwyn could see nothing of the Duke's

face. Even his form was impossible to make out. He appeared bent
and aged in the darkness—like some strange creature out of a song.
His voice, deep and resonant, seemed to echo out of the river.

"Innes was a fool not to accede to your demands," Menwyn
said meekly. "Half the Renné lands; it is a bargain, I think."

"Half the Renné lands," Vast said, "and the right to any other
estates I can conquer upon the western shore."

Menwyn took a deep breath. He knew it was outrageous, but
he also knew he had no choice. The Renné had beaten them upon
the Isle, and Menwyn feared that they would do it again. He lay
awake at night wondering where they would land their forces upon
the eastern shore. Wondering what day he would wake to find a
Renné army bearing down on him, that indomitable Toren Renné
at its head.

"I agree, Vast. But first you must help me defeat the Renné."

"That I will do, but does Hafydd not control the Prince's army?"

"Hafydd is gone. He took a small company of guards, Beldor
Renné, and a few others, and disappeared. A captain of his guards
was left to command the army, but that will change this night.
There aren't a hundred guards, and they are hated. It is all
arranged."

"Ah, Menwyn, your reputation is well deserved. But what will
you do when Hafydd returns?"

"Hafydd and a handful of guards can't stand against a whole
army of Innes and Wills men-at-arms. Unlike that fool of a Prince,
I am not under Hafydd's spell. I will happily have him killed if he
dares return." Menwyn thought he saw Vast nod in the darkness.

"Then let me tell you this, as a show of good faith," Vast said.
"Lord A'denné is a traitor. He made a bargain with the Renné. I
know this because I was there. And one other bit of information:
Prince Michael of Innes lives. He is in Castle Renné as we speak
and has offered his service and knowledge to Lord Toren."

Menwyn cursed. "That isn't good news. A'denné I don't care
about. His son, Carl, ran off, and Lord A'denné was taken by
Hafydd, for what reason I don't know. But Prince Michael . . . he

will have supporters among his father's army and among his allies. . . ." Menwyn cursed again. "I wonder if we might not find an
assassin who will solve this problem for us?"

"The Renné aren't fools. The attempt on the life of Lord Carral has them wary. Prince Michael will be well guarded."

Menwyn cursed again. "We will have to spread the rumor that
the Prince is dead and that the Renné claim otherwise to undermine our confidence."

"Yes, that might be believed," Vast whispered, "for a while. Perhaps long enough."

"What will you do now?"

"I will return to Westbrook and learn Toren's intentions. It is almost certain that they will hear of the Prince's death and Hafydd's
disappearance. They will try to move an army across the river to
take advantage of this confusion. I will send you a message telling
you the time and place. Your army is larger and better prepared. Let
them land by night, and at first light drive them into the river. One
short battle, and the Renné will be ruined. We will cross the river
and besiege Castle Renné, then divide their lands between us."

Menwyn reached out and put a hand on the Duke's large shoulder. "Vast, your name shall ever be honored among the Wills."

"Yes, I shall be known as the great traitor, but in two hundred
years who will care?"

Twenty-three

Samul woke to a jangle of keys and the ancient lock of his cell turning. The door creaked open on rusty hinges, and a lantern swung into view, its smoke-stained glass emitting only the vaguest light. He propped himself up on one elbow, shading his eyes against the glare.

"Light a candle," a guard said. A servant hustled in and set a tray on the small desk to take up one of the candles sitting there. He lit this from the lantern and put it back on the desk, where it flickered fitfully. A second servant laid a suit of clothes over the back of his chair. Somewhere high up above, the castle bells tolled—four in the morning.

"What is this?" Samul asked groggily.

"It is your last meal," the guard said. "Eat up and dress. You have an appointment with the executioner at five."

The servants turned and bustled out, the guard behind them.

Samul bolted out of bed.

"But I've been told nothing of this!" he shouted.

The door thumped into place, and he heard the keys jangle again. "I know nothing of that, your grace," the man mumbled.

"Call Lord Dease!" Samul shouted through the barred window. "I must speak with Dease!"

The guard withdrew the keys from the lock. Samul could hardly make out the man's face in the poor light.

"Lord Dease has gone off with Lord Toren. No one knows when they'll return. I can take him no message." The guard lumbered off down the passageway, the dim light of his lantern disappearing into the dark tunnel.

They came to fetch him before the bell tolled five. Samul wondered if this was a nightmare, for nothing felt real. Every little sound was heightened, the stones in the walls all seemed to stand out in the dim light. Two others were taken from their cells then; a noblemen and a small, dark-haired man.

"Lord Samul, I expect . . . ?" the nobleman said.

"Lord Carl—I see your face at last."

The two bowed to each other. Samul saw that the little man was trembling, near to collapse. Lord Carl put a hand on his shoulder.

"So this is what I've brought you to. I can't tell you how much I regret it, Jamm."

"It would have come to this eventually," the little man said, trying to steady his voice. "At least I go in good company." He tried to smile but failed.

It was a silent procession—at least there was no speech. Every footfall seemed like the note of a dirge to Samul. Even the pendulous creak of the lantern swinging on its handle was as clear as a lark's song in the early morning.

The company made their way in near darkness up a narrow stair. At the top a small company of guards waited. Without pause they went on, marching in step down the corridor.

Samul thought the Renné blue of the guards' surcoats was the most beautiful color he had ever laid eyes on. As beautiful as the sky on a summer's day. A dim gray light illuminated the high windows.

"Will we be executed before the sun rises?" he asked the guard. He had not seen the sun in days, and suddenly it was important to see it once more.

"I don't know, sir," the guard answered softly, no doubt breaking his orders not to speak with the condemned.

Samul made every effort to bear up, not wanting anyone to say he faltered at the end. He had made his decisions and now must accept the consequences, but at the same time a small voice within him cried, *These cannot be my last minutes! I'm not ready to make an end of it yet. I'm not ready!*

Doors opened into a small courtyard. Samul knew the place: "the bone yard" it was called. It was a cheerless square of gray paving stones and empty-eyed walls, for only a few windows stared down into the place. No one wanted a room with such an outlook. No garden softened the harsh rectangle, no tree offered shade, or climbing vine broke the blankness of the stone.

The little company turned and passed through the doors. Carl's companion sobbed once but then took hold of himself and bore up. Samul looked over at the young nobleman. His back was straight, and his hands were steady. There was a pale sheen of sweat upon his brow, and his eyes were wide, like a man surprised, but otherwise he carried himself with admirable dignity. Samul only hoped that his own appearance did not suffer by comparison.

A scaffolding, hung with black cloths, stood at one end of the courtyard, and below the cloths, three baskets waited side by side. Samul's nerve almost failed then, but he tore his eyes away and walked on, his feet hardly seeming to hit the ground. Each step seemed to happen slowly, the heel of his boot striking, the ball of the foot touching sometime later.

Fondor waited at the bottom of the steps, his face grim and filled with sadness. Samul remembered that Fondor had been his protector when he was a small boy, shielding him from the bullies among his larger cousins.

The company stopped at the foot of the wooden steps. Fondor drew a ragged breath. "Have you anything to say, Cousin?" he asked.

Samul leaned near to the larger man, so that he might whisper close to his ear. "It was Dease who was to have murdered Toren," he said, "but he would not shoot, for he knew it to be Arden. Beld knocked him down and took the shot himself, believing it was Toren." He stepped back and gained some small satisfaction from the shock on Fondor's face. "Thank Dease for all the concern he's shown me."

Samul turned away and mounted the stairs, Carl and his guide close behind.

It was dark within the black hangings, but in the dim light Samul could make out the executioner in his black hood, axe in hand. More guards hovered over three wretched-looking men who stood with their hands bound, one rocking quickly from foot to foot, so frightened he could barely stand.

They will execute common criminals on the same scaffold! Samul thought indignantly. It was an intentional insult, he realized. A final message from Toren, who had certainly ordered it.

High up in a narrow window stood the messenger from the Duke of Vast. He had been brought here that morning, having arrived soon after his lord had heard that Carl A'denné had made his way across the river to Castle Renné. The aging Renné counselor who stood beside him cleared his throat.

"You will take Lady Beatrice's thanks to the Duke. This young traitor might have done much harm if the Duke had not found him out."

The messenger nodded. "The Duke will be much gratified."

"There is also a small gift—a token of Lady Beatrice's affection."

The messenger performed a small bow.

A dull thud was heard through the dirty glass, and a head toppled into a basket. Another dull report with the same result, then a third.

"That is the end of A'denné, his young guide, and also Lord Samul Renné. What a time of treachery we live in," the old counselor added.

"So it is, but you have paid these traitors back in full." The messenger hesitated, glanced once more through the smudged pane, then turned away.

The two men proceeded down the hall thinking about breakfast.

Samul's gaze turned toward the three blocks set out at the edge of the scaffold. His eyes closed involuntarily, and he turned his face up toward the sky. Opening his eyes, he saw only the featureless gray of the early morning. No hint of blue.

"Lord Samul . . . ," a guard said, "this way."

A hand touched his shoulder, and Samul tore his gaze away from the sky. The guard gestured toward a stair that led back into the castle.

"What?" Samul said stupidly.

"This way, sir." The guard took his arm gently and led him down the stairs.

Samul glanced back once to see the first criminal led forward to kneel before the block, then he was inside.

Fondor waited there in flickering lamplight. Behind him came Carl A'denné and the little thief who served him. They were hustled past and down the passageway.

"Wh-what goes on?" Samul stammered.

Fondor leaned close to him and spoke in a harsh whisper. "Samul Renné is dead. You will cease to use that name, and you will never—never—return to Renné lands. I have a task for you, Cousin, and if you will perform it, Toren will not feel he let you go in vain."

"Whatever it is," Samul said, "I will do it." His knees buckled then, and he would have fallen had not Fondor reached out and kept him on his feet.

★   ★   ★

Carl A'denné could not quite catch his breath. He and Jamm were hustled into a small dim room, and the door slammed behind them. A single window, barred, was set high into a wall.

Jamm began to sob, shoulders shaking almost silently. "What trick is this they play?" the little man lamented.

"I know not," Carl answered, gazing around—a tallyman's room, with tables and ledgers. The sound of the executioner's axe came dully through the door. Jamm collapsed against a wall.

A moment later the door opened, and Fondor Renné stepped in, his manner grim and determined.

"What game is this?" Carl demanded angrily.

"Vast will think you dead," Fondor said. "One of his minions had a poor view of your execution from a high window. Though the head that fell into the basket was not so fair, it would pass as yours in such poor light." Fondor leaned back against a table and crossed his arms. "I'm sorry not to have warned you, but there are spies within Castle Renné and you had to look like men going to your deaths. Anything less would have been remarked upon."

Carl leaned back against the wall, bracing his hands on his knees.

"Take a moment to compose yourself," Fondor said kindly. "It was a cruel trick, but you are alive this day, and the Renné have no thoughts to end your lives."

Carl forced himself to breathe. Another dull "thwack" was heard—the third, he realized.

"Who were those men?" Carl said weakly.

"Criminals who had been sentenced to die. Don't concern yourself—the Renné are not so cruel as to have taken innocent lives to preserve yours."

"But what now?" Jamm asked.

"Under the circumstances I will excuse you for not addressing me properly," Fondor said. He rocked back against the table, which creaked from his weight. "My family have a proposition for you. The Isle of Battle is ours still because of your warning, Lord Carl, but that is not enough to earn the reward you asked." Fondor put a hand to his chin and seemed to consider his next words. "The world has changed since we made our bargain. The Prince of Innes was assassinated and his son, Prince Michael, has become our ally. When we made our bargain with your family, Lord Carl, the Prince of Innes was our enemy, and we gladly agreed to cede you half his estates. But now . . . now his son is our ally and his estates have all been taken. What are we to do?" He raised a bushy eyebrow. "And there is more. Even with the element of surprise on our side and Hafydd off somewhere, our armies are no match for the armies of Innes and Menwyn Wills. We won on the Isle of Battle because they were not expecting us to land in force, but they won't allow themselves to be humiliated again. They will attack in greater numbers in a place where we will not have a canal to protect us." He gazed at Lord Carl a moment, his face lined and serious. "We are desperate. That is the truth."

He glanced at Jamm and offered him a small smile of encouragement.

"Here is our proposition," Fondor went on. "Prince Michael has nothing, as he well knows. Even the information he has offered is of small value. Without Renné support he has no hope of recovering his estates. So we have made a bargain with him. If he will travel east of the river and make contact with men he believes will be sympathetic to his claims—officers who served his father, and other allies—and if he can bring these men over to our cause, then we will support his claims after the war." Fondor took a long breath. "But if you will aid him—if you will be his guides and his guards, Lord Carl, you will receive from Prince Michael estates enough so that yours will equal his."

"He will never keep such a promise."

"Oh, I believe he will, and I think you will believe him yourself once you've spoken." Fondor opened the door and motioned to someone outside. A young man dressed like a poor traveler came in. Carl had met Prince Michael before, but this young man, though certainly the prince, appeared older, less full of himself. He was certainly not smirking, as Carl remembered him.

"Prince Michael," Carl said, and bowed badly, still shaken.

The Prince bowed in return. "Lord Fondor has told you of our bargain?"

Carl nodded.

"What estates my family had are now in the hands of Hafydd or Menwyn Wills. Hafydd is gone off somewhere, we're told. Anything might happen with my father dead. There might be fighting between his allies, ambitious generals who see a chance to take some lands of their own. If the two of us can preserve my estates, then I will gladly give lands to you so that our holdings will be equal. Better half of something than all of nothing, I say. But even more importantly, if some of my father's allies can be persuaded to fight against Hafydd, then we might have a chance of defeating the sorcerer." Prince Michael looked at Carl closely, and Carl thought he saw some sympathy there. "There are greater forces at work and larger things at stake, Lord Carl, than the estates of the House of Innes—or A'denné, for that matter."

"There is not much time," Fondor said. "We must get you out of the castle before it grows light. Yea or nay, Lord Carl. Lady Beatrice would have your answer."

"What will we offer Jamm, for to be honest I would never have managed my escape without him. If he will not guide us, we will almost certainly fail." Carl turned to the little thief. "Or would you even take the risk of crossing the river again?"

"What is it you want, Jamm?" Prince Michael asked.

The little man did not answer right away, but cast his gaze around the room like a man looking for a way out.

"I know nothing but the roads," the little thief said, thinking. "Drays. Drays and teams to pull them. There is always much to be moved from the river inland and never the wagons to do it." He nodded. "A dozen large drays, new built, and teams of my own choosing."

"If we succeed, they will be yours," Prince Michael said.

Carl looked at Fondor and nodded.

"Horses are waiting," the Renné lord said, and waved them out.

Carl still felt as though he were not quite on the ground, and more than once preserved his balance with a hand against the wall. He noticed that Jamm did the same.

He lost his way in the dim corridors and later could not tell you how far he'd walked or how long it had taken, but they arrived at the stables, where saddled horses were waiting. Samul Renné was there as well, looking like a man who'd just been told his home and family had burned. He nodded to Carl but did not seem capable of speech at that moment.

Fondor gave them clothes to change into, and when they were done they looked like highwaymen.

"Here is the fourth member of your company," Fondor said, nodding to Samul. "Three of you are believed dead, so no one will be looking for you, but if you're caught, better to fight to the death, for if Menwyn Wills learns you are alive, he will know that we believed you, Lord Carl, and not Vast."

In a moment they were led out a gate and were riding into the now-graying morning. Overhead the sky began to change to blue, and twice Carl noticed Samul Renné turn his gaze up, his eyes glistening.

"Do you think he told the truth?" Lady Beatrice noticed herself in a mirror, every wrinkle around her eyes standing out in high relief. She tried to smooth away the pain, but with only partial success.

"It is difficult to say; certainly Dease was there, and when one looks back one wonders why."

Lady Beatrice could see that Fondor was as troubled as she. "Perhaps he had tried to force Dease into helping him escape and when Dease wouldn't. . . ."

Fondor shrugged. "It would not really be like him. Samul was never known to be vindictive."

Lady Beatrice nodded. The alternative, however, was harder to accept: that Dease had conspired to murder Toren, was to be the murderer, in fact. And where was Dease now but off with Toren somewhere? The thought chilled her.

"Is Toren in danger?" she asked numbly.

Fondor shook his head. "I don't think so. They were to murder him because he was trying to make peace with the Wills. Toren is at war with the Wills, now. Unlike Beldor, Dease was not acting out of malice, I don't think. But where have they gone, Dease and Toren?"

Lady Beatrice handed him a hastily scrawled note.

"It doesn't say much. What does this mean, '. . .there are more important battles to be fought.'?"

Lady Beatrice shook her head. "Sorcerers," she said, her voice harsh, "All this talk of things from the past, servants of Death." She looked at Fondor helplessly, and shrugged.

"I hope he knows what he's doing."

"And I for one would feel better if Dease were not with him. *Dease* . . . ," she said sadly. Lady Beatrice touched fingers to her brow. "I would have said that Dease loved Toren. They were always very close. But they were rivals for a certain lady's affections, though Toren might not have known it. . . ."

This silenced Fondor for a long moment, a crease appearing in the center of his heavy brow. "I had not thought of that." His scowl darkened. "Let us pray that Dease was not so inspired. Toren would never for a moment suspect it, for he is as innocent of this rivalry as a baby of his brother's."

Twenty-four

They came down from the high valley, wending their way among trees that cast long, serpentine shadows across the slope. With the sun beginning to drop toward the western hills, even Tam's shadow was worthy of a giant.

It had been an uneventful day. No minions of Hafydd had caught them, and they had encountered no one as they made their way across the lands of the Dubrell. Wolfson told them that his people had dwelt in this area long ago, but the incursions from the borderlands had driven them all away. Only the border patrol still lived there, and they moved constantly, never spending two nights in the same place. They were wary, Wolfson said, never knowing when they might be attacked by the unnamed horrors that slipped out of the borderlands.

An hour before dusk they found the bottom of the hillside and would have made better time had they not been so tired. Tam felt as though he could sleep in the saddle, and he noticed Fynnol slumping down, his eyelids slowly drifting closed.

A wolf howled in the distance. Tam barely noted the sound, but then he realized Alaan and Crowheart where whispering, suddenly very alert. Tam snapped awake, blood pounding through his veins.

"What is it?" he whispered.

"Wolves," the giant said, striding up beside him. "Some of my people are nearby. They patrol the border." Gesturing to Alaan to slow his pace, Wolfson walked out ahead, shafts of sunlight falling across his path.

A wolf appeared before him, then another. His own pack gathered around him, their hackles up, growling. Wolfson spoke firmly to them, and they wagged their tails and licked his hands.

A birdcall Tam did not recognize echoed through the wood, and Wolfson put a hand up to his mouth and answered in kind. A moment later the bushes parted, and two of Wolfson's people stepped out of the wood. They cast wary glances toward the mounted men, but Wolfson went forward, his palms out, speaking their rapid, heavily accented dialect.

The giants met in a small clearing, talking surprisingly softly for men so large. Much nodding of heads, then one of the giants pointed, and Wolfson came trotting back to his companions.

"Come," he said, "there has been a nichmear hunting here these last two nights. Come quickly before it grows dark!"

Tam did not know what a nichmear was, but he dug heels into his horse's sides and followed the others. The giants were trotting along now, covering ground more quickly than Tam would have thought possible. They did not seem to tire, and Tam guessed they might keep up such a pace for half a day or more.

They trotted along through the shadows and low shafts of light, branches swatting them as they passed. The bars of sunlight suddenly faded, as though someone had snuffed a candle, the sun having fallen behind the western hills. Twilight drifted through the trees like smoke.

Just before darkness fell, and the stars sprang to light, the companions broke out of the trees to find a ruin of tumbled stone, much overgrown, but one section of wall had obviously been repaired; and it was there the giants led them. One of the Dubrell dropped his pack and weapons and climbed over the wall, clearly knowing where to find purchase for feet and hands. A moment later the oak doors swung open, and they entered. In the falling darkness Tam could see they were enclosed within a thick stone wall, roughly square and maybe twenty-five paces across. Two shed roofs had been built against the stone, one enclosed by a fence and clearly for horses, the other covering a hearth set in the wall. Four sets of stairs led up to ramparts with a rough parapet. One giant went directly up to the ramparts and walked a slow circle, staring into the gathering darkness.

Tam dropped down onto the packed dirt and weeds that made up the floor of the place. Realizing how tired the little Vale-man was, Crowheart took Fynnol's mount. Horses were soon rubbed down and watered. Two of the giants took scythes that hung in the rafters and went out into the clearing, coming back shortly with a small mow of grass between them. The horses munched happily on this, though Tam thought they were skittish and wary.

A fire was kindled in the hearth, and men and giants were soon eating dinner—rabbits and partridge they'd killed earlier. Benches—tree trunks with one side flattened by an adze—were arranged around the hearth, and the Dubrell and their guests threw themselves down on them. Fynnol lay on his back with his knees drawn up and was immediately asleep.

"You came a distance at a good pace, Wolfson," the giant named Beln said.

The three giants, who called themselves sentries, were all young, or so Tam thought. He found it difficult to judge the ages of these giants partly because their faces were hidden by thick beards, and their voices were all dungeon deep.

"There is no time to waste," Alaan answered.

The three sentries glanced at each other, then one of them asked, "What's this we've heard of men forcing the north pass?"

Wolfson was slicing onions, his eyes watering. "We put them to rights," he said. "I don't think they'll follow us farther."

"Don't be so certain, Wolfson," Alaan said. "Hafydd's servants are more afraid of him than of us."

"Hafydd . . . Who is that?" one of the giants asked. He was the one who smiled often. Tam had divided them up thus: the one who smiled, named Pounder; the vigilant one, Beln (he kept jogging up onto the ramparts to search the darkness); and the sullen one, whom they called Teke. He sat a little apart from the others and said little.

"A sorcerer," Alaan said. "One you don't want to meet."

"What is it you are hunting here?" Tam asked.

"A nichmear," Pounder said. "Though it is the nichmear that will be hunting us." He looked up at the sky. "The smoke and the smell of cooking should draw it. The pack will start to howl when it arrives."

Tam bent over and retrieved his bow and quiver. He strung the bow quickly.

"Don't worry," the giant said. "Only one's ever made it over the wall."

"But what is this thing?" Tam said.

"Nichmear," Wolfson said. " 'Nightmare' in the tongue of men. It is a massive thing. Two-legged, but with the horns of a bull. It has a tail that cuts like a whip and claws that can tear through mail." His face became strained and anxious. "It is thrice your height, or very nearly, and would take the lot of you and smash you against the wall with one swipe of its claws. It comes out of the twilight, and is never abroad by day, and is the more frightening for it. We have killed one once before, and wounded others, always at heavy cost." He looked around the small group of giants. "One of us will be dead before morning if the nichmear comes."

"You hadn't us to help you before," Cynddl said.

This caused the giants to turn away or back to their work, not quite hiding their smiles.

"I think you will find that Cynddl is not boasting," Alaan said. "They have fought the servants of Death before . . . and won."

A howl carried over the wall, and the giants all stopped, suddenly alert.

"Eat up, now," Pounder said. "Death has no servant more terrible than this."

Tam was too nervous to eat much, but forced a few mouthfuls down. They were all up on the ramparts in no time, armed with whatever weapons they carried. Pounder hefted a great iron ball on the end of a thick oaken handle. In the hands of a giant it would shatter bones—it would break rock, he was sure. The giants didn't seem much interested in bows or arrows, though they leaned spears against the wall, and some of these were for throwing. They also kept a pile of good-sized stones, and Tam guessed these were to crush whoever might attack from below.

The wall of their small keep was not high, about three times Tam's height—the same height Wolfson had given to the nichmear. Tam hoped the giant had been merely trying to scare him with his description.

Beyond the ruins of what once had been a fair-sized keep was a broad meadow, which ran off to the south out of sight in the dark. On the other three sides a forest stood, nearer in some places than others. Tam could make out little in the cool light of the stars and the thin crescent of moon.

Wolves darted along the border of the wood, dodging in and out of shadow. Tam nocked an arrow and tested the pull of his bow. They were all silent, giants and men—listening. Tam could feel the sweat on his hands and worried that his bowstring might slip off his fingers. Fynnol and Cynddl were to one side of him, both with their bows ready. Beyond them stood Alaan and Wolfson, and the three giants waited to Tam's left.

"Will the pack attack this thing?" Tam whispered.

In the faint light he saw Wolfson shake his head. "They're afraid of it, and you'll soon see why."

A small breeze moved Tam's hair, and he almost jumped. The cracking of wood sounded somewhere out in the dark, and Tam raised his bow.

"It's still some way off," Beln said. " 'Tis the single thing we can

be thankful for when it comes to the nichmear: they know nothing
of stealth."

"It isn't really so big as you claimed, I assume?" Fynnol said.

" 'Tis every bit as big, but in the dark, of course, it looks bigger."

"Of course," Fynnol said. "Don't we all?"

Small clouds sailed across the dark ocean of sky, passing before
the waning moon, throwing shadows down on the meadow and the
half-fallen walls of the keep. Tam began to see movement in every
shadow. The giants posted themselves on the four corners of the
keep, but left the outsiders facing south as it was the most likely
place of attack, they said. Tam felt vulnerable the moment the giants were gone. There was something comforting about having
four men the size of Slighthand standing beside you. And only the
giants had fought these things before.

"Is that something?" Fynnol whispered, and pointed out into
the darkness.

A cloud had passed before the moon a moment before, and the
shadows spread out like pools of water. Tam strained to see into the
darkness—like staring into the night river.

"It is your imagination," Alaan whispered.

"I think Fynnol is right," Crowheart said. He pointed at the
tallest section of wall. "There. Do you see."

The horses began to mill around in their small enclosure, whin-
nying nervously.

Tam's eyes began to water from staring into the dark. There was
something there, he was almost sure of it. A darker place in the
shadow. Alaan called Wolfson. The giant came pounding along the
ramparts.

The cloud blew off then, and the faint light grew, spreading over
the ruins. The dark shape seemed to take on an outline.

"River save us!" Fynnol whispered.

It was immense and coming at great speed. Its feet, pounding
on the earth, could be heard now; a deep drumming that shook the
stone beneath their feet. Alaan cursed. He raised his bow and drew
back an arrow. The others did the same.

Wolfson came up beside them, and called urgently to the others, who all converged on the center of the south wall.

Run! Tam's brain screamed. He struggled against his desire to flee, muscles in his legs and arms twitching. *Run!*

Fynnol fired an arrow at the "thing" converging on them. And then it was near, a blur of pumping limbs. Tam let his arrow fly then, but he miscalculated the speed of the thing, which seemed to have materialized out of darkness. A glimpse of horns, a malevolent face, then it lowered its head and smashed into the gates below. Tam was thrown off his feet and would have fallen to the yard below, but Wolfson caught his shoulder and dragged him up.

The sound of splintering wood, the scream of iron hinges wrenched out of shape. Pounding like hooves on a barn floor, and the thing was in the yard below, casting its gaze around and snorting like a bull.

It spotted the horses and charged the enclosure. Alaan's mount, Bris, leapt over the fence first, and the others scrambled to follow, knocking each other down in their panic. The nichmear smashed through the fence, pinning a screaming horse to the wall. As it thrashed and fought the shed roof collapsed, burying gored horse and monster both. Pounder had run around the wall and jumped down on the fallen roof. Lifting his hammer, he smashed it down on the shingles, splinters of wood flying up all around. The creature howled and stood up, throwing the roof and Pounder off. The giant landed on his side on the hard-packed dirt, and struggled to his knees, dazed.

The creature looked around, extricating itself from the ruin of the horse pen by breaking away the roof with its claws. In the harsh darkness Tam could not make it out clearly—lethal-looking horns on a massive head, shoulders muscled like a bulls. It tore its legs free of the debris and spun around, tail snapping like a whip.

Struggling to gain his feet, Pounder faltered and fell to his hands and knees. Beln leapt down from the wall and put himself between the monster and his companion as Tam and the others rained arrows down on the creature.

"Shoot at its face!" Alaan cried.

Tam pulled an arrow back to his shoulder and let it fly, aiming at what he hoped was an eye. The creature bellowed and put an arm up to protect its face. Beln had dragged Pounder to his feet, and the two of them stumbled toward the stair. But the creature ignored them, bounding straight across the yard toward the men on the wall.

Tam and the others kept firing, but the creature did not slow. It swept the two Dubrell aside with one backhanded swipe and threw itself at the stone wall, using the debris from the gate as a step.

"It is after the outlanders!" one of the giants shouted.

Alaan cursed. Tam fired a last arrow at the horns he saw rising from below and drew his sword. Claws scraped up onto the stone of the ramparts, and Tam swung at what he hoped was the creature's hand. But it was quicker than he and snatched its limb away. Grasping Tam by the ankle, it threw him off the ledge so that he slid down the creature's back, barely missing being gored.

It is after Alaan, Tam realized.

He fell hard on the ground, driving his knees into his chest. His sword lay a few feet away, and Tam rolled and snatched it up, despite being shaken and hurt. On the parapet above, Tam could see shapes jumping aside as the creature tried to bull its way up onto the ledge.

Tam jumped up onto the fallen gate, which lay at an angle, still connected at a top corner by one hinge, bent impossibly out of shape. The gate shuddered and heaved beneath him as the creature struggled to climb up against the resistance of the men above. Taking no time to think, Tam drove the point of his sword into the back of the creature's leg joint. It howled so loudly that Tam was frozen for a second. When he tried to pull his sword free he found it lodged. The creature swung a clawed hand at him, and Tam dived off the swaying gate just as the beast came tumbling down, tearing the gate away from its last hinge.

Pain shot through Tam's shoulder, and he struggled up. He stepped back and stumbled over Pounder's round-headed hammer. He swept up the handle and discovered it was all he could do to heft the thing, pain cutting through his shoulder like he'd been stabbed. He swung at the arm of the monster as it fell full length. Whatever he hit gave, snapping like a thick board. The monster bellowed and looked up, fixing its terrible gaze on the frightened Valeman.

"Run, Tam!" Fynnol shouted.

Tam bolted for the narrow stair, but he stumbled and fell. The creature would have been upon him had someone not dropped down from the wall above, landing between Tam and the monster.

"It is me you want," Alaan said calmly. "I'm the one your master sent you for."

Tam got slowly to his feet as though not to draw the monster's attention. A sword landed point first a few feet away, and stood there quivering. Tam yanked it free and braced himself, not sure what Alaan might do.

"I'm at your back," Tam said softly.

"Move away," Alaan whispered.

The creature had risen to its full height, more than twice that of Alaan, and thrice the body weight of the largest giant. Before it, Alaan looked like a child holding a toy sword. But the creature eyed him warily, snorting. It hobbled, the sword still lodged in its knee, so it would not charge headlong, but even so it was the most horrifying monster Tam had ever seen. Against the stars, horns pierced the darkness.

"Come, you stupid beast," Alaan muttered. "Your master is waiting."

"I speak, sorcerer," the beast hissed, its voice like rocks rumbling down a chasm.

"Then I am the sorcerer once known as Sainth, son of Wyrr. Alaan men call me now. Your master has sent you to find me. Why is it you wait? Can you not work up your nerve?"

The thing began to circle to the left, hobbling painfully on its injured leg.

"I know you, sorcerer," the creature said. "You have been to the gate before, but this time it is opening. Can you hear it? The sound of grinding bones?"

It stumbled and went down on one knee, but as it came up it hurled something in the dark. Alaan threw himself aside, and Tam's sword clanged off the stone steps. The beast was upon him, seemingly unhurt. Alaan was rising from the ground as it leapt forward. He put up a hand, and there was a flash of white light, so bright Tam staggered back, blinded.

A terrible scream echoed off the stone walls and rose up into the dark sky. Tam tried desperately to see, but the flash had stolen his vision. He found himself against the wall, blinking furiously, sharp pain cutting through his watering eyes.

It was a moment before his vision began to clear, and then he could see only vague silhouettes, odd shapes. Finally, he began to make out something large, prostrate on the ground, a small shape—Alaan—standing over it.

Tam groped forward, the scene coming slowly into focus.

"You killed it," he said to the figure standing there.

"If you can kill something that came from Death's kingdom," Alaan answered wearily. "Yes, I killed it. You kill a charging bull by dodging aside and driving your sword between its shoulder blades."

"You've done it before?"

"No, but Sainth had. The thing was blinded, luckily, which made it a bit easier. Let's see who's injured."

Alaan put a hand on Tam's shoulder, guiding him, for Tam could still see little. The giants came down from the wall. They had no taunts for the outsiders now, but kept glancing from Alaan to the dead creature, and Tam wasn't sure which unsettled them more.

"It spoke to you . . . ," Pounder said.

Alaan nodded.

"It knew your name," one of the other giants said very quietly. "Death knows your name."

"It is a long story," Alaan said. "And you would rather not hear it." He was walking toward one corner of the keep, where they found Crowheart soothing the horses.

"We lost a packhorse," Rabal said, stroking the neck of a shaking mare. The horses gathered around him as though he would protect them.

"I don't imagine we will be bothered again this night," Alaan said, "but we should try to do something about the gate."

The giants all jumped to the task with a will, still glancing now and then at Alaan. Tam couldn't tell if they were more awed or frightened. Sometimes he wondered himself.

"Wolfson?" Alaan said, interrupting their work. "Tomorrow we will go into the shadow lands. You needn't travel farther than this."

The giant nodded quickly, then went back to his work, obviously relieved.

Twenty-five

They waited several silent hours for cloud to wrap the moon, then slid their boat into the Wynnd. Samul didn't like what they were doing. It reminded him too much of his foray east of the river with his cousin, Beld, when they had been on the run after their failed assassination of Toren—and murder of Arden.

The company was better this time—he had to admit that—but the situation was more desperate. Fondor had dressed them as poor travelers, though they looked like nothing so much as highwaymen. It didn't take a great deal of wit to see why he'd done that. They could not travel openly for fear of being recognized, and highwaymen were forced to slink about, keeping to secret paths and out of sight. If they were to run afoul of soldiers of Innes or of the Wills, they would have to fight for their lives, for highwaymen were, more often than not, cut down where they were found and never came before a magistrate. If they were caught, Fondor clearly hoped, they might be buried before any recognized them.

The two watermen who manned the oars were frightened, and could not hide it, which didn't increase Samul's confidence. A glance at Lord Carl told him nothing in the darkness. He sat very still, though—listening, Samul guessed—and stared into the night. Lord Carl and his servant-thief had already been on the run across the Isle of Battle, and the two of them looked terribly haunted and wary. Samul guessed that he would soon become equally wary—if he lived long enough.

Jamm was recovering from injuries and illness and had that vulnerable look common among the sick. Samul wondered if the little thief, in his present condition, would be able to guide them successfully through lands controlled by the Wills family and the House of Innes.

Better this than death, he told himself. He glanced up at the moon, which could just be seen behind a thin veil of racing cloud. "Faster," he whispered.

But the watermen didn't change their pace, and the Renné realized that greater speed would make more noise, and they couldn't afford that. He glanced up again. A patch of cloud, illuminated from within, grew brighter as though the cloud stretched and thinned. At any moment the moon could break through.

Samul turned his gaze back to earth, seeking the eastern shore. A band of shadow was probably a line of trees, but how distant it was he could not say. The watermen kept dipping their muffled oars, the smell of their sweat mixed with the river musk. Wind tore the cloud to rags, and the moon broke free, turning the water to silver. Before he thought, Samul threw himself down. It didn't matter; their black hull would be impossible to miss on the glittering river.

There was nothing for it now but to race for the eastern embankment and get ashore as quickly as they could. They would have to trust to Jamm to slip them away before they were found.

Trees loomed out of the dark, and the boat slid almost silently up on the mud. Immediately, Michael and Carl leapt ashore. He could see their blades gleaming in the moonlight. Jamm scurried after them, crouching low, casting his gaze anxiously this way and that. Samul made his way past the watermen, wanting to keep his boots dry if at all possible. He stepped ashore as something erupted out of the trees.

A horseman, sword high, went straight at Prince Michael, who barely got a blade up in time. Two other riders and men on foot crashed through bush, milling about in the tiny clearing.

Samul turned back toward the boat, but the watermen were already twenty feet out into the river and pulling for their lives. Arrows began thudding against wood, but Samul saw no more as he dove aside to miss a blow designed to take off his head.

A horse screamed, rearing high, as Jamm yanked a sword free of its ribs. The rider was thrown down at Samul's feet, and he plunged a sword into the man's throat before he'd gained his knees. Carl and Michael were in a fight for their lives, leaping this way and that, keeping the horses between themselves and the others. The confined space worked against the riders, and in a moment the four fugitives were stumbling through the dark wood, the shouts and curses of their hunters right behind.

Samul felt someone grab his arm and pull him hard to the one side, where he was dragged over a large log to land on top of his fellows. He could hear their harsh breathing as the hunters came thundering by, five men on foot and two horsemen, he judged. For a moment they listened to the men go charging into the darkness, tripping and falling as they went.

"Follow me," Jamm whispered. "Stay down."

They went off across the mossy forest floor on hands and knees, stopping every twenty feet to listen. Men were shouting not far off, and others answered. Samul could see torches waving through the trees.

They had stopped again, and Jamm drew them all close.

"That is the road," he whispered, "where the torches are. If they can keep us this side of the road until sunrise, they'll trap us here. We have to pass over, no matter the cost."

Samul nodded in the dark. Sunrise was only few hours off. There wasn't much time to waste. They followed Jamm, creeping a few paces, stopping, then moving again. The little thief was more stealthy than a spider. Such a man could slip in your window, steal anything he desired, and slink out again. Good reason to keep dogs, the nobleman thought, before remembering that he possessed not a thing in this world but a good sword, a dagger, and a fast-beating heart. He felt his resolve harden then. If they were forced to fight their way across the road, he didn't care—no man-at-arms was going to stand between him and another dawn.

Three horsemen thundered by, far too close, and Samul pressed himself into the ground, hardly daring to breathe. They were hard up against the road now. Horses clattered by, their hooves just feet from his head, and torches bobbed past in the near distance, a bitter haze left hanging over the lane to sting his eyes. Here and there a bit of moonlight found its way through the trees, illuminating the cart tracks, though Jamm had picked the darkest section he could find.

Carl A'denné was beside him and leaned close to Samul's ear. "Jamm says to be ready to run across, all at once, as quick as we can."

Samul nodded and dug his fingers into the detritus of the forest floor. Every time he felt the others brace themselves to sprint, a horsemen or a small company of infantry would appear. Too many men were swarming the area. Apparently the Wills took spies rather seriously, though there must be enough of them around—on both sides of the river.

Just as Samul began to the think the light in the eastern sky was not imagined, Jamm leapt up and dashed across the road, his legs a blur in the poor light. The others were only a few paces behind, diving into the wood opposite. Samul hit his head so hard on a branch that he was driven to his knees. Carl dragged him up, and the two of them went blindly on, blundering into boulders and tree trunks.

Thirty feet farther they dropped to their knees again, crawling quickly to their right. A company of foot soldiers came crashing into the wood, a single torch lighting their way. They stopped not fifteen feet away.

"Listen!" their captain ordered, and the soldiers stood there, trying to control their breathing.

Samul and the others stayed as still as they could, afraid the torchlight would find them in the dark, for they could see the soldiers fairly clearly through leaves and branches.

Other men were calling into the wood from the road, then they too came crashing through the underwood: Samul could see the torches flickering, turning the tree trunks a dull orange. They were in trouble, now.

Jamm stood up a little, raising his arm. He let fly a good-sized rock, which struck one of the men with such force that he dropped the torch. Chaos erupted, men stamping out a fire that had started, others crashing in from the road.

In the noise and confusion, Jamm led them off. They did not go quickly, but they never stopped, and in a short while the torches were lost from sight, and the shouting of the men grew distant and unintelligible.

Even with daylight Jamm kept them moving, until he finally crawled into a spreading thicket of spiny bushes. The path they took forced them down on their bellies, and even then they were scarred and scratched repeatedly. A little "room" lay in the center of the thicket, the bushes arching over them so that even a hawk wouldn't know they were there. Here they lay in the sparse grass, not daring to move, listening to men pass all morning and on into the afternoon, before the search moved off to the south.

Samul could see the look of wariness disappear from Jamm's face, and he tried to smile at the others.

"Well you did it again, Jamm," Carl A'denné whispered. "Did you know of this place?"

"I was shown it once, but we should not talk. A few words can be worth your life, sometimes."

They slept in shifts that day, eating the little bit of food they carried. Jamm did not like to bear more than a mouthful of water, saying that it sloshed about and made noise at the most inconvenient times, so they were all parched by sunset. Jamm, however, did not seem much concerned about their thirst, and when Samul mentioned this to Lord Carl the young man put a finger to his lips.

Leaning close, Carl whispered. "If not for Jamm I would be dead many times over. If you are hunted, do as the fox does."

Samul tried to ignore his dry mouth and cultivate patience.

When the night was good and dark, Jamm crept out to the opposite edge of the thicket from the place they'd entered. After what must have been an hour, Samul leaned close to Carl.

"He's run off," he whispered.

Carl shook his head in the near darkness. "*Patience*," he whispered.

Eventually Jamm returned for them. They crawled out of the copse with a hand on the boot of the man in front. For a few moments they crouched in the shadow of the thicket, then slunk off— Samul could think of no other word for it—through the long grass of a fallow field.

Jamm was a master of finding shadow—beneath a hedgerow, alongside a drystone wall. He went often on hands and knees, and even on his belly, when he was forced to cross open areas where the moonlight fell. He stopped frequently to listen and watch for lengthy periods. Hilltops were things to be feared in his world, and he eyed them with a deep, abiding suspicion.

A few hours after their march began, he led them to a spring, though not before circling it once and watching it for some good time before he deemed it safe. Despite what Lord Carl had said, Samul was certain there was no fox so wary as Jamm.

They skirted a small village and left farm buildings in the distance. Once they went out of their way to avoid a couple furtively making love in the shadow of a hedge. By the time the eastern sky began to show a hint of coming morning, Samul Renné could hardly have gone another yard. Fortunately, the little thief led them to a cliff, up a steep, narrow gully, across a bit of a ledge, and into a shallow cave that angled down into the rock, like a pocket.

"You can't see this from the ground," Jamm whispered. "Only a few know it's here."

They ate the last of their food as they lazed there, and drank the little bit of water that Samul had left in his skin, the others as reluctant as Jamm to carry water. The day spread out below, and Samul crept up beside Jamm, who lay on the stone, his eyes just above the rim, surveying the lands. They were fairly high up—not because the cliff was high but because the land sloped up from the river—and they were afforded a view for half a league, Samul was sure.

"Stay as still as you can," Jamm said. "Movement can be seen at some distance."

"But is anyone looking for us?"

Jamm raised a hand to the rim of the stone and pointed. Some distance off, on a road that cut north to south across the patch-work of fields and woods, a column of riders in purple-and-black livery, rode slowly south. The longer Samul looked the more signs of war he saw—troop moving, trains of wagons lumbering north, but there were men-at-arms and huntsmen out on the fields and woods too.

"They're searching for us?" Samul asked.

"Perhaps," whispered Jamm, then pointed again.

A figure dodged out of little stand of scrub and went haring along the edge of a field, slipping into the bush to avoid a group of riders.

"And who might that be?" Samul wondered aloud.

Jamm shrugged. "Highwayman, thief, deserter . . ."

Samul watched a little while, then slipped back down into the cave, no longer feeling so secure.

For a few hours he slept but woke to a hand over his mouth, Jamm looking down at him, a finger to his lips. There was some sound coming from above, and then a stone bounced off the lip of their hiding spot and went tumbling on. Laughter from above was a relief to them all, for these were children. A rain of rocks and sticks fell for the next hour, then Jamm was suddenly alert, slipping his sword from its scabbard. Samul was afraid the children might be climbing down. What would they do about that? But a moment later he heard the thud of a horse's hoof, the creak of leather. Riders stopped below the cliff; and the children ended their rain of rocks.

"Boy!" a man called from below. "Seen any strangers hereabout the last day or so?"

"Not today, sir," a child's voice came from above. "But we saw three men on horses yesterday morning, just after dawn. They were slanting cross-country and not taking the roads. My father said it was a strange way to travel."

"Where were they going?" the man called.

"Southeast, sir. Toward Crofton, or so we thought."

"Thank you, lad," the man-at-arms called back. "Is there a way down from up there?"

"There is, sir," the boy answered, though reluctantly.

"Then I'll leave a coin for you. By this tree."

The horses moved off. Samul could hear the boys clambering down the same little gully they had ascended. Did these children really not know the cave was there? He hoped they didn't; especially now that they knew the soldiers were looking for strangers. But the children went quickly by, hardly more than a dozen feet away, apparently unaware. The coin was found, to great delight, and the boys set off, hotly debating the uses for such a great sum of money and marveling at their good fortune.

The moon was waning and did not rise till late, so they were forced to make the climb from their eyry in the sparse light of the stars. Samul's respect for Jamm went up then. He had thought Jamm a timid little man, but there was little question whose nerve was tested to tackle that climb in the dark. When his feet finally reached the ground, Samul regarded the thief with newfound respect.

"I didn't much like that," Samul admitted to Lord Carl. "Though it didn't seem to bother our guide."

"He was never trained in arms, as we were, but he does not lack courage when it's needed."

"Where do we go, now?" Carl asked Jamm.

"I was going to ask you that same question," the thief whispered, always wary. "Where am I to take you? The army was gathered east of the Isle, a few days ago. Is that our destination?"

"I have been thinking about this," Prince Michael said. "Not so far from here I have a cousin who married a nobleman. He is older and won't be involved in the fighting, but he profited much from his marriage into our family. He could contact my father's allies—the ones I think will be loyal to the House of Innes. I need such an intermediary, and A'tanelle would be perfect."

"Are you prepared to trust him with your life?" Samul asked.

"I am."

"Where must we go?"

"South a league, more or less, and a little inland. His estates are near the town of Weybridge."

"My father," Lord Carl began hesitantly, "did not hold A'tanelle in the highest regard, for what it's worth."

Samul glanced over at Prince Michael, whose face shone nagar-pale in the starlight.

"A'tanelle is an opportunist, I admit, and a bit more cunning than I would like, but he is my kinsman by marriage and has enough authority to sway the undecided to our cause." The prince threw up his hands. "And if not A'tanelle, then who?"

"I can't answer that," Carl said. "I'm only telling you my father's opinion."

"I don't think you need worry, Lord Carl," Prince Michael said, though he looked concerned himself. "A'tanelle rose in the world because of his connection with the House of Innes. His future depends on us. Despite his shortcomings, he is intelligent enough to know that. And you mustn't forget his wife: she is beyond reproach, for beauty, sentiment, or reason."

Carl made a little bow.

"Weybridge," Jamm said. "We'll not reach it this night." The thief led them off at a good pace, not abandoning his practice of staying to shadow, crossing open land only when he had to. Without a torch to light their way, the going was difficult and slow, punctuated by many stubbed toes and tumbles on the uneven ground.

Parties were still out searching the countryside, even by night, and they found two encampments of huntsmen and men-at-arms, giving both a wide berth. Several times Jamm stopped them to listen and watch the countryside carefully from the relative safety of a shadow.

The fifth time he did this Samul could stand it no more and whispered close to the little man's ear. "What is it, Jamm?"

The thief shook his head. They were skirting a small wood of oak and beech, and Jamm pointed down the border. "Wait for me at the end of the wood," he whispered. "Go quietly."

Samul hesitated, but Carl, who had utter faith in Jamm, marshaled them on. At the end of the wood they crouched among the bordering trees. The night air vibrated with the sounds of insects, and the leaves whispered sleepily in the low breeze. Off in the distance, a dog's bark pummeled the night.

"What is Jamm up to?" Samul asked. Despite Carl's obvious loyalty, Samul had never trusted Jamm. Once a thief always a thief, he believed. People didn't change their natures any more than a fox could become a sheep.

He half expected Jamm to abandon them there and run off. No doubt he'd turn them in for the reward if he wouldn't face a noose himself. Samul found himself shifting from foot to foot, eager to be off.

They waited an inordinate length of time. Samul fixed his eye on a point on the western horizon and counted the stars that slipped behind the distant hills. When Jamm did appear he contrived to do it with such stealth that he made them all jump, appearing in their midst.

"I could hear you breathing from twenty feet," he told them softly. "Quick now!" And he was off again—along the edge of the wood, then on his belly through a field of oats. They "surfaced" in the shadow of a spreading cherry tree, then slipped through an orchard, the barking dog closer now.

Hedgerows were Jamm's highways. Farmers habitually carted the rocks they removed from the soil and piled them along the borders of their fields. If the fields were used for pasture, the rocks might be made into drystone walls to contain livestock, but more often they were merely piled, and whatever grew over or near them was left untouched. Wild apple trees, chokecherries, vines and bushes of all kinds, many armed with lethal thorns. These hedgerows grew thick and tall, providing a network of shadow roads across much of the night landscape.

Of course those same shadows could hide their enemies; but Jamm was so wary and had such matchless night vision that he held the advantage there. He led them on through the night, stopping often to listen. Samul could not help but notice Jamm was paying more attention to what might lie behind them than he had been formerly. Carl had noticed this too, Samul was sure, and the young noblemen had taken up traveling at the rear of their column and casting his eyes back often.

Jamm led them up a small hill crowned with a wood. There they hunkered down in the edge of the trees, and Jamm watched the shadowed countryside with the intensity of a hungry hawk.

"What is going on, Jamm?" Carl asked.

"We're being stalked. I'm sure of it."

"By whom?"

Jamm shook his head. "Someone more wary than I, and more skilled in woodcraft, too. But I've heard him now, several times, and I've caught glimpses of him—just a shadow slipping into cover— more than once." Jamm fell silent, his manner grim, unsettled.

"Is this some huntsman of the Wills?" Samul asked.

"I don't know what his game is," Jamm said. "I suspect he's known where we've lain up at night, yet we've not been disturbed. Explain that."

"Perhaps he is some old friend of yours, Jamm," Carl suggested.

"If he was a friend, he'd have shown himself before now. No, this one's up to something. . . ." It was clear the little thief didn't know what.

They hid in the wood that day, staying deep in the shadows. Jamm slept a little while Carl stood watch, but then he was up, prowling the wood's edge. Twice Carl caught glimpses of him, bent over, a hand to his cracked ribs. He was hiding it, but he was still not healed, and Carl wondered how long he would be able to keep this up.

"Is your thief patrolling our borders," Samul asked Carl, "or is he trying to catch sight of this imagined huntsman who's stalking us?"

"I think he's doing both, though I doubt that Jamm is wrong. If he thinks someone follows us, then someone follows us."

"But it doesn't stand the test of reason. If someone were following us, he would have turned us in by now, especially if he knew where we hid by day. It's Jamm's imagination and fear, though perhaps these are not bad things. They might be the reasons that he's lived so long."

The day crept by, a low overcast washing across the sky by midday. Light rain spattered down through the leaves, and a wind, cool and ghostly, rustled through the wood. Samul found it difficult to sleep. Rain, in rivulets, streaked his face, and just as exhaustion closed his eyes, the wind would moan through the trees, waking him with a start.

Crows found an owl roosting in a pine, and soon a dark army had gathered, crying and cawing from every perch. Finally, Samul sat up, cursing.

"I'm hungry, thirsty, and foul-tempered," he announced, "and now these bloody crows have come to ruin my sleep, as though the wind and rain were not accomplished enough at that particular task."

"Everything you say is true," Prince Michael answered, not rising from his prone position, "but you are alive, and there is much to be said for that."

Samul could not deny this, and hardly more than a day ago that had been in doubt. "I'm tired of sneaking through hedgerows and sleeping in ditches," Samul said. "I would rather a horse and a battle. I wish Toren had allowed me that. Such a death I could accept."

"Better than the life of a spy?" the Prince chided, but then he nodded. "You speak like a true man-at-arms, Lord Samul. But we've made this bed of discomfort and dishonor for ourselves, so we must try to sleep in it, crows and all."

Samul smiled unhappily. "Perhaps I've made such a bed for myself, Prince Michael, but neither you nor Lord Carl can make such a claim, I'm afraid. You've merely been the victims of misfortune."

"But we are all equally desperate—dispossessed, almost friendless, our worth measured by our ability to convince my father's old allies to rebel against this sorcerer and Menwyn Wills—which might make our worth very small."

Samul considered this. The Prince seemed to be bright enough, and in an unusually candid state of mind. "Tell me honestly, Prince Michael. Are there men among your father's officers and allies who remain loyal to you?"

The Prince almost squirmed where he lay. Samul saw that Carl A'denné was awake and listening carefully.

"To be honest, Lord Samul, my father did not create alliances out of loyalty. I'm not sure he believed in it. He preferred to employ threats—force when needed. You can ask Lord Carl. His father wanted no part of this war, but my father coerced the A'denné into our alliance even so, driving them into their desperate bargain with the Renné. I'm not sure that I am any more respected than my father, but I'm sure our allies and my father's officers will not be happy serving either Hafydd or Menwyn Wills. I'm placing my hope in that."

"Do you mourn your father?" Carl asked suddenly.

Prince Michael looked over at Carl, his look not so much offended as surprised by the question—as though he'd not considered it. "The Prince," Michael said, "had little respect for me, and for my part, I felt the same toward him." He hesitated, the look on his face unreadable. "And yet, he was my father. He bore me on his back as a child; my wild charger as I slew imagined enemies with a wooden sword. The truth is, I mourn the man he never was more than the man he became."

Samul would have to recast his opinion of this Prince—who was neither coddled nor foolish, as he had at first assumed. His visit to the Stillwater had matured him greatly, and a good thing too.

"I . . . I find myself mourning my father," Carl said, suddenly interested in the handle of his dagger. "And must remind myself that the Renné believed him still to be alive when we set out. I pray that he remains so and that we will see each other again."

"I met Lord A'denné on several occasions," Prince Michael said. "He was a man worthy of esteem. I hope that you will see each other again, so he can tell you how proud he is of all you've accomplished."

"I've accomplished little," Carl said. He looked up at the sky, which seemed to be growing dark at last. "Dusk is finally coming."

As if they'd heard, the crows took flight; a winged cacophony swarming south.

"The owl will be on the hunt soon," Carl said. "Smart crows to fly now."

"Smart perhaps, but ill-mannered," Prince Michael said quietly. "We should follow their example and be off soon."

Jamm returned half an hour later, shaking his head. "It will be too dark to travel this night without torches or lantern, and we can risk neither."

"You mean we have to spend another night here?" Samul said, unable to hide his frustration.

"There are many worse places than this, your grace," Jamm answered. "My only complaint of this wood is that someone has been here, too recently, cutting trees. I hope they don't come back until we are many days gone."

They made a small meal of the last of their food—bread going stale and cheese turning moldy. It didn't help the mood much. Samul found the rhythm of his sleep had been ruined and lay awake after darkness, listening to the forest endlessly dripping with rain. A fitful wind kept the trees from sleep, and far off, lightning tore at the sky.

Samul had nodded into a strange dream of food and a warm

fire, when a hand on his shoulder brought him back to damp reality. It was cellar-dark, and the rain was falling in earnest.

"We're found!" Carl whispered. "They're coming up the hill."

Someone came crashing back into camp then. "At least a dozen men coming up the hill with torches!" Jamm said, his voice rising in fear. "We'll have to go down the north side, as fast as we can. There is no cover there, just open pasture cropped by sheep." He didn't wait for the others to collect themselves but set out. Samul came stumbling behind, dizzy from just waking.

Beneath the trees there was no light, and they went forward like blind men, groping and flailing with their hands. Samul smashed his shins on a large boulder, fell, and left too much skin behind. The close wood claimed a great deal of blood and skin that night, but finally they reached the far side. Jamm stopped there a moment even though they could see torches had reached the edge of the wood behind them. The landscape was utterly impenetrable, areas of black contrasting with areas of near black.

"Jamm, we have no time!" the prince complained. "They're in the wood."

"They might not be the only danger," the thief said.

The sounds of their hunters crashing through the underwood could be heard.

"All right," Jamm said. "Keep low to the ground. There are hedgerows straight on. They funnel into a lane way with a gate at this end. It's easy to get off your course in the dark. When you reach the hedgerow follow it down hill, and we'll find each other at the gate."

Beneath their feet the short grass was slick with rain. Samul's feet went out from under him first, then Prince Michael's, or so he thought—it was difficult to tell in the dark.

They slid and tumbled down the hill, getting farther and farther apart. The ground finally began to level so that Samul could run without fear of slipping, though the odd boulder or patch of thistle would trip him as he went. He glanced back once to see the torches coming out of the trees.

Somewhere ahead and to Samul's right, Jamm cursed. The hedgerow loomed out of the dark, and he plunged into a thick cedar. Disentangling himself, he turned right and hurried on as best he could, someone only a few feet ahead.

"The gate," Carl called.

"Where?" Jamm's voice came out of the darkness.

"You're through it, I think," Carl answered. "It's open."

"It was closed at dusk. . . ."

A torch appeared twenty feet behind them, coming out of some hole in the thick hedge. Then two more ahead of them, casting light on the narrow lane way. There were men before them and behind. Samul heard a sword being drawn, then another. The third was his.

"We go down the lane," Samul ordered, taking charge. "Cut down the men with the torches first."

The hedgerows to either side would be impenetrable, he knew. These men weren't fools. There were only two ways out, and they were outnumbered from both before and behind. Samul raised his sword and shouted, running at the dark forms of men who appeared in the dull torchlight. Rain continued to fall, making the footing treacherous. Even the pommel of his sword was slick.

They had only a moment to fight their way through the men in the lane before the others would be upon them from behind, and they'd be trapped and hopelessly outnumbered.

The clash of the two companies meeting was loud in the narrow lane. Samul went straight at the nearest torchbearer but two of his company intervened, then they fell back, parrying and dodging, hoping to slow Samul until the others were on him from behind. Prince Michael and Carl were having no better luck, the men before them doing the same. Samul could hear the pounding of boots behind.

"I'd drop those blades, lads, if I were you," the man with the torch called out. "Unless you'd rather die he—" But he did not finish. A sword through his ribs sent him reeling forward, lumbering into one of his fellows, whom Samul disarmed and ran through. A shadow wielding a sword threw their enemies into disarray, men plunging this way and that to escape the blade, Samul, Carl, and Michael slashing at the men as they tried to escape. Torches tumbled to the ground and in a second they were running for all their worth down the dark lane, the sounds of pursuit close behind.

"Here!" Jamm called in the dark, and Samul followed Carl and Michael over a gate. There were horses there, with one man guarding them. One look at the numbers coming over the gate and he dropped his torch and fled into the dark. Samul was on a horse, slashing at the reins of the remaining mounts, taking the nose off one horse in the dark. In a moment they were galloping over open pasture, rain still pouring down, running into their eyes.

Someone—Jamm, Samul thought—had taken up the fallen torch, and Samul tried to keep that in view, almost colliding with Carl in their headlong dash. A low stone wall loomed up, and Samul almost lost his saddle as his mount leapt it at the last second. Jamm slowed their pace then, the will to self-preservation overcoming his fear. He slowed almost to a stop, his horse dancing about so that torch waved wildly.

"Are they behind us? Are they behind us?" the little man called.

They all reined in their mounts, listening. The rain drummed down, and far off they could hear shouting.

"I think they've lost sight of us," the Prince said.

Jamm threw his torch into a narrow ditch, where it sputtered out, leaving them in utter darkness again.

"Let the horses go," Jamm said, and Samul heard the thief dismount.

"But they will overtake us!" Samul protested.

"Not this night," came Jamm's answer out of darkness.

Samul cursed as he heard the others following the little man's orders. He dismounted reluctantly.

"Do as he says," Carl whispered. "You'll be caught in half a day without Jamm."

Samul heard Jamm smack his mount and send it trotting off, and he did the same. He couldn't see the others a few feet away.

"Follow me," Jamm said, just loud enough to be heard over the rain and the sound of retreating horses.

"But where are you in this pitch hole?" the prince asked.

"Follow my voice. That's it," whispered Jamm. "Are we all here? I will lead. Put a hand on the shoulder of the man before you."

They set off like a train of blind men, and in three steps had blundered into the ditch. Samul started to climb out when he realized that Jamm had no intention of doing so. They sloshed their way along, water running about their knees. Progress was slow as they fought the current, but Samul realized their would be no boot prints to follow. Three times they stopped while Carl and Jamm made forays out into the dark, leaving false trails to where, Samul couldn't guess.

Above the splatter of rain, they could hear men on horseback, and even see their torches. They pressed on desperately, falling often on the slippery ground or tripping over objects hidden by the dark. Patrols rode by while they were crossing open fields, and they were forced to lie down and press their faces into the wet grass and dirt.

They passed over the land like a silent pack, wary and wild. At the corner of three irregularly shaped fields Jamm stopped to survey the gray landscape. How he could see anything beyond a few feet, Samul did not know. They were crouched in long orchard grass that dripped with rain. Cold, wet spiderwebs clung to the nobleman's hands, and fireflies danced through the air. In the distance, cattle lowed, and nighthawks cried forlornly.

"Do you smell something?" Carl whispered to Jamm.

A tiny breeze did carry a foul odor.

"Dead animal," Jamm said quietly.

When the thief was satisfied that they could press on he went quickly over the wall and into a field of oats. Samul came behind, thinking this would be as wet as wading through a lake. Immediately he tripped over something soft. Pressing the oats aside with his arm, he cursed.

"What is it?" Carl asked.

"A dead man."

A second man lay a few feet away. In the dark it was hard to tell how they'd been killed, but it was hardly by accident. They wore mail shirts and surcoats.

"These men served the House of Innes," Prince Michael said, crouching over the corpses in the dark. "Our crest is embroidered on their shoulders—you can feel it."

Jamm rummaged the stinking bodies but found neither purses nor weapons, and then he led his companions off, clinging to the shadow at the field's edge, a new urgency in their pace.

Twenty-six

It crouched high in the dead branches of a tree. In the diffuse gray light the creature cast no shadow, but Tam could see it was thin-boned and angular—almost human. It appeared narrow-chested and thin-necked, bent like a stooped old man, but it leapt nimbly to another branch, swung one-handed, and landed in the crotch of a nearby tree, its long tail curling around a branch like a fifth limb.

Whatever beast it was, it stared down at Alaan through the leaf-less branches, its eyes large and dark, almost hidden in short, ash-gray fur.

"Have you kept your word?" it hissed. "Have you?"

"Can you keep yours? That is what I wonder," Alaan answered.

"She will be angry," the creature said very softly, as though someone might hear. "If she finds out, she'll cast another spell on me."

"She'll learn nothing from us." Alaan dug into a pocket and produced a leather pouch dangling from a cord. He reached up, the cord entwined in his fingers, the dull little pouch twisting slowly.

For a moment, the creature stared solemnly at Alaan, then came creeping down the branches, more sinuous and nimble than a squirrel. It reached out a paw tentatively toward the pouch, almost afraid to touch it, Tam thought. Just as its fingers were about to snatch it, Alaan seized the creature by its wrist and yanked it bodily from the tree. It tumbled down upon him, throwing its thin arms around his neck. It bared its fangs and would have bitten him had Alaan not been expecting such an attack.

"Don't you dare bite me!" Alaan hissed, grabbing the creature by the throat.

"Liar!" the beast hissed. "Liar."

"I just want to be sure I get what you promised," Alaan said. "The potion is yours, but you must do what I've asked." He put the pouch into the creature's hand and closed the bony fingers around it.

"How do I know that it will do what you promised?" the creature accused.

"It will, on my word."

The creature stopped struggling and stared at Alaan's handsome face, so close to its own. "I will put you on the right path," it conceded.

Alaan let the creature crouch on the saddle before him, for it would not sit like a man, despite its ability to speak like one.

It pointed, and Alaan gave his horse a heel. The others followed in single file, dumbfounded by this latest strange twist in their journey.

"What manner of creature is that thing?" Tam heard Fynnol whisper to Crowheart.

"A man—or so it once was."

"That is no man!" Fynnol argued, but the creature turned and glared at him, and Fynnol fell silent.

Whatever it was it had good ears, Tam decided.

They continued on through the dim wood, the barren and broken trees like creatures burned to a hard shell, their arms flung out, thin fingers grasping the air in agony. The ground itself was barren sand and rocks, though a little darker soil could still be seen around the exposed roots of the trees.

Every so often the creature would point, and they would change direction, though how it found its way in the featureless landscape Tam did not know. He pulled his cloak close against the cool breeze and bent low to offer less of a target. The mane of his horse whipped about with the occasional gust, and sand stung his eyes.

The horses were restive and wild-eyed, and if not for the attentions of Crowheart might have bolted—all but Alaan's Bris, who seemed to be frightened by nothing.

After several hours of riding through the desolate landscape, they came at last to a broken hill. Out of a mouth in the rock poured a little rill of dusky water. The creature jumped down from Alaan's horse and crouched low to slake its thirst from the murmuring stream—as though he drank in the words of this forsaken land.

"Drink. It is good," he said, standing and wiping his mouth with the back of a meager wrist.

No one moved to dismount, but Alaan let his horse drink a little. Tam thought they'd all go thirsty before they'd drink such water, but their waterskins weren't empty yet.

The creature gazed down at the pouch in his hand, the cord tangled in his thin, almost human fingers. Then he stirred himself. "What is in it?" he asked, holding up the pouch.

"The breastbone of a sorcerer thrush, ground to powder, among other things."

The creature's eyes went wide. "You killed a sorcerer thrush?!"

"Even I'm not such a fool. A falcon killed it. I merely waited for it to pick the bones clean. Wear it around your neck."

The creature hesitated, gazing at the bag, the almost human face unreadable. Eyes closed, it lifted the cord over its head, letting the pouch settle against the gray fur of its chest. Its posture changed, becoming more erect, almost human, and the dark eyes flicked open to stare at its hands. "It does nothing!"

"Be patient," Alaan said. "A spell such as yours cannot be broken in a moment. It will take several days, perhaps a fortnight, but you will be yourself again, Waath. You have my word."

The creature closed its fingers around the pouch, as though trying to feel the magic, then pointed down the path of the little trickle of water. "Follow this," it hissed. "The stream will lead you where you want to go. But mind what you say! She will be very angry with me. Very angry." It glanced down at the pouch, then up at the men. "Luck to you Alaan," it said. "Come visit when I am myself again. You shall see—I was a man of some dignity, once. . . ." He tried to smile—a terrible misshapen grimace.

"Perhaps I will, one day, Waath." Alaan nodded to the creature, and they set off, following the meandering track of the little stream.

Tam looked back and saw the creature staring down into the small pool that formed below the spring. In one fist he held the pouch tightly, his manner so hopeful and pathetic that Tam had to look away.

They rode for some few hours—Tam didn't know how many, for the light never seemed to change in this place, no matter the time of day or night. Eventually, they began to hear a sound like wind or water, and finally they decided it was water, running water. A good stream of it, Tam guessed.

But before they reached it, they found a pool—too large to throw a stone across but not by much—around it a screen of bleak trees, some fallen or shattered. Here and there Tam saw stunted plants, gray-green in color: a desperate fern, a lily, some clumps of grass.

"Do you know where we are, Alaan?" Cynddl asked. He looked around, and shivered.

In answer, Alaan lifted an arm and pointed. Against the far shore something moved. A swan, Tam realized, a black swan. He could see the graceful curve of its neck, the wings held high.

Alaan swung quietly down from his saddle and handed the reins to Crowheart. As the others dismounted he gestured for them to stay back, going forward only a few paces himself. There he crouched, looking out over the slick, dark water.

The swan disappeared behind the black bole of a tree, then appeared again, barely there against the dark water and burned shore. Alaan did not move, but waited, still as a stalking cat. The swan finally made its way around the pond, and when it drew near to the place where Alaan waited, the traveler spoke.

"Hello, Grandmother," he said softly.

The swan stopped, then darted behind a tall rock. Alaan did not move to give chase but bided his time. After a long moment a shadow appeared on the water's edge, half-hidden by a tree. A human shadow, Tam could see—a young woman by form and movement.

"You are a child of Wyrr?"

"Sainth, or so I once was," Alaan said, "before I slept an age in the river."

She gazed at him a moment. "What you have done is unwholesome. It is wrong to take another—"

"It was forced upon me—or him rather, for Sainth is but a part of me, now."

The woman came forward a step, and Tam could see her more clearly, thick, black hair to her waist, a face that would thaw the heart of Death himself.

"Why are you here?"

"Why are *you* here, I might ask," Alaan said. "No one has yet passed into Death's kingdom and returned. You wait in vain."

"What I do is my business. You have not traveled here to lecture me about matters of which I know more than you."

She stepped behind a thin tree so that she was half-hidden. Tam saw Cynddl move forward a little, his face alert.

"I have come seeking my father," Alaan said.

"Wyrr sleeps in the river, as you must know." She disappeared behind a larger tree.

Alaan rose to his feet. "Caibre will create a soul eater at Death's bidding. He is seeking Wyrr, and I fear he knows where he rests."

A swan appeared, paddling along the shore, its webbed feet stirring up the water in its wake. It passed behind a rock, and on the other side emerged a shadow, slipping gracefully across the barren earth.

"You disturb me, son of Wyrr," she whispered, her voice clear and musical. "Do you know what lies beyond the river? A place without human warmth. These twilight lands are verdant compared to Death's kingdom, yet once he was just a man—if a sorcerer can ever be called just a man. Mea'chi was his name then, and the friend of his heart was named Tusival. Both were in thrall to the arcane arts and learned much. They laid the foundation for the arts as they came to be known in later years. But Tusival was full of life, nearly bursting with it. You have never met a man so vibrant, so utterly alive. And Mea'chi was wounded by living. Everything scarred him, good or bad, and he withdrew into a world of his own—first a room in a tower, a dark lifeless place, then the castle entire. Soon the lands around began to die, trees withering away, fields barren of crops. The pain and fear of Mea'chi were like a spell, spreading outward, killing what could not run, chasing everything else away. Tusival tried to bring his friend back, back to life, but he could not. In the end Tusival was forced to wall Mea'chi into his kingdom, where he preys on the souls of the dying, breathing in the last whiff of life from those who pass through his gate." She turned and pointed a finger off toward the sounds of the river. "That is where he took my daughter, only a child, breaking every pact he had ever made. And then he created that . . . *thing*, that monster." She seemed to wither away then, collapsing into a crouch, arms across her knees, a hand hiding her lovely face. "And he took my Tusival away . . . into that lifeless place. Tusival, whom time could not touch." She began to weep softly.

"And now he will take Wyrr as well, and eventually Aillyn," Alaan said softly. "That is his plan. And Sainth's brother, Caibre, will create the monster for him."

She wept on, seeming not to have heard, or to have cared.

"Mea'chi has one of your children," Alaan said. "Will you let him take the others? The children Tusival vowed Death would never have?"

She stirred a little, moving into a patch of shadow, and there was a swan again, paddling slowly over the black pond, away from them.

"Meer," Alaan called, "will you not help me?"

The swan hesitated, turning its elegant neck and looking back at the man standing on the shore. For a moment it drifted there, pushed by the small breeze, turning slowly, then it came back toward the shore, disappearing behind a tree.

Tam expected the beautiful woman to appear again, but only her voice was heard.

"The resting place of Wyrr is on a branch of the river. A high island where it is said Pora awaited her lover, who never returned."

"I know that place!" Alaan said. "But where on the island was he laid to rest?"

"Look for the Moon's Mirror," the voice said. The woman appeared again, Meer, and came toward Alaan.

"There is a stone," she said intently, "a green gem, that once belonged to my Tusival. It passed to Wyrr, then to Aillyn before it was lost. I seek it."

"Why?"

"Because it belonged to my love, and it would be a danger if it fell into the hands of mortal men."

"Certainly any spell placed upon it would have faded by now."

She shook her beautiful head, gazing intently into Alaan's eyes. "Not these spells."

"I don't know it," Alaan said, his gaze dropping to his feet.

She regarded him a moment more, her look a little mad and unsettling. Reaching out, she touched his face and pressed her own cheek close to his. For a moment they stood thus, then she turned and blended into shadow. The swan appeared swimming on the pond, never looking back. And then it was lost in darkness on the far shore.

For a long time they all waited, but the swan did not return, and, finally, Alaan turned away. "There, Cynddl," he said, "you have found many stories of ancient times, but you've never met one of the figures from that age."

"I have met you," Cynddl said.

"I am but a youth compared to Meer, or rather, Sainth is but a youth." His eyes lost focus for a moment, and he hesitated as though suddenly lost.

"Where is this place she spoke of?" Cynddl asked.

Alaan gave his head the smallest shake. "It is on the hidden river. Few have traveled there. I doubt even our intrepid Theason has wandered so far. Sainth was there long ago. It is a place made famous in an old tale: the Isle of Disappointment, it has been called, and the Isle of Waiting. There is said to be a ghost there though Sainth did not see it."

"But . . ." Cynddl's voice trailed off as he gestured toward the pond.

Alaan turned to the story finder and nodded. "Yes," he said softly, "she has been here all this time. There is a story of grief for you. Or madness." Alaan took the reins of his horse from Crowheart. "We have journeyed this far—come gaze on the final river. On the other shore lies Death's kingdom. The gate is not far off, above the steps of an ancient quay. But we will not go there this day."

Alaan did not mount but led his horse through the twilight wood. In a short distance they came to the murmuring river, which ran like gray ink through the doomed landscape. The far shore was lost in shadow, though if he stared Tam thought he saw more barren trees, perhaps a cliff, he could not be sure.

"Is there a more oppressive place than this?" Fynnol wondered aloud.

"Yes," Alaan answered, "but no one returns to speak of it."

"I thought to see this place only once," Cynddl said, his manner distant.

"Innithal, it was called in ancient times," Alaan said. "River of tears or perhaps river of sorrow. But men do not name it now, if they even believe in its existence. Be sure your ashes are spread upon the Wynnd before your body is cold. Then you will follow the black wanderers, Cynddl's people, back to the breathing sea. Better to lift upon the breast of a wave beneath the sun than pass into the darkness." He turned away, and the others followed, more than one glancing back. As Tam did so he realized Fynnol still stood gazing out over the river.

"Fynnol . . ." Tam whispered, jarring his cousin from his reverie. The little Valeman turned away. "Come on," Tam said. "Let's be shut of this place."

They mounted horses and followed Alaan, an empty wind plucking at their clothing.

Twenty-seven

Dusk brought the town of Weybridge into view. Jamm hid them in a small wood not far from the manor house of Prince Michael's cousin.

"You won't want to appear by day, your grace," Jamm said, as they hunkered down in a small copse.

"Hunger is tempting me to take that risk," the Prince answered, his gaze wandering to the mansion house.

"I think Jamm is right," Carl offered. He had slumped down with his back against a tree, a tired, disreputable-looking nobleman if there ever was one, Samul thought. "You can't trust their servants or the freemen who work their land. Better to go hungry another few hours than be handed over to Menwyn Wills."

"I'm sure you're right, but if I don't eat a real meal soon, or preferably several, I shall fall into a state of unreason." The summer sun floated up, bringing a hot, windless day. The wood seemed close, but the shade was a welcome relief. All day they could see the comings and goings of the people who lived on the estate. The dairymen and their dogs took the herd out to pasture after milking,

and hay was cut on a field not too far off, men and women swinging their scythes beneath the hot sun. The bright skirts of the
women and girls showed up at a distance, though their faces were
hidden by straw bonnets. The previous day's cut was raked and
pitchforked onto wagons that rolled slowly back to the barns and
stables.

Samul felt a growing envy of these people, whose lives seemed
so simple and untroubled by great decisions.

The day crept by, hunger taking a grip on all of them, and more
than once Samul was doubled over with stomach cramps. Sunset
seemed worthy of celebration to Samul, and he almost smiled as
the first stars appeared.

"I have been wondering all day," Samul said, "who will accompany Prince Michael? Shall we all go?"

"I won't go," Jamm said quickly.

"Then should the three of us go?" the Prince wondered.

Carl A'denné shook his head in the gathering gloom. "Are you
known in that house? Would the servants recognize you?"

"Certainly, yes."

"Then there is some risk in what you do."

The Prince considered this. He was brushing his coat in a vain
attempt to make it presentable. "I would like to take Lord Samul
with me. After all, I shall make the claim that I have made agree-
ments with the Renné. Having a member of the family with me will
be of some benefit."

"Unless, of course, they know my recent history," Samul noted.

"There is that," the Prince said. "You were to have lost your
head. . . ." He thought a moment. "But I can introduce you as some
other Renné, can I not? There seem to be so many of you."

"Archer. I shall be my cousin Archer. We look much alike and
few know him, anyway. He keeps to himself and hasn't entered a
tournament since doing grave injury to his back, some years ago."

"Lord Archer you shall be."

The two noblemen set off down the hill toward the manor
house, the thought of a meal, and perhaps a bath, lifting their spir-

its. As they departed from their friends, Jamm called after them. "Say nothing of us!"

The door to the house was answered by a footman, who, out of respect for the state of the world, wore a sword.

"Sir?" he said, regarding Michael by the small light that shone through the barely opened door.

"Would you tell Lady Francesca that her cousin is here?"

"Do excuse me, sir, but may I say which cousin?"

"I'd rather surprise her, if you don't mind."

"As you wish, sir. If you'll excuse me."

"Well, he didn't recognize you," Samul said, "or he wouldn't have left you standing out in the dark."

"We'll hope for better luck with Franny."

"When did you last see her?"

"Oh, not a year ago. We have always had great sympathy, she and I."

A noise from within silenced them, and the door creaked open, a distinctly feminine eye regarding them through the crack.

"Franny? It's Michael."

The eye widened. "Michael!" A chain rattled, and the door was flung open, light flooding out. A lovely woman threw her arms about Michael's neck as though he were a lost son. "We thought you were dead," she said, her voice betraying her emotion.

"Nearly, and more than once, but I survived."

She pulled away, all joy swept from her face. "Your father—"

"Yes, I know."

"Who is there?" came a male voice from inside.

"Look, Henri!" Franny said. "Look who's returned from the grave!"

"River save us!" the man said as he caught sight of Michael. "Michael! You are a sight! Come in. Come in at once!"

Food was brought to the two vagabonds, and baths promised. Samul Renné tried to restrain himself, but feared he ate like a starving soldier rather than the nobleman he was. Henri A'tanelle paced back and forth across the kitchen, where Samul and

Prince Michael sat, and Franny bustled about keeping their plates filled.

"First he formed a secret alliance with your father's allies and senior officers," Henri said. "By this means Sir Eremon's guards were either destroyed or driven off. Menwyn then arranged a coup, displacing the ruling council he had created himself. There is no one now to oppose him. All have sworn allegiance to the Wills—to Menwyn Wills, that is—and anyone suspected of sympathy to the claims of Lord Carral Wills have been eliminated . . . brutally."

"And what will he do when Sir Eremon returns, I wonder?" Prince Michael asked between bites of food. He stopped a moment to drain his almost empty wineglass, which his cousin Franny immediately refilled.

Henri paused, placing an arm on the high mantelpiece. For a moment he stared into the fire, a portrait of a troubled man. "Menwyn will have no choice but to fight—and he will have a great army on his side . . . against Sir Eremon and a handful of his guards."

"It doesn't matter how small Eremon's force," Samul said. "He will win any battle against Menwyn and his armies. If Sir Eremon returns, Menwyn and his supporters will die."

Henri and Franny glanced at each other. They were frightened, though of what Samul was not sure.

"The Wills are demanding the greater part of everything we harvest, and we don't hold out much hope of payment," Franny said, filling Samul's glass as well. She was quite a lovely woman, Samul thought, with a warmth and ease of manner that was unlike the pampered ladies of Castle Renné.

"If Menwyn Wills has made himself so unpopular, then it should ease our task," Prince Michael said, not without satisfaction.

"So it would seem, but the truth is, anyone you might have counted on in such a situation is either dead, in a cell, or has joined Menwyn Wills." Henri still stared into the fire, shaking his head. "There are a few we might speak to secretly, but any one of them might give us over to the Wills. Menwyn has been doling out portions of your father's estates—your estates—to his supporters, and promising even larger tracts of Renné lands." Henri turned away from the fire and offered the prince a tight-lipped smile. "But we will see. There is no doubt in our minds where our loyalties lie," he said, and looked at his wife, who nodded firmly. "I will sit and think this night and make a list of men who I believe will be loyal to the House of Innes, or those who might think to gain by Menwyn's fall, and we will go over it together in the morning. But you, cousin, and Lord Archer, must have rest this night. Baths have been drawn for you, chambers made up. Until the morning."

Twenty-eight

Not all of Hafydd's guards could fit in the boat, what with Hafydd himself, Beldor Renné, the mapmaker Kai, and his manservant. Lord A'denné watched the legless man carefully. If he had an ally in this place, it was Kai—whom Hafydd called "Kilydd." Ever since they had entered the boat and set out along this unknown river he had felt some tension grow between the legless man and Hafydd. There was some history there, Lord A'denné thought; some ancient history, if he was to believe the things he was hearing.

He looked around, the river stretching broad and slick beneath a low leaden sky. The forest there was almost unbroken, only the occasional meadow interrupting the dense tangle of green. If men had ever dwelt there, it was a long age ago.

Kai shifted on the plank thwart, the Fáel pillows that had lined his barrow getting soiled and wet, their beautiful fabrics ruined.

"Do you recognize this place?" Lord A'denné asked.

Kai shook his head, drizzle running down his round, pink face. "I traveled here once, long ago—with Sainth. Several generations of trees have come and gone, embankments crumble, even the river might change its course over so many centuries—but this is the way, all the same."

Lord A'denné glanced over at Hafydd, who sat in the stern by the helmsman, if that's what you would call the black-clad guard who anxiously clutched the tiller. No one spoke much in the knight's presence, but his attention seemed to be elsewhere, and A'denné refused to be treated like just another one of Hafydd's servants. He might feel the same fear of the man that everyone else did, but he would be damned if he'd show it!

"Where is it we go?" the nobleman whispered.

Kai glanced at him, then away, like a truant schoolboy. "An island. There is an ancient, sacred spring there. Hafydd is looking for the resting place of his . . . of Caibre's father—the great sorcerer Wyrr. It is his plan to give him up to Death."

Lord A'denné shook his head. "I seem to have fallen into a nightmare. *Death?* Is this not a creature of fable? An artifice of the balladeer?"

Kai closed his eyes, a faint smile flickering over his lips. "I wish it were so. The creature we call Death was once a sorcerer, like Wyrr—or perhaps more akin to his father, Tusival. But his mind turned into unwholesome paths and over an age he grew into the creature we now call Death—as real as you or I."

A'denné felt a shiver run up his back and along his arms, his hands twitching once involuntarily. "Why has he brought me?" he asked a little desperately.

A hard rain spattered down on the river then, a sound like hail on gravel. The legless man turned and looked at him, his face glistening and running with rain. "Hafydd does not carry his enemies with him in hope that they will convert to his cause, that is certain. You are to be sacrificed, Lord A'denné. That is what I think. Beldor Renné knows something of this, and he is not clever enough to keep knowledge to himself. You might learn something from a conversation or two with the Renné—"

"A'denné!"

It was Hafydd, glaring forward over the pumping oarsmen.

"Your turn at the sweeps."

The nobleman made his way aft, stepping gingerly over the baggage they carried, his hands on the wet gunwales, rain pounding down upon his back, running inside the neck of his coat. He took the offered oar from one of the guards and tumbled into place, setting the sweep between the tholepins, hesitating only a second to catch the rhythm of the others, then digging his oar into the rain-battered river. The slick wood slipped between his fingers, and he gripped it more tightly, his hands cold and stiff from sitting. He glanced out at the passing riverbank, tree branches drooping down, heavy with rain.

You are to be sacrificed. The words echoed in his mind. *Sacrificed!*

Hafydd sat staring darkly at the shore, his manner grim. Lord A'denné wondered if it would be possible to kill the knight. Certainly the guards would immediately bring down any man who managed it, but what of that? A'denné believed his life was forfeit anyway. If he was to be sacrificed, let him choose the cause he would be sacrificed for. How to manage it, that was the difficulty. Hafydd was vigilant and possessed powers of which others knew little. Others but for Kai . . . Kai knew more than he was telling, he was certain of that.

Sacrificed!

Hafydd stood and drew his sword from its scabbard. Lord A'denné almost lost pace with the oarsmen, his eyes fixed on the blade, but Hafydd sat down again and thrust the smoky blade into the river. For a moment he sat, eyes closed in concentration, and then he cursed with such perfect rage that everyone on the boat was overcome by fear.

No one could clearly see what Hafydd was doing. The knight was all but hidden by trees and bushes, and though it was not yet night, the thick cloud and shadows beneath the wood held almost all the light at bay. He performed some arcane ritual involving fire, for he could be seen walking around a blaze—and once he had walked through it! Apparently he had suffered no harm, for the ritual continued.

Some hours later he stumbled into the camp, his guards rushing to support him. They lowered him on a log, where he slumped with his head down between his knees.

Lord A'denné realized at that moment that here was his opportunity. Everyone's attention was on Hafydd, even while men tried to look busy at their appointed tasks. He went quickly to the fire and ladled some thick stew from a pot into a bowl. No one paid him the least attention, and A'denné set the bowl down for a moment, waving his hands in the air as though the bowl had been too hot to hold. He took up bit of cloth that lay there and used it to carry the bowl, hoping no one realized the cloth had been thrown down on a sharp kitchen knife.

A'denné could hardly catch his breath, and had to exercise firm control to keep his hands from shaking.

You are dead anyway, he told himself. *What better way to die than killing this sorcerer?*

He felt as though he were pulled half out of his body—so that he both animated his limbs and was someone else, watching. His vision narrowed so that all he could see was Hafydd, bent over like a man exhausted beyond measure. His head was bent so his face was hidden, only the oval of dull gray hair apparent. A'denné knew that he would have to get the knife into Hafydd's throat where the major blood vessels ran. Nothing else would do. One chance; that was all he would have. He made himself breathe and tried to concentrate his will as he had so often in tournaments. It would be like the joust—one opportunity and no room for errors.

The guards glanced at him as he approached, then, seeing the food, let him through.

"Sir Eremon?" A'denné said softly, bending over and offering the soup.

Hafydd raised his head, his gaze out of focus, clearly confused, but then he raised his hands to take the bowl. The second Hafydd began to take the weight of the bowl, A'denné drove the point of his blade toward the exposed throat.

He felt his hand stop, clasped in a grip like stone. Hafydd looked up at him, his eye suddenly clear, the stew, unspilled, in one hand, A'denné's wrist in the other. The nobleman dropped the knife unwillingly.

"You were too respectful, A'denné," the knight said. "You gave yourself away." Hafydd shook his head, a look of disgust, perhaps even disappointment, crossing his face.

A'denné was dragged back by two guards, and Hafydd took up the spoon from the bowl and calmly began to eat his stew, as though nothing untoward had happened. A'denné thought he would be killed then, but instead he was thrown roughly down on his bedding and left, as though he were so little threat they needn't do more.

For a moment he gazed at the little group surrounding Hafydd, but then he realized someone regarded him, and turned to find Kai staring at him evenly.

"Why didn't you speak to me?" the legless man demanded softly. "That was your one chance, and you've wasted it!"

For a day Hafydd slumped in the stern of the boat, like a man too ill to care where they went or why. Seldom did his head rise, and when it did his eyes were not focused, and his flesh was an unhealthy gray. His head soon fell forward again, and he appeared to sleep fitfully. His guards hovered over him like nursemaids, their faces filled with concern.

A'denné was seated in the bow with Kai and his servant, Ufrra, when he was struck with a thought. He turned his head away so that none might see his lips move and leaned toward Kai, speaking as softly as he could.

"We might overturn the boat," he whispered.

Kai leaned to one side so that he was hidden from the oarsmen by the large bulk of Ufrra. "He cannot be drowned, even if this could be done by only three of us."

Lord A'denné turned away, staring at the passing riverbank. The sky remained obscured by cloud, but the position of the sun could be found now, as it struggled to burn away the haze, illuminating a circle of cloud with a faint urgent glow.

"How much farther?" Hafydd demanded. He was much recovered after a day of utter listlessness, but his mood was black.

They made a camp by the river in small clearing among willows. The dark, threatening sky was breaking up, revealing the last of the day's light, a sky of fading blue, high up, thin wisps of orange-pink.

Kai shrugged. "A day. Two days. I can't be sure. It was an age ago that I came this way."

Hafydd glared down at the legless man in his barrow, who alone among them appeared to have no fear of Hafydd and his temper. "If I find you are sending me on a merry chase, Kilydd, I shall cut off your remaining limbs. I will shatter your eardrums and pluck out your eyes, too. And you may live that diminished life as long as you desire." Hafydd turned and walked away.

Kai watched the dark figure go into the gloom, his face an impassive mask. Then he turned and smiled at Lord A'denné. "When you are a cripple, long past being of interest to the fairer sex, and not inclined toward drink, you must take your pleasures where you may."

Twenty-nine

"**I** wonder how the Prince has been received by his cousin?" Carl said. He and Jamm sat eating apples and raw carrots they'd stolen from the nearby orchards and garden.

"You don't seem to hold the cousin in high regard," Jamm said between bites. Carl could hardly see him in the dark, but the sounds of his munching were loud and clear—unusual for the silent Jamm.

"My father judged him harshly, and he was seldom wrong about men."

Jamm continued to eat. "Then I say we move our camp. There is an old barn foundation in a stand of trees overlooking the road. We can keep the manor house under our eye there."

"Why would we move?"

"You can never be too careful," the thief said, and he began collecting up the apples and carrots, being sure not to leave any apple cores behind.

★　　★　　★

Carl woke to cold steel at his throat, the dark shape of a man looming over him.

"Tell your companion not to move, or I'll cut your throat," a voice said softly.

"Jamm . . . ?" Carl said, but he could hear that Jamm was already awake.

"I won't move," came a voice out of the darkness.

The man sat down on a stump, his blade still at Carl's throat. "You travel with two men I know: Prince Michael of Innes, whose father is said to have been murdered, and Samul Renné. Both men have recently been allies of Hafydd, or Sir Eremon, as some know him." The man was silent a moment. "Your father I knew by reputation, Lord Carl, but you keep strange company. So I wonder what you are doing in these lands. Make your answer convincing because I will kill both you and your friend without much hesitation."

Carl swallowed hard. Was this some ally of Hafydd's? He thought of the dead men they'd found in the grass and the stranger who rescued them in the dark.

"You haven't time to contrive an answer, Lord Carl. Speak now, or you will have no throat to speak from."

"We are enemies of Hafydd," Carl said, praying he read the man right. "And have crossed the river in hopes of finding allies for our cause among the Prince's friends and family."

"So you say, but both the Prince and the Renné traveled with Hafydd not so long ago."

"I don't know that whole story, but certainly the Renné trusted Prince Michael, and as for Samul, he made some bargain with his cousins."

"No doubt. He has made several bargains in recent weeks," the shadow said, but Carl thought he felt the pressure of the blade lessen a little.

"That was you who helped us that night when we were trapped in the lane . . . ?"

"Yes. Menwyn Wills allied himself with a sorcerer, making him an enemy of mine. His troops were trying to kill you, making you a possible friend . . . but it is difficult to tell friend from foe these days. Samul Renné has changed allies too often. If I had been Lord Toren, I would have sent him to the gallows, as the rumors said he had—along with Lord Carl A'denné." He fell silent a moment, thinking. "But if Lord Toren saw fit to let you live—to feign your death—then he must have either had good reason or been entirely desperate." The man removed the point of his sword from Carl's neck but held the weapon still so that he could use it instantly—and Carl was not going to test this man's reflexes.

"You've not told us your name . . . ," Carl said.

The man considered this a moment. "Pwyll, I am called."

"Pwyll?—who won the tournament at Westbrook?"

"By Lord Toren's generosity and sense of fair play—yes."

"I have been secretly Lord Toren's ally," Carl said. "It was I who warned him of the invasion of the Isle of Battle."

"Was it, indeed? I was far away when that happened, or I might have ridden with the Renné myself."

"Then you are an enemy of Menwyn Wills?"

"I am an enemy of Hafydd's, and at the moment so is Menwyn Wills, though for all the wrong reasons, I suspect."

"May I sit up?" Carl asked.

"Slowly. I can see your hands even in the darkness," the man said. "Keep them away from your sword and dagger. That goes for you, too, master thief."

Carl sat up, trying to shake off both sleep and fear. It seemed his throat wasn't about to be cut. They might even have found an ally—a formidable ally.

Pwyll shifted on the stump. "Tell me, Lord Carl, do you trust Lord Samul and the Prince?"

"Prince Michael has worked against Hafydd even while his father was in the sorcerer's thrall. I don't doubt him in the least. Despite present alignments, the Renné are still the main enemies of Hafydd, and Prince Michael is trying to rally allies to their cause. Michael believes that Menwyn will not win a battle with Hafydd despite the size of his army."

"The Prince is right. Men-at-arms won't stand and fight a sorcerer for a captain like Menwyn Wills. He does not have either their respect or their love. The first signs of sorcery, and they will break and run. Hafydd will gather them all together again in a few days and command them out of fear. Menwyn will not survive this war. But if we are to defeat Hafydd, he must be denied that army."

"And that is the Prince's purpose."

"There is a small problem that the Prince did not foresee. . . ."

"And that would be?"

"His kin sent out a rider soon after he arrived, and a troop of men-at-arms wearing Wills livery arrived at the manor house not half an hour ago."

Thirty

The river had narrowed and increased its speed while the cliffs
had fallen way to rolling banks, which rose and dipped a little as
they passed. To either side, dense forests of pine and fir mixed
with oak and maple, beech and ash. There were trees growing
there that Dease Renné had never seen before: a tree with bark
white as a wave crest and branches that hung down like the weep-
ing willow, a maple with leaves larger than platters. He watched
the hidden lands roll by between his turns at the oars. No one
who could manage a sweep was exempt. Even Elise, he noticed,
took her turn, and the men in her boat were hard-pressed to
match her pace. *A gift from the river*, she called this strength, but
it was arcane, Dease knew, and it unsettled the men-at-arms, even
A'brgail's Knights.

"Do you smell smoke?" A'brgail asked, sitting up and turning
his head, nostrils flaring as he tested the air delicately.

Toren turned and gazed back the way they'd come. "Wind is in
the north, so it must be coming from behind. Did we pass a camp-
fire?" Dease saw Toren reach over for his sword, which he now kept

buckled to a thwart. Hafydd was somewhere on this river before them, or so Elise claimed.

"The winds eddy and twist among these hills, Lord Toren," Theason said. "The smoke might be coming from anywhere." He too sniffed the air. "Forest fires can occur in summer. I have seen the places where they've burned—vast stretches, soon green again with new life, but the skeletons of the great trees stand for many years, like gravestones." Theason was silent a moment, then went on. "Do you know, the name Eremon, which Hafydd uses still, is the name of a shrub that grows up where fire has destroyed the forest? The seeds of the eremon bush can lie dormant in the ground for two hundred years, but the heat of the fire cracks their shells, and they sprout up only days after the fire has passed."

No one had any response to this, and the boat fell silent.

"Do you smell the smoke?" Elise called a moment later. She was standing in the stern of her boat, wrapped in a Fáel cloak, her hair wafting in the breeze. She twisted it into a rough tail and tucked it behind an ear, and then inside the collar of her cloak—a practiced motion that was all Elise. Sianon, Orlem had said, cut her hair short.

"Yes," A'brgail called, "but where is it coming from?"

Elise shrugged. "The wind comes from all directions."

And so it did. North for a while, then from the west, then south by southwest. It even veered east for a time. The smoke seemed to be carried on any wind, now stronger and more pungent, then weaker or gone altogether.

They rounded a bend in the river, and Dease's eyes were stung by smoke, the smell even stronger. Flakes drifted down from the sky, like snow, but this was a gray snow.

"Ash!" Theason said.

"Bring the boats together!" Elise called out. She had unsheathed her sword and thrust the blade into the river.

"Is it Hafydd?" A'brgail asked, as the boats came alongside, oarsmen swinging high their sweeps and taking hold of the other craft's gunwale.

Elise did not answer but held her blade in the back of the river, eyes closed, her head cocked to one side as though she listened intently. Then she shook her head, drawing her sword from the water and drying it in a fold of her cloak, all in one motion.

"He is ahead of us yet—and some distance, too. But still, fire is his greatest weapon, and we must be wary."

"Theason said he has seen forest fires in the hidden lands before," A'brgail offered.

Elise nodded. "Then let us hope this is such a fire and nothing more," she answered, but she stood again in the stern of her boat and surveyed all that could be seen, her manner stiff and apprehensive.

Ash continued to snow down, dappling the water, where the flakes soon became a leaden scum spread over the surface. Smoke could be seen now, hanging among the low hills that bordered the river.

"Rain would be welcome," Theason remarked.

"Fire is a way of rejuvenating the forest," Eber said, "for it sweeps away the ancient trees, cleanses the soil, and allows the long cycle of growth to begin again." He held his son, asleep in his lap, and Dease thought the old man looked overwhelmed by sadness. "Young trees appear, flourish, and are replaced by others, like generations, until you again have the mature forest we see here. It is the natural cycle and keeps each breed of tree strong, for the forest is full of scourges, even for the oak and the willow."

"If anyone is wearing mail, he should take this opportunity to shed it," Elise said, but work at the oars was hot, and mail shirts had long since been rolled into oiled sheepskins and put away out of reach of water.

The smoke was thicker ahead, a cloud of it wafting out over the river, casting a shadow on the dark waters.

"What is it you fear, Lady Elise?" A'brgail asked. "Something I think."

But she answered with a question of her own. "Who among you can swim?"

A few voices answered in the affirmative—not enough, Toren thought.

"Those of you who cannot swim find another who can. Do as he says and do not let fear get the better of you."

Eber turned in his seat in the bows, fear across his face. "But what of my son?" he said, his voice shaking with anger and apprehension. "You swore that you would protect him."

"And I will," Elise said. "Pass the boy back to me."

Llya was wakened and passed quickly down the row of oarsmen to Elise, who took him up gently, smiling at him and caressing him as though he were her own.

"Don't be afraid," she said. "I am of the river. No matter what happens, you will be safe with me."

The boy made some sign with his hands, and Dease wondered if he had understood at all.

They rounded another bend, and there the smoke was thick. Fire climbed a tree in the distance, branches breaking away and tumbling in flames. Despite cloaks stretched over mouths, smoke burned into the lungs all the same, and everyone coughed. The boats drifted into a gloom, like a dry fog. His eyes stung and watered so that he could see almost nothing. The heat began to grow, so that Dease's face ran with sweat, and he could feel it spreading down his sides beneath his clothes.

"Douse your cloaks in water!" Elise yelled.

Dease pulled his cloak off and thrust it into the river. In a moment he had it over his head, crouching within this small tent. He could feel his cousin beside him, hear him coughing.

Dease was racked by a fit of coughing himself as the smoke tore at his lungs. He opened his cloak a little and tried to pick out anything in the obscurity. To run ashore would be a disaster.

"Flames!" he yelled. A wave of heat struck him like a blow, knocking him into the bottom of the boat. His cloak was quickly steaming itself dry.

"Into the water!" he heard Elise yell, and Dease threw himself blindly over the side. The cool water washed over him, drawing off the scalding heat. He struggled out of his cloak and threw the sodden mass into the boat. He kept one hand on the gunwale, but the wood was growing almost too hot to hold. Quickly he switched hands, splashing water up onto the wood.

In the water beside him were others, faces blackened and obscured by smoke. Something burned his wrist, and he drew his hand away from the boat, only to find the burning did not stop in the water, and he scraped away at his skin for a moment before he was free of the scalding material.

Paint, he realized. The paint was bubbling off.

"Splash water on the boats!" someone yelled, but Dease turned quickly around, staring into the smoke that burned his eyes. The boats were gone!

Flame appeared overhead, the heat unbearable. Dease dove beneath the water and swam. The forest fire, if that's what it was, leapt the river. The desire to cough was strong, but he fought it down, pressing himself forward into the cool water. To surface there would be to die. There was no light in the water, though he swam with his eyes opened. He didn't even know for sure that he was swimming downstream.

When he began to see black spots about the edge of his vision, Dease rose toward the surface, emerging into a smith's forge, the heat searing his face, wet though it was. Even the water seemed hot, steaming around him. Flames shot out of the smoke, and the sound of fire was deafening.

He drew in a lungful of smoke and coughed uncontrollably. The heat was more than he could bear, but he could not dive without air, and there was nothing to breathe but smoke.

Dease rolled on his back, gasping and hacking. Water choked him, but he could no longer find the strength to struggle. The world seemed to recede, fading, darkness swirling out of the air.

The river took hold of him, and he was pulled down, down into the waters. He did not resist, nor could he have, but slipped into a dream, a cool dream where he drifted within the river, held gently in its maw, carried off, where he did not know.

*   *   *

Toren felt they were in an oven, close, utterly dark, hot as a bed of coals. He could hear the others breathing, coughs echoing beneath the overturned hull. For a moment he rested, clinging to the inwale with his fingers. When he felt he had enough strength he reached an arm out and splashed water onto the hull, his fingers roasting in the heat of the fire.

In a moment he pulled the hand in again, dousing it in the quickly warming water.

"Call your names . . . ," A'brgail said, almost at Toren's elbow.

Names were croaked in the darkness.

"Dease?" Toren called. "Dease? Are you here?"

There was no answer. One of A'brgail's Knights was missing as well—their numbers down to eight. Toren cursed between fits of coughing. He didn't think anyone would survive outside the boat, the heat was too great, the smoke overwhelming. He took a breath and ducked under, surfacing in a kind of purgatory, flame and smoke roiling overhead, hotter than a blazing hearth.

"Dease!" he called. "Dease . . ." For a moment he listened, then went back into the relative safety of the overturned boat, drawing in a lungful of smoky air.

The current seemed to be infinitely slow, and the fire spread over a greater area than he had hoped. It even occurred to Toren that the boat might be circling in an eddy, not escaping the fire at all. He reached a hand out into the oven and splashed water up onto the hull, as did the others, but still it was growing dangerously hot. He reached up and pressed his palm to the planking— then pulled it quickly away. The wood was almost too hot to touch.

"It can't be much farther," someone lamented.

"How big can such a fire be?" a voice asked.

"Very great," came a small voice in response. "I have seen a fire scar the hillside for leagues."

"We'll not survive for leagues," A'brgail said low to Toren. "Another few moments, and this shell will be on fire, and all the turtles will be forced out into the flames."

"Let us hope . . . ," Toren said. But A'brgail was right; another few moments, and they would be gone. He dipped his head under, for the air beneath the boat was growing hot. As he surfaced something scalding-hot dropped onto his cheek, and he wiped it away— *pitch* from the seams between the planks! He heard someone surface into the boat.

"We're afire!" Theason gasped.

Toren ducked under the gunwale and surfaced into the swirling smoke. He rubbed at his stinging eyes, trying to clear them with water. Squinting, he could see flames spreading over the turtled hull. He stripped off his shirt and beat at the flames.

"The paint is aflame!" he called to the sooty face that surfaced beside him—Toren could not begin to guess who it was.

Whoever it was followed his example, and after a moment they had doused the flames. They ducked back into the boat, gasping, choking, his scalp feeling as though it had been seared.

"The paint," he managed. "It is aflame. We have to beat it with sodden shirts."

Three men-at-arms ducked under immediately. A dull thumping sounded on the hull. When these three returned, three more went out—not a shirker among the group.

"I think the smoke is not so thick," one said as he returned, and Toren felt his hopes rise. Perhaps they would not be baked after all.

But it seemed a long time, even so, before the air began to clear, and glimpses of sunlight heartened them. They were a bedraggled lot when finally they washed ashore upon a narrow strip of mud and sprawled upon the grass. Smoke still filled the sky, drifting up in great, molten clouds. The air, however, could be breathed without promoting spasms of coughing. One of A'brgail's Knights called out, and Toren sat up to see the other boat, overturned, men clinging to it. It was brought ashore with some effort.

Dease was not there among the smoke-stained faces, though Eber, his white beard dirty gray, crawled out onto the bank.

"But where is my son?" he rasped. "Is he with you?"

"No, but he was with my mistress," Orlem Slighthand said. "He will be safe. Don't waste a moment in worry."

A head count turned up two others missing besides Dease—one of A'brgail's Knights and a Renné man-at-arms.

The tall man from the wildlands was soon up, assessing the damage to the boats. Most of the gear was lost, though weapons and some other necessities had been tied to the thwarts, and these had not been jettisoned when the boats were overturned.

Toren was on his feet, but Slighthand had assumed control and was seeing to the men, tallying their weapons and tools—a natural leader. He stood overlooking the boats with Baore.

"Can they be put to rights?" Toren asked, feeling small between the youth from the wildlands and the giant.

Baore tugged at his sparse beard, thinking. "I will take a day to make them somewhat riverworthy. Some of the pitch melted out of the seams, and the paint is gone. The wood is scorched black in places, but not to any depth, luckily. We might find some of our oars washed up along the bank; otherwise, we shall have to fashion them with an axe. They'll be rough, but serviceable."

"I'll lend a hand," Orlem said. "I'm not a stranger to wood, though I'm no shipwright."

Toren waited until Baore had gone off a few steps, then said quietly to Orlem, "What has become of Elise? The old man is worried to the point of distraction about his child."

The giant crouched and ran his hand over the blackened planking, rapping it with a knuckle. "The fire was not natural," he said in his deep rumbling voice. "Caibre created it to destroy us—to destroy Sianon . . . Elise. I cannot say what other snares he might have left to catch her. Caibre was brutal and cunning. I only hope she was equal to his art." The giant glanced back up the river. "I don't know how long we'll be safe here. The fire is spreading south. It will soon catch up with us. Whoever has skill with wood or boats should lend Baore a hand. A meal would hearten the men-at-arms. I don't know if we have a bow that can be used, but Baore has hooks and line. If there is a fisherman among us—other than Baore, who cannot be spared—then we should set him to finding food."

Someone called out and pointed. Toren stood to find Elise, her golden hair awash, swimming toward them.

Eber sat watching over his sleeping child. The child who had emerged from the river sickly pale, his lips blue—looking too much like a nagar for anyone's liking. But he was alive and sleeping gently as though nothing had happened, his natural color restored. Eber kept glancing over at Elise, who sat apart, wrapped in her Fáel cloak. She might have saved Llya, but Toren thought you would not know it by the looks Eber gave her—as though she had violated his son in some way or turned him into a monster.

He had been kept alive within the river, Toren thought, *kept alive in its dark depths.* Many a man among them would have chosen death instead. Toren was not sure what choice he would have made. He was as disturbed by the arts as many of his less-educated men-at-arms.

The nobleman looked up into the night sky. Tendrils of dark cloud wafted over, blotting out the stars—smoke. It appeared to be growing thicker, and Toren feared the north wind was carrying the fire down upon them. He wondered what had become of his cousin. Had he been consumed by the fire? Poisoned by the smoke, for certainly they had only survived beneath the protection of the boat, and even that had been a close run thing. Poor Dease. He seemed to Toren to have been afflicted by ill luck since he had been struck by Beld. His whole manner had changed, as though he blamed himself for Arden's death. Guilt seemed to consume his life's fire. And now he was gone. Lost to the unfathomable river.

Orlem, Baore, and some others slid the first boat into the river to groans and halfhearted cursing. Toren walked over to see if he could lend a hand in any way, though he had no skill as a woodworker or shipwright.

"The seams have opened up from the heat and from losing

much of their pitch," the young giant from the wildlands announced. "The other is no better. The planks will take up after a
while, but I don't think we can bail fast enough to keep them
afloat, now."

Elise rose up from the shadow where she rested. She strode
down to the water where the boats lay and stood looking at them a
moment, her manner more imperious than Toren remembered.
The shy girl of memory was gone, replaced by this woman who unsettled everyone—frightened them, in truth.

"Carry the other boat down to the water," Elise ordered, and
she shed her cloak, letting it slide to the ground in a pile.

The other boat was borne quickly down and hissed over the mud
as it splashed into the river. Without taking notice of anyone, Elise
continued to drop her clothes onto the riverbank, and in a moment
she had splashed into the water. There, she spread her arms and
seemed to hum, her palms flat on the surface. At intervals she
scooped up a double handful of water and splashed it into one boat
or the other. The water where she moved her hands appeared to become faintly green and luminescent, as Toren had once seen in the
wake of a boat on the open sea. The planking of the boats took on
this greenish cast and glowed softly. The water in the boats receded,
appearing to drain through the cracks between the planks, and in a
moment the boats were bobbing gently upon the waters, glowing as
though bathed in faint green moonlight.

Elise came out of the water, where Orlem immediately wrapped
her in a cloak.

"Load the boats," the giant ordered as he supported Elise, who
appeared weak, her knees wobbly. Orlem bent and scooped up her
clothing, bearing her up the low embankment. In a moment the
two returned, Elise dressed and tightly wrapped in her cloak, her
gaze cast down and shoulders slumped, like one overwhelmed by
fatigue.

The men-at-arms stood about the boats, no one wanting to step
into a craft that had been bespelled. Toren could see the men, looking down, none meeting Orlem's eye. Toren stepped forward and

shoved the first boat out into the water, scrambling aboard and taking up one of the oars that had been found adrift. A'brgail followed, taking up an oar himself. Eber set Llya down in the bow of the other boat and climbed aboard after him.

Orlem turned to the men-at-arms, who still hesitated on the shore. "There will be no harm to any of you," he said reassuringly. "Do not fear." He pointed to the north. "But you will be hard-pressed to outdistance the fire on foot through this dense forest. Any who cannot bear to encounter the arcane arts might be better taking his chances with the fire. Before this journey is over you will see arts enough, that is certain."

Reluctantly, and with many a measuring look to the north, the men climbed into the boats, taking their places, shipping the oars. They all appeared apprehensive but in a moment they were in the current and striking out for the south, in the wake of Hafydd, who had tried to kill them with fire. They were silent boats passing beneath the stars, and still very faintly aglow.

Toren looked back, seeing tendrils of smoke reaching out toward them, but thinning and breaking apart before they could come so far. He dug in with an oar and thanked the faint stars that he had not been washed up at Death's gate. Not yet.

Thirty-one

They traced a small tributary down from the hills and followed its turnings through the forest. A silent company: four men, one beneath a crowd of crows, and a Fáel who was neither young nor old.

Late in the afternoon of the third day, they rode out of the wood into river bottom: gardens surrounded by tall lattice fences made of saplings covered the open valley. In some gardens, men and women bent over their plantings, but all rose to see the strangers riding through. Silently, they watched the outsiders pass, their looks apprehensive, though not hostile.

Half an hour brought them up to a small village, the houses of honey-colored stone, weathered and worn, the roofs densely thatched. There was no sign of paint. The door planks were weathered gray, window sashes the same. But everywhere there were flowers in pots and long troughs, climbing vines and trees in blossom. It was as though the flowers had escaped the fenced gardens and were invading the village, and overgrowing it slowly. Men and women emerged from doorways at the sound of horses. They too stared silently at the outsiders. Children were captured by their mothers and sent quickly inside.

Crowheart's winged army swarmed from roof to roof, scolding the silent villagers, who shrank from them visibly.

"They are a friendly lot," Fynnol said to Tam.

"I don't think they see outsiders often," Tam answered. "Like our own people."

In a few moments Alaan had led them down to a much larger river, where boats were drawn up on the shore. The crow army settled on the gunwales and on the ground, cawing raucously.

"Baore would like to see this," Cynddl said. "These boats are hollowed-out logs."

Alaan dismounted and raised his hands, palms out, to three men who were carving designs into a newly made boat. None of the men answered, but only stared, the nearest stepping back.

"Do nothing sudden," Alaan said quietly to his companions. "Draw no weapons, even if a crowd forms." He turned to the three men. "I'm Alaan. I visited your village once before."

"We remember you," one of the shipwrights said. "But then you traveled with a whist. Now you bring a company of enchanted crows."

"You need not fear them," Alaan said, and smiled reassuringly. "We've come to trade horses for a boat."

If Alaan had proposed "diamonds for dung," he could not have provoked a greater reaction.

They had not taken the best boat in trade—it was too large for their company—but very nearly. Horses, it seemed, were rare and highly valued to the villagers, and they were only too happy to provide a boat and whatever else the outsiders wanted. It was pretty clear to Tam that the man who traded for the horses thought he'd taken terrible advantage of the outsiders, and he couldn't have been happier about it.

The traveler divided the company into two watches, and each

Sean Russell

watch paddled turnabout for the rest of the afternoon, driving the
boat south. They were, Alaan told them, on the River Wynnd, or
one of its "many branches," and had a good distance to go. The sun
plunged into a range of blue hills, and the stars appeared among
scattered clouds that looked like plaster scraped over the sky.

"The moon is waning," Alaan said, "so the night will be dark.
But the river is broad and lazy. I think we should try to make some
leagues by morning. We'll give up paddling, but we'll have to stand
watches. I think the greatest danger will be getting swept up to the
shore and running aground, which will slow us—something we can
little afford."

Alaan organized three watches for the night: Tam and Fynnol,
Cynddl and Crowheart, and Alaan by himself.

Tam drew the middle watch and made a place for himself to
sleep, laying out his bedding and clothes on the floorboards, worn
smooth by use. Settling on his back, he gazed up at the stars, the
tar-black sky. The moon appeared late, drifting up from the eastern
horizon, a thin silver crescent, like the night's earring.

He thought of Elise Wills, who, Alaan said, was on the river before them. He couldn't forget the night they had lain in the grass,
a soft rain falling upon them, though he had hardly noticed. Her
kisses had been so knowing, yet at the same time she seemed as
awestruck as he by what was happening.

She is both ancient and young, he reminded himself. He closed
his eyes and felt desire course through him as he remembered Elise
moving beneath him, remembered her cries of pleasure, choked off
lest they be discovered. With these memories drifting through his
mind as he fell asleep he was surprised to be wakened later from a
very dark dream.

"Your watch," Alaan whispered.

Tam could barely make out the traveler in the darkness. The
moon had drifted into the east and was aground, and tilted oddly,
on a small island of cloud. He sat up and rubbed his eyes, trying to
shake off the nightmare. He'd been drowning, but not in water, in
some dark air.

"There is cloud in the south—quite black," Alaan said. "Perhaps a storm coming in off the sea. Be a bit wary. The river can become surprisingly rough in a storm."

Tam roused himself and stood, surveying the night world: the shadow river, glittering here and there with stars and ribbons of moonlight; black embankments and vague hills; stars still thrown high against the night. Here and there floated thin ovate clouds, but in the south Tam could see the gathering storm Alaan had spoken of. Yet it did not look quite right to him. The clouds were dark, but high and thin, tingeing the stars nearby so that they appeared almost crimson.

"Wake me if there is any trouble," Fynnol whispered.

Tam prodded his cousin with a toe. "Up, lazy Fynnol. There is a sorcerer adrift on the river. We dare not sleep."

"Sorcerer be damned," Fynnol whispered in exasperation. "What has he to do with me? Let me sleep . . . just a little more."

Tam prodded him again, this time not so gently.

"Tamlyn!"

"Up, or it's a bowl of water next."

"Ahh!" Fynnol rolled up and sat digging knuckles into his eyes. "There. Satisfied? You have ruined my perfectly lovely dream. I shall never have another like it."

"I'm sure you will have many like it," Tam said.

"No, I was so . . . adored. By everyone. Women wanted to shower me with favors—if favors can said to be showered. My every remark was repeated over and over. I could not go anywhere but people were courting me. Ah . . . it was a lovely dream."

"Better than mine. I was drowning in some dark . . . air. I can't explain it. I was so glad to have Alaan wake me."

Fynnol stretched his arms out. "Let us hope my dream is prophetic, and yours is not. Ooh! I'm sure this bed is much harder than the beds in my dreams. But then the beds in my dreams were padded with comely women, so I did not properly notice the mattresses. Hmm . . . Perhaps another visit to that wondrous place is in order."

"Not for three hours, at least. We are on watch. What do you make of these clouds in the south?" Tam could hardly see his cousin in the darkness, but was sure he turned to look down the river.

"They seem the ordinary type of clouds. You know, high in the sky, obscuring the stars. Admirably doing their job, I would say."

"Yes, but they seem a little . . . odd to me." Tam shrugged. "Perhaps you are right. Ordinary clouds. Alaan thinks it might be a storm coming in off the sea."

"We could use a little rain, Tam. I haven't had a bath or laundered my clothing in days. Do you notice how much we have come to be like the animals? Bathing when the rain falls or when we are forced to ford a river. Eating what we can catch. We have become a pack of men. Soon we shall have reverted to the wilds entirely— like the wild men of stories we heard in our youth, appearing one day out of the forest, unclothed, unkempt, snarling and grunting our idea of wit."

"Worse things could happen," Tam said distractedly, a shiver running up his back.

"Yes. We've seen it," Fynnol said, suddenly serious. "I shall never look at a river the same now that I have gazed across the final river and into the darkness beyond. Nor will I ever fall asleep without thinking of the claws of Death's servant snatching me up. If not for Slighthand I would dwell in the darkness yet—whatever that would mean. Do you ever wonder, Tam, what lies beyond the final gate?"

"Anyone who is not a fool must wonder at sometime or other. But it is a futile endeavor. Even Alaan does not know."

"Or so he says," Fynnol said softly.

Tam looked at the shadow of his cousin in the dark. "What do you mean?"

Fynnol hesitated a second, perhaps wondering if Alaan's even breathing meant he was asleep. "I felt there was something odd in his conversation with the swan lady. If stories are to be believed, she lived before Death made his kingdom. Back in the age when he was just a sorcerer. Death once loved her, Alaan claims. If anyone knows what lies within Death's kingdom, it is Meer. And who is Alaan but her grandchild—or at least Sainth was. There seems to be a quantity of family knowledge—kept from mere mortals—but known to the descendants of Tusival."

Tam had not thought of that before, but had to admit that there was some ring of truth to it. He remembered the woman they had seen, changing into a swan and back, but beautiful and youthful still. How long had she been living there, in that dying wood? How long did it seem to her, to someone who did not die? "Did she seem mad to you, Fynnol?" Tam asked.

"No . . . no, not really. Not in the way that I've seen madness, though I can't claim any great experience in that matter."

"She did not seem mad to me, either."

The Valemen fell silent, the river spinning them slowly beneath the stars.

"Do you see that cloud?" Tam said. "Is it not drawing nearer? See how much more of the sky it blocks."

Fynnol stared a moment at the sky. "I think you're right, though there is precious little we can do about it. We might find a hospitable bit of riverbank in the dark, but we're just as likely to find cliffs or a swamp. Maybe even a wood of stone trees, as we did before. Who knows what this river will offer next."

"You're right. We should stay our course till we have some light, which is still two hours off at least."

But within the hour the smoke reached them, and it quickly grew thicker. Tam woke Alaan, and everyone was soon roused by the caustic smell.

Alaan stood, gazing off into the south.

"It is a big fire, I think," Tam said standing beside Alaan. "Given how few people seem to live in these lands, I would guess it's the forest burning, not a village or a farmstead."

"Yes, I'm sure you're right, Tam," Alaan said. "But is it a natural fire?" Alaan found his sword, crouched, and pushed the blade into the river. For a while he stayed like that, still as a hunting heron. "Hafydd and Lady Elise are still some distance off and traveling more quickly than we." He dried the blade.

The eastern horizon began to brighten, and the sky overhead grew both lighter and darker at once, as their craft drifted beneath the cloud of smoke. A blackened land appeared around a bend in the river, the very earth charred to cinder, black skeletal trees standing here and there, many others fallen, misshapen stumps pushing up like arms broken and burned.

"Well, here is a scene of desolation," Cynddl said softly.

A lone bird flitted low over the dark earth, landing on a charred stump.

Whist, whist, it called.

"Yes, Jac . . . it is like a battlefield with death and destruction all around. One of many where Hafydd has ridden away unharmed, leaving devastation behind. And there will be too many more if he is not stopped, for he has allied himself with monsters, now."

"Did Hafydd cause this?" Cynddl asked.

Alaan nodded. "So I would say. He tried to slow Sianon . . . Elise and kill her followers, though I think he succeeded only in the former. Elise is not like Sianon. She will not sacrifice her followers for her own safety. Perhaps Hafydd knows this, too."

"But she is alive . . . ?" Tam whispered.

Alaan looked at him oddly. "Yes, Tam, she is alive. Fear not."

Here and there flames still flickered, finding some fuel on the darkened earth. A stand of trees, missed somehow by the all-consuming fire, burned slowly, flame climbing through the branches, which fell away one by one, spiraling slowly down like torches. No creature stirred in the bleak landscape. The companions stood up in the boat, gazing at the black hills, rolling back as far as the eye could see.

A shout surprised everyone.

"There," Crowheart said, and pointed.

A man waved from the shore. He was as blackened as the surrounding lands, his clothes smoke-stained, his face and hair dark as charcoal. The companions maneuvered their craft up to the shore, and the man limped along until he reached their landing spot.

"Alaan!" he said as he came. "Rabal! Tam!" He stopped when he realized no one recognized him. "Dease Renné, at your service," he said, and tried to smile. "I daresay, I look a sight."

"Lord Dease!" Alaan said, splashing ashore. "What has happened to you?"

"I was separated from my companions," he replied, sitting down on an inky rock. "We had all gone into the river to avoid being turned to cinders. I let go my grip on the boat a moment because the paint had bubbled beneath my hand and when I turned around, the boats were lost in the smoke."

Smoke appeared to have worked its way into all the fine lines of his face, even into his pores. His hair was singed in places, as were his clothes, which were in rags.

"I don't know what happened then, for I seem to have lost consciousness. I awoke in a little backwater, lying in the shallows, fire all around me. The bank I was on was not so hot as the other, so I crept along through the shallows. Diving under to avoid the flames and heat. Going as far as I could, then surfacing for a few lungs of smoke before diving down again. I didn't expect to survive. It seemed like hours before I was out of the worst of it. I waited for the fire to move south before I dared follow, and even then I've stayed to the river, for the land is still hot, with pockets of flame beneath the fallen trees and underwood. You step down, and flame erupts around you. Not at all safe for travel. I've been in the river, but it has not cleaned me, or so my reflection says. I fear I will be smoke-stained for the rest of my life."

"You're lucky to be alive at all," Alaan said. "But tell us who you were traveling with."

"Elise Wills and Orlem Slighthand. Your friend Baore is with them," he said to Tam, "as are Gilbert A'brgail, Eber, and his son Llya. My cousin Toren. And Theason came to conn a boat. Some Knights of the Vow and Renné men-at-arms. Perhaps twenty in all, though I have fallen by the wayside."

"No, you have just moved to the livelier company," Fynnol said. "It is an indication of your superior taste and judgment."

"But how did you find your way into the hidden lands?" Alaan asked.

Dease shifted on his rock. "Llya, Eber's son, led us. He came to the Fáel saying that he knew where Wyrr was buried and could lead us there."

"There is always some unexpected twist," Alaan said. "Where did a child learn this skill? And why didn't he tell us this before? He might have saved us a journey."

Dease shrugged. "He is a child of mystery, that one. Who can claim to understand him?"

Alaan shook his head. "Come aboard. We have to press on, fire or no."

"But can we pass the fire?" Fynnol asked. "Will we not be burned?"

"It has burned itself low now," Alaan answered, digging a paddle into the bank and straining to push them off. "There are some rocky hills not far off. Even Hafydd's fire will be hard-pressed to find fuel there."

Dease clambered aboard, rocking the boat as it slowly gained way.

"I can't quite believe that I should find a such rough-hewn boat a luxury," the nobleman said, "but after the last day, it seems the most comfortable craft afloat to me."

"Find yourself a berth, Lord Dease," Alaan said. "We will need you to take a turn at the paddles." Saying that, Alaan dug his own paddle into the river and sent the log boat quickly south.

Thirty-two

Samul woke to armed men entering his chamber, swords drawn. He was allowed to dress, his hands were bound, and in a moment he was hustled down the stairs to the front entry, where Prince Michael waited. The men wore the evening-blue surcoats of the Wills family, and were not, by the look of them, men to be trifled with. The Prince had his hands bound behind his back, as Samul did, and a look of sadness and rage on his face.

There was a disturbance on the landing above, and Franny appeared in her nightclothes, her husband catching her at the top of the stairs. They struggled there a moment.

"No, Henri! He is my cousin!"

Henri had an arm around her waist and held one hand by the wrist. "The Prince of Innes is dead," he said. "Michael cannot help us now. We have different allies. There is no going back." He pulled her away, sobbing and cursing her husband, trying to scratch at his eyes.

And then Samul and Michael were pushed outside and hoisted into a cart.

It was still dark, but Samul could see his companion by the light of torches. He thought there might have been a tear on his cheek, but then he hung his head and was silent. The driver shook the reins, and the cart rolled forward, a mounted troop of Wills men-at-arms falling in around them.

Thirty-three

Dawn was not far off, Carl thought. He crouched behind a tree, bow in hand, staring at a dark vein of road curling off into the wood below.

"Shoot the torchbearers last," Pwyll said. "The driver of the cart I'll shoot myself."

Carl pulled back the arrow he had nocked, testing the bow Pwyll had given him. His heart was pounding madly, not from fear, but because they had run like madmen to reach this place before the men carrying off the Prince and Samul Renné. The ever-resourceful Pwyll had bows and quivers of arrows he had taken from some unlucky men-at-arms—perhaps the two they'd stumbled over in the oat field.

Carl could hear Jamm gasping nearby. The thief was frightened. He wasn't much for a fight, especially one where they were outnumbered by trained men-at-arms, but Carl knew he would do his best, all the same. Pwyll, however, could not have seemed more calm. There were only eight men after all. Just a fair fight by his estimation, Carl was sure.

The drumming of horses and the clatter of wheels sounded dully through the wood, then torches appeared, bobbing and waving. The smell of smoke was carried down the dell by a night breeze.

Carl did not know the bow he was holding and would be lucky to hit anyone at all. But horses were large, and if the men rode close together, he might find some luck. He hoped only to miss his companions in the cart, which was why Pwyll insisted the driver be left for him—he'd used his bow.

Carl pulled the feathers back to his shoulder, feeling the bow flex. "Not yet," Pwyll whispered.

Around the torches shadow horsemen began to take shape, riding out of the gloom. The cart appeared, then the driver. Carl strained to see Michael and Samul in the back, but the light was too faint. He hoped they were lying down.

The riders drew nearer, growing in size it seemed.

"Now!" Pwyll whispered, and they let fly their arrows, pulling two more free. A horse rose up, and the riders drew their blades. Two more arrows flew, and at least one man toppled from his saddle. A horse spun around and crashed into another, an arrow in its face, Carl thought. A torch fell to the ground, then another was thrown, the riders realizing the light was their enemy. Several spurred their horses forward as the driverless cart shot ahead. Carl got one more arrow off, then drew his sword. The cart horse tumbled to the ground below them, the cart turning over on top of it. Two more riders went down, their horses tripping on the doubled rope Pwyll had tied across the road.

Carl followed Pwyll down the slope, where the men-at-arms were trying to get up among panicked horses. Pwyll jumped into the midst of this, his sword swinging this way and that, men falling before him.

"Michael!" Carl called in the dark, afraid of slaying the men he meant to rescue. He cut at the head above a dark surcoat and felt the sickening thud of a sword striking flesh, then bone. Dodging a horse, he threw himself on another man, though this one had found a sword. Two missed strokes, then the man went down, his leg cut from under him by Pwyll. And then all was silent but for the pounding of horses speeding into the dark. Jamm ran off and came back a moment later with a torch, examining each fallen man and taking his purse.

"They're not here," Pwyll said from the ruin of the cart. He dispatched the horse, which could not rise, with one quick, sure blow.

"Michael!" Carl called again.

"Here!" came the reply.

"Up among the trees, I think," Jamm said, and held his torch aloft.

Samul and Michael came stumbling down the slope, their hands bound behind them. Jamm cut them free.

"Who's hurt?" Pwyll asked.

"I've twisted my ankle," Samul said, and Carl could see the Renné grimacing in the poor light.

"Can you walk?" asked Pwyll.

"Yes, but I don't know how far."

"Pwyll?" the Prince said, recognizing the knight. "Are you our mysterious protector?"

"So it seems," the man-at-arms said. "You need weapons."

Swords and daggers were quickly found, as well as a basket of food in the ruins of the cart. They set off, first along the road, then through a field of high corn. Samul was hobbling, and Carl and Michael helped him where they could.

Pwyll drove them on, silently, over the starlit land. If anything he was more wary than Jamm, and seemed to know the land almost as well. By sunrise Jamm had led them to one of his hiding places, beneath a curtain of willow branches in a dense copse of trees. A little stream ran nearby, and if they had not been hunted, Carl could hardly have imagined a more pleasant spot. Jamm unwrapped the food that had been packed in the basket, and he and Carl fell on it like carrion crows.

"Well at least we got a meal and bath out of it," Samul said, eyeing his hungry companions.

Prince Michael did not seem quite so philosophical. "I hope one day I have the chance to roast poor Franny's husband over a hot forge." He glanced at Carl. "Your father was right about Henri—thrice-worthless scoundrel!"

"I will take no satisfaction in that," Carl said. "If A'tanelle was our best hope, what are we to do?"

"The army," the Prince said. "I will go directly to my father's army. Let's see how the men-at-arms feel about Menwyn Wills usurping my father's place."

"Lord Menwyn will know by now that you are on this side of the river trying to undermine his control of the army," said Pwyll, keeping his voice low. "He'll send many, many more men to find you. It is only a matter of time until we are caught."

"Then we must make all haste," the Prince said, his voice shaking with rage over his betrayal. "Where is the army of Innes, now?"

"They were east of the Isle of Battle," Carl said, "when we escaped a few days ago."

"They have moved south," Pwyll said, and when the others looked at him. "I questioned some men-at-arms not two nights past. One had a great deal to say."

Samul remembered the two men they'd found in the oats, remembered their pale, still faces in the starlight.

"Armies don't move swiftly," Michael said. "We'll catch them."

They fell silent for a while, each man alone with his thoughts. Samul took off his boot with difficulty and soaked his swollen foot in the cool waters of the stream. His jaw was sore from gritting his teeth.

"How did you come to be on this side of the river, Pwyll?" the Prince asked.

The knight shifted where he sprawled, raising himself up on one elbow. "I wish I had an answer for you, your grace—"

"Call me Michael. We're a company of beggars, here."

Pwyll plucked up a long stem of grass and began to chew on the soft end. "After nearly being drowned in the Stillwater, I was spewed out into the river on a dark night. I'd lost my sword and boots and was battered and bruised; it was all I could do to stay afloat. Fortune sent a log drifting my way, and I managed to keep hold of it until I found the shore.

"I slipped up the bank and lay for a time in the trees, gathering my strength. When the sky began to brighten I realized I'd washed ashore on the wrong side of the river and went looking for a boat, too tired to manage the long swim. I thought I'd row across by night, but before I had gone a mile huntsmen happened upon me and seemed to think I was some kind of Renné spy. We had a dispute over that, as you might imagine, and I was forced to kill them with my dagger. Fortunately, they weren't skilled with the swords they carried. One of them gave me his boots and another his sword."

"How many of them were there?"

"Oh, four or five," Pwyll said. "Are you going to eat all that food yourselves or will you give a bit to me?"

Carl and Jamm moved the basket so Pwyll could reach it, and he went on with his story as he ate.

"There were no boats to be had, and I learned that the Prince of Innes had tried to invade the Isle of Battle and been defeated in this endeavor by Kel Renné. I knew then that all the boats on this side of the river would be gathered together and well guarded, which left me to swim the river. Unfortunately, the huntsmen I killed were found, and the countryside was suddenly swarming with men-at-arms, looking for me . . . or so I thought. It turns out they were looking for some spies who'd crossed the river a few nights later. I was forced to go inland, hiding by day and skulking about the countryside by night. And then I saw the four of you— two of whom I knew—so I followed you to see what you might be up to. You know the rest."

They slept and stood watch by turns during the morning. Just after the sun reached its zenith they began to hear men calling out in the distance. Samul could see that both Jamm and Pwyll sat up, turning their heads this way and that listening to every small sound. If fortune smiled on them, these would be field workers or herds-men, but then they heard horses and, far off, a horn on the wind.

Pwyll was in a crouch now. He parted the curtain of willow branches, watched for a moment, then moved a dozen feet and did the same. Jamm looked out the other way.

"Should we climb up?" Samul wondered, gesturing to the tree, but Carl shook his head and motioned for silence—perhaps being treed was not such a good idea.

Carl had one of Pwyll's bows in hand though only a few arrows remained. Samul slipped his sword from its scabbard, feeling his mouth go dry. There were only four of them, and even with Pwyll on their side they wouldn't be a match for even a small company of mounted men. Pwyll and Carl had prevailed over their guards because of surprise—the guards didn't know how many men they faced in the darkness—and because of the ferocity of their attack. A dozen men would take the five of them down quickly—though not without losses. Samul squeezed the hilt of his sword. This is what he'd wanted—a clean death in battle. An end to all his folly, where every decision he made seemed to go awry.

Horses could be heard.

"They're coming up the stream," Jamm whispered, and plunged through the branches opposite. Samul followed, trying to go as quietly as he could. They wormed into a dense underbrush, but too late. A shout went up, and horses galloped toward them.

Samul heard arrows, and realized Pwyll and Carl were shooting. He leapt up from where he hid and saw the horsemen coming through the bush. Two went down but the others were on them instantly. Samul dodged and parried a hard blow that nearly took the sword from his hand. His bad ankle collapsed under him, and he went down awkwardly. A horseman aimed a stroke at him, but his horse stumbled, falling forward and throwing the rider. Samul struggled to his feet but the rider was up quickly, fending off Carl A'denné. The man found his balance and began to drive Carl back. Samul waded in, on the man's sword side, swinging at his arm, feinting at his knee. Despite his immense strength the man realized he was in trouble, up against two trained swordsmen. He shouted for help, but Carl managed to slash his forearm so that he dropped his sword. The man raised his hands in surrender, but Carl drove the point of his sword into man's exposed throat, yanking it free before the man fell.

Carl turned to Samul, his face grim and determined. "There are no prisoners in this war," he said, and went to the aid of Jamm.

In a moment it was over, six men down, their horses milling about but for two that had been hamstrung and lay thrashing. Prince Michael dispatched both of these cleanly, turning to the others, his face contorted in fear and rage, sweat glistening on his cheeks. Jamm was finishing off the men who still lived, which Samul could not bear to see. This was not the kind of warfare he had been trained for.

"If the sounds of this little melee have been heard, every man-at-arms within half a league will be upon us," the Prince said grimly.

"Quiet," Jamm ordered. "Listen."

They all stood gasping for breath, Samul favoring his injured ankle. It had almost cost him his life a moment ago. Pwyll and Carl caught the remaining horses and brought them under the cover of the willow.

"Samul?" Pwyll said. "Can you help?"

The Renné went to the aid of his friends, calming the horses.

After a moment Jamm appeared. "I think fortune has smiled on us," the little man said. "Though we'll not be this lucky twice."

"We're traveling too slowly," Pwyll said. "We need to put leagues between ourselves and this place. Sneaking about by night can only take us a small distance each day." He shook his head. "Not enough."

"I agree, but what else can we do?" Samul asked.

"It is time for a bold stroke," Pwyll said, tying two horses to the tree. "Help me strip these corpses. We'll hide them in the bushes. Wash the blood out of their surcoats, and ride out into the daylight. There are companies of riders going this way and that, we'll hardly be noticed. At a distance we could be anyone. Up close . . . well, four of us can pass for men-at-arms. Jamm will do if he doesn't speak."

"It's a crazy risk," Jamm said urgently.

"So is staying near here this night," Prince Michael said. "I agree with Pwyll."

"Someone will find these dead horses," Jamm said. "What will you do with those?"

"Use the other horses to drag them into the wood," Carl said.

"Anyone who sees the flattened grass and bush will want to know what caused it." Pwyll considered a moment. "There might be nothing better to do than leave them where they are and hope no one discovers them."

After some debate, they cut down bushes and hid the horses as best they could. The smell would give them away soon, anyway, as it was a warm day. They stripped the dead men and washed the blood out of their clothing as best they could. Jamm found a needle and thread in a saddlebag and turned his hand to mending the rents caused by blade and arrow.

Samul Renné felt good to be a man-at-arms again, even if he was dressed in the purple and black of the House of Innes.

"There you are, Michael," Carl said, gazing at his companion. "A Prince of Innes again."

"Just a renegade man-at-arms, I'm afraid," the Prince said.

They let the horses drink, and rode out of the protection of the trees. Pwyll led them up a nearby hill, where they could survey the countryside for some distance. Parties of riders and men on foot could be seen searching the hedgerows and woods.

"We'll have to make a show of searching as we go," Pwyll said. "But we must also make our way south with all haste. Once the dead horses and men are found the search will be on for men-at-arms dressed in purple and black. We need to be far away by morning."

Pwyll and Jamm contrived to keep them distant from any other companies they saw that day, and when a company was in view Pwyll and the others would make a show of searching along hedgerows and under thickets. Near dusk they stopped at a peasant's cottage and bought food enough for dinner and to break their fast in the morning. As night fell they stopped to eat and let the horses graze awhile. Soon after, they were riding, under a clear, starry sky. If they were seen crossing the open fields, they would appear to be men-at-arms searching the countryside—and the local people didn't interfere with men-at-arms.

In this way they approached the Isle of Battle by morning. Pwyll kept them going, tired as they were, over the dew-slick pastures. Cocks crowed as the dairymen drove their freshly milked herds out to pasture. In the east, a few strands of cloud were awash in orange and crimson.

"A perfect morning," Lord Carl said to Samul Renné.

"It is incongruously peaceful. But even so, you're right. When you believe you're seeing your last graying dawn, each one after seems a miracle."

Carl nodded, and then said quietly. "I'm concerned that Prince Michael is becoming desperate. That he might do something reckless."

Samul let his eye stray to the Prince, who rode ahead with Pwyll. A grim determination had come over him, Samul thought, as though he would either succeed or die in the attempt. "Sometimes it is the act of reckless bravado that wins men over," the Renné said.

"And sometimes it gets you killed. I've seen it."

"Yes, but this was a desperate endeavor from the beginning, Carl. The army Menwyn Wills now commands is too large, and too well equipped and trained. All the forces the Renné can muster cannot stand against it in the field. And that is without Hafydd. If he returns—and I don't know how you kill a man who has made a bargain with Death—they will roll over the land between the mountains like a winter storm. If Prince Michael can't succeed in breaking off part of that force, we will all soon be dead anyway. Dead or, if we run, dishonored."

Thirty-four

It stood in the center of the river, rising like a tall ship, stone sails billowing in the filtered light of later afternoon.

"There is your island, Sir Hafydd," Kai said. "The Isle of Waiting. The Moon's Mirror is said to lie there, though I did not see it when I traveled here with Sainth."

Hafydd rose up in the stern of the boat, staring down the river. He glanced around toward the west, shading his eyes and gauging the height of the sun. "Sunset is still some hours off. We will go ashore and find this mirror."

The island proved to be farther off than they first thought, its great height creating the illusion that it lay closer, but in time they reached its shore. Beneath the massive cliffs and towering ramparts Lord A'denné thought they must look like a water insect, skimming the green surface of the Wynnd.

"There is a landing place at the far end," Kai said, "or there was—an age ago."

What had appeared at a distance to be great billowing stone sails now proved to be the remains of walls, and all about, stairways went winding up, their stone treads weathered and worn away. Trees broke through the stone in many places, roots heaving up steps and paving stones, reaching out from between the stones of walls, doing what siege engines could likely never have done when the fortifications still stood.

As the boat passed, the men stared up at the stoneworks above. It was a quiet place, apparently dry, for many leaves had turned reddish brown, and a thin carpet of the fallen lay upon the ground and the ruined battlements. In the filtered light that fell through the high overcast of smoke, autumn seemed to have come to the isle—as though it lay outside of the time that governed the rest of the world.

At the southern end, a small, man-made lagoon welcomed them, and they drove their craft over the still waters up to a half-submerged stone quay.

Lord A'denné climbed out stiffly, stretching his back, cramped from his unaccustomed duty at the oars. As usual, the black-clad guards gathered close about their master. Another stood a few paces from the noblemen, and A'denné did not need to be told what duty he had drawn—they would never leave them unwatched again, or let them near their master without Hafydd's express command. He had wasted his one chance—and, worse, he felt that Hafydd had made a fool of him, feigning weakness to lure him into the attempt on his life. If it were possible, he hated the sorcerer even more.

Kai was lifted out of the boat and set in his barrow, where his servant tried to make him comfortable. The legless man was in agony, A'denné could see. Hafydd held back the herb Kai needed to govern his pain and portioned out just enough to keep Kai in near-constant torment. There was no reason for this cruelty that the nobleman could see, but then such viciousness was not founded in reason.

Hafydd turned on Kai then. "This is the place . . . ," the sorcerer said. "You're certain?"

"Yes. This is the place Sainth brought me," Kai said, "an age ago . . . when I still walked upon the earth."

"Then I wonder what use I have for you, Kilydd . . . ?" Hafydd said softly.

"None," the little man answered, "unless, of course, you wish to return to the land between the mountains."

Hafydd nodded to the flowing river. "Oh, I think this branch will join the Wynnd eventually."

"I wouldn't wager gold on it. This place is like no other. It lies on the border between the hidden lands and the world that we know. You will see when you climb up. The stairs do not lead where they should, nor even to the same place twice. Even Sainth was confounded. As for leaving . . . You might set out down the river, but you will soon fetch up on the shore of this island again. The Isle of Waiting, Lord Caibre. Without me you will wait here an age or more."

Hafydd turned to his guard captain. "Search him for weapons! See that he does himself no harm." Hafydd turned back to the man in the barrow but still addressed his guards. "He has harbored his pathetic life this long, I hardly think he would chose to end it now—but we will take no chances." For a moment more the knight stared at Kai, who met his gaze and would not look away.

"Haul the boat up on the quay and make it fast to a tree. We don't want to be swimming when we leave." Hafydd turned brusquely away and mounted the stair. Lord A'denné helped Ufrra and Beldor Renné bear Kai's barrow up, and it was not light, even with Ufrra taking half the weight.

There were two stairways ascending from the quay, and Hafydd chose the left. The stair wound steeply up through the autumnal trees, its uneven treads allowing not a moment of inattention. The bootblack tried to help with the barrow where he could, but was too small and almost more of a hindrance, getting under the feet of the others, until Beld warned him away. Finally, the stair crested at a landing. The bases of columns could be seen there, in a field of dried mustard-colored moss. The view over the winding river was beautiful, Lord A'denné thought. The thin light upon the treed banks, the glittering waters. Everyone caught his breath after the climb, then Hafydd turned to Kai. He gestured down what appeared to be an old walkway that sloped up and curved out of sight, cliffs both below and above.

"Where does this lead?"

Kai shrugged. "Not to the same place twice. That is the truth. I spent almost a fortnight here with Sainth, and soon gave up trying to understand the place myself. But Sainth was more tenacious, exploring every inch of the island, coming to some understanding of the maze, if anyone could understand it." The little man shrugged. "Let me warn you—do not let your company become divided, for you will not soon find each other again."

Lord A'denné saw the black guards glance at each other, apprehensive, he thought.

"We don't have a fortnight," Hafydd said, and set out along the mossy walkway.

The trees were strange, yellow trumpet flowers hanging down from some, others with whirling silver bark and leaves the colors of sunset. Beneath their feet a carpet of leaves crunched as they walked. Light filtered down through the stained sky—smoke from Hafydd setting the world afire—and the silence of the place was lulling. Lord A'denné found himself slipping into daydream, and he wanted nothing so much as to lie down and sleep.

Part of the bank had fallen away so that the pathway narrowed. Only one might pass at a time, so the entire company fetched up there, sorting themselves into single file.

A'denné fell in behind Kai, the bootblack, Stil, behind him, followed by Beldor Renné and Hafydd's last guard. The embankment had eroded away over the years and in places become so narrow that Ufrra bore Kai upon his back, while his barrow was moved with difficulty by Lord A'denné and Beldor, with Stil trying to help and getting in the way, more often than not.

At a particularly narrow point, the bank broke away beneath Stillman's feet, and the boy lost his balance and fell. Before Lord A'denné could react, Beld threw himself after the boy, the

two of them going over the edge. A'denné spun around to find
Beldor clinging to a thick root, his fist locked around the boy's
arm. A'denné and Ufrra hauled the two of them up, Beld cursing and swearing.

"Stay out of the damn way, boy!" the Renné said, brushing the
dirt from his clothes.

Lord A'denné realized that Kai was doing as he was—staring at
Beld in wonder. The cripple and the nobleman shared a look. This
was the boy who, a few days before, Beld had threatened to kill if
Kai did not lead Hafydd to this very place. And now he had almost
lost his own life trying to save him. Lord A'denné could not begin
to explain that. The man had tried to murder his own cousin. Why
would he care about the life of a bootblack? Unless there was something about young Stillman that they did not know. Or something
about Hafydd's plans.

They carried on for some time along the western shore of the
island. At last they found a stairway, though it led down. In half an
hour they arrived back at the quay on the south end of the island,
having traveled in, more or less, a straight line north. Hafydd glared
at Kai.

"It was not my doing," the legless man said evenly. "That is the
nature of this place—paths lead where they should not, where they
cannot, most would say."

"And this mirror—you don't know how to find it? Look at me
when you answer."

Kai gazed up at the knight. "If Sainth found it, he said nothing
to me—which was not unlike him, as you would know. I brought
you here, but I can do nothing more than guide you back."

The sun fell in among the hills in the distant west, setting the
river ablaze. Firewood was gathered and a rough camp pitched
there on the broken quay. Hafydd relented and gave Kai some of
the mysterious seed to subdue his suffering, though Kai did not ask
for it, nor did he ever complain. He was clearly never going to show
weakness to Hafydd.

"Tomorrow I will leave you and your servant behind with the

boy," Hafydd said to Kai over their meager supper. "A'denné, you will come with us, as will you, Lord Beldor."

A'denné spread his blankets upon the hard stone and laid his aching muscles down. He desperately needed sleep, but thought how poor such sleep would be upon this hard mattress, then he knew no more. Morning was upon him in what seemed like an instant.

The men broke their fast quickly, some bathing in the lagoon. Kai caught Lord A'denné's attention as he readied himself for another strange expedition.

"There is a flower growing here. I have seen it. It blossoms blood red and grows in little patches. It is the seed I require. If you have a chance to steal some away . . ."

Lord A'denné nodded. It was a measure of Kai's desperation that he would beg such a favor—for certainly Hafydd would be in a rage to learn anybody supplied Kai with the herb. But A'denné did not care. He was going to give his life for something, and if it could not be Hafydd's death, then relieving Kai's agony would be his cause.

Hafydd had them bear two things with them that day—a wooden box, which was trusted to Beldor Renné, and a large earthenware pot, stoppered by a cork sealed with wax. This burden Hafydd almost entrusted to A'denné, but then changed his mind and gave it to one of his guards with an admonishment not to drop it. A'denné wondered what might be carried in these two containers, and whether it might be worth his while to send either of them over a precipice—if such an opportunity were to be offered.

They went up the same stair, but at its crest found not the walkway of the previous day but another stairway branching to the right. For a moment Hafydd gazed at this, his black-clad guards glancing one to the other, shifting about uncomfortably—showing some human weakness after all.

Hafydd made up his mind quickly and led his company up, his guards scurrying to surround him. The path curved around the southern end of the island, running almost level for a time, then another set of stairs took them up. After a time they came to a place where a stair branched and climbed what appeared to be a cleft in the natural stone. It was all but overgrown, roots, and even mature trees shouldering the stones apart, breaking through to daylight. Hafydd sent two men along the now-level pathway they had been following, to see if it continued much farther, but they did not return within the hour as he ordered.

"Shall I go search for them?" Hafydd's guard captain asked.

"No," Hafydd said, shaking his head. "I should have heeded Kai's warning. Hopefully they will find their way to us again." He pointed up the stair. "We will try this way."

They climbed the stair in the warm sun, wondering what manner of place they had been carried to—where paths led off . . . but did not bring you back again.

Kai sat in his barrow in the shade of a tree that leaned over the ancient quay. Occasionally a golden flower would fall near him—like a trumpet dropping from the sky—though they made only the softest sound when they fell. The day so much resembled the one previous that Kai had the strange feeling that days were merely repeating themselves. A thin light fell through the film of smoke that still spread over the sky, and a soft breeze from the south caressed his face and carried the musky scent of the river.

Ufrra busied himself about the encampment. His big hands piled firewood that he and Stil, the bootblack, had collected. Hafydd's guard had spent the morning pacing back and forth across the broken quay, but now he sat in the sun, his back against a large block of stone. He wore no helmet, and strands of his black hair wafted in the breeze, tickling him into partial wakefulness— but then he would fall back asleep again.

A lull in the breeze hushed the whispering of the trees, and Ufrra stopped his labors. Kai nodded to him, and the mute picked up a heavy stick of firewood. He crossed to the slumbering guard without hesitation and raised the club high. Something warned the guard, and his eyes snapped open as Ufrra swung his cudgel down. The guard rolled aside, the blow glancing off his shoulder. He reached for his sword as he came to one knee, but a second stick caught him hard on the temple and stopped him cold. For a moment he seemed to hang there, frozen in time, then Ufrra struck him on the skull with a second blow, driving him to the cobbles. A third blow caved in the bone, and the guard lay still—still as the stone that made his deathbed. The boy, Stillman, stood wide-eyed and panting, his bloodied club gripped by white fingers.

"Thank you, boy," Kai said.

Ufrra crouched before the child and pried the club from his hands. The child burst into tears, and, for a moment, the mute took him awkwardly in his arms.

"Can you launch the boat yourself, do you think?" Kai asked, as the boy pulled free, wiping his eyes and nose on a sleeve.

"I'll help him," the boy volunteered.

"I'm sure you will," Kai said, "but it is a cumbersome craft for so few."

Ufrra could barely get the heavy boat to move, but they quickly levered it up and found some round sticks to lay under it to act as rollers. Kai watched the stair apprehensively as this went on.

"I think I hear voices," he whispered, as Ufrra and the boy pushed the boat toward the water. It slid the last few feet and splashed into the lagoon.

"Get the guard's sword and dagger," Kai whispered to the boy, as Ufrra wheeled his barrow toward the boat.

There was no question by then—there were voices coming from above, and they could hear footsteps thumping down the stair. Ufrra tumbled his master aboard, then dashed back to snatch up an axe and some bedding. Stillman vaulted over the gunwale as the mute shoved the boat out into the waters.

A black robe appeared at the foot of the stair then, and the guard shouted. Ufrra fit oars between the tholepins and dug them into the waters, turning the boat sluggishly about.

The guard ran to the water's edge but there he stopped, cursing—clearly unable to swim.

By the time the other guard ran out onto the quay, Ufrra was rowing out of the lagoon into the broad river. The guards found bows and came running out onto the crumbling seawall, sending arrows after the quickly retreating boat. A small rain of them spattered down around them, one lodging in the floorboards between Kai and his servant. The bootblack ducked down in the stern, trying to hide himself beneath a thwart. Fewer arrows were landing near, by then.

"We are almost out of range," Kai said to the boy. "In a moment you'll be safe."

Just then a missile came hissing down and lodged itself in Ufrra's thigh. The mute faltered, letting go one oar which thudded about between tholepins then pivoted overboard. Stillman made a dive over the side and fetched it, dripping, from the river.

He placed it back between the wooden pins and, manning that oar two-handed, helped Ufrra take them out of range, the current assisting in this endeavor. The men on the shore gave up shooting, and as they watched their prisoners escape, shouted imprecations and threats.

"Where is Hafydd?" the boy gasped as he pulled at his oar.

"Still wandering about the island," Kai said. "It seems he didn't listen to me when I warned him to keep his company together—all the better." Kai glanced down the river. "Help me into place, and I will man an oar if I can," he said. "Hafydd will be in a rage when he learns we've escaped, but even so I don't think he'll come after us. He has his master to serve. Revenge on Kilydd will have to wait—a very long time, I hope."

The island was a maze contrived by a madman—a sorcerous madman. Hafydd led them up steps and along pathways that disappeared when they tried to return. Once, they were forced to scale a near cliff, and arrived atop a ruined parapet to find a place they had passed earlier, though all were sure it had been lower down and to the south.

Hafydd took out his sword there and ordered the others to leave him in peace. He was heard muttering and chanting to himself, then he struck the flat of his blade upon a stone, making it wail and quaver like some tortured spirit of the dead.

Lord A'denné rested on a fallen log, trying not to look too interested in what Hafydd was doing. If this were magic the knight performed—and it most certainly was—then perhaps Hafydd would be weakened afterward. The nobleman glanced casually around. Hafydd's guards had been ordered to leave their lord in peace, but they had staked out a perimeter around him—ever vigilant, their eyes on the nobleman. If only there were some other to perform the assassination while the guards watched him—but there was only Beldor Renné, whose loyalty might not be certain. He had risked his life to save a bootblack. Would he not risk it to save the land between the mountains?

Hafydd turned in a circle, holding out his wailing blade. The sound made A'denné shiver, so haunting and otherworldly did it seem. Then Hafydd stopped. A'denné could make him out through the leaves. He stopped, and his eyes sprang open.

"Sianon," he whispered.

Thirty-five

They found, on the western shore, a narrow landing place from which they could climb a broken spine of fallen boulders to the low shoulder of the island above. With some effort they dragged the boats up and hid them beneath low-hanging trees.

"I don't much like putting our boats up here, where they can't be launched quickly." Orlem glanced around, a look of disapproval on his ancient face.

"We've no choice, Orlem," Elise said. "We can't leave them where they'll be easily found. And I don't think it will be the last thing you don't like on this journey. Hafydd is here before us, I'm sure."

Orlem loosened his massive sword in its scabbard and unrolled the sheepskin that held his shirt of mail. As Toren watched the giant don the rippling garment he felt glad to be on his side. If his mail weighed that much, he would be worn-out in an hour.

The others spread out the few belongings that had not been lost to the river. Some weapons had been saved, two axes, a few shirts of mail, two bows, and perhaps two dozen arrows. Baore said he could make more, for they had the heads, and he was skilled with his hands, but there was no time for that at the moment, and Toren feared there would be no time later either.

Eber, of course, was too old to wield a weapon, and Llya too young. Theason did not seem inclined to warfare, though he knew a great deal of healing, which the Renné lord was afraid would be put to use. A'brgail was a formidable warrior, as were his few Knights, and Baore had apparently been chased down the length of the Wynnd by Hafydd's guards, winning several skirmishes on the way, so there was more to him than his farm boy appearance suggested. Even with Elise and Orlem and his own men-at-arms, though, Toren feared they would be no match for Hafydd. And who knew what would stop a soul eater?— whatever that was.

Elise did not seem to need either food or rest and was soon ready to go, though most of the others were tired and hungry. Even so, they picked up what weapons they had and stood ready to follow, trying to push fear and exhaustion aside with pure will.

Elise crouched on one knee and smiled at the boy, Llya. "Do you know where we're to go now?"

Eber made some signs with his hands to be sure his son understood, but the child hardly took his eyes away from Elise. Llya shook his head. Elise messed his hair and kissed his cheek. "You have done enough."

"Lady Elise," Eber said softly, averting his face a little so his son could not see his mouth move. "I fear my son is in danger here."

Elise nodded, her face pensive. She rose to her feet and for a moment was lost in thought. "You could take a boat, perhaps with Theason, and go off down the river, but there will be no one to protect you then."

Llya seemed to register what Elise was saying and tugged on his father's robe. Quickly, he made words with his hands.

"What is he saying?" Elise asked.

"He says he must find the sleeper in the river," Eber said, a sigh present in his voice. He too crouched down so that Llya could easily see his face. "It is dangerous here," Eber said, slowly and deliberately.

But Llya shook his head and began moving his hands again, his manner surprisingly determined.

Eber did sigh then and looked up at Elise, who raised an eyebrow. "He says there is danger everywhere, now. Llya thinks we should stay with you and Baore, who he thinks is a great warrior."

Elise smiled. "Baore *is* a great warrior. He and his companions fought a company of Hafydd's guards and men-at-arms of the Prince of Innes and won. Not many could do that. They even fought Hafydd himself, as we escaped that forbidden swamp. Baore is fearless. We will make him Llya's guard, for I have other matters that will take my attention. Baore . . . ?" she said, turning to find the young man from the wildlands. "You will be Llya's guard now."

"But I am your guard, my lady," the quiet youth said.

"Yes, but I'm more able to defend myself than is Llya. Can you not look after him so that I do not worry?"

Baore bowed his head. "If that is what you wish."

Elise favored Baore with a smile that would melt many a man's heart, Toren thought. She turned back to the others. "Hafydd is here. Be wary. Speak only when you must, and then quietly."

Much of the day had slipped away, and the island cast a long shadow over the eastern shore. Toren had never been anywhere that had such a strange . . . "feel." The island was inordinately silent, apparently caught in an everlasting autumn. Even the light seemed thin and golden, as though summer wound slowly down. He expected flights of ducks and geese to pass over, chasing the descending sun into the south.

The day had been spent wandering over the isle, mounting stairs that seemed to lead them back to where they began, following paths that did not take them where they should. If Toren had not once traveled to the Stillwater by an impossible road, he would have been very disturbed by these events. But instead, he was not surprised. This place was magical—he could feel it.

They had stopped to rest at the base of a cliff on the island's northern tip, where they stood staring down the river. A tiny rill sparkled there as the water ran quickly down.

"What do you say, Orlem?" Elise asked. She stood looking around as though it were a plot of land she considered buying. "I think this is as good a place as any to make camp. There is water, and we can defend ourselves well enough."

Orlem stood and turned in a circle. They were on a rounded point of land cliffs or very steep slopes falling off to three sides. Behind them, the stream had cut a narrow gully through the rock. This was choked with branches and the trunks of fallen trees.

"It is less than perfect," Orlem pronounced, "but we might wander until darkness and not find anyplace better. I think we should not light a fire," he said.

"Yes. We have little enough to eat anyway, and there doesn't seem to be much game for the archers."

Hard, salted beef was put to soak in cups, and a berry-picking company was formed and went scouring the nearby hillside under Elise's watchful eye—for she had warned all of the pickers to keep her in sight. Theason filled his vest with edible mushrooms, and roots he said tasted like cinnamon, though no one but Eber would try them, so foul did they look. Hard little apples were plucked from a stunted tree, and Theason gathered rose hips, explaining that they were both of admirable flavor and healthful. In the end it was not such a sparse meal after all, though most could remember better.

Orlem and Elise discussed exploring the gully for a little distance, but dusk put an end to that endeavor, though Toren realized it would be their path of retreat should they be surrounded where they were. The Renné lord drew first watch, which he stood with A'brgail. Stars were clear overhead, but by the end of the first hour, they began to blur, then were obscured entirely. A cool wind arose from the south and soon began to gust through the trees, tearing away branches and spinning up little whirlwinds of leaves.

"We shall see some rain," Theason said. "Within the hour, I should say."

"Let it pour," Elise answered. "Hafydd is only half as formidable without fire." She looked around. "We might find a bit of shelter there, where the cliff overhangs."

The company moved their few belongings to the place she indicated, though there was barely room for them, let alone any place for a man to lie down and sleep. Elise went to the small stream and bent to drink, just as lightning tore open the horizon and thunder tolled across the hills.

Hafydd appeared to follow where his blade led, pointing down toward the earth. They rounded a buttress of stone where a flash of lightning illuminated a small, round pool. Hafydd stopped there, turning in a small circle.

"I sense him," the knight whispered hoarsely, and thrust his blade into the small stream leading from the pool. A flash of lightning illuminated his stark face, eyes open in surprise.

A'denné watched as the knight ran his blade back up the narrow little stream, as though cutting it carefully in two. The blade reached the small pool where the water ran thin over an ancient stone weir. As his blade entered the pool, Hafydd stopped. For a moment he crouched there, eyes closed, holding the blade utterly still with both hands. His eyes opened after a moment.

"There you are, Father," he whispered. "Death comes stalking you, at last. Can you feel him? Can you feel a son's loathing?"

"Hafydd!" Elise hissed, and leapt clear of the little stream, her sword already in hand. Rain drove down upon them, and wind whipped around the headland. She had gone to the stream to drink and staggered back suddenly.

"He is above us . . . ," Elise said, her voice low and urgent.

Orlem gazed up the stone buttress, one arm raised as though to ward of missiles. "Does he know we're here?"

"Almost certainly. I sensed him. He must have been drinking from the stream above. I can't imagine he didn't sense me as well."

They all crowded under the overhang, pushing up against the cold wall, waiting for boulders to begin dropping from above. But only wind-borne leaves spattered about them. Lightning flashed—even nearer—and thunder battered them. Rain washed out of the sky and ran like a curtain of beads from the lip of over-hanging rock.

For a long while they waited, Orlem standing over the stream, gazing up the gully, sword in hand. At each flash he raised his blade, and the others stiffened, ready to spring to his aid. Elise too, stood out in the teeming rain, her golden curls plastered straight against her glistening face.

Lightning flashed, and Elise was gone. Just as the light faded Toren found her by the now-overflowing stream, her blade in the water. A darkness of wind and thunder returned, the storm howling around them. Toren was beginning to feel chill but could not stand beneath the low-hanging rock. He felt the need to move, or he would begin to shiver and stiffen, so he pushed himself out into the weather, rain finding him immediately. It ran in slow, cold streams down his neck and back.

"He's gone . . . ," Elise said, as a peal of thunder faded.

"Gone where, my lady?" Orlem asked.

"I don't know, Orlem. He is traveling away from us, and quickly."

"It is not a trick?"

A flash of lightning and explosion of thunder interrupted conversation. The light revealed Elise, still with her sword in the water.

"I don't think it's a trick. Hafydd knows what Sianon could do with water . . . but even so, I wouldn't wager that he is running."

Darkness descended, and when the lightning flashed next, Toren saw Elise, her wet cloak fluttering madly in the ferocious wind, climbing up into the mouth of the gully, which ran deep with water.

"Come!" Orlem called the others. "We can't wait for the storm to subside." He paused, his face changing. "I'm sorry, Eber, but I don't think we can leave you and your son here."

Toren and A'brgail took up their position again at the rear of the column, and they went wading and slipping up the raging little stream. Water had risen to midthigh and ran with surprising speed and force down the ravine. Where they could they climbed above it, straddling the torrent, but often there was no purchase, and they had to force their way against the stream. Many times someone slipped and tumbled down on those below, and it was only a wonder that they didn't all end up in a broken heap at the bottom. A'brgail's Knights ended up carrying Eber between them, and Llya rode Baore's broad back, clinging to the Valeman's neck. They waited for each lightning flash, then moved as quickly as they could, trying to memorize a few feet ahead. Once, the heavy clouds parted to reveal the speeding moon, and they all scrambled up as best they could before the clouds shut, stealing the faint light away.

Toren didn't know how long the climb took, but when he reached the top his feet were numb, and he fell down on the trampled grass, gasping for breath. The rain continued to batter them without respite. Only Elise and Orlem were on their feet, exploring the ground carefully, wary as animals.

The clouds still raced overhead, a faint blemish of light waxing and waning where the newly risen moon flew. In this faint light Toren could make out Orlem, crouching by the pool.

"Do you see these boot prints?" Orlem asked. He bent low, his face inches from the ground. "They come to the water's edge, but I can't find where they lead away. . . . And these as well."

"As though they went into the pool . . . ," Elise said softly, her words snatched away by the wind.

"They must emerge on the other side," A'brgail said, rising with some difficulty.

Orlem beat the knight to the opposite edge, but then he walked around, pausing in each flash of lightning to look closely at the water's edge. "I can't find them," he said after a moment.

At that moment the moon passed through a thin patch of cloud, and Orlem stopped in his tracks.

"*The Moon's Mirror,*" Elise said, and dove into the waters, as graceful as a swan.

Thirty-six

Alaan came quickly up the stairs, careful to make no sound. "There are three of Hafydd's guards below," he whispered, "one sleeping."

Tam looked at Cynddl, whose face was suddenly grave. They had come there hoping that Elise might be found, for this was the island's ancient landing spot. But Elise was not here.

"We can't leave them here," Alaan whispered. He saw the reaction of his companions; they did not like to kill men in cold blood. "They might come upon us from behind"—he looked from Tam to Cynddl—"and they will not hesitate to kill us."

Cynddl bent his bow and dropped the bowstring into its notch. Tam took a long breath and did the same. He hadn't much stomach for what they were about to do.

They nodded to Alaan, and he started down the stair, silent as a breeze. The others followed, careful where they placed their feet, Cynddl watching their backs as they went. After a brief descent Alaan stopped. The river could just be made out through the leaves of trees. Tam thought two dark shapes must be Hafydd's guards, but could not be sure.

Alaan leaned close to his ear, and whispered. "Come down a little farther where you can see them better. Wait until I reach the bottom of the stair, then shoot the guards. If somehow one escapes, I'll see to him." Alaan paused. "They'll be wearing mail shirts."

Tam nodded, and Alaan whispered the same thing to the Fáel. All three climbed down a few more stairs, where Tam could not mistake a black tree trunk for one of Hafydd's guards. He nocked an arrow and placed three others within easy reach. A glance up told him the stair above was still empty. Cynddl caught his eye and turned down his mouth. Neither liked what they were about to do, but these were the same men who had shot Baore and tried to kill them more than once. It was a war, after all.

The call of a sorcerer thrush wafted through the wood—almost enough to make Tam smile. He pulled back the arrow, sighting carefully, not forgetting that they shot downhill and need not allow so much for the arrow's arc.

"Ready?" Cynddl whispered.

Tam nodded, and they let their arrows fly. Tam heard them flash through the leaves but hardly looked to see whether they found their mark. Instead he snatched up another arrow, and set it in place. Beyond the curtain of leaves, a dark form staggered, bent double, but before Tam could shoot again he saw another moving, quick and direct. Alaan dispatched the man in a stroke and went after another. Cynddl put an arrow in the sleeper, who had not wakened, or moved at all.

When Tam and the story finder reached the bottom of the stair, they found Alaan crouched over one of Hafydd's guards, who had an arrow in his chest, the Fáel bow proving stronger than links of iron once again.

"We don't know," the man whispered, trembling with the pain. He choked and spat up blood, then gasped horribly. "We were separated . . . lost."

Alaan took the point of his blade away from the guard's throat and stood up.

"The third man was already dead," Alaan said, a dark look crossing his face. "Kai was here, but escaped in the boat after the guard was killed." He gazed down the river.

"What of this one?" Cynddl asked, afraid to hear the answer.

The man lay, eyes closed, jaw clenched against the pain, sweat bathing his face. He choked again.

"I promised him a clean death," Alaan said. "He's seen men drown in their own blood before."

Cynddl and Tam turned away but had not taken a step when they heard the unmistakable sound of a blade cutting into flesh. Tam closed his eyes.

"Come," Alaan said, his voice subdued. "We'll give them to the river."

The three bodies were dragged to the western shore, crows calling from the trees, scolding the men. Alaan took the guards' swords and daggers and peeled off their mail shirts so that the bodies might drift downstream. One at a time they were slipped into the river, the current taking them in its soft fist. For a moment they lay, half-submerged, then they slid beneath the surface, into the cool, dark depths of the River Wynnd.

"Their war is over," Alaan said gently, as though they were not his enemies. "But ours is not."

They reached the bottom of the stair, and Alaan stopped, looking up at the sun, appearing to listen carefully. "Quick now, before the stair leads somewhere else."

They went bounding up the uneven treads.

"But how do you know where it leads when?" Cynddl asked as they ran.

"It is the gift given to Sainth by his father. Though even so, it took Sainth some study to get the lay of the land here. It is an island in flux, the destination of this stairway changing even as we climb it. Hurry, if we don't reach our companions soon it will be a long wait."

They found their friends at the top of a short, overgrown cliff. While Alaan and the others were away, they had thrown ropes over stout branches that overhung the river, and using them like ships' davits, had hauled the boat up where it swung gently, well hidden from anyone on water or land.

Crowheart, as always, appeared quietly fascinated with anyplace they traveled. Dease, still gray-faced with smoke, climbed up onto the island's low shoulder and smiled weakly at Tam. The Renné had not yet recovered from his ordeal in the river, and their hours of paddling had left him utterly exhausted. Tam thought Dease went forward only on pride.

Gear was quickly gathered up and portioned out, and as they packed their gear, Fynnol came over and began fussing with his pack beside Tam.

"So, what happened?" he said quietly. "You look as grim as I can remember, Cousin."

"We found three of Hafydd's guards, though one was already dead. We shot them and Alaan finished the last of them after he'd answered some questions."

"One of Hafydd's guards divulged information about his master!"

"Nothing particularly useful."

"Ah." Fynnol hefted his pack up and swung it into place. "And where are we going now?"

"We are following Alaan. And I would stay close if I were you. This island is like the River Wynnd; its paths don't always lead where you're expecting, or even to the same place twice."

"Should we be on the lookout for this soul eater?" Cynddl asked Alaan.

Alaan stopped packing his gear. "Not yet. It can't exist by day. Hafydd will create it after sunset, and by the last hours of darkness it will have begun to die, passing the peak of its strength in the middle hours between sunset and sunrise."

Tam shivered. "How do we fight this monster?" he asked.

"You don't. It can't be harmed by any weapon devised by men.

Its skin is more impenetrable than the finest mail, and it's stronger than the nichmear, though not as large, or so the stories say." Alaan looked suddenly troubled. "Listen, all of you. This thing that Hafydd will make is of the ancient world and more powerful than we can understand. You cannot hope to stand against it. It killed Tusival, the most powerful sorcerer who ever lived. If we can't stop Hafydd from creating it . . ." He did not finish; nor did he need to.

"I suppose the question, then," Fynnol said, "is, how do we kill Hafydd?"

"A more reasonable proposition," Alaan answered, "but still not easily done. If Elise is here, we might prevail against Hafydd, the two of us, but if he finds us one at a time, we shall be lucky to survive."

"He has never caught you yet," Crowheart offered, breaking his silence.

"No, not in this life," Alaan said softly. "There is one possibility. The spell to create a soul eater would be very complicated—too complicated to perform from memory. It will be written down, in a book, most likely. Even the book would not be easy to destroy, but if we meet Hafydd, that book would be more important than any of our lives—mine included."

Thirty-seven

Menwyn Wills stood at his field desk studying a map of the River Wynnd. His finger traced the gently winding river, seeking a small creek.

"Vast has earned his reward," he said.

A counselor of the Duke of Vast stood looking on. "He has kept his part of the bargain, your grace."

Menwyn straightened, gazing down at the map, seeing the land the way an eagle might from high above. "Unfortunately, the Duke hasn't given me much warning."

"It couldn't be helped, your grace. The Renné debated too long."

"I'm sure they did." Menwyn tapped a finger on the map. "Vast is certain this is the place?"

"Yes."

"Then we'll prepare the welcome." Menwyn moved slowly around the table, his eyes still fixed on the map. He crossed to the western shore, Renné lands, and began noting the names of towns, the borders of estates, which had been drawn on the paper so that he could begin dividing up the lands.

"If the Renné were smart, they would stay on the western shore and wait for us to cross. They might defend the river against us . . . for a time."

"They are wagering everything on a quick strike, your grace."

"It is more than that. After the debacle on the Isle of Battle they think me a bungler. But it was Innes who planned that . . . and your Duke was with the Renné then. If the Prince had listened to me, Vast would have been on our side, and he would have turned the tide of that battle in our favor. That mistake has been corrected." Menwyn Wills put his finger on the Westbrook, tracing it from its source to Castle Renné, near its mouth. "Can you carry a warning to Vast? Is it possible?"

"It would be difficult. Time is short, and the riverbank is watched."

"You must try, all the same. Prince Michael of Innes appeared at the home of his cousin not a day ago. He was seeking supporters among his father's officers and allies—hoping to wrest control of the army from me." Lord Menwyn glanced up from the map to see the reaction of this man. "Fortunately, this cousin had decided to join the victorious side sometime before. He sent word, and a company of men-at-arms was sent to his house."

"Luck sides with the virtuous."

"I hope you're wrong. The Prince was rescued while being brought to me. We haven't managed to find him yet, despite all our efforts."

The man had no platitude for that but shifted uncomfortably.

"The odd thing about this was that the young prince was accompanied by a Renné—Lord Archer Renné, apparently." He looked up at the man. "Do you know him?"

"Only by reputation. He is . . . reclusive. It's said he suffers from an injury he received in the tourney some years back."

"Exactly. The Prince's cousin thought this man looked remarkably like Samul Renné. In fact, he thought it was Samul

Renné, though he had seen him only once before and some years ago."

"Samul Renné was executed, your grace. I witnessed it myself."

"Then you're certain? You saw Lord Samul die?"

The man hesitated a moment. "I saw the head fall into a basket. I was some small distance off, in a window." He thought. "The gallows was obscured by black hangings—a custom of the Renné, I was told."

"So you didn't see the axe fall?"

"No. I saw Lord Samul and Carl A'denné led up onto the gallows platform, along with a thief who had assisted in Lord Carl's escape. They were men going to their deaths—I could see the fear, even though they bore themselves well. A moment later the executioner went to work and the heads fell rather gruesomely into a basket. It could have been no other."

"Would you wager your life on it?"

The man stood looking foolish, blinking rapidly. "I did not examine the heads up close. It was early morning, just before sunrise. The light was poor."

"Then you should pass this along to Vast: if Lord Samul's death was feigned, then Carl A'denné's might have been as well. And if that is the case, the Renné believed Lord Carl . . . and are playing Vast for a fool. Warn the Duke of that, and find out if Archer Renné sits safely at home. I need to know if this information Vast has given me is true—or if it is a Renné deception." He put his finger on the small creek where it met the River Wynnd. "When I meet the Renné I don't want any surprises."

Thirty-eight

The white eye of a nagar gazed at her, then blinked closed.

The moon, Elise realized, *slipping behind a lid of clouds.*

She was sinking through liquid so black, it was like the space between the stars. And then she was falling, hard, like a stone through the air. She struck and lay for a moment, dazed.

"Orlem? Orlem . . . ?" Her whisper echoed in the dark. She pushed herself up into a sitting position, the world spinning. "But I was with Slighthand. . . ." A flash came from above, and she looked up.

"Impossible," she heard herself say. Another flash a moment later showed the same thing—what appeared to be water, but above her, as though she looked down into a pool. It took a bit of an effort to gain her feet, for her leg had been hurt in the fall. Elise tried to reach up, but what appeared to be water was too high— just out of reach. Another flash revealed her surroundings. She was in a round chamber with walls of natural stone—but the floor . . . the floor was an ancient mosaic, partly buried in sand and pebbles and old leaves. A dark arch led into a tunnel and opposite it a narrow stair had been carved from the natural stone. It followed the curve of the wall up into the pool overhead. Darkness returned.

Elise shook her head, trying to clear it, and hobbled stiffly in the direction she hoped the stair lay. Her hands found the stone wall in the darkness, then another flare of lightning illuminated the chamber. She had missed the stair by a good distance.

"I'm half in a daze," she muttered to no one, and felt along the wall until she encountered the stair. It was almost impossibly narrow, forcing Elise to climb with her back against the wall and her toes off the treads. She moved up, one step, then another, her stiff leg threatening to collapse each time she put weight on it. In a moment she reached the water, which, when illuminated by a glare of lightning, appeared to wash back and forth above her like water in a glass. She took a step up and felt cold liquid touch the top of her scalp. Another step, and she was in water—Sianon's natural element for the last age of the world. A few more steps, and she kicked free, swimming up, up toward the world above.

"Bring the child to me," she said, gesturing to Baore.

Toren Renné and his companions stared at Elise dumbly for a moment. A flash of lightning revealed her, up to the waist in water, skin unnaturally pale, eyes waxen and strange. The appearance of this half nagar among them disturbed the men-at-arms, who all stepped back. Some made warding signs.

"We have no time for superstition," she snapped, climbing out of the water and approaching Eber and Llya. "The pool is an entrance to a tunnel. Below the water, perhaps eight feet, there is air, the water suspended overhead by a spell the likes of which I have never seen. I will take the child, then Eber, but the rest of you must jump in. Carry your weapons or something heavy. Let yourself sink down, and be prepared to suddenly drop another eight feet onto a smooth stone floor." She swept up Llya. "He will be safe with me, don't worry," she assured his anxious father.

Elise took two steps and plunged, feetfirst, into the pool. No one moved to follow.

"We must do as Lady Elise says," Orlem announced. He sheathed his sword and leapt into the waters behind her, disappearing in a splash.

Thirty-nine

The water glowed pale green, like the wake of a ship in the summer sea. Elise began to knead the liquid with her hands, humming or chanting all the while, and the water took on substance; a pale opalescent jellyfish. The passageway, the faces of their companions, all turned a soft green in this light. Toren felt as though he were below the water—which in a sense he was; below the water in a bubble of air.

Elise plunged the blade of her sword through the glowing mass, and withdrew it, glistening green. She passed the mass to Orlem, who did the same. The giant offered the mass to A'brgail, who, Toren noted, hesitated only a second before doing as Elise and Orlem had done. It seemed even A'brgail could become accustomed to the arcane.

"It will stick to iron or steel, less well to brass. Your hands might glow faintly for a few moments after you've touched it, but that will quickly fade. Run the blade of your sword or dagger through it quickly."

A'brgail handed the mass to Toren, who was surprised at the

coolness of the "witch water," as Elise called it. Very quickly they had a number of blades aglow, casting an eerie green light over the smooth stone.

Elise pointed to the floor of the tunnel, which was wet. "Hafydd is before us," she said. "Here is his track."

She led them at a jog, her glowing blade held ready.

The tunnel quickly proved to be a hallway, for a distance carved out of the island's bedrock, then the right-hand wall became enormous blocks of tightly fitted granite. Here and there a kind of writing could be seen carved into the wall, and though Elise stopped to regard this, if she could read it, she did not say.

The passageway descended and curved slightly to the left. After perhaps two hundred feet, side passages began to open up, first to the left, then to either side. Elise stopped at each and lifted her sword high, illuminating the writing over the openings.

"Do these signs mean anything?" A'brgail asked.

Elise shook her head, her tangle of wet hair spraying drops of water into the air. "It appears to be an early form of an ancient language that Sianon knew. Some words I recognize, a few others I can guess at. This passage we are in seems to have been called the 'east nool.' Nool, I would guess, means passage or hallway. Have you ever seen such signs before, Orlem?"

"I have not, my lady."

She glanced down at the wet floor. "It does not matter. We follow Hafydd's track. Let's hope we are not so slow that their clothing dries." She set off again at a jog.

But in a hundred yards Hafydd's trail disappeared at a blank stone wall.

Orlem tapped his pommel on the stone and examined the edges by the glow of his blade. "It appears to be seamless . . . solid rock. Not a slab that has been rolled into place."

Elise nodded, her look pensive but not surprised.

"What devilry does Hafydd practice?" A'brgail asked.

"It was not Hafydd," Elise stated evenly. "It is this place. Even the passageways change." She touched a hand to the wall. "Orlem?

You have some of Sainth's ability to travel the hidden paths, can you find your way here?"

"I cannot, my lady. Even Sainth might be confused in such a place."

"I fear you're right. Let's hope that Hafydd fares no better. We must make a map as we go. We might have to explore many passages before we find what we seek."

"I'll make the map, Lady Elise," Theason said, with something near to enthusiasm. He took from his jacket a small notebook wrapped many times in heavy, oiled cotton. "Hardly wet at all," he assured everyone. He found a writing implement and began drawing immediately, reminding Toren of Kai—the man they called the mapmaker.

"There was a branch not far back—let's see where it will take us," Elise said.

The company retreated in their bubble of pale green light, A'brgail and Toren Renné bringing up the rear, listening for any sounds behind them.

"Have you ever seen such a place?" Toren whispered to A'brgail.

"No. Even the great ancient fortresses of the Knights were small and crude compared to this."

Toren nodded. "They must have had mighty enemies to make such a stronghold."

"Or mighty fears."

The tunnel was wide enough for three to walk abreast, though they went in groups of two, dripping water behind from their plunge through the pool. Elise stopped suddenly, crouching down. Toren pushed through the group until he could see. The floor was wet there, a thin stream of water seeming to emerge from the wall.

"Is it our track or Hafydd's?" Toren asked.

"Hafydd's," Elise said, rising. "I can't find Orlem's boot print here." She dashed on, her light footstep echoing in the ancient hall.

Hafydd stared at the floor of the tunnel as though it had somehow offended him. He crouched, and Beldor Renné half expected him to smash the floor with his fist, but instead he reached out and rubbed his hand over the water that lay there in droplets and small pools.

"We are wandering in circles," A'denné pronounced. Unlike everyone else he ignored Hafydd's dark moods and spoke whenever the urge struck.

Hafydd appeared not to hear but rose to his feet and motioned for his captain. "Pick two good men for rear guards. Sianon is here and not alone." He spun on his heel and set off down the hallway.

In fifty yards they came to a splitting of the way—three passages going off at different angles. Hafydd held a torch aloft, examining the writing. "I shall kill Kai when I find him next," he said evenly. He waved his torch. "This way."

The passage went less than a hundred feet before it branched in two. Sianon had apparently gone left. Hafydd hesitated only a moment, then took the right-hand passage, which appeared to lead down. Fifty feet along, three side passages opened up, two to the right, one to the left. Hafydd took the second opening to the right.

The tunnel split again not far off. Hafydd stopped here for some moments, examining the marks on the walls. He even took out his sword and banged it once against stone, so that it rang an unholy note, echoing and distorting off the walls. But divining did not seem to offer an answer, and after a moment he sheathed his sword again. Beldor could see that Hafydd's mood had become more than dark. Even A'denné had the good sense to stay quiet.

The left passage was chosen this time, and it soon curved sharply around and angled slightly down. A'denné caught Beld's eye and raised his eyebrows, then shrugged. Beld thought it was as articulate as one could get about this place, which appeared to defy reason.

An odd, distant sound reached them, echoing strangely against the stone, but no one knew what it was. The passage ended in a narrow opening, and beyond was a circular stairwell that wound steeply down. Hafydd stuck his head through the opening, and with no further hesitation, started down, his footsteps echoing and distorting back up the well. Beldor thought they sounded almost like words.

After thirty steps Beld began to feel as though he had entered an icehouse, and his breath appeared. "Autumn outside, winter inside," he muttered to himself. Stairs, endless and ancient, kept appearing before him, curving vertiginously round and round, and the strange sound, almost a ringing, grew louder and louder.

At the bottom of the stair they emerged into a massive domed hall, eight-sided and lavishly decorated, though the light from their small torches illuminated it only dimly. Beldor stopped and turned a slow circle, while Hafydd continued out into the center of the hall.

"It is a lovely bedchamber, Father," Hafydd whispered. "But I have come to wake you, at last."

Alaan stood staring at the pool, which they had finally reached after an endless hike up and down stairs and slopes drenched by rain. Dease was so tired he fell down on the mud and wet grass and hid his head in his arms.

"Where are we now?" Crowheart wondered.

"This is the place I was seeking." Alaan crouched, looking at the ground. Lightning flashed off in the distance, offering its faint light. "But someone is here before us."

"Who?" Fynnol asked.

"Orlem, certainly," Alaan said, pointing out a massive boot print. "And with luck that means Elise Wills as well." He gazed at the ground a moment, awaiting the little flashes of light that came from far away. "But there are many footprints here. I fear Hafydd found this place before us."

"And where have they all gone?" Fynnol asked, looking around.

But Alaan did not answer; he stared at the pool a moment, as though the sight of it robbed him of speech and reason.

"*Into the pool*," he whispered. "*They've gone into the pool.*" He walked quickly around the water's edge, examining the ground by lightning flash. "And not come out again. . . ."

They began to find storage rooms as they reached the lower level: an armory; a spirits room where casks still stood against the wall; a bakery with a great hearth.

Toren lingered there a moment, as though he could almost hear the former inhabitants. He closed his eyes and listened.

"Do you hear it?" a voice asked.

Toren opened his eyes to find Eber and Llya, halfway out the door, gazing at him.

"Hear what?" Toren responded.

"The whispers," Eber said. "As though he were trying to speak to us in the smallest breezes, the silences."

Toren shook his head. "I hear nothing."

"Lord Toren? Eber?" It was A'brgail calling. "We mustn't become separated from the others."

Toren nodded and pushed quickly past Eber and his son, feeling the child's large, knowing eyes on his back.

The vastness of the maze began to make itself clear as they walked, miles passing beneath their feet, though they arrived nowhere.

"Do you think we're still on the island?" Toren wondered aloud, as they stopped to consider another side passage.

"I think we are, Lord Toren," Elise answered. "Though it is only a feeling—an intuition." None of the urgency had gone out of Elise's step. Though Toren knew that facing Hafydd frightened her, the fear didn't seem to dim her determination.

They made their way down this new passage, descending at a shallow angle. After a short while a soft metallic tinkling reached them. It echoed and distorted up the tunnel, never growing louder though occasionally fading almost completely, only to return as they progressed.

Passages opened up sporadically, and at each Elise would listen carefully, then choose the tunnel from which the sound seemed to emanate.

"What could that be?" Orlem asked, as they stopped to listen at another opening.

"Water running, I hope," said Elise.

"But it sounds like small bells ringing," the giant said.

"I pray you're wrong, Orlem," Elise said. "We can't drink bells, and our waterskins are rapidly emptying."

The giant glanced down at the waterskin that hung from a strap over his shoulder, it sloshed when he walked, less than a quarter full.

"Do you know what I find odd?" Eber said softly. Llya had fallen asleep riding on Baore's back, his head bouncing on the Valeman's shoulder. Eber himself looked ready to fall asleep.

"What, Eber?"

"Though we have traveled all about, we have never found our way back to the pool where we entered the tunnels."

Elise nodded, her look thoughtful. "The maze has not done with us yet."

"Or people who find their way in here never leave . . ." A'brgail said prophetically. He met no one's eye after offering this bit of speculation.

"I doubt anyone has been here before us, Sir Gilbert," Elise said. "The place is too well hidden."

"Unless someone who had not the skill to stay afloat fell into the pool . . ." Eber suggested.

"Hurry on," Elise said. "No amount of speculation will change the task we have come here to perform. Hafydd has to be stopped whether we are to find our way out or not." Her eye fixed on Llya, asleep on Baore's shoulder, his face the epitome of innocence. She reached out as though she would touch his cheek, but then stopped, sadness and regret overwhelming her look of resolution. Quickly, she turned away and set off down the passage, the metallic tinkling echoing softly around them.

At length the passage ended at a narrow opening, ornately decorated with signs and symbols they had not seen before. Elise held her blade aloft for a moment, examining them, but then shook her head and thrust the blade into the opening, leaning in to see what lay beyond.

"It's a stair," she announced, "circling down. A cold stair."

Elise pushed through, and Toren could hear her steps echoing against the unforgiving stone. Slighthand followed, forcing his large frame through the narrow opening. The rest went in turn, one man at a time. When Toren's turn came he found himself in what looked like a well, perfectly round and vertical, but with a winding stone stair circling down. Unlike the other tunnels, this well was as cold as an icehouse, and he quickly learned not to touch the frigid walls for balance. His own blade lit the way for him, and he followed the retreating back of Gilbert A'brgail, round and round. It was impossible to guess how far they descended—a very great distance, Toren thought, and he was sure it grew colder with each step.

Baore stopped momentarily to drape his massive cloak over Llya, who stood blinking and rubbing his eyes, the cloak flowing onto the floor around.

"Winter appears to await below." Toren helped Baore arrange the cloak over the child. "Damn, it is cold!"

Baore scooped the child up again. "I'm from the north," the Valeman said. "Cold is afraid of me."

They went more quickly then, round and round, trying to stay warm with movement. Toren caught sight of Elise's retreating back, tangled yellow hair bobbing. She went swiftly, as though their long march and time on the river had not tired her at all. The others straggled behind, Eber supported by Theason.

"There is light below," someone called up the well, and the column slowed its descent, suddenly wary. Toren saw the glowing swords below rise up, ready to do battle, faces appeared in the cool light, drawn and pale.

A few more steps, and they stopped entirely. Someone waved a hand at them. "Lord Toren. Sir Gilbert. Please, come down."

The others pressed against the ice-cold walls to let them pass.

Elise waited below. Above the murmur of what was clearly running water, a voice droned though Toren could not make out the words. Elise looked up at them, her face a ruin of anguish.

"Hafydd makes the soul eater," she said, her voice colder than the air. "We must sacrifice everything to stop him . . . if we're not already too late."

Forty

The army camped in a broad coomb through which ran a clear stream. The ridges to the north and south were steeply wooded and alive with swift streams that burbled and whispered to each other day and night. Samul gazed down at the army below and felt a shiver course through him. It was larger than he imagined. Three or four times greater than any force the Renné could muster.

"Now I understand why my cousins were so desperate," he whispered. "Look at Menwyn's army!"

"It is Hafydd's army," Pwyll answered softly, "as Lord Menwyn will learn to his dismay."

"It was the army of the Prince of Innes," Prince Michael said, "and will be again."

"Whoever it is loyal to, this is an army preparing to go into battle," Lord Samul offered. "They're forming ranks and getting ready to move. Either they are about to cross the Wynnd or they think the Renné are approaching. They'll slaughter Fondor's army if he is foolish enough to cross the river."

"He's not so foolish," Carl said, glancing at Samul, but he said no more.

Prince Michael turned to the others where they crouched, staring out from behind a fallen oak. "What I must do next I must do alone. Against these tens of thousands, even Pwyll's blade will be of no avail." He turned to Carl. "You have fulfilled your part of the bargain—you and Jamm. You brought me here. Though we could not have done it without you, Pwyll. You have all done your parts. Now I must do mine."

He went back through the wood and found their horses. From the saddlebag of one he took a banner of the House of Innes and fixed it to a pole cut from the forest. Nodding once to each of them, he mounted his horse, and, swinging the banner high, set off down the hill.

His feet pushing hard against the stirrups, Prince Michael felt the shoulders of his horse working as it went slowly down the path. Emerging from the trees, he angled across the meadow directly for an opening in the ring of stakes. A dozen men-at-arms stood guard there. They saw him coming from a distance, but thought nothing of it, for riders came and went regularly there.

The Prince wasn't sure how he would handle this moment. He doubted that Menwyn Wills had left orders for how to deal with a sudden appearance of the Prince of Innes, but one could never be sure. If the guards recognized him, he would simply ride through, hoping surprise would grant him that moment's reprieve. If they didn't recognize him, he would have to improvise. He couldn't let himself be taken quietly to Menwyn Wills—that would be the end of him.

The Prince felt an odd sense of floating as he rode toward the unsuspecting guards. As though he watched the entire proceedings from somewhere else—from up on the ridge with his fugitive companions. The sound of his horse seemed to come to him from afar—the creak of his saddle, the banner fluttering in the wind. The pale, silent faces of the guards seemed to loom up before him, staring, as though they had seen a ghost.

"I am Prince Michael of Innes," he said to them from afar, "remain as you are."

"Your grace . . . ," one of the men whispered, his face white with surprise.

"You cannot pass," another guard said, stepping forward and reaching for his sword. "We have orders—"

But a third guard restrained him with a firm hand on his arm. "It is the Prince, you idiot. He does not need papers."

The guards bowed their heads quickly as he passed, but one went running ahead. "The Prince!" he called. "Prince Michael has returned."

The men had been formed into ranks, but then allowed to sit and talk quietly among themselves while they awaited orders to march. Down the long lane that divided the camp, the Prince rode, lines of infantry to either side. He wore the stolen livery of the soldiers of Innes, and over his head fluttered the banner of his House. The calling of the guard who ran before drew the men's gaze, and many who knew him rose to their feet. A murmur swept down the ranks, like a wave, and the men began to rise to have a better view. To either side a sea of disbelieving faces. And then he saw a man he knew who had once been a house guard.

"Rica," he said, and nodded.

"Your grace . . ." the man said, his eyes suddenly gleaming. "We were told you were dead."

"Too many lies have been told in my absence. Find twenty men you trust and fall in behind me."

"But, your grace," the man said, "we have been ordered into ranks. . . ."

"And now you have been ordered out. Do you take orders from the Prince of Innes or Menwyn Wills?"

The man drew himself up. "I take orders from the Prince of Innes," he said, and began calling out names.

Another two hundred feet the Prince rode, his newly formed

guard falling in behind him. There, almost in the encampment's center, he stopped. The army of Innes was in such a state that the men almost broke ranks to see if the rumor were true. Michael stopped a moment, turning his mount in a slow circle, letting the men get a good look at him. Down the lane he could see officers and men of high rank striding quickly out to see what this fuss could be. Michael knew he had only a moment. He stood up in his stirrups.

"I am Prince Michael of Innes," he declared loudly, "and I have returned to you by a difficult road. I know it was said that I had died, but you were also told that my father was assassinated by his own guard—which we all know was a lie. He was murdered by men who claimed to be his allies. The same men who thought I had been killed . . . , but I escaped and came back to you."

A hush had fallen over the army, though far off the rumor still traveled, like distant surf. The officers and noblemen were all but running by then. One of them was shouting, but the sudden roar of the army drowned him out. The men broke ranks, pouring over the field toward the Prince. Rica and his twenty guards formed a circle around him, trying to hold the men back a few feet at least. Michael could see all the faces gazing up at him in wonder, returned from the dead, as it must have seemed—and was in ways these men would never know.

Men he knew began to shout their names to him, and he waved these closer, saying, "Let them through."

The noblemen, once allies of his fathers, and officers, were hopelessly cut off. Michael could see the group of them hemmed in and being tossed about like a boat on a storm. The Prince knew that if he pointed at them and denounced them now, they would be in great danger, but he hoped there were some among them who were still loyal to his House, and he didn't want to risk their lives. He would need them yet.

Now was the moment to confront Menwyn Wills and his cabal . . . if he could move this mass of men, for he had earlier picked out the banners of Menwyn Wills flying at the far end of the encampment. He began pointing with his banner and moving his horse that way. The men around him quickly understood and started calling out. "To Lord Menwyn! We go to address Lord Menwyn Wills!"

Progress was almost imperceptible, but inch by inch Michael made his way down the length of the camp, the center of a roiling mass of men, all of whom wanted to get a look at him, and who called out his name over and over. Many reached out and he touched their hands as though to prove that he was not a ghost.

The strangeness of it all was not lost on Michael, who had never been so loved when his father was alive. But now these men saw him as their rescuer—freeing them from the dominion of Menwyn Wills, and maybe the sorcerer Hafydd as well. He was suddenly the good prince who had come to save them from circumstances they did not understand, come to lead them to victory and to be sure they got their share of the rewards, which was in question under the Wills, who would no doubt look to their own first. Perhaps most of all, he had come to take control of the largest part of the army, making them again preeminent, and not at the beck and call of Menwyn Wills.

Several large pavilions had been erected near the eastern end of the encampment, Menwyn keeping his allies close and separated from their own armies so that a situation like the one he was about to face could not occur. Men-at-arms in evening blue had quickly formed up before the tents, though they were vastly outnumbered. The men of Innes divided the men of Menwyn Wills into two parties, forcing a column through their middle to the tents beyond. It took some time for Michael to make his way through, and when he did the men who jostled there fell silent. Perhaps three thousand men in dark blue were ranged before the tents. Not nearly as large a force as the men of Innes, but Michael wasn't sure how many would fight for him if it came to that, and he was vulnerable there, with so many of Menwyn's guards nearby, some armed with bows. Of course Menwyn could not be sure of the situation either, which Michael was counting on.

An officer emerged from the largest tent—a tent Michael was sure had belonged to his father—and bowed to him. "Prince Michael," the man said, acknowledging Michael's claim—not that he had much choice. "You have no doubt traveled far. Lord Menwyn invites you to dismount and join him." The man gestured toward the tent, smiling tightly, trying to hide his distress at this turn of events.

"I will speak with Lord Menwyn here," Michael said. "After what befell my father I don't wish to go anywhere without my guards, who are too numerous to fit inside Lord Menwyn's pavilion." It was a terrible insult, but Michael heard a growl of approval from his men.

The officer tried to smile. "We are, my Prince, at war. Much that should be said is of a sensitive nature."

"I trust any man wearing purple and black with my life," Michael said. He was pretty sure that if he stormed the tents at that moment he would be killed by an arrow, but he was equally sure that Menwyn Wills would die as well. "Please ask Lord Menwyn to do me the honor of attending me here." He had chosen his words with care. The Prince would be honored by Menwyn's presence, but Menwyn would be attending him. He was the Prince of Innes, not some out of pocket noble with two hundred swords at his command.

The officer stood a moment, uncertain, and then retreated inside. Nothing happened for a moment, and a grumbling began among the men in purple and black. The situation could quickly spin out of control—Michael could feel it.

The doors to the pavilion were drawn back, and Menwyn Wills strode out, a dozen minor noblemen at his back—former allies of the House of Innes, for the most part. Many of Michael's father's officers were there as well. Menwyn was making a statement.

"Prince Michael!" Menwyn said, smiling broadly. "I cannot tell you the joy we feel to see you returned! We thought that blackguard, Sir Eremon, had left you dead."

"And so he no doubt thought," Prince Michael answered, "but he was wrong."

"It grieves me to tell you, Prince Michael, that your father, the Prince of Innes, was not so fortunate. Hafydd had him murdered." Menwyn paused a moment, his gaze going respectfully down. "But with the assistance of these noble men"—he gestured to those around him—"we drove off the last remnant of Hafydd's force and wrested control of the army from them."

"And for this I thank you," Prince Michael said. "I have returned, it seems, just in time to resume command."

"For which we are thankful. We will, my Prince, go to war this very day. I fear that you will not be able to take up your rightful place immediately, for the plans are all laid and the command of each company has been assigned and each officer knows his part. But you should ride with me and our chief allies, for this day we will destroy the armies of the Renné and prepare the way for our victory."

"I will surrender the command of my army to no one," the Prince said, and a loud murmur of approval came from the men of Innes. He prayed the company of the curious that followed him would look enough like a loyal and resentful army that Menwyn would not dare insult them.

Menwyn indeed did look like a man on shifting ground. "But my Prince"—he almost stammered—"we will fight a major battle this day upon which all of our future success depends. With all due respect, no man could assume command of such a large force on such short notice. All of our carefully laid plans would be in danger."

"Then send my officers to me so that I may be informed of your plan. I will be with my men." He bowed courteously and turned his horse. A passage opened up before him, the men pressing back all the while nodding and whispering approvingly among themselves. "Return to ranks!" the Prince ordered, and this call was taken up down the length of the encampment.

Slowly the men returned to their places, officers of lower rank stepping in to organize. Michael suspected that if he had a loyal following, it would be here, among the men and junior officers. "Rica?

You are now the captain of my guard. Find me fifty loyal men and give them an armband or some kind of insignia so that I will know them." He pointed to the center of the army of Innes. "Find a pavilion and pitch it there, in the center, but leave the walls rolled up so that all may see me. Find four banners and raise them up on poles—nothing ostentatious—I just want my presence to be felt. Then bring me the junior officers, five at a time. Do you know them?"

"Many of them, sir, though not all."

"I will have you stand by and tell me something of each of them . . ." But he was drowned out then as the men called for three cheers for their prince, the valley echoing with their voices. He hoped that Pwyll and the others heard this, for they would be wondering what had happened.

A small pavilion was quickly erected. Surcoats of the disbanded house guards were found, and Rica mustered the men for their master's review. The Prince walked among them, speaking quietly. "There have been many betrayals of late," he said. "Friend and foe are no longer easily recognized. You must therefore be prepared to follow my orders without question. If I order you to cut down some captain, even one who has served our house for thirty years, you must do it without hesitation. Is there any man among you who cannot do that?" The men responded quickly, as he'd hoped they would. The Prince of Innes had been murdered—a failure they did not want to repeat.

"Rica," the Prince said, as they returned to the pavilion, "place only a single guard at each tent post. I want the men in ranks to be able to see me and to see that I trust them utterly." The Prince looked around at the men sitting in ordered rows, many a curious eye turned his way.

Rica quickly arranged the guards, the bulk of them seated in a square around the pavilion. He came back to the Prince, who stood watching men erect a map table beneath the canvas shelter. "Your grace should know that the captains of all the companies have been replaced by men loyal to Menwyn Wills."

"What happened to my father's officers?"

"Many were demoted into the ranks, your grace. Others were ejected from the army, some few left in shame, unable to accept this treatment."

"Bring all of these new officers to me and find as many of my father's company commanders as you can, or their immediate subordinates. I will replace all of Menwyn's officers within the hour."

"Your grace," said Rica, "some of these men will not acknowledge your authority."

"Give them one warning. Any insubordination will be punished by summary execution. If they so much as hesitate after that, you must cut them down. If we wish to take back control of the army, we cannot falter."

Rica saluted and gathered a small company to follow him. The Prince cast his eye back toward the pavilions of Lord Menwyn. No doubt there was quite a heated debate going on there at this moment. The longer it lasted—to a point—the better. Michael needed some time to reverse the coup Menwyn had staged. Some men would have to die, he feared, but it could not be helped. If the army wasn't firmly in his control within the hour, then he would fail, and the hours of life left him would be few.

The officers appointed by Menwyn came sullenly to the pavilion, grumbling among themselves, looks of apprehension and resentment on their faces. Rica had them stand out in the open and placed guards with swords drawn around them.

"All of you appointed in my absence by Lord Menwyn deserve the gratitude of the House of Innes. But I have, upon the order of Lord Menwyn Wills, resumed command of the army of Innes. Your services are no longer required. You are hereby dismissed and may return to your former officers—immediately." The Prince nodded to them in a kindly way, then gestured to Rica, who marshaled the stunned captains away before they might think of doing something foolish. Another group of men were quickly gathering—these in the purple and black of Innes. They fell in before the pavilion, and the Prince had each of them give his name, rank, and former command. The situation was not as bad as it could have been, for a number of former commanders still remained. The other positions were quickly filled by men the commanders recommended. Michael had them swear an oath to him and warned them to take orders from no one but himself or Rica until he had filled the ranks of senior commanders—at which time the Prince would make these officers known to them. These men were sent off to organize their companies.

He did not yet have in place a structure of command—there was a broad layer of senior commanders missing—but he was making quick progress.

"So tell me, Captain Rica, who is left among my father's former allies and senior officers who might either be loyal to the House of Innes or hate the Wills enough to side with me?"

The man stood with one hand on the map table. "It is difficult to say, your grace. So much has changed and so rapidly. After the Prince, your father, was murdered, Hafydd took control of the army, placing his own men in all but a few key positions. When Hafydd left, Lord Menwyn drove the black guards off and put his own men in their stead. Everyone was forced to swear an oath of loyalty to the Wills. The few who refused were stripped of their positions, thrown into cells, or 'disappeared.' Of the noblemen who were your father's allies I think only T'oldor and Quince might side with you against Menwyn. Your grace must realize that these men were all promised large areas of your estates. They will not give up that promise easily. I would let none of them stand at your back."

Michael nodded. It was unfortunate that his father did not command loyalty. Now his son would pay the price for this short-sightedness.

"Your grace. They are coming."

The noblemen and officers who had been given control of the army of Innes had elected to travel the length of the camp on horseback, banners flying, perhaps hoping this display would give them legitimacy in the eyes of the men. When they reached the army of Innes they spread out, only six approaching the pavilion,

the rest riding out among the mustered companies. They began
calling out orders immediately.

Six minor noblemen reined in their horses. "My Prince," one
said with feigned urgency, "the army marches. Come with us, and
we will inform you of the design as we go."

Michael did not answer, praying that the soldiers would not
move without command from their newly appointed officers.
He held his breath. Not a man stood or acknowledged the
shouted orders of the horsemen. Michael had to stop himself
from smiling.

"This army," he said, "goes nowhere without my express command. And within the hour I will command it to return to my estates. Now get off your horses and order your officers back, or you
may go tell Menwyn that he meets the Renné alone." Michael
crossed his arms and stared at the six men.

The noblemen retreated to confer among themselves, whispering and casting glances toward the prince.

"Captain Rica," Michael ordered. "Do you see these horsemen
trying to give orders to my army? Warn them that if they do not de-
sist immediately and remove themselves from my ranks, I will treat
them as enemies trying to undermine my command."

Rica seemed to have anticipated this and had several small companies ready. These ran off, each bearing a banner of the House of
Innes. They soon reached the shouting officers, some of whom had
drawn swords and were threatening the soldiers. Two or three refused to remove themselves, and swords were drawn, companies of
soldiers leaping to their feet at orders from the Prince's captains.
One horseman was chased out by armed men, haughty even in retreat, the rest realized that their lives were in danger and acted ap-
propriately.

The six noblemen still conferred.

"Captain Rica?" Michael said loudly. "Drag these former allies
off my father's off their horses and bring them to me."

The six noblemen separated then, two quickly dismounting.

The other four were surrounded by armed men on foot, and they too dismounted, and all were brought before the Prince.

"Who among you will renounce your claim to the parts of my estate that Menwyn Wills has promised and swear an oath of loyalty to me?" The Prince regarded the six men, all of whom he had known since childhood. Apparently they still thought him a child. They had not been witness to the events of the Stillwater, when Prince Michael had been forced to come of age.

"I will take an oath, my Prince," Lord T'oldor said, dropping to one knee.

"As will I," responded Quince, whose estates comprised a small tract of mountains and meadows to the north—far too small for a man of such ability and character, Michael thought.

"I lived beneath the heel of your father's boot for thirty years," said Lord Farwell, "I will not live beneath yours now."

"No one need live beneath the heel of my boot, but the estates of the Prince of Innes are not for the taking. This army that my father created is mine to command, and I will not commit it to the field until I am satisfied that it is not being sent to ruin. If you will not swear loyalty to me, then go back to Lord Menwyn and demand that he pay you what he promised out of his own purse. It won't be coming out of mine."

T'oldor and Quince swore an oath to the Prince, with all of the army there to witness. The other noblemen and their officers rode back the way they had come, having failed in their attempt to seize control of the army of Innes.

T'oldor watched the men go, then turned to Prince Michael. "It is well that none of them offered to swear an oath to you, my Prince. I should never have trusted them."

"Nor would I, T'oldor, but the offer had to be made. They were the allies of my house for many years."

Rica had unrolled a map on the table, the corners weighed down by stones. Michael wondered what had become of the silver weights his father had used. In someone's purse, no doubt.

T'oldor, an elegant ruin of a man, sketched in the design. His white hair hung in carefully arranged ringlets, and the lace of his collar and cuffs was as unblemished as new snow. For all that, he was a brilliant old scoundrel, as Michael well knew.

"Menwyn's spies tell him that the Renné intend to land tonight where this valley meets the Wynnd." T'oldor placed a finger on the map. "He plans to move his army into position surrounding the landing place, then let the Renné disembark their army before driving them into the river, preferably at first light, though our presence might not go undiscovered for so long."

"Show me the disposition of our forces?" Michael asked.

The old man laid a few quick marks on the paper with a stick of charcoal.

"But the army of Innes has all the forward positions!" Michael said, more in anger than surprise. "Menwyn's army is only the reserve."

"That is true, my Prince," Quince agreed, his manner very subdued.

"Then we are to fight this battle against the Renné and suffer all the casualties?"

The two noblemen nodded.

Michael stared at the map a moment. Of course he didn't want to fight the Renné at all, but he was certain that his officers and his men wouldn't readily accept that. His hold on the army and on the loyalty of these noblemen was tenuous.

The prince took the charcoal from T'oldor and redrew the lines. "Menwyn's forces will array themselves here, to the south, we will arrange our armies here, to the east and the north. That will put him in the forefront of the battle across a third of the area to be contested. He will have to fight. I will not take all the losses and he all the gains." He turned to Lord T'oldor. "Will you go to Lord Menwyn and tell him this?"

"Gladly, but it might be better if I don't go alone, as I am now a traitor to the Wills."

"Take forty men with you—mounted, if you like. Tell Menwyn

that once his armies have taken up the southern position, I will move mine into the positions I have indicated. Don't allow him to argue or prevaricate. I will march my army home before I will let him use it so."

The riders were quickly formed up and they followed Lord T'oldor down the long aisle between the armies. Michael stood looking around the field. He wondered if he would be forced to fight the Renné before he could do away with Menwyn Wills. One thing was certain, he would not give up control of his army at any cost. The moment he did that he would be dead.

"Rica?"

"Your grace?"

"Bring me our four most experienced captains. They are about to receive promotions."

"Immediately, your grace," but despite his promise of immediate action, he stood there awkwardly a moment.

Michael turned to the man. "You have something more to say, Captain?"

"If I may, your grace. There is one young captain whose abilities are far beyond his years. He is, perhaps, the strongest of all your subordinate officers."

"Then bring him as well. Rica? You have my permission to speak your mind whenever you deem it necessary."

"Your trust is an honor, your grace."

"And you may call me Prince Michael."

"My Prince," the man said, making a quick bow before hurrying off.

Lord T'oldor returned to find Michael going over the plan of battle with his new officers, deciding how the companies would be arranged, how they would move to their places, and how they would be supplied both with food and arms. Moving such a large force even a short distance, which was what they intended, took a great deal of planning. Men who had been fed fought better than those who were hungry. And men who believed in the abilities of their superiors fought better still. The army of

Innes would have no idea of the abilities of the Prince. He would have to prove himself. They didn't know he had fought the servants of Death in the Stillwater and wouldn't believe it if they were told.

"And what said Lord Menwyn?" Prince Michael asked Lord T'oldor.

"He was not pleased and there were accusations of infamy all around." The man smiled like the rake he was. "I have seldom more enjoyed being the bearer of bad news."

"Then he will do what I require?"

"You control the superior force, my Prince. If you refuse to fight, Lord Menwyn and his allies will be outnumbered by the Renné. They will be driven from the field." The man looked up at the sun. "We will know within the hour for he must soon begin moving his army to the river, or retire."

"It will be a long hour. Captain Rica? What became of Lord A'denné's men-at-arms?"

"They were distributed among the companies of the Wills and of Innes, your . . . my Prince."

"Is it possible to find a man who served in Lord A'denné's personal guard?"

"I believe it could be done."

"Good. When you find such a man send him up that hillside and have him wait at the crest. The men who aided me in my journey here are hiding in the trees. If he had a banner or some token of the A'denné that he could display, it would be useful."

There was a moment's silence, then Lord T'oldor spoke. "Prince Michael, Carl A'denné was a traitor to your father's cause. He is widely blamed for our failure on the Isle of Battle, for we believe he warned the Renné of the invasion."

"Lord Carl was the enemy of Sir Eremon, who had my father under his sway. He is still the enemy of Sir Eremon, which makes him my ally. Tell this man you send up the hill to bring my companions to join us after dark. There are some secrets that it would be better Lord Menwyn not know."

"My Prince," Rica said hesitantly, "you told me that I must speak my mind when I felt it necessary. . . ."

"Yes, Captain. Please say what you will."

"Your men . . . they are ready to lay down their lives to fight our enemy, the Renné. Many of your soldiers lost comrades and kin on the Isle of Battle. The lust for revenge is strong. It is true that they resent Menwyn Wills, who they believed supported Sir Eremon in the murder of your father, but their real hatred is reserved for the Renné. A change of alliances would be a dangerous thing right now. You might lose the army."

"Captain Rica," Michael said, "I chose well in you." He turned to the serious man-at-arms, and all of his other newly appointed officers. "I traveled far in the company of the man you call Sir Eremon—though his real name is Hafydd and he was once in the service of the Renné. He has made alliances with . . . powers we can't understand and has become a sorcerer of great skill. Killing him now would be almost impossible. If he comes back. . . . No. *When* he comes back, he will kill Menwyn and me and take over this army, with which he will overrun the land between the mountains. And this man—this sorcerer—is loyal to no one and to no thing. Better a hundred years under the rule of the Renné than a year under Hafydd. But we don't have to war with the Renné—they will ally themselves with us against Hafydd." Prince Michael watched the faces of the men. They looked at him darkly, mouths drawn down, their arms crossed. How to make them understand? "Menwyn Wills, unfortunately, hates the Renné above all things and will never give up his feud, and this weakness will allow Hafydd to return. We can only hope to defeat Hafydd if we have strong allies and are prepared for great sacrifice—perhaps our own lives. I believe the Renné are those allies. And Menwyn Wills? He would lick Hafydd's boots for another ten minutes of life." He looked from one man to the next, meeting their eyes. "I know Hafydd. A more heartless, cruel man has not been born of woman. If this army will not give up its desire for revenge against the Renné, and make them our allies,

then you will bend a knee to this sorcerer, and he will lop off
your heads and the heads of your families, for he will not suffer
any to oppose him."

"But Prince Michael," Lord T'oldor said softly. "Captain Rica
is right. Your army wants revenge on the Renné. Talk of sorcerers
will only frighten them."

The man-at-arms who had been a guard of the late Lord A'denné
brought the small company down the hillside and, using the passwords, escorted it into the presence of Prince Michael of Innes.
Not long before, the sun had plunged into the western hills, setting
the horizon aflame, and dusk crept out of the east like spreading
smoke. The armies had arrayed themselves in a half circle around
the Renné landing place, and waited in utter silence, the penalty for
speaking being death.

Dressed in their stolen mail and surcoats, Pwyll, Lord Carl,
Samul Renné, and Jamm appeared in the failing light. Michael
stood with his senior officers on a small rise in among a few trees.
Around him his runners crouched, ready to carry orders to the
company captains. His guards were there as well, though not many
in number. Prince Michael felt safe with his army around him, and
now with Pwyll and the others he breathed a great sigh.

"What goes on?" Pwyll whispered. He had realized immediately
that the unnatural silence was no accident.

"The Renné are about to land," Michael whispered.

"Vast . . . ," whispered Carl.

Pwyll leaned close so that none of the officers might here. "But
they are your allies," he whispered.

"Yes," Michael said softly, "but my army desires revenge for
their losses on the Isle of Battle. I have had no choice but to bring
them here. Pwyll, I don't know what to do."

Carl A'denné had leaned close to listen. "You must withdraw
your army," he said urgently.

"There will be a mutiny if I do."

"But the Renné will not land here," Carl said. "They will have sent false information through Vast, whom they know to be a traitor. The Renné will land either north or south and fall on your army from behind, driving them into the river."

Michael put both hands to his forehead. "I wrested control of my army from the Wills. Now how do I wrest control from the soldiers?"

Forty-one

Vast sat on the gunwale of the boat as the oars dipped silently. He could just make out the other craft, all painted black, their passengers still and silent. A horse whinnied softly on the western shore. Barges would bring them across as soon as the Renné had landed and established a perimeter. It would take several hours to move all the men, their mounts and equipment. He wondered how long Menwyn Wills would wait before ordering the attack. No doubt he would want to destroy the Renné army, not just drive them back to the western shore. It would take patience and nerve. He worried that Lord Menwyn possessed neither.

The Duke could almost feel the men around him in the darkness. Feel the living heat of them. Many of his own men would cross over the river that night. The final river. His heart sank at the thought of it. They would die because of his bargain with Menwyn Wills. Because the Renné did not offer him enough. Never enough.

As for the Renné . . . by morning they would be a noble house in hiding, those that were left. They would have to be hunted down to the last child—none left alive. Otherwise, their genius for hatred would bring a terrible revenge.

He looked up at the stars, then at the dark shadow of the eastern shore.

"Is the current not setting us too far south?" he whispered to the massive shadow that was Lord Fondor Renné.

"No," Fondor answered. "We are exactly on course."

Vast felt himself nod, though none could see in the dark. He gazed fixedly at the shoreline again. He knew the river hereabout as well as anyone, having traveled it all his life. They were already south of the stream mouth where they planned to land. Disaster was about to be born of incompetence.

He touched Fondor on the shoulder. "We are too far south. I'm sure of it." He leaned toward the riverman who held the boat's tiller. "We must go north—"

But a blade at his throat stopped his speech.

"Say not another word, Duke," Fondor whispered.

Vast found himself staring down into the water, ten thousand points of light wavering across the surface. He wondered if he'd ever see such a sight again. Traitors were never shown mercy. He swallowed hard. He had made his choice and now the price would be exacted. The wavering stars drew his eye again, the sheer beauty of them.

I'm crossing a river of stars, he thought. But it was the darkness that seemed to draw his eye, as though he could tumble out of the boat and fall endlessly into the night.

Forty-two

Hafydd did not concern himself much with the beauty or the wonder of the chamber, but Beld found himself staring like a peasant in a palace. The room was vast, yet not a single pillar supported its dome, which curved overhead like an ivory sky. Across the floor spread a great mosaic, the pattern eight-sided like the chamber itself. The walls were highly decorated, but the faint light of the torches barely touched them, and Hafydd wouldn't have much patience for him wandering off to admire the art. Near the far side, the floor was bisected by a narrow channel that ran with water, and on their side of the channel, was a small, round pool, faintly aglow and half-obscured beneath curling vapor wraiths.

"He will ask you to kill me, now," A'denné whispered, slipping quietly up beside Beld.

Beld looked over to Hafydd, who stared into the steaming pool. No guards were within hearing. "I cannot," he whispered.

"You must," A'denné said softly. "Only you might get close enough to murder him, but if you refuse to"—the man swallowed hard—"end my life he will never trust you."

"How do you know I would want to kill him?"

"Because I have watched you, Beldor Renné. I don't know what happened, but some . . . understanding has come over you. . . ." He struggled to find more words but could not. In his face, Beld saw resignation and a visible struggle to control his fear.

Beld touched the stone beneath his shirt. "He's too careful."

"With me, yes, but he suffers you to come near. When you kill me show not a trace of remorse. Strange to think that he would trust such a man more, but I believe it's true."

"Lord Beldor . . . !" Hafydd called out, his harsh voice distorted and eerie in this place.

Beld hurried over. Hafydd stared into the pool, his hands clasped behind his back. White light streamed up from below, and an intense cold knifed through his clothes and into his skin. Hafydd didn't look up, and Beld found himself gazing into the pool, wondering what so fascinated the old warrior.

"Do you see him?" Hafydd whispered.

Beld bent a little closer. The veils of steam swirled slowly over the surface, and the light from below caused him to squint. *There . . .* ! What looked like a face—raven-haired and bearded— eyes closed, lips so faint they were all but colorless.

"I think I do see . . . a man's face."

"The great enchanter," Hafydd said softly. "Wyrr, encased in a coffin of perpetual ice."

"What will you do now?" Beldor heard himself ask.

"We have bargains to keep, Beldor Renné. Bring the book, the earthenware jar, and Lord A'denné. You've kept your blade sharp?"

"It is always sharp, Sir Eremon."

Hafydd turned and looked suddenly into his eyes. "Then have it ready. You will kill A'denné for me. I will tell you when and how."

Hafydd summoned his guard captain. "Have someone bring me two of those chairs," he ordered.

*   *   *

Beld stood frozen to the spot. He had killed many men—his own cousin, even—and felt no misgivings before, nor any guilt after. . . . But now he felt suddenly light-headed, strange, as though it were he about to die. Beld fingered the green gem beneath his shirt. Had he fallen beneath a spell? Was this what others felt when they went into battle? He was flushed, hot, breaking out in a sweat. He watched Hafydd with a growing sense of horror.

The knight opened the wooden box containing the book, and Beld noticed that everyone took a step away, as though they could feel the malice, the coldness—colder than the ice that encased Wyrr. Laying the box over the backs of the two chairs, Hafydd opened the book. Beld felt a sudden weight inside him, like a stone dropped into the winter river. There was no cheating Death. You could only pass through the gate with your honor intact or without it. He saw that now. Toren had always understood it instinctively. Even Dease knew it in his way. It was the only thing one took from this world. Nothing else passed through the gate—not even love. Beldor knew. He had groveled before the entrance to Death's kingdom, stripped of all pride and property . . . and of his honor, as well. That had been his deepest regret. He would go honorless into that dark place, to be remembered for nothing else.

With the utmost care, Hafydd laid a rope in a circle, perhaps thirty feet across. A small sackful of gray dust he emptied evenly over the rope's entire length. In the center of this, the sorcerer made another circle, two yards in diameter, and from it, eight lines were marked on the floor with gray dust, cutting the circle evenly.

"Bring the earthenware jar and your sword, Lord Beldor. Step not on the lines! And Lord A'denné . . . . We will need you as well."

Beldor took up the jar, surprised by its weight. A'denné approached them, as if in a daze. Beld had seen men go to the gallows before, and they looked much as A'denné did now—disbelief mixed with grief and horror.

Beld tried to concentrate on the actions of the sorcerer—anything to keep his mind off A'denné and what he was about to do.

Hafydd took the jar from Beld, his face betraying nothing. Two guards had followed A'denné, and stood behind him to either side. The nobleman struggled to control his fear. Many, Beld knew, broke down at this point.

Hafydd took out a dagger and cut away the wax seal around the large cork that stoppered the jar. Using the dagger's point he levered the cork slowly out, and the smell of strong spirits touched Beld's nostrils—mixed with something more bitter.

Hafydd pulled up his sleeve and reached into the liquid, drawing out a dripping, stillborn infant by its tiny feet. A'denné choked back a sob, earning a disdainful glance from Hafydd. The tiny creature was set in the center of the circle, where it lay in a puddle of spirits, eyes closed, waxen, as still and silent as morning.

"Lord A'denné . . . ," Hafydd beckoned with a finger.

The nobleman took three measured steps and stopped within reach of the sorcerer, his black honor guard close behind. His eyes blinked rapidly several times, perhaps stung by the smell of spirits.

"Lean over the stillborn child," the sorcerer said, and the guards took A'denné by the arms, as he leaned forward from the waist. Hafydd nodded to Beld, who drew his sword. He could feel his heart hammering in his chest, his face flush red.

"Cut his throat, Lord Beldor," Hafydd said, backing away, out of sword's reach. "Quickly!"

A'denné glanced up at him, ashen with fear, but even so he gave the smallest nod. Beldor hesitated only a second, the eyes of the guards on him. One swift cut and A'denné went limp, held up by the guards, his blood pouring out, a crimson stain overspreading the tiny infant. The salt smell of blood, like the distant sea, assaulted his senses, and Beld reeled away, nauseated and unsteady.

"Your part is done, Lord Beldor," Hafydd said. "Be careful where you place your feet as you leave the circle."

Beldor backed away, the scene burning into his vision like a flame; Lord A'denné bleeding out his life onto the stillborn child, which lay, half-human, half-maggot, in the center of Hafydd's web. The dead and the dying, and the life not yet born.

Turning away to hide his reaction, Beld stepped out of the circle as Hafydd opened the book, using the box over the chairs for his reading stand. He began immediately to murmur, then to chant. Beld covered his ears, but the words did not stop. They beat upon his eardrums like drops of water—one by one by one.

The guards dropped the body of Lord A'denné and retreated from the ring, escaping just before Hafydd set it afire. Beld turned away, but a dark fascination drew his gaze back. Among the lines and circles of flame he saw the smallest movement—the fingers of the stillborn child opened and closed, then it threw back its head and opened its mouth as though to scream.

Elise did not hesitate at the bottom of the stair but rushed out, cutting down the first of two guards. The second guard Orlem ran through, but not before the man called out a warning.

The giant and Elise raced toward a ring of fire that flickered and smoked, across the floor of a massive chamber. Toren forced himself to keep pace, his feet hammering the hard surface. A step behind and to his left, Gilbert A'brgail matched his pace, sword glowing green in the smoky air.

Hafydd, it could be no other, stood beyond the flame, chanting. His guards formed a line between their master and his sorcery and the onrushing company. Elise and Orlem raised their luminous swords and bellowed like animals as they struck the line of black guards. Toren threw himself on a man who tried to circle to Elise's left, and then all order was lost in the frenzy of battle. Evading this stroke, countering that, cutting a man's legs out from under him, the feel of his blade slashing into flesh. As he fought a larger opponent, Orlem stepped back into him and sent him sprawling at his enemy's feet. He could feel the sword rise above him for the final blow, then the man toppled onto him, twitching and writhing. The weight came off and someone dragged him up, and Toren found himself facing his cousin—Beld—who had been swept up into the air by Death's servant.

"You're too late," Beldor shouted over the clamor. "He is done."

A tongue of flame flared out among them, setting cloaks afire and chasing both guards and their enemies in all directions. Toren felt the floor shiver, and he was thrown off his feet. Among the ring of flame something hideous rose. It spread out its arms and bellowed, shaking the Isle to its very roots.

A giant leapt the line of flame, bounding into the circle, a great blade raised. He struck the creature a blow that shook the air and shattered his sword, but the monster brushed him aside with a single swipe and turned its back on the pitiful scuffling of mortal men.

"We should never have left the stairwell," Eber said. He clutched his son's hand tightly and gave it a little shake. "Don't leave my side again! Look at the danger you've put us in!"

Theason glanced over at the small man, who was trying to shield his son from the battle, as though his ancient body might stop a blade. The fighting ranged over the floor of the great chamber, careening this way and that. It drove them around two sides of the left wall, where they slunk along at the edge of the floor, hoping to go unnoticed.

"What is going on, Eber?" Theason whispered. "Do you see?"

In the center of a flickering ring of red flame, something large was moving just perceptibly.

"It's feeding," Eber said, his voice flat, frightened.

"On what?"

"The carcass," Eber whispered, "of a man—"

"River save us."

The light was poor, and the tide of the battle could not be guessed. Hafydd collapsed suddenly and was supported by two of his guards. The others fought a ferocious battle against Elise and her company, Orlem driving the black guards back wherever he went. The giant leapt the flame and attacked the soul eater, but it sent him tumbling back through the flames.

And then a tongue of fire struck out at the fighters, scattering them this way and that.

"You have lost, Sister!" a voice cried over the fighting. "Go back while you can."

The fighting seemed to waver, the black-clad guards gathering about their master, Elise and her company standing defiantly across the floor. Theason could see her there, tall and straight-backed, undaunted and proud.

"I shall bring this cavern down upon us first!" she called out.

Raising her sword she struck the ground with it, a blow that shook the walls and threw them all down upon their bellies. Thea-son scrambled up and helped Eber to his feet.

"Where is Llya?" the old man said, looking around frantically. "Where is Llya!"

A second blow, greater than the first, and Theason was thrown hard against the wall and lay for a moment, dazed. A deafening rending, and he opened his eyes to see massive broken blocks of stone tumbling down from the ceiling.

The shock of their landing buckled the floor, throwing the little man into the air for a moment, then slamming him down. He thought he heard someone whimpering and realized the voice was his. Something fell so close that he was tossed up again, and again smashed down. Smoke stung his nostrils, then darkness fluttered over him, like a fall of black snow.

Beldor felt something jerk around his neck, and then slide over his hair. He thought he moaned. He slipped away for a moment, then woke again, darkness, but not far off, a little light. His vision was blurred, and he tried to shake his head to clear it. The murmur of a soothing voice.

A rubble of stones ranged around him, and Beldor lay in some space between. He moved his arm and felt down his side. There was no feeling there, as though the flesh belonged to someone else. He struck his hip but felt it only in his fist.

"What has happened to me? I can't move."

His vision blurred, darkness bleeding in around the edges. But there, in the center of the darkness, he could see a figure hunched down in a faint light. A voice, very distant, murmured, like water running over stones.

"There, granddaughter," it said softly. "Death shall not have you this day—you or the poor girl who bears you."

The figure rose, a woman. Gracefully, she slipped down a narrow passage between fallen stones. He could almost see her face.

"Can you help me?" he whispered, his words poorly formed.

The woman hovered over him an instant, as though weighing his request.

"You made your bargain with Death," she said at last. "I will not interfere." And she turned away.

"Please," Beld heard himself say. "At the end, I forsook my bargain."

"Too late, man-at-arms," she said. "Too late."

"No," Beldor whispered. "Not too late. . . . Not for me."

Darkness dribbled across the scene, like ink over glass, and Beldor felt a sudden warmth spread through him. He exhaled a long breath—and did not draw it in again.

Tam held his torch aloft. A rubble of boulders, half the size of houses and greater, spread over the floor of the cavern. Smoke wafted about the place as though it could not find an escape, and a burble of water echoed eerily.

"What happened here?" Fynnol asked.

"We came too late," Alaan said, and cursed. "Caibre . . . Hafydd and Elise fought."

"Who survived?" Tam said.

"Perhaps no one. Come let's look."

A crash shook the chamber, and Tam flinched, almost burning Fynnol with his torch. A great chunk of the ceiling had fallen, breaking boulders beneath. They began to search among the rocks, ducking down as they went, fearing the ceiling would collapse at any moment and bury them all.

Tam dropped down a crack between two boulders and found himself in a narrow passage.

"Are you all right?" Fynnol called down from above.

"Yes. Stay up there, Cousin. I might need your help to get out."

"Easy for you to say. The ceiling will kill me first."

"Yes, but it will kill me second. I will trade places with you if you wish?"

"No, Tam. Go on as you are. We'll search together."

Tam wormed his way between the stones, getting down on his belly here and there to push himself through small openings. Every few moments he met a dead end and was forced to find another way, but Fynnol proved useful scouting the route from above.

"Fynnol? I thought I heard something—like a voice."

They both stopped and tried to quiet their breathing.

"A moan. Yes! This way, I think."

Tam tried to follow his cousin, who leapt from boulder to boulder, quickly finding his way. A tight squeeze, then he tripped over something soft.

"I found someone!" Tam pushed himself out of the cleft between the stones and crouched, holding the torch so that he might see.

"Who is it?"

"A man—dead, I fear." Tam turned the man's head a little, the eyes staring at him vacantly. "You know, Fynnol, I think this is Beldor Renné."

"No. He was taken by the servants of Death in the Stillwater. Don't you remember?"

"Nevertheless, I think this can be no other."

"Tam?" came a faint whisper.

"Well, Tam, if you thin—"

"Fynnol! Quiet!"

"Tam?" came the voice again.

The Valeman held his torch aloft and swept it this way and that, throwing its light down the narrow crevices between the fallen ceiling.

He leapt up. "Elise? Elise?" He forced his way between two close stones, tearing away cloth and flesh. And there he found her, lying in a void between the fallen boulders.

"Elise! Fynnol! Call Alaan!"

He dropped down, wedging the torch into a crack, and took her head in his hands.

"Can you move? Where are you hurt?"

"It is all right, Tam. I'm unharmed . . . or at least healed from all my hurts. Give me a moment," she whispered, close to tears, "and I'll get up."

"Oh, Elise," he said, unable to contain his feelings. "I thought never to see you again."

Her hand slipped, small and warm, into his. "Something keeps throwing us together, Tam," she said softly, "no matter the distances between."

Alaan appeared above. "Ah, there you are! How badly is she injured, Tam?"

"I'm unharmed," Elise said, though she did not open her eyes.

"That is a miracle," Alaan responded, leaning over the opening, his face appearing in the flickering light of Tam's torch.

"Perhaps. Someone healed my hurts, or so I dreamed. What of the others?"

Alaan did not answer, and Elise suddenly rose to a sitting position.

"Tell me," she demanded.

"We found Slighthand . . . crushed beneath a stone."

Elise covered her face, tears running out between her fingers, like blood from a wound, but there was no sound.

"Who else?" she whispered.

"Some Renné men-at-arms. Knights wearing gray cloaks."

"Toren? A'brgail?"

"We have not found them yet."

Her silent tears continued. "He had survived for so long," she whispered, haltingly, "and given up the sword. If Kai had not found him, and sent him after you—"

"We might all have perished in the Stillwater," Alaan said, interrupting her gently.

"He saved me when Death's servant had me in its claws," Fynnol said sadly.

"Slighthand saved many from death," Alaan said, "but we have no time to mourn him now."

A distorted shout from some distance silenced them all.

"Can you climb up?" Alaan asked, reaching down as far as he could. "I think they've found some others."

Alaan and Fynnol pulled them both up. Elise swayed, supporting herself on Tam's shoulder.

They made their way across the rubble, jumping from boulder to boulder, until at last they reached a place where the ceiling had not fallen, though the floor was buckled and broken. Here, a small company huddled, some lying, others sitting propped against the wall. A channel ran with water, and a small distance off, a round pool steamed, glowing faintly white.

Some of the gathering were wet through, and others lay still, injured, or dead, or sleeping.

"Thank the river," Elise said with feeling, "not a few have survived."

Baore rose as he saw them approaching over the rubble. His carriage was bent to one side as though he favored an injury there. Three gray-clad Knights also found their feet, raising weapons as though ready to defend themselves, though they looked like they could hardly stand. There were two in Renné blue, neither of whom could rise, little Theason, and Eber, his back against the wall, knees up, and a hand over his face.

"You need not fear us," Alaan called out. "It is Alaan. And we have found Elise unharmed amid the rubble."

One of the gray-robed Knights came forward, and one of the two in Renné blue.

"Sir Gilbert," Elise said. "I am heartily glad to see you unharmed."

"None of us have gone unharmed," he said, as they drew near, then nodded to the old man leaning against the wall, "though none of us have received so great a hurt as Eber."

Elise had climbed down onto the buckled floor, but there she stopped. "Llya . . . ," she breathed as though the wind had been knocked from her lungs.

"*Gone*," Eber said, the word coming out as a sob. "Washed into the channel by a wave formed when the floor was broken. It rose up and swept him off. Gone before I could even gain my feet." He began to sob, his face hidden by his knees and a bent gray hand.

Elise went forward, crouching down on one knee before the old man. "Eber. I'm so sorry. . . . I said I would protect him—"

"And you did not!" the old man said, pulling his hand away from his face, fierce with grief. "What kind of father lets a child— hardly more than a baby—lead warriors in search of a monster?"

"Eber," Elise said, drawing back a little, "there was no one else to lead us. Hafydd had to be stopped."

"But we did not stop him. I gave up my son's life for nothing! His precious life!" Again he was overcome by grief and sobbed as though there were no one there to see.

None of the others would look directly upon Eber, but all turned a little away, their faces filled with sorrow and pity and guilt. Elise came slowly to her feet, tears running down her cheeks. Tam could see the accusation had cut her deeper than a blade ever could. She hesitated, as though seeking something to say, something to do, and turned away.

Theason caught her eye with a gesture. "Theason saw it happen. Hafydd's terrible creature leapt into the pool and broke through the ice, dragging the limp body into the river, his master close behind."

"His master?" Elise said.

"Hafydd," Theason said. "It grew very dark then—a cloud of dust thrown up by the falling ceiling—but Theason thought he saw a woman. At first Theason believed it was you, Lady Elise, covered in dust and dirt, but it was a dark-haired woman." He looked suddenly a bit hesitant, even embarrassed. "She went into the river. It will sound mad, but she seemed to change as she went. Certainly it was only the poor light, the dust in Theason's eyes—"

"She appeared to turn into a swan," Alaan said.

Theason looked at him, surprised. "A black swan, yes."

Alaan nodded and walked to the pool, where he crouched, staring into the water.

Toren Renné came forward and embraced his cousin. "We thought you dead," Toren said, pounding Dease on the back.

"I don't know how I survived. The fire tried to burn me, the smoke to choke me, and then I was found by Alaan, a coal spat out of the fire, stumbling along the bank." The two pulled apart.

"I cannot tell you how glad I am to see you. How your loss has preyed upon my mind when I should have concentrated upon other matters. . . ." Toren ran out of words.

Dease met his eye, moved by this show of feeling. "I am here, Toren, and largely unharmed."

Toren nodded, pulling himself up a little and trying to smile. "Yes, we have other matters to concern us. Other losses."

Elise picked her way across the broken floor to Alaan's side.

"He's gone," Alaan said. "Theason is right."

"We failed utterly—and murdered poor Llya in the bargain." She dropped down to her knees, staring into the steaming pool. "Would Elise Wills have used a child so, I wonder? Or is it only the part of me that is Sianon that would do such a shameful thing?"

"We have no time for remonstrance. Hafydd and his monster are escaping."

"What can we do against that thing?" Baore asked. He, Tam, and Cynddl all had come to stand a few paces off. "It tossed Slighthand aside like a child." He winced at his choice of words.

Alaan stood. "The soul eater begins to weaken soon after it is born. If we could catch it before it passes through Death's gate . . . It is a vain hope, but I would not want to see Llya die for nothing."

Elise looked up at Alaan. "Is there any chance at all?"

"A slim chance. Sainth can take shorter paths than the soul eater."

"Then while we have breath we must try," Elise said firmly. She scrambled to her feet. "If nothing else, we might have revenge for Llya's death."

"Spoken like a true Wills," Alaan responded.

"It will take us hours just to reach the surface again," Cynddl said.

Alaan pointed down the channel, which disappeared into a round tunnel. "We will go this way."

"But not everyone can swim."

Alaan turned to make a quick head count. "There are enough of us who can to get the others out. We have a boat hidden near the end of the island to bear us on."

Cynddl glanced back at the others. Eber had lapsed into silent tears, his face hidden again. "Everyone is injured and exhausted beyond measure."

"Only those who can still travel with speed need join us." Alaan looked down. At his feet, carved into the floor, were words in a tongue Tam did not know.

"What does it say?" he asked on impulse.

" 'Here sleeps Wyrr, son of Tusival, until the ending of the world.' "

"Nothing turns out as planned," the Fáel said, crouching down to run his hand over the letters, "not even for the great and powerful."

"Especially for the great and powerful," Alaan responded. "Come, let us make haste."

No one complained or even muttered when Alaan roused them. Elise went into the water first and returned a few moments later.

"It empties into the river not far off, and, though it's dark, there is air all the way but for the last twenty feet." Her skin had become as white as snow, and the color seemed almost washed from her eyes. Tam found her appearance disturbing and looked away.

"Tam?" Elise called out. "Would you bring me Slighthand's sword. No one else could bear it out. It's too heavy."

"It's broken," Alaan said. "Perhaps it should stay here?"

"No, I will have the hilt at least, so never to forget him and all that he did."

Tam brought the hilt of the heavy sword to her, and she took it, its weight not seeming to affect her at all as she floated in the channel.

She gestured with a hand. "It is a fitting burial chamber for Orlem Slighthand, though not as grand as it was."

A cracking sound reached them, and a massive boulder tumbled from the ceiling, crashing down on the stones below, spraying dust and debris a hundred feet.

"We must be gone from this place," Alaan said.

He and Tam took Eber between them, and Toren and Dease Renné helped A'brgail, who had already learned much of swimming in the tunnels of the Stillwater. Mail was shed, and they climbed stiffly into the water. The current took hold of them, and Tam looked back once at the ruined chamber. What pride these sorcerers had to make themselves such places to lie in death. But then Wyrr had not seemed wholly dead. Some part of him had been half-awake . . . until Hafydd came.

They went from the dim light of the Wyrr's chamber into the darkness of the tunnel, though some of Elise's party had blades that glowed faintly green and offered a little light.

"Stay together," Alaan warned, his voice echoing hollowly in the tunnel. In a few moments they came to a place where the stream disappeared into rock. Alaan bore Eber through and Elise took A'brgail. The others managed on their own, the current speeding them along and spewing them out into the night river.

Tam surfaced to summer air—warm water around him. The crescent moon was high, and the stars sharp and bright. The storm had blown over. Was that last night or this? Tam didn't know. He had lost all sense of time in the caverns.

"It is like a warm bath after being out in the snow," Fynnol said nearby.

"Yes," Tam said. "You talked to Baore; how is he?"

Tam could just make out his cousin's face in the moonlight, and his look was not happy. "He has not been himself since the nagar began to haunt him, far up the river. His silence . . . has changed. It is brooding and dark now. I worry for him."

Tam felt himself nod as he treaded water. None of them had been the same since they were hunted down the river and traveled the Stillwater, but Baore had turned inward, his mood too despairing.

"Our boat is not far," Alaan said from a few yards away, "but it won't carry us all. Some will have to stay."

A log floated by, and the swimmers all took hold of it. They drifted on the current, a human raft, faces haunted and ghostly in the moonlight. Spinning slowly, they ranged down the side of the island, the warmth of the river restoring them. Tam thought he could put his head against the log and go to sleep, bobbing on the water beneath a blanket of stars.

He was roused from his reverie by Alaan, who led them to a spine of rocks curving up into the trees. It was not easy climbing in the dark, and Eber was passed from hand to hand, until they all found themselves on the grass above.

Alaan and Elise were conferring as the Valemen began lowering the boat that had been left hanging in the trees. Toren Renné and Gilbert A'brgail approached Alaan.

"We are ready to go with you, for you will need skilled fighters," Toren said.

"We will need skilled watermen first," Alaan said. "I'm sorry, Lord Toren, but there is not enough room in the boat, and though you try to hide it, I can see you are injured. We'll take the northerners. They grew up on the water and traveled the great river all the way from its source."

"But what will you do when you find Hafydd? These young men aren't trained men-at-arms."

"They are more formidable than you know, and I'll never catch the soul eater without them. There is no time to argue. If we don't return, you will have to build a raft and go south. The river here is very strange . . . But Crowheart will lead you. Good luck to you,

Lord Toren." He gave a nodding bow and turned away. "Tam? Are all of you ready?"

"We're short of arrows, but otherwise, yes." Tam went to the edge of the embankment to begin the climb down, but as he went to swing over the edge he saw Elise crouched before Eber.

"Eber . . . ?" she said softly, caressing the man's cheek. "I will get him back, if I can."

"And how will you do that, Lady Elise?" Eber asked. "He has passed through the gate into Death's kingdom, from where none return."

"Perhaps, but I will try all the same. He gave voice to a river—much should be sacrificed for such a child." She hesitated a second then rose, turning quickly away and striding purposefully toward Tam, and the way down to the river.

Forty-three

Alaan steered from the stern, and Elise and Baore drove them on, setting a pace that soon had the others gasping. Even so, they did not relent, but kept it up, passing through a river of stars scattered across the waters. Tam had a feeling that all was in vain, but his respect for Alaan and his feelings for Elise kept him plunging his paddle into the river, thinking each time, *Just one more. Just one more.*

But after two hours even Baore began to falter, and Elise bid the three Valemen to take a rest, and she and Alaan continued to push the boat on. Tam was nearest Alaan in the stern and, as he slumped down trying to catch his breath, fighting the cramps in his arms and shoulders, he asked the traveler, "Is this not futile, Alaan? The soul eater has taken Wyrr. Is there any hope that we can catch them?"

"None if we chased after them, but I will take a quicker way, though it won't be much to your liking, I fear. It doesn't matter. If Wyrr is lost, then who is left to repair the spell that walls Mea'chi into his kingdom?" Alaan looked down at Tam, collapsed on the floorboards. His face was only barely visible, but Tam imagined his look was kindly. "It was always you, Tam, who buoyed the spirits of your companions, no matter what befell you. You must bear up a little longer."

"I will try. . . ." Tam searched for something more to say, feeling very low that he had disappointed Alaan.

"Don't worry, Tam," Alaan went on, "the soul eater has not the gift that Wyrr gave to Sainth. He can't travel the hidden paths. There is a chance we will reach the gate before him."

Tam sat up again, and Alaan and Elise slowed their rhythm a little, realizing that they were better to have the Valemen and the Fáel with them then to paddle alone, for even their stamina would diminish eventually. Tam didn't try to measure the time that passed, but it seemed like hours. Surely dawn would soon break on the eastern shore?

They passed into a mist, stirred by their paddles and their passing. The shores disappeared, and then the tops of the trees, so that only a few bright stars could be seen overhead—then these too drowned. A coolness settled around them, and the sounds of their paddles rippling the water sounded loud and strange.

"Can you find your way through this fog, Alaan?" Cynddl asked.

"Yes. Don't fear. But keep a lookout ahead. I can set our course but not see the dangers that lie along our path."

Fynnol glanced back at Tam, who could see that his cousin didn't much like the sound of this. The Valeman loosed his sword in its scabbard and readied his few arrows. Fynnol did the same. Moonlight touched the mist, and it appeared to glow faintly around them, swirling slowly and reaching out thin tentacles toward them.

Something large loomed out of the fog and darkness, causing Fynnol to start.

"A tree," whispered Elise, who was in the bow.

The apparition came abreast, grey-barked and massive.

"A stone tree," Tam whispered. "We have passed through such a place before, but far up the river."

"There is only one such place in all the world that I know," Alaan said. "The Stone Forest, and it is near the gate to Death's kingdom. If you found such a place before, then you were nearer death then than at any other time. Something must have saved you, perhaps unknown to you, or greater luck was with you, for most who see the stone trees never again lay their eyes upon the world of men."

"You say the most comforting things, Alaan," Fynnol said. "How much farther?"

"The quay will appear soon."

"Certainly you haven't been there before!" Fynnol whispered.

"Twice, and both times I found reprieve. I don't know if I can count on such luck again."

Fynnol might have answered, but Alaan bid them be quiet, and they paddled on in silence, gray-cloaked trees looming out of the night, water lapping eerily about their bases.

They had slowed their pace, perhaps afraid of running into one of the stone trees, though Tam suspected they were all unsettled by the place—even Elise and Alaan. Baore had shrunk down in the boat, and though he paddled with the rest, he was barely stirring the waters. Fynnol looked quickly this way and that and back again, as though afraid something lurked behind him. Tam thought of the monster they'd seen in the chamber—Hafydd's soul eater—and he felt his own breath start to come short.

Calm yourself, Tamlyn, he told himself. *That monster is not after the likes of you.* But he could not escape the feeling that the soul eater would smash up through the bottom of the boat at any moment.

He heard Elise catch her breath, and he looked up quickly, to see some greater darkness ahead, and in a few strokes a line appeared like a distant horizon.

"We are here," Alaan whispered.

A horrible grinding noise began then, and Baore stopped paddling altogether, staring straight ahead. "It is opening," he said, so softly Tam barely heard.

Tam realized that only Alaan continued to paddle, pressing them forward. The terrible grinding went on and on, so that the Valemen all covered their ears. And then it stopped. A hollow wind moaned, and a ruin of a voice echoed out of the darkness. "Why are you at my gate? Will you give up this life at last?"

Tam could not catch his breath and looked around in panic, as though there might be somewhere to hide.

"I have come with an offer," a woman's voice answered, "that even you will not refuse."

Tam could not have been more surprised if he'd heard his own mother's voice, there in that desolate place. The line before them began to take on depth, and Tam realized the quay was only a few yards off. Then, in the slow-whirling mists, figures appeared. One wore a hooded black cloak. Another lay upon the quay: the soul eater, writhing and swaying by the body of a dark-haired man.

The boat struck the step and Elise and Alaan leapt out onto the dark stones, but Tam was too frightened to follow. He and his companions knelt in the boat while it knocked gently against the quay. He felt a tear slip down his cheek and it was all he could do not to sob openly, so exhausted was he. All their efforts had come to failure.

A darkness fell on the stones before the gate, a shadow so black that it seemed to draw all light toward it. Tam closed his eyes a moment, then opened them again as the soul eater made a terrible moaning sound. The Valemen flinched back, and Tam snatched up his blade. The monster, dragging the body of Wyrr, began crawling toward the darkness, unable to lift its belly from the ground—a wounded beast creeping toward its hole.

The ruined voice echoed out of the shadow. "And where is the son of Wyrr? Where is Caibre?"

"He went back to make his kingdom among the living," the woman said.

Tam knew that voice. . . . *Meer.*

"But I am here, with a treasure above value, though my price will not be small."

"What is it you do, Grandmother?" Alaan said, stepping forward, but a gesture from Meer stopped him.

She held up her hand, and as her sleeve fell away, a gleaming gem appeared in her hand dangling on a chain. "The Stone of Remorse, it was once called, but each sorcerer who possessed the stone laid his own spell upon it. This is the smeagh of Aillyn, and in it he wove the designs of the great enchantments: the spell that split the One Kingdom, and the spell that sealed you behind these walls. It was to be given to a child of Wyrr, when it was needed. Long I tried to possess it, but I could not. Aillyn knew what use I would make of it."

There was a stirring in thc darkness inside the gate and Meer held out the stone before her. With the other hand she pulled back her hood and shook free her hair.

"There is no one alive who understands the spell that keeps you within these walls, Mea'chi. But the designs are here, within this stone—and I will give it to you . . . for a price."

"What is this price?" came the voice, so broken and ancient that it seemed a dry wind among stones.

"You will return the daughter you stole from me," she said, letting these words hang in the air a few seconds, "or I will give the stone to Sainth, and he will remake the spell that holds you, and there you will dwell in the darkness for another age."

A ripple and splash behind caused Tam to jump, and he turned in time to see a small figure climbing out of the waters.

"Llya!" Elise said, almost jumping in surprise. But then her face fell. "Go no farther," she said, crouching down. "I will pass through in your stead if Mea'chi will allow it."

"I will allow it," the ancient voice said quickly.

"But I will not," Llya answered quietly.

"River save us . . . !" muttered Fynnol, his eyes wide in surprise.

"I am unharmed," the child said, his voice clear and youthful and surprisingly mature. He faced Meer with a confidence beyond his years. "And that stone, Mother, is not yours to give. It is mine, and even without it I will remake the spell."

"Oh Llya, no!" Elise said, her eyes closing as though a knife pierced her heart.

But the child appeared not to hear. "You have failed, Mea'chi," he called into the darkness. He turned to Meer, "And so have you, Mother, though you would give me up to my father's enemy to have what you wanted."

"I knew the soul eater bore only a sack of skin," Meer said, backing away from the child. "But Wyrr . . . you should not have done this. He was only a child. . . ."

"You should never have wakened Caibre and set all that followed in motion." Llya's look softened, and he shook his head sadly. "Give me the stone, now," he chided gently. He took a step toward Meer, who shrank from him. "You know I can take it if I must," Llya said, the threat quiet but sure.

Meer looked at the gem, still dangling from her white fingers, and a tear trembled on her eyelashes. "It is the one thing he wants most in the world. . . ." she whispered.

"No," the child answered. "You are the thing he wants most."

For a few seconds she didn't move or even blink, a look of utter sadness passing over her face.

"You have given in to our enemy twice, now, Mother," Llya said.

She closed her eyes, tears glistening on her dark lashes. "Out of love," she whispered.

"And weakness. Mortal we were, who should never have been. And now you would unleash Mea'chi and his hunger upon the lands of the living." Almost tenderly, Llya untangled the chain from her fingers, placing it over his head so that the stone hung, glittering, upon his breast.

They faced each other, the child undaunted. A tear slipped down Meer's cheek, and then another. She reached out a hand as though she would caress the boy, but stopped, her gaze unreadable. She nodded once, as though agreeing with something only she had heard. Ever so slowly, she turned and walked toward the shadow; a picture of grace and dignity and sorrow. As she passed through, a raven-haired girl emerged from the darkness, blinking as though she had just wakened. A sob did escape Meer then, and she reached out, but something seemed to have hold of her and drew her into the shadow, where her sobs were suddenly distant, then gone.

"You have what you want," Llya said. "Close the gate. No more of us will pass through this day."

Nothing happened for too long, then the gate began to grind closed again, and just as it stopped, Tam thought he heard a sob from within, or perhaps it was a name called out in despair. Before the gate, where the impenetrable shadow had been, lay the black-haired man and the already-shriveling carcass of the soul eater. Tam gazed at the body of the dead sorcerer, so perfectly preserved that he looked as though he might wake. It was a handsome face, youthful and strong. Even in apparent sleep the beauty of Wyrr struck him. He could not imagine what presence the man must have had in life.

A movement drew Tam's attention. Elise Wills wrapped her cloak about the girl-child and knelt down to draw her close.

"She is cold as snow," Elise gasped.

"Colder," Llya said. "But you will warm her."

The girl buried her face in Elise's shoulder, and Tam thought she wept, though he could not be sure.

Alaan came and crouched before Llya. "What you do is wrong. He's only a child."

"You never had faith in me, did you Sainth?" Llya said softly.

"I had utter faith in you," Alaan answered, "to do whatever served you best."

Tam thought Llya looked hurt by this, his eyes glistening. "I will go back into the river and, in time, the child who bears me might forget the memories I leave behind. Let us hope." Llya took the stone from around his neck and, with his small hands, placed the chain over Alaan's head, then leaned forward and kissed him on both cheeks. "All the silent years we shared this world . . . How I regret them now." Llya placed his hands on Alaan's shoulders. "You must remake the spell. Mea'chi can never be unleashed upon the land of the living." He smiled sadly, too knowing by half, then turned to the others. "Leave this place, and may you not come here again for many years."

He went to Elise then and kissed her, then embraced his sister, though she seemed confused, unaware of who he might be. Releasing her, he waved a hand at the body of Wyrr. "My body must go back into the waters," he said so softly Tam barely heard.

Llya stood a moment on the quay, gazing at Elise and Alaan, as though reluctant to let them go. Then he turned away and waded into the waters, sinking quickly from sight. Tam stirred himself then and helped Alaan slip the body of Wyrr back into the water. The face of the ancient sorcerer appeared so serene, as though he slept, and dreamed only the fairest of dreams.

Cynddl looked on, distressed. "But I thought he said he would release the child."

"Wait a moment," Alaan said. "One thing you could say about Wyrr, he always kept his word."

And in a moment Llya emerged, spitting up water and splashing wildly. Baore waded quickly in and fished him out, setting him beside Elise in the boat. Another cloak was offered, and she wrapped it around the boy. He went to make a word with his hand, but then stopped.

"Thank you," he said haltingly, and a tiny smile flitted across his face.

The others climbed eagerly aboard, and Tam took up his paddle. They set off into the mist, Alaan guiding them. Elise sat upon the center thwart, an arm around a child to either side. The children leaned their heads against her, as though weary beyond measure. And then their small hands found each other in the near darkness, and the fingers entwined, clinging tightly—two children who had seen too much.

"We have no time for rest," Alaan said. "And I am sorry for it. But Hafydd can still bring ruin to the land of the living."

Forty-four

Menwyn kept his hands clasped behind his back lest their trembling betray his fear. As the night deepened, his anxieties intensified. The call of an owl seemed a bad omen to him, and the relentless creaking of the crickets was a torment almost beyond enduring.

"Is there no sign of the Renné?" he asked his lieutenant for the hundredth time.

"None, sir."

Menwyn glanced up at the sky. Dawn could not be far off. "Could the Renné have been warned?"

"There is still time," one of the noblemen said.

A rider came thundering up the valley in defiance of all orders.

"Who is that blunderer?" Menwyn snapped.

"I don't know, your grace," a junior officer responded. "But we'll find out." He ran to intercept the rider, and in a moment brought the man, flushed and gasping, back to Lord Menwyn.

"Well?" Menwyn said, trying to keep his voice low despite his anger.

"Your grace . . . ," the man managed between gasps. "A company of riders comes down the valley." He pointed back the way he had come. "Black-clad riders. It is Sir Eremon, and he is gathering companies to him as he nears."

There was no hope now of keeping his hands still. They flew up like fluttering birds. "Is no one resisting?"

The man shook his head. "As he comes he is calling out that the Renné are behind him, that we must form up and turn to fight."

"It is a lie! A ruse to frighten the men-at-arms into joining him."

"Your grace . . . ," the man said softly. "There is a large force coming down the valley not far behind Sir Eremon."

"No," Menwyn said stupidly. "Vast told us they would be landing here. Here . . .at the mouth of the Llynyth."

The sounds of horses reached him then.

"Form a mounted company!" Menwyn shouted. "Hafydd must be met on the field! Did you hear?"

But no one moved to deliver his order. A dozen men broke and ran for their horses—officers and noblemen.

"Cut them down!" Menwyn ordered. "No one deserts his post on pain of death!"

Chaos erupted around him, men running this way and that, scuffling over horses. Swords were drawn, and fighting broke out.

"Your grace!" It was Menwyn's equerry, holding the reins of a horse, blood running down his face. "You must go to Prince Michael. He's our only hope." Menwyn hesitated, unable to believe what happened around him. Men were killing each other over mounts. He caught sight of the approaching riders then—torches bobbing in the darkness illuminating the black horsemen.

Death himself would appear so, Menwyn thought.

He snatched the reins from his equerry, vaulted into the saddle, and, drawing his sword, rode off into the darkness.

Another company of riders could be heard far up the valley. This second force was much larger than the first they had seen, passing like shadows.

"Why is Menwyn moving riders into the draw now?" the Prince whispered to those around him. He looked up at the sky which he thought showed some sign of growing light. "The Renné can't help but hear all this. They will know we're here."

"This is a very large company," Pwyll said turning his head to listen. "Has Menwyn been hiding cavalry from us?"

Four horsemen loomed out of the dark and spoke the passwords to Prince Michael's guards.

"Ah," the prince said. "Now we'll learn what goes on."

One of his guards ran up. "Your grace," he said. "Lord Menwyn."

Michael glanced over at Pwyll, who seemed as surprised as he. Lord Menwyn was led quickly through the circle of guards.

The Wills nobleman ignored all polite convention, striding up to Michael. "Hafydd has returned!" he hissed. "Returned and seized control of my army. Vast betrayed us. . . ." Menwyn gestured wildly up the valley. "The Renné are at our backs."

No one responded, or even moved. Menwyn stepped closer to Prince Michael.

"You must attack Hafydd, Prince Michael. If he survives this night there is no place where we can hide from him."

"But this army wants revenge upon the Renné," T'oldor protested.

"The desire for revenge has led us to this pass!" Michael said angrily. "No plague has ever caused more suffering or spread its contagion more easily." He turned to his officers. "I will go from company to company. The men must understand that we take up arms against a sorcerer to preserve more than our lives. It is to preserve the world we know."

A great echoing clash resounded down the valley as the Renné army met Hafydd's force.

"There is no time!" Lord Menwyn protested, grabbing the Prince's arm.

Michael shook him off. "There is no other way." He snatched a newly lit torch away from a guard, but before he'd gone many steps he stopped. Turning back to the others, he pointed at Menwyn. "Put this man in the forefront of the cavalry and be sure he has a sword."

"But I am Menwyn Wills—"

"Yes, and you are as responsible as any for the plight we find ourselves in this night. All the suffering your conspiracies have caused, and you thought never to pay the cost."

Vast rode in the center of a small company of Renné guards. They'd taken his sword, stripped him of his mail, and tied him to his saddle, leaving his hands free. He was wearing a surcoat of Renné blue so that his own allies would kill him. The Duke found himself wondering how long he would last in battle. Perhaps the Renné had laid bets. Certainly a few moments would see his end. He thought tenderly of his wife then. Of their palace and gardens. Of the fields where he liked to ride and see the grains grow.

Torches appeared ahead. A bit of light made shadows out of darkness. And then a line of horsemen loomed out of the night. The Renné let out a great shout, and the two lines of cavalry struck like a hammer to an anvil.

There was fighting all around. Vast ducked his head and wheeled his horse. He saw a man in a Wills surcoat raise his sword to deliver a stroke to a Renné and he tore the blade from the man's hand, knocking him from the saddle with a blow to his helm.

He turned his horse in time to parry a slash from another Wills rider. In desperation he cut the man down. The irony was not lost on him. He was fighting for the Renné whom he had tried to betray. Fondor wasn't such a ponderous fool after all.

Michael of Innes rode down into the valley at the head of his reluctant army. No one knew if they would engage the enemy or turn and flee the field. Perhaps the men-at-arms didn't know themselves. Michael found air came into his lungs in shallow gasps. If the army would not fight he would be left alone on the field with a handful of loyal men, all of whom would soon be dead.

I survived the servants of Death, he told himself. *Armed men cannot frighten me.* But he *was* frightened all the same. Frightened of the darkness, of sorcery, of the shadow land that lay just out of sight of the living.

Down the valley, a terrible battle was being fought. At this distance, in the poor light, it was difficult to be sure what went on, but the battle was moving away from the river, and he was sure that wasn't a good sign. The Renné were being driven back, slowly, relentlessly, despite having the element of surprise and superior numbers. In the thick of the battle, what had at first appeared to be a waving torch, the prince now realized, was a flaming sword, cutting this way and that. *Hafydd.*

Bodies began to appear on the ground, their limbs twisted, as though they had been thrown down from the sky. Riderless horses galloped among the dead, frightened and lost. Little knots of wounded staggered past, bearing each other up, and the clash of arms could be felt now, like blows to the chest.

Michael raised his sword and glanced to his left, where Carl A'denné did the same. To his right, Pwyll took up their cry, lowering a lance. They spurred their horses forward, and behind he heard their cry echoed. It seemed to carry him forward, almost lifting him from the saddle. And they were upon the rear of Hafydd's army. The Renné line had broken, and they fought in isolated companies, the sky-blue of the Renné surrounded and assailed by evening blue.

The army of Innes fell upon the forces of evening and the small companies of black clad guards. The Prince cut down his first man, throwing him from the saddle, then caused his horse to kick another, the shod hooves snapping a rider's leg. A black guard appeared before him, and the Prince's guard divided before him, the fear of Hafydd's magic clinging even to his servants.

The rider fell upon the Prince, strong and skilled. Michael was driven back, parrying each stroke, the sword almost flung from his hand. He quickly realized that he'd met a superior swordsman and rider when a second black guard appeared and attacked him from the other side. The Prince spun his horse and slashed this way and that, looking for a chance to flee, for these two would kill him in a moment. But then a horseman of Innes appeared, and one black guard was thrown down and trampled. It was Pwyll, Michael realized, as the knight engaged the second rider, forcing him back, countering every trick the man used. In a moment the second guard was lying on the ground, bleeding, unable to rise.

"You saved my life, Pwyll," Michael called out.

"You may not thank me," Pwyll shouted over the din. He pointed with his blade. Among the whirling dust and smoke from torches, Prince Michael saw Hafydd bearing down on them, his sword ablaze. Men fled before him, and a company of black guards rode behind, falling on the fleeing men from behind, slaying all in their path.

A black guard rode at the Prince and Pwyll, perhaps expecting them to turn and run, but Pwyll cut the man from his saddle with three quick strokes, then, using the flat of his blade, he drove the man's horse back into Hafydd. The two animals collided, and as Hafydd tried to control his mount, Pwyll took out its eye with the point of his blade.

The warhorse stumbled and fell, Hafydd going down in a sheet of flame. The sorcerer's guards drove desperately toward Pwyll, but Michael and a handful of other riders pressed forward to meet them. Pwyll tried to ride over the fallen Hafydd, but the sorcerer held the horse back with his flaming sword as he staggered up.

Pwyll would have engaged Hafydd, but his horse kept shying from the flames and the presence of the sorcerer. Pwyll finally leapt down and let the horse run. He strode toward Hafydd with his sword high.

"So there is one man among you," Hafydd called out. "Too bad you fight for the wrong lord." The sorcerer raised his blade and in one quick motion threw flames over Pwyll, setting his surcoat afire.

Hafydd stepped quickly forward to finish the knight, but even aflame Pwyll raised his own blade and turned the blow aside. He staggered back, then desperately tried to wipe flame away from his face. The sorcerer came forward again, watching, awaiting a clear opportunity. Pwyll could no longer see and stumbled back, almost falling.

Michael saw Carl A'denné jump from the saddle and go after Pwyll. Michael spun his horse and made it kick, its hind legs lashing out toward Hafydd, the flame hidden from its view. Once, twice the horse kicked, and Lord Carl tore away Pwyll's surcoat and led him, running blind, away. Prince Michael spurred his horse then, out of the reach of Hafydd's sword.

He rode into the darkness and the chaotic fighting and killed a Wills man-at-arms who had engaged one of his own riders. It hardly mattered; if no one could face Hafydd, he would carry the day. Already he could see men breaking and running. Flame caught in the grass and the trees along the valley's edge. A small barn burned not far off, and smoke lay in the valley like morning fog. He realized then that defeat was certain. It was only a matter of when.

Forty-five

Elise held her blade in the water and pointed. The paddlers turned the boat toward the darkened shore. Tam had no idea where they were. It seemed like they'd been driving the boat forward for half the night, but with Alaan aboard, that effort could have taken them anywhere. They might not even be in the land between the mountains. A wash of gray seeped up from the eastern horizon, staining the sky. Along the near shore, however, night lingered beneath the trees. A distant din reached them over the waters, and the smell of smoke clung to the air.

"What is that sound?" Fynnol whispered.

"Battle . . . ," A'brgail answered.

"Hafydd is here," Elise said, her voice empty and lifeless. She took her blade, dripping, from the water, and rose to her feet, staring off at the shore, not fearfully, but not with hope either.

Alaan pulled his sword from its scabbard and glanced back at the others. Lifting his paddle inboard, Tam flexed his back and shoulders, trying to work out the knots. The boat came gliding up to the bank, and Elise stepped ashore, Alaan right behind her.

"Baore—please," Elise said. "Will you guard these children? I will not fail Eber twice."

Baore did not meet her gaze. "There is a battle, my lady. You will need me."

"I can't leave the children unprotected. Take them out into the river if you must. Please, Baore . . . ?"

"As you wish," he replied softly.

To the others she said. "Come, any who will. Hafydd is here, and despite brave hearts there are none on the field who can stand against him."

A narrow band of trees grew at the end of the valley, along the bank of the Wynnd. There it was dark, the damp voice of the river clear and soft, the ground beneath their feet redolent with decay.

Over the voice of the river, the tumult of battle could be heard. Tam tightened his grip on his sword. In his other hand he held a bow, though only a precious few arrows remained.

Emerging from the trees they saw chaos, riders and men on foot locked in ferocious battle. Tam could see others retreating into the trees, the valley was afire, and men, their clothes burning, came running out of the smoke, screaming.

Horses materialized out of the cloud, blind with fear. Some ran right at them, only turning away at the last second. There in the dust and smoke, barely lit by the still-distant dawn, stood a warrior with a flaming sword.

"You will leave Hafydd to Alaan and me," Elise said, glancing once at Tam, though speaking to all. "Heroism would be foolish here. If we can bring Hafydd down, his army will break and run."

"We'll try to keep back his guards," Cynddl said.

As they all set off across the field, Elise reached out and grasped Tam's arm. "I wish I could have left you safe at the boat," she whispered. "You have risked enough in this war."

"No more than many others," Tam said. Their fingers found each other and clasped for a second, then they were running, running against a tide of fleeing men, some afire. Hafydd was winning.

Alaan found Tam in the smoke, and shouted, "The men of

Innes and the Renné are in flight. They are the enemies of Hafydd. The dark surcoats are the Wills, and Hafydd's guards." He slapped Tam once on the shoulder and was gone, following Elise into the smoke.

Tam sheathed his sword and drew an arrow. In the smoke and false dawn it was hard to tell friend from foe, but he let fly at a rider clothed in dark and watched him fall, the Fáel bow proving stronger than mail at short distance.

He tried to stay close to Fynnol and Cynddl, as they all followed Elise into the smoke. They were forced to skirt areas of burning grass, the flames in places reaching higher than their heads. Men appeared out of the clouds, some fighting, others looking for their enemies. Tam fired at any dark surcoats he saw, but the smoke billowed and whirled, revealing men for an instant, then hiding them again a second later. He feared some arrows went into the ground.

A flame appeared in the smoke, then a man wielding it.

"Hafydd!" Alaan shouted to Elise, and pointed with his sword. Heat seemed to emanate from the knight—it seared his face and stung his eyes, forcing him back, looking about madly. Horsemen rode out of the smoke and Tam would have been cut in two by one, but Alaan took the man from his saddle in one stroke. Elise had another, and Cynddl put an arrow in a third, and the rest were gone, devoured by the clouds.

Hafydd saw Elise and came striding toward her, the wave of heat driving Tam and the others back.

"Fall back to the stream!" Alaan ordered, and Tam began a retreat to where he hoped the creek lay. There was no sound of water to be heard over the din of battle, the cries of men, and the searing crackle of fire.

Alaan and Elise raised their swords and, two-handed, drove the points into the ground. Tam was thrown onto his back as the ground beneath him heaved, and a deep, rending sound rolled across the valley. He tried to get up but was thrown to his knees. A dark, jagged rift snaked along the ground, which then parted, tearing open like a wound. Alaan and Elise both scrambled to their feet, separated by the opening ground.

Two dozen feet away, Hafydd tumbled into the fissure. Elise and Alaan drove their swords into the ground again, this time to either side of the crack. Tam braced himself and felt the earth shudder, grinding as it moved. The crevice stuttered closed, leaving an ugly, dark scar across the ground.

The tremors stopped, and Tam could see Alaan and Elise, both leaning on the pommels of their swords, heads hanging down as they gasped for breath. Alaan forced his head up, spotted Tam and tried to smile. The sound of battle had ceased, and a strange silence fell over the valley.

"He is dead!" a voice cried in the smoke. "The sorcerer is dead!"

Alaan staggered to his feet, but was thrown back as the ground exploded, and a column of fire erupted out of the earth. Cynddl dragged Tam up. His eyes were filled with dirt, and he wiped at them with one hand, his bow still tightly grasped in the other. A figure emerged from the fire: Hafydd, his sword still in flame.

Tam thought Alaan and Elise looked at each other, not so much in surprise but as though Hafydd's return was inevitable, somehow. Tam remembered that Sianon had given her life to destroy Caibre, and he heard himself whisper, "*Not this day.*"

Tam nocked an arrow, shouting to Cynddl. "Elise will die to kill him if we can't help."

Tam tried to sight Hafydd along the shaft, but he was still half-blind from the explosion. He let the arrow fly, not sure if it was even close to the mark. Smoke and flame surrounded Hafydd, as though he himself were afire, and he was never wholly in view. Tam rubbed at his eyes, backing away as Hafydd came toward them. Even Alaan and Elise were retreating, half-blind.

Cynddl and Fynnol both let arrows fly at Hafydd.

"I swear they burn to ash before they reach him," Fynnol cried.

Tam stepped back, almost falling into the stream. He felt the cool water run down his boot.

"Elise!" he shouted. "The stream!"

She turned and ran toward Tam, leaving Alaan. Tam could see the traveler stop retreating. He took a fighting stance and raised his sword. Alaan, Tam knew, was far stronger than he appeared and full of deceptions and guile, but Hafydd appeared so much more powerful than he, billowing flame as he stalked the traveler.

"You cannot stand against us both," Alaan cried out. "Better to lay down your sword and go into the river than through the black gate."

"The gate will not open for me," Hafydd shouted. He raised his flaming sword and came toward Alaan, who did not recoil.

Elise stumbled down into the river, thrusting her blade into the water. Tam could hear her mumbling rapidly. In the smoke, Tam saw Hafydd aim a great stroke at Alaan, and though the traveler looked as though he would stand and meet it with his own blade, he dodged aside at the last second and let Hafydd drive his sword into the ground.

Alaan swung at him, his blade arcing into the knight's side. Hafydd was knocked down but rolled to his feet, nimble and apparently unharmed, his mail having turned the stroke.

Tam soaked an arrow in the stream and let it fly, watching it bury itself in Hafydd's shoulder. The knight staggered a step, then threw flame at Alaan, and at Tam. The Valeman leapt aside, stumbling into the water, trying to keep his bowstring dry. He lunged up, and reached for another arrow, but they were gone—spent.

"Fynnol!" he cried. "Cynddl?" He must have more arrows, but his companions were not in sight. Smoke seared his lungs so that a spasm of coughing gripped him. He could see only Alaan, locked in combat with Hafydd. The wander's cloak caught fire, but he tore it off with one hand and threw it aside. It hardly seemed to have touched the ground before it rose, as though caught by a wind, and flew at Hafydd's face.

Alaan ducked low and cut at Hafydd's leg, catching him just below the knee. Hafydd staggered but did not fall, and the cloak was thrown aside. It flared for a second, then whirled away.

"I know all your feints, Brother," Hafydd taunted. "Have you nothing new to show me?"

A broad snake of water slithered out of the river, running ankle deep through the blackened grass. It reached Hafydd in a heartbeat and surged up his leg, smothering flame as it went. The knight looked down in surprise, as the tendril of water circled his waist, then ran up his arm and extinguished the flaming sword.

"Only the inside of a grave, Brother," Alaan said, and waded in with his sword, driving the limping Hafydd back. The knight had only one good arm, from Tam's arrow, and Alaan hewed at him two-handed, the force of his blows almost driving the blade from Hafydd's hands.

Elise leapt from the stream, running toward the two men. She raised her sword, and Tam thought that certainly Hafydd would fall now.

As Elise was about to strike a blow, Hafydd spun in a circle, fire spraying from his blade. He threw a circle of flame around the three of them, and Tam was sure he heard the sorcerer shout in triumph. The flames leapt up, and smoke billowed out, driving Tam down onto his haunches on the stream's far shore. He realized that the battle was still being fought, riders clashing furiously, knots of men hewing at each other, screaming in rage and pain. It all seemed so distant.

Elise was blinded by fire and smoke, holding up an arm to protect her face from the heat. Hafydd was lost in the fire, as was Alaan. She had been here before . . . long ago.

She remembered.

The walls had been thrown down, gates torn from their hinges. He had dammed up the river . . . with a spell, until the stream bed itself ran dry, and his armies came swarming over what had once been an impenetrable moat—her great defense. Armies fell upon each other and were consumed in fire and magic.

The memories came back to her, drifting back.

Smoke and flame everywhere, stone burning, exploding from heat. And he had pursued her up into the ruin of a tower, where there was no escape but into the air. Sianon had backed up the broken stair, Caibre in pursuit, hobbling where she'd wounded him—wounded him at great price, for he'd run a sword through her left arm, which hung useless, blood oozing through the rag she'd tied around it.

His helmet was silver, reflecting the fire of his sword: she remembered that—and his face contorted in rage. She shrank away, toward the shattered wall, hardly a parapet.

Caibre stopped at the stair head, looking quickly around, realizing then that she was trapped. "Come, Sister," he said, his voice soft and malevolent, "I will send you to join your beloved brother. . . ."

"A place I would go gladly," she said. "But not alone. . . ."

Dim figures appeared in the smoke; Hafydd and Alaan, locked in battle. She lurched forward to support Alaan, but they were gone, swept away in the whirling smoke.

Caibre used his great sword two-handed, like Slighthand, but she had only one good arm and was forced to rely on quickness and guile. She leapt onto the wall and almost landed behind him, for he was hobbling and slow—if it wasn't all an act. Caibre was ever cunning and duplicitous.

A horse and rider, entirely aflame, raced by, and Elise barely jumped clear. The heat was unbearable and she choked and coughed, the smoke burning her throat and lungs, searing her eyes. A black billowing cloud forced her to turn, driving her to her knees.

She had stumbled at last, despite her swiftness, and barely rolled out of the way of Caibre's stroke. His sword rang on the stone beside her head.

The smoke clung to her, as though it had claws, but a small breeze tore it free, and Hafydd stood before her, sword raised. She was about to leap aside when she realized he was turned away from her, and there, barely visible, Alaan braced himself, sword high. Elise did not hesitate, but sprang forward, slashing at the back of Hafydd's knee. But at the last second he moved, and drove the pommel of his sword into her head.

The memories burned inside her. . . .

He had trapped her in the tower, and no matter what she did, kept himself between her and the stair. Several times their swords met, and even one-handed she did not falter. She kicked his good foot out from under him, sending Caibre crashing down on the stone, but with only one good arm she could not finish him. He turned her blows aside, rising slowly, finally finding his feet, still limping and slow, but formidable even so. She cut his forearm, and saw him bleed, and he struck her good hand a glancing blow with the flat of his blade, cracking a bone. The afternoon bore on to evening, the sorcerers in the tower locked in combat, burning stones tumbling down the walls, where they bounced and rolled into the riverbed and lay hissing in the damp earth.

Elise fell forward, dazed, but some shred of awareness told her hand to hold on to the sword. The world seemed to draw away, the sounds of fire and battle fading. She expected the final blow—the point driven into her heart or the blade slicing through her neck—but it did not come. And then the sounds of battle came drifting back, the blistering heat. She opened her eyes, and saw a hand, bleeding, holding a smoky blade. She forced herself up on one knee, where coughing and nausea stopped her. For a moment she reeled, then forced herself to stagger up. Alaan could not stand against Hafydd alone. She knew.

She tried to turn the blow aside, but it struck her sword full force . . . shattering the blade, leaving her with a foot of steel. Sianon leapt back, looking desperately around. Caibre lumbered forward, driving her into a corner with his flaming sword, too long to elude.

"Ah, Sister," he said. "You disappoint me. Sainth put up almost as good a fight . . . before I cut him down." He raised his blade, a faint smile appearing.

Elise stumbled forward, barely able to raise her sword two-handed. She felt the memories inside her, body memories of battles and individual combat. Many lifetimes of warfare. A deep breath and she opened the gate, letting the memories surge to the surface of her consciousness. Without Sianon, Elise Wills would not survive this day. A rage came over her, a bloodlust. She felt her grip tighten on the hilt of her sword, though she had not willed it. The rage was beyond her understanding, like a poison coursing through her veins, like acid. It focused her mind as though she saw the world through the keyhole of this hatred. Everything else was cast aside. There was only the battle. The chance for revenge.

The rage was molten in her veins, the world reduced to her brother, standing over her with a sword. But he savored the moment too long. She drove the broken point of her blade into the stone, shivering the rock. There was a cistern below them, unknown to Caibre. It exploded like dust ignited in a granary. Caibre stumbled, his stroke falling wide. The tower lurched and crumbled, tumbling into ruin, bringing down the curtain wall below. Sianon fell among the battering stones. Darkness. . . .

And then the ripple of water.

Tam circled to the right of the wall of fire, trying to see through the flames and smoke, all the while glancing over his shoulder where riders would appear, and disappear, horses running wild. A dark silhouette materialized out of the smoke—a black-robed guard. Without hesitation, Tam went at him with all the fury he could muster—there was no place for half measures in battle. The fight was brutal and surprisingly short, the guard going down after Tam slashed his knee, then put his blade through a gap in the guard's mail and into his throat. He went back to circling the fire, trying to see what happened beyond. Shadows and dark shapes would appear faintly in the flame—apparitions, Tam thought, only clouds of billowing dark smoke.

He kept hoping beyond hope that there would be a gap in the flames that would let him through.

Hafydd loomed out of the murk, standing over someone prostrate on the ground. The knight lifted his sword high, and Elise stepped forward and drove the point of her blade into Hafydd's shoulder, rending the iron rings. Hafydd stumbled, half-falling over Alaan.

Elise jerked her blade free, then just barely dodged a blow, as Hafydd spun and slashed at her face.

Alaan rolled to his feet, shaking his head. Without a word, Alaan began to circle away to Hafydd's left, Elise to his right, staying as far apart as possible.

"You've stopped taunting, Brother," Alaan said. "Can you not catch your breath?" He feinted toward Hafydd's head, and Elise cut toward his leg. But Hafydd was equal to it, dodging aside, almost catching Elise with the tip of his flaming sword.

Hafydd stamped his foot, and a column of flame jetted up from the ground, blinding Elise. She leapt back and to one side as Hafydd's blade slashed through the air a few inches from her throat.

Dense smoke rolled over the field, blinding Elise for a moment. Hafydd was there . . . then he was not. She crouched low, sword ready, turning this way and that, expecting the flaming blade to strike out of the smoke. A figure appeared and she stopped her blade before it severed Alaan's arm. He flinched, then realized it was her. They turned back to back, each guarding before them and to their right.

"I don't know how he broke my spell," Elise said, her eyed darting this way and that, trying to peel back the dark haze.

"He was ready for us," Alaan answered. "More prepared than we were for him."

"We need to escape the fire ring," Elise said.

"Not with our lives we won't. Either we kill Hafydd, or we die here—"

Fire blossomed to her left, rising up to the height of a man. They sidled quickly away.

"Where is he?" Elise whispered. "Why is he waiting?"

A shroud of smoke wafted over them, as dark as night. Elise could hear Alaan coughing. They pressed back to back, not wanting to lose each other, and to her horror, Elise felt desire course through her. She stumbled and scrambled back up, staggering away from Alaan. She drove the feelings down—her own brother! Repelled, she pushed back the rage, the consuming hatred . . . and then she was alone. . . . Elise Wills, standing on a seething field of battle, stalked by a sorcerer. She did not know which way to turn, what to do.

"*Alaan!*" she called out. "*Alaan?*"

Flame swept out of the darkness, burning into Elise's side. She fell into the smouldering grass, her sword gone, and a smothering pall swept over her.

For an instant the smoke thinned, and Tam saw Hafydd standing over a figure, who was trying to rise. And then the smoke enveloped them again.

"Elise?" he whispered. "Elise!"

Tam drew his sword and was about to charge the wall of flame, when something caught his eye. He thought it was a trick of smoke and poor light, but then it appeared again—among the fighting men and riderless horses—a small child walking uncertainly through the madness. He spotted Tam and turned toward him. For a second the smoke washed over the child, and Tam saw a horsemen ride through, swinging down with his sword, but a second later the child emerged, unscathed.

"*Llya* . . . ," Tam said. He ran, smoke burning his lungs, and reached the child in a few strides. "Llya! Where is Baore?" Tam asked.

"He waits by the river." The boy held up something—an arrow laid across his small hands.

"It must go into his eye," he said in his child's voice. "You cannot miss."

For a second Tam didn't understand, but then he snatched the arrow, set it in place and drew back his bowstring. He stared into the whirling clouds, his eyes watering from the smoke and fire and heat. Figures appeared—unrecognizable silhouettes. Alaan he thought, and waited. How would he ever put an arrow in a man's eye through this? Even on a clear day with the target standing still such a shot would be nearly impossible. Like shooting a coin at thirty paces.

Hafydd appeared in the smoke, like a shadow, his blade raised. Tam couldn't tell if he faced away or toward him. It can't be done, he thought. Not one time in a thousand. And then he felt a small hand reach up and come to rest on his hip, the touch both fragile and reassuring.

"The river carried you here for a purpose," Llya said.

Tam drew the arrow back a further inch and let it fly at the shadow. The smoke billowed over again, swallowing everything.

Tam lowered his bow. "I missed," he said, the words almost a sob. "There was no shot."

The wind backed and buried them in caustic smoke and ash, so that Tam crouched down and tried to protect the child, drawing him near in the burning darkness.

The smoke rolled aside again, and two figures appeared—Elise with her arm over Alaan's shoulder, leaning on him heavily. Her eyes were closed and her face twisted in pain.

Tam went quickly forward and put an arm around her, helping Alaan to bear her up. A dozen steps, and they lowered her into the little creek, where the water ran around her. She nodded her thanks, eyes shut tight and jaw clenched. She held a hand to her side, and Tam realized blood seeped between her fingers.

"Elise!" Tam cried, and crouched in the water, reaching out to pull her hand away.

She leaned her face into the crook of his neck, wet with sweat and tears.

"You must bring your brother," Tam heard Llya say. "Your father vowed long ago that Death would have none of you. I remember."

There was no answer. Tam could see Alaan. He had fallen down by the stream's edge and gasped for breath.

"Sainth . . . ," Llya said, his child's voice urgent.

"Cynddl?" Alaan called. "Fynnol? Can you help me?"

Alaan and Fynnol set off, but Tam remained, holding Elise, her face, bruised and bleeding and slick with tears. Cynddl came and stood guard over them, though he looked near to collapse.

Tam felt Elise take his hand and press it to her soft breast. "I must go into the river, Tam," she said. "You cannot follow."

She kissed him once, then let him go. She slipped beneath the surface, and Tam saw something ghostly in the waters. It fooled the eye with its speed, passed swiftly through the shallows, and was lost to sight.

Cynddl dropped to his knees in the shallows. Reaching out, Tam put a hand on the Fáel's shoulder. He tried to speak, but no words would come.

"It's over," Cynddl rasped finally. "Hafydd is dead."

Alaan and Fynnol appeared out of the smoke, dragging the black-robed Hafydd. They dumped him unceremoniously into the creek, splashing Tam and Cynddl. The body sank into the shallow water, mouth slack, the shaft of an arrow still protruding from one eye.

"Pull up his mail," Alaan said, bending over the fallen sorcerer and tearing at his clothes. He and Fynnol pulled the armor up under the dead man's armpits and Alaan took his sword and drove it through the body's chest. Even Tam was horrified. With all his weight, Alaan pressed the blade down until it pinned Hafydd to the creek bottom.

"Caibre might go back into the river," Alaan said, dropping down on the bank and wiping a hand over his smoke-stained face. "But Hafydd goes onto the pyre."

Hafydd's corpse went rigid suddenly, the back arching. Fynnol scrambled up, snatching a sword off the ground. A milky fluid appeared to ooze from the sorcerer's pores. It swirled off downstream—taking a vaguely human shape—then it too was gone.

Something caught Tam's eye, and he looked up and started. One of Hafydd's black clad guards sat on a horse, staring down at his former master. When he saw Tam's reaction he held out a hand, palm out.

"He's dead," Alaan said to the ominous rider. "If you lay down your arms, you will be treated with mercy."

The guard continued to stare, his face unreadable, then turned his horse and disappeared into the smoke. The sounds of battle were dying away. A riderless horse thundered out the murk and was gone just as quickly. Men began to limp by, toward the river, and the smoke thinned.

Tam realized that morning had dawned without him noticing. Above the smoke and dust it might even have been a clear day. Alaan asked Tam's help, and they tumbled the body of Hafydd out onto the shore, limp and ashen. A small pool of water formed around the corpse. Alaan rummaged the body like a thief, but took only a dagger in a sheath.

"He's dead?" Fynnol asked. "Truly dead?"

"Yes," Alaan said softly. "The nagar has fled into the river. We'll burn the corpse to ash. This time there will be no reprieve."

Tam collapsed on the riverbank, feeling a sob well up inside. But he forced himself to breathe and swallowed it down.

A company of riders appeared, all in soiled Renné blue. A double-swan banner fluttered in a new breeze.

"I'm told that Hafydd is dead?" said a large man, as smoke-stained as the rest. He lifted a helm from his head and hung it from his saddle.

Alaan gestured to the corpse. "And who are you, sir?"

"Fondor Renné," the man said, then nodded to another rider. "My cousin, Lord Kel. If you killed the sorcerer we are deeply in your debt."

Alaan shook his head. "The arrow wasn't mine." He glanced over at Tam, then Cynddl. "One of you, I expect?"

"We all played our part," Tam said. He looked down at the child who had gravitated toward Fynnol and stood leaning against the small Valeman with a familiarity that only children could conjure with their chosen protectors. "Llya found the arrow. . . ." He glanced up at the Renné noblemen and thought that they did not need to know more about the boy who had become the voice of a river.

Men-at-arms began to converge on the place—to see the dead
sorcerer. They were battered, exhausted, a look of horror in their
eyes. They emerged out of the thinning smoke like spectres, quiet
as the dead. A second group of riders appeared. These wore the
purple of the House of Innes—a livery Tam could not see without
a flash of apprehension.

"Is that Prince Michael?" Fondor said, a little surprised.

"Lord Fondor," the young Prince said. "I'm thankful to see you
unharmed." He nodded graciously to Lord Kel, then looked over
at the others. "Alaan? You look like you have walked through fire."

"And so I have, my Prince," Alaan said. "We have managed to
kill Hafydd for you, though it would never have been done without
Lady Elise."

"And where is she?" the Prince asked quickly.

"She has gone to tend a wound. I don't think you will see her
again this day."

"But she will recover?"

"So we hope."

Fondor was gazing over at the prince's party. "Samul?"

"I don't believe this is Renné land," Samul said quickly.

"No," Fondor said softly. "These are the estates of the House of
Innes. You have only the Prince to answer to, here."

"Samul Renné has permission to travel my lands freely. To settle here, if he wishes. Without him and Jamm and Carl and Pwyll,
I should never have survived to take back my father's army."

"Pwyll!" Alaan said. "Where is he?"

"He was wounded—burned, in combat with Hafydd."

"Where?"

"In the shade of the trees." Prince Michael pointed.

Alaan scrambled up. "I must see to him." Alaan turned to the
others. "I haven't even asked if any of you are hurt?"

All were injured in minor ways, but all shook their heads. On
such a day a broken arm would be considered good fortune.

Alaan looked from one Valemen to the other. "We owe a great

debt to you, Cynddl, and to you northerners. This was not your war, yet you have been in the center of it from the beginning."

"It was no one's war," Fynnol said. "It was just the echo of a struggle that began before history. A feud over . . . what I still don't understand. A child, perhaps. A sorcerer who succumbed to madness. A spell that contained that madness." He shook his head. "Perhaps it is about a swan that did not want to die." He looked up at the story finder. "Maybe you will make sense of it, Cynddl. And put it all into a story."

"There isn't one story," Cynddl said. "There are myriad tales to be told, all different and puzzling. It is vain to ask them to make sense. Rath taught me that: just tell the tales. They will speak for themselves."

Forty-six

The day was spent separating the wounded from the fallen. All through the morning boats plied back and forth over the river carrying the wounded to the healers and returning those who were beyond the healers' skill. A great pyre was built for the dead beside the river, and silent companies of the living carried their fallen brothers there. Orlem Slighthand was not there to be mourned, but his friends made a small ceremony by the river, and Cynddl told a story of Slighthand and his home in the hidden lands. The massive sword, rescued by Elise, was claimed by A'brgail as a relic of his order, for it was Slighthand and Kilydd who had secretly formed the Knights of the Vow so many years before.

"Elise should have been here," Fynnol said to Tam. "It was Elise he loved and followed, even more than Alaan."

"It was Sianon he loved," Tam said, "and she's gone."

A cloud of sooty terns wheeled and dived into the river, bobbing up and taking once more to the air to call mournfully. The sun was over the other shore now, its light glittering on the dancing river.

Boats passed back and forth with news and families looking for their loved ones. The pyre was soaked in oil and lit, the smoke streaming straight up for some hundred feet, then drifting south on a high wind.

Tam thought he should feel lucky to be alive, but he felt nothing at all. Sounds seemed to echo hollowly from some distant place, and even his thoughts seemed not quite his own, surfacing randomly and often going nowhere. He and his companions walked up the bank a little, where they stripped off their smoky clothes and dived into the river. Tam floated there, on his back, cradled by the cool water, the summer sun caressing his face.

"Is it over?" Fynnol asked after an age of silence. "I mean really over?" The little Valeman floated a few feet away, his eyes closed.

"Caibre has returned to the river," Cynddl said, "and Alaan took an ancient dagger from Hafydd's body—a smeagh, I would guess—then burned the corpse. The Wills and the Renné have met in battle and the usurper, Menwyn, is dead." He paused. "And a child returned from the shadow kingdom—returned as no one ever has before. If Alaan can repair the spell, then I think we can say it is over . . . at least over for our lifetimes."

They drifted like that for a time, listening to their own quiet breathing and the distant crying of the terns. Alaan appeared on the bank and called to them, and they swam reluctantly ashore.

"How fares Pwyll?" Cynddl asked.

"Well enough. He tried to fight Hafydd on his own." Alaan shook his head. "Of all people he should have known better. He's with the healers, now."

"Where are we going?" Fynnol wondered.

"Across the river. I want to go see the Fáel. They sent word that Eber is there, and he doesn't yet know that Llya is safe."

"And how will you explain what happened? That the child he knows is gone, replaced with a. . . ." Fynnol let the sentence die, and glanced at Alaan, afraid that he had offered offense.

Alaan didn't seem to notice. "I will tell him the truth; Wyrr went back into the waters but his memories remain." Alaan shook his head. "Llya was never born for an ordinary life, poor child. I don't know what will become of him."

Tam pointed to the crowds converging on the far shore. Pavilions were being raised. It looked like a fair. "What goes on?"

"The Renné are gathering—to celebrate a victory, I would guess."

"How can any celebrate this?" Fynnol asked, waving a hand toward the still burning pyre. "Thousands lost their lives this day— thousands, from all sides. If any won, I don't know who it was."

"The survivors won," Alaan said, then reached out and put a hand on the little Valeman's shoulders. "You, Fynnol Lowell." But then the smile disappeared. "But we have all been delivered from Mea'chi and Hafydd. Few will ever know or understand, but the living have cause to celebrate."

A large boat was waiting to carry them across the river. The girl, Sianon, and Llya waited there under the eye of a kindly Renné guard. She squinted and blocked the sun with a hand, but Tam had yet to hear her utter a single word. Perhaps the now-vocal Llya would have to teach her the hand speech.

Prince Michael of Innes, Carl A'denné, and several Renné noblemen stood by, all still smoke-stained and grim. They didn't look like men who had won a war.

"There is a rumor," Prince Michael said, "that one of the men from the wildlands shot the arrow that brought down Hafydd."

"It was Tam," Fynnol said, making a little mock bow toward his cousin.

Prince Michael did smile then. "The river didn't bring you so far without purpose," he said.

"Why *did* you venture so far south?" Fondor Renné asked.

"We agreed to take Cynddl a fortnight's journey down the river," Fynnol said, "in exchange for horses, but we got . . . lost."

"Lost on the river?" Fondor said, and he and the other Renné laughed as though Fynnol made a joke. "Prince Michael tells us

that you have fought many battles against Hafydd and his guards."
He made a little bow to them. "You will always be welcome among
the Renné."

"And in my home as well," the Prince said. "My estates are
quite reduced, but I think I can still make you comfortable."

They thanked the noblemen and settled aboard the boat. The
watermen set out for the distant shore, angling up the river. A little
breeze swept down the channel, and Tam closed his eyes and imagined that it carried some scent of home, of the mountains and the
hay fields. He wondered what his grandfather would be doing in
the late afternoon. Walking out to gauge the growth in the orchard,
perhaps, or checking on his prized bees.

He could see the people thronging the bank and hear music
being played. Banners and streamers fluttered in the breeze, and
costumed men walked like herons on high stilts. There was an at-
mosphere of holiday in the air.

"It seems like another world," Baore said, staring. "Like some-
place in the hidden lands that knows nothing of our troubles."

"There has been pain enough," Llya said softly. "Let there be
joy for a while."

The men in the boat all shifted in their seats, glancing at the boy.
It seemed this new Llya would be as disturbing as the old—though
in a different way.

Tam noticed three women walking along the bank, one not
twenty years of age. They wore dark gowns and black scarves over
their hair—widows. They went so slowly, as though time had
changed its pace for them, while behind all was chaos and color.
The young woman turned her gaze out over the water and Tam
imagined that their eyes met, hers soft with tears.

He remembered the man-at-arms they'd found floating in the
river with Tam's arrow in his chest. It seemed like so long ago, and
so distant. Did his widow bear her grief with such dignity? Tam
thought of all the men he had killed—so many he'd lost all count.
He'd fired hundreds of arrows at distant faces, never knowing if
they brought a man down or missed their marks. He remembered

the final river, an ink-gray artery running through the twilight. How many men had he sent into the darkness, and how long would they haunt his dreams?

He shook his head and looked away, realizing that he would have to brave his dreams because he was desperate for sleep. The Fáel encampment was subdued. They were making preparations to have their archers return, for a company had crossed the river with Fondor Renné. Hardly enough to turn the tide of a battle, but welcomed all the same. The Fáel had given up their long held neutrality in the wars of men, and Tam wasn't sure that was a good thing.

As they were in the company of Cynddl, they weren't required to explain themselves or what they wanted, and Nann, the elder, strode quickly down to greet them. Tam still thought her the most un-Fáel-like woman he had ever seen: practical and sober where the others were exotic and filled with mirth and mischief.

"Send word to Eber," Nann said to a man standing nearby. "Tell him his son is safe." She crouched before she greeted anyone and gazed a moment at the two small children.

"And who are you, child?" she said to the girl.

"This is Sianon," Llya said softly, causing Nann's eyes to grow wide. "She came out of the dark land and doesn't speak."

"And you do, I see," Nann said, glancing up at Alaan.

"It's a long story," he said in answer.

Nann stood slowly, looking a little unsteady on her feet. "I see there is much to tell. Come, let us find Eber and remake his broken heart."

The Fáel did not look at them as they once had—like intruders—but smiled and nodded to the strangers as they passed. There was palpable relief that Cynddl had survived. They did not want to lose their most gifted story finder and heir of Rath. A young woman brought him a bouquet of white flowers, which Cynddl received graciously.

"White flowers," Fynnol said. "Does white signify love or perhaps that you owe that young lady money?"

Cynddl smiled, his ancient face showing its true youth. "Red signifies love, but we would never give red flowers after a battle where much blood was shed. White flowers are often given to a story finder because they signify high purpose and contemplation."

"They will bring you wild roses, Fynnol," Tam said, "signifying no purpose and thoughtlessness."

"Would you leave the wit to me, Cousin?" Fynnol said. "I have kindly left the heroics to you and try never to walk on your turf."

"Is that what you do in the north?" Alaan asked, his mood lifting. "Neatly divide your areas of endeavor?"

"Yes, Baore gets feats of silent strength and loyalty; Cynddl 'high purpose and contemplation,' as you've heard; wit and the admiration of women are my province; and Tam, obviously, gets heroics, like the slaying of sorcerers and such."

"Who does the common work?" Nann asked, "like hunting and cooking and gathering firewood?"

"*Cynddl!*" the Valemen all said at once, and laughed.

"And after he's cooked supper, and cleaned all the dishes," Fynnol said, "if we're satisfied with his efforts, we let him tell a story."

Eber appeared from behind a tent, striding toward them as fast as his ancient legs would go. Tears immediately appeared, and Llya sprinted forward and threw his arms around his father's neck. For a long moment they remained motionless, Eber crouching with his arms wrapped around the small boy, his eyes tightly closed, tears glittering in his beard like frost on snow.

"I thought I'd lost you," Eber said at last, his voice breaking a little.

"No, Father," Llya said, his face still buried in his father's beard. "I knew just where I was."

Eber's eyes sprang open. Unwrapping his sons arms from around his neck, he gazed into the boy's serious face.

"Llya," he whispered, "you spoke . . ."

The boy nodded. "The whisperer in the river did it."

"He gave you your voice . . . ?"

Alaan crouched down so that he was on the same height as
Eber and his son. "Llya made a bargain with Wyrr—a temporary
bargain. Wyrr went back into the river, but he left Llya with a
voice."

Eber could not hide his horror. He gripped his son by the
shoulders and gazed into his eyes. "He's gone?" he said to the
child. "The whisperer is gone?"

Llya nodded. "Yes, but he left his stories in my head."

Eber looked confused.

"Memories, I think he means," Alaan said, his voice full of
concern.

"But he is only a child," Eber said. "The memories of a sorcerer
were never meant for him!"

"No, they weren't, but I think they'll fade in time." Alaan's gaze
came to rest upon Llya. "I'm sure they are a jumble to him, without meaning. From my own experience I know that imposing order
on them is not easily done. I think a child will just forget them."

Eber clasped his son close. "Why did this have to happen to
you?"

"We had to trick the soul eater and get the jewel back," Llya
said, as though explaining something to another child. "Alaan had
his part, and Elise hers, and I had mine. And then I made a special
arrow by putting it in the river, and Tam used it to kill Hafydd, who
is also called Caibre, and that is how we won the war."

Tam laughed at this outpouring, unable to stop himself. "It is as
good an explanation as you will find, until Cynddl turns his hand
to it, I suppose. But even his story will not have more charm."

"You all look fatigued beyond measure," Nann said.

"I think we're more hungry than tired," Cynddl said. He looked
down at the girl child. "And this child must eat and drink, and find
her voice."

She still squinted at the light and looked more than a little apprehensive. Tam wondered what the girl was thinking. Did she remember anything from all the long years she had spent inside

Death's kingdom? Could she tell them, at last, what lay beyond the gate?

I will go into the river, Tam thought. He'd learned that much on this journey. There would be no dark gate for him; his story would be added to the river's.

A high, squeaking sound pierced the air, and Kai appeared, wheeled by the silent Ufrra, a boy walking at his side. Unlike the others who had traveled to the Isle of Waiting, this trio looked unharmed, almost refreshed.

"Kilydd!" Alaan exclaimed. "It must have been you who brought everyone home."

"It was I. We were hiding on the bank and saw Toren Renné and Eber, and all those you left behind. We loaded them all into our boat, and I still don't understand how, but we returned here more quickly than I would have thought possible."

"The river has many branches, my friend, and no two the same."

"So it is said." The two men joined hands, their eyes meeting for a moment.

Tam couldn't imagine what they were thinking, these two ancient men, their memories stretching back into another age of the world. What journeys these two had shared!

"And where is Slighthand?" Kai asked suddenly, looking around.

"Gone," Alaan said softly. "Into the river at last."

Kai touched the fingers of one hand to his forehead. "I tore him from his quiet life to go seeking you in the Stillwater. It was my doing."

"Orlem was a warrior, Kilydd. He chose this cause. And who better than Slighthand knew the dangers? He had served Caibre and Sianon, then was the companion of Sainth's travels for many years."

"Yes, he understood the dangers. . . ." Kai's voice trailed off. "But he has gone into danger so many times and returned unharmed."

"Even Slighthand's luck had to run out," Alaan said. "Don't blame yourself. Certainly Orlem wouldn't blame you, Kilydd, I'm sure of that."

The man in the barrow looked up at Alaan. "I am Kilydd no more. Kai, they call me in this age. No one remains who saw the armies of Sianon and Caibre and lived through all the years of this age while the children of Wyrr slept in the river. I am alone."

"And for this you should be honored. If I have my way you will be an outcast no more, Kai."

Three riders in Renné blue came into the camp, accompanied by Fáel guards. They were led to Alaan, where they dismounted and bowed.

"Are you Alaan?" the captain asked.

"I am."

"Lady Beatrice and Lord Toren invite you to join them, if you would," the captain said. "They have pitched pavilions by the river." He gestured south. "They have also asked me to find the men who felled Hafydd, for they would give them their thanks."

Alaan glanced over at Tam and the others. "Maybe sleep will have to wait."

The Renné guards had brought horses with them, and even though it was but a short walk, they all rode to the Renné camp. On the way they passed the spontaneous fair that had grown up beside the river. Men-at-arms were returning from the battlefield on the eastern shore, all of them welcomed and given drink and food. Women were searching anxiously among the men disembarking from boats, and many an unself-conscious reunion took place.

They entered a narrow, tree-lined lane that ran along beside the river. Not far off, a flock of crows swarmed from tree to tree, and in a moment a solitary figure appeared. He'd lost his great hat, but Crowheart met them still wearing his leather coat festooned with the treasures his crows had brought him. He looked out at them from behind his inky beard, and smiled, deep crow's-feet appearing at the corners of his eyes.

"And where is it you go, Master Crowheart?" Alaan asked.

He gestured with a staff. "There is still much to be seen in this world. I have concentrated too much of my effort in one area, of late," he said.

"Beware," Alaan said, leaning upon his pommel and smiling down at the traveler. "If you are descended from Sainth, you might never settle."

"And was Sainth unhappy with his lot?"

The smile wavered on Alaan's face. "Sometimes."

"But I suppose the same can be said of men who spend all their days in one place."

"You can be sure of that," Fynnol joined in.

"Then I will take my chances. Fare well, Alaan," Crowheart said. Then he made bow to the others. "Perhaps I will come to the north one day and visit the lakes."

"You would be welcome," Tam said.

He saluted them with his staff and set off, his company of crows crying and fluttering from tree to tree. Tam and his companions watched him go, until he stepped off the road, no doubt to avoid the festivities ahead.

"Well, we shall not meet another like that," Cynddl said.

"What will become of him?" Fynnol wondered. "He seems to belong nowhere."

"I'm afraid you're right, Fynnol," Alaan said.

"Maybe he is like Cynddl's people," Baore said, "at home everywhere."

"My people are at home because we carry our village with us," Cynddl responded. "Crowheart has no possessions and only his noisy crows for companions."

"And yet, even a crow finds a mate and makes a nest one day," Alaan said. "We might hope the same for Rabal."

They spurred their horses on. Across the river, the pyre still burned, a dark pillar of smoke rising into the sky. Tam couldn't bear the sight of it, and thought how easily he could be there, among the silent dead, staring empty-eyed at the smoke stained sky.

The Renné camp was in a field behind a line of trees. Pavilions had been pitched in the shade, and guards formed an almost solid ring around the area. Over the pavilions, banners fluttered, black swans winging across the sky blue.

They were led past the guards and into the presence of Lady Beatrice, who rested beneath a spreading oak. Immediately, she rose from her chair to greet them, and Toren Renné joined her. His arm was in a sling, and his face was pasty-pale, but he seemed otherwise unharmed by his ordeal.

"So here is the mysterious Alaan," she said. "Toren tells me you have been the prime mover in this war—the enemy of Hafydd and his . . . allies."

"I have been the enemy of Hafydd, but so have many others. Lord Toren, Lady Elise, Lady Llyn, my friends from the north. Cynddl, of the Fáel."

"Yes," she said, regarding Alaan's companions. "I understand that I've met them, though they were costumed at the time."

"It was Tam, I'm told, who brought down Hafydd, in the end," Toren said.

Lady Beatrice took Tam by the hands. "My family owes you a great debt."

"It was just a lucky arrow," Tam said. "And it would never have even reached him, if Alaan and Elise hadn't been taking up all his attention."

"Modesty is a virtue," she said, and kissed Tam on the cheek, "but such deeds should not go unrecognized. We've been told that you began your journey to acquire horses . . ." She nodded to Toren, who waved his good hand at someone. From behind a pavilion came grooms leading four horses—and what horses they were!

"These are the finest saddle horses in our stables," Toren said. "Swift and of admirable temperament. Of course if you would rather horses for the tourney, I can offer you others."

"We aren't men-at-arms," Tam said. "We're just travelers, too far from home." He bowed to Lady Beatrice and Lord Toren. "This is a generous gift."

"Hardly a beginning," Lady Beatrice said. "You will each sit with me for a time and tell me what more we might do for you. And Prince Michael has something in mind for you as well. He said he traveled far with you and assures me that your part in all of this was great."

She let go of Tam's hands and took the hands of each in turn, kissing them on both cheeks. "You I remember," she said to Baore. "You were a giant then, and your stature has only increased. Thank you."

Her smile turned almost mischievous when she stood before Fynnol. "When last we met you were a highwayman, and now look what's become of you!"

"After what I've seen, ma'am, I shall be most happy to return to my former trade."

"Stealing kisses, wasn't it?" Lady Beatrice laughed. "Well, I remove my former ban. You may steal all the kisses you can bear. And you may have a place in my hall for all the rest of your days, if you wish. Your wit would be welcome."

"I thank you, Lady Beatrice, though I fear I've lost my wit. I feel nothing but a terrible sorrow, and loss."

"So we all feel, good Fynnol, but that will pass in time, and our laughter will return. I have not seen a winter yet that spring did not follow."

She came next to Cynddl. "Ruadan? Of the magic pipes, I think."

Cynddl gave a small bow of acknowledgment.

Lady Beatrice kissed his cheeks. "But it is not you who captured the heart of a lady, I'm told?"

Cynddl glanced at Tam.

Lady Beatrice pretended not to notice. "You are honored among your people," she said. "And we would be honored to have you ply your art beneath our roof. There is a great story to tell, now, and I've only heard parts of it."

"It will take me some time to find, then order it all, but when I do, Lady Beatrice, I shall be most happy to come to Castle Renné and tell the tale of the Swans' War."

"I look forward to it."

More gifts were brought then. Mail and helms from Toren Renné, shields and swords from Fondor. Lord Kel sent them saddles and tack, all of the finest craftsmanship. Ladies gave them bolts of fabric and clothing fit for noblemen. Such riches were never seen in the Vale—not all in one place, anyway—and the Valemen were overwhelmed.

Minstrels played, and a table was set beneath the branches so that the travelers could rest and eat and slake their thirst. The late afternoon wore on to evening, and the sun plunged into the western hills, turning the sky into a pool of red. There was a murmur among the Renné by the river, where boats were still landing and departing, and then a ghostly form appeared in the last light. Tam jumped up from the table, as everyone stared.

"Elise?" he said.

"Tam," she answered, her voice so soft he could barely hear. Without seeming to notice the others, she came and buried her face against the Valeman, her hands gently on his chest. She seemed small and fragile to him as he took her in his arms, and she was cold as a winter stream.

"Are you . . . healed?" Tam asked.

"As much as I can be," she said. And then she pulled gently away. "I have something I must do." She turned to the others, her eyes, like moons, unsettling everyone. "Alaan . . . if you would go with me."

Alaan nodded immediately, not even asking where or why. They were on horses in a moment and riding off. Tam stood watching them go, unable to hide his distress, then he realized that Baore stood beside him, looking just as unhappy. The big Valeman put a hand on Tam's shoulder and tried to smile at him. For a moment the two friends regarded each other and turned back to the table. There was no animosity in the look Baore had given him, just a sense of loss and sadness. Tam wondered if Baore understood that Wyrr had given his daughter this gift—that men would serve her out of love—but that it came with a price: she loved none in return. The heart didn't care much for truth, Tam thought. Baore might harbor hopes despite what he knew.

"What will the Renné do now that the war is over?" Fynnol asked, trying to pick up the thread of the conversation.

"The war is never over here," Kel growled. "We have been fighting the Wills for generations—"

"And it is time we stopped," Toren interrupted. He hadn't said much their entire visit, and Tam suspected he was in pain.

"You tried to put an end to it, cousin," Kel said, "but there was a war anyway. There is a lesson there."

"Yes, and the lesson is that Menwyn was not the man we should have been dealing with, nor was the late Prince of Innes. Lord Carral and Prince Michael are men of great integrity."

"I think you're right," Fondor said quietly, "but what of their sons? Their grandsons? This feud has skipped a generation before, but it is like a fire in the forest that goes underground. It smolders there, sometimes for years, then springs up again. We might have peace during our lifetimes, but the feud will not go away. It never has."

"It is but an echo of an ancient feud," Cynddl said, "going back to a struggle between sorcerers who were born before the mountains formed. It's a story one can find in some form or other the entire length of the Wynnd."

Toren's jaw stiffened. "I won't accept that this is some affliction of the Wynnd Valley—a pestilence that abides in the soil. We have to make an end to it."

"And how do you propose to make a lasting peace?" Fondor asked.

"It is all a matter of what we are willing to give up," Toren said.

Dease woke just after dusk, and went unsteadily out of his tent, into the cooling air of evening. A faint wash of color still hung in the western sky, and the brighter stars appeared overhead. Dease tried to shake off the sleep that clung to him, his mind fuzzy and his temper foul. He had washed and changed out of his smoking clothes, eaten a little, and fallen asleep. The whole journey on the river seemed like a nightmare to him now. He remembered the monster in the chamber. How could that have been real? But it was. Dease had seen too much that was strange and would be unbelievable to anyone who did not see it themselves. It made him feel a little mad—like Toren's father, afraid of the darkness because of the visions he saw.

"Dease?" His cousin emerged from the shadow of a tree.

"Fondor! Are you well?"

"Unharmed, but for a mass of bruises. Hardly worth a mention." He looked off across the river to the still-burning pyre. Dark smoke twisted up, then bent south like a dark river among the stars.

"The casualties were many?" Dease asked.

"Yes, though we lost few among our own family. Menwyn Wills was killed, and Vast seems to have escaped. I don't know how. Many among the dead were burned beyond recognition, but Vast's armor was distinctive."

"We'll find him soon enough."

"Yes, I suppose." Fondor still stared at the fire. "Dease, when Samul thought he was being taken to his execution he asked for you. When he learned that you had gone off he told me that you were part of the plot to kill Toren. He said that you had realized it was Arden in the window, and wouldn't shoot, which was when Beld knocked you senseless, then killed Arden, believing it was Toren."

Dease took a deep breath.

"Don't say anything," Fondor interrupted. "I have only one question for you. Are you a threat to Toren or any other Renné?"

Dease closed his eyes. He wanted to weep though he didn't understand why. "No," he said with difficulty. "I'm not."

"Not even if Toren seeks peace with the Wills?"

"He has my blessing to do whatever he thinks is right. I will not oppose him in word or deed." Dease did feel tears on his cheeks then.

"That's all the answer I need," Fondor said.

"Who else knows of Samul's accusation?" Dease asked.

"Lady Beatrice. No one else. Toren has asked for our presence within the hour. A council of some sort." Fondor turned and started to walk away.

"Fondor?" Dease said, stopping his cousin. "What will you tell Lady Beatrice?"

"That I confronted you with Samul's accusation and that you denied it. I will say I believed you."

"But that isn't the truth."

"She has had enough pain, Dease. Enough disappointment. Within the hour, Cousin. Don't be late." And he walked off into the gathering dark. For a long while Dease stood looking at the flames on the distant shore. Later he would say that the smoke stung his eyes, though that was not the truth either.

Lord Carral wondered if he would ever hear music in the night sounds again. The frogs sang. The insects hummed. Wind stirred and murmured sleepily in the trees. None of these things enchanted him as they once had. He had heard music in everything— once.

Darkness had fallen. He could tell by the cooling air. Carral walked alone in Llyn's garden, his thoughts a jumble. He had lost his heart, there was no doubt of that. But the woman he had lost it to was less certain. Oh, she loved him, that was certain, but there was another. She had never said it, but Carral wasn't utterly foolish with love. She loved Toren Renné as much as she loved him. Perhaps more.

Lord Carral had so many different reactions to this that he could not keep them straight. He loved Llyn utterly and could understand why anyone would feel the same—even someone young and imposing, like Toren. Of course Toren had never seen Llyn. Or perhaps it would be more accurate to say that she had never allowed Toren to see her and likely never would. To Carral, who had never seen another human being, this obsession with another's appearance was incomprehensible. He had spent his life among the sighted, and had often been surprised to find men attentive to the most tedious women, only to be told that they were beautiful. But this refusal actually to be in the same room with someone did seem a rather large impediment to a marriage. Toren might feel the same way.

But then Llyn might have been waiting for Toren to declare himself, to tell her that the burns that had forced her into exile within Castle Renné meant nothing to him. And perhaps that was the truth.

Carral shook his head. His mind seemed to whirl through a cycle of thoughts over and over again, to no avail. This cycle of thoughts led him to one conclusion over and over again. Llyn would never marry him while there was hope that Toren felt toward her as she did toward him.

He should have felt anger toward or resentment of Toren—his rival for Llyn's affections—but he wasn't sure that Toren was even aware of this rivalry. The young nobleman certainly wasn't acting like a man who felt threatened by some other. He went about his business as though this never entered his thoughts, visiting Llyn with the same infrequency that he apparently always had.

Nor did Carral feel any anger or resentment toward Llyn. In truth, he felt pity for her. She was tortured by this division of loyalties, by her love for two men.

But I am the one who loves her utterly, Carral thought. She must see that. She was sighted, after all.

He stopped suddenly. Someone hovered a few feet away; he could hear their breathing

"Father?" The voice was so small he could barely make out the word.

"Father?" the voice said again, no stronger.

"Elise?"

Footsteps sounded on the gravel, but they were not Elise's—were they? She was in his arms, damp and musky, as though she had come out of the river. Her hair was cold and moist, a mass of uncombed curls. He breathed in the scent of her all the same, felt her in his arms, thin and fragile.

"You-are-alive, you-are-alive, you-are-alive," he said over and over.

They did not move for the longest time, but stood holding each other close. Carral drank in her presence, felt the air move in and out of her lungs. He thought he could almost feel the beating of her heart.

"Father . . . I'm sorry I didn't send word that I was alive, but—"

"You never need apologize to me, Elise. You wouldn't have done it without good reason."

They were silent again for a time.

"I must go away again," Elise whispered, her voice laden with regret.

"Will you be gone for long? I've missed you so."

Elise pulled back a little, so she could see his face, Carral thought. "There is no place for me here—"

"But we'll go back to Braidon Castle. . . ."

"I can't go back." She drew him near again, pressing her cheek against his chest as she had when she was a child.

"But Elise, I will take up my place as the head of our family. I will need your help. And you are my heir—"

"I renounce this foolishness," she said emphatically. "There is no throne, Father. There never will be. I can't live here among our people. Too many know what I have done—what I've become. I made a bargain with a nagar, father. There is no going back."

Carral felt tears, not just at what she said but at the despair in her voice. "Where will you go?"

"North, to a house on the river. It is a place where I might heal, and there are two children there who will need my guidance."

"I'll visit you there if you'll let me."

"I would and gladly, but it is a hidden place. A place you cannot find."

"A place only Alaan might travel?" he said.

"Alaan, and a few others."

"Will we never be together again?"

"I hope we will. We'll see where the river takes us." She kissed his cheek with great tenderness, then drew away. He felt the loss of her the moment she left his embrace—almost more than he could bear.

"I have brought you something," she said, her voice barely more than a whisper. She placed an object in his hands.

Carral ran his hands over it quickly. "It is a mask."

"Yes."

"Why is it wet?"

"It has been in the river."

"And what am I to do with it?"

"It is not for you, father. It is for Lady Llyn—a gift of the nagar. If she will wear it, and not remove it, her scars will be healed." Elise paused. "She will be whole again—beautiful."

"Ahh," Carral said softly, but his first thought was, *then why would she love a blind man like me?* She would marry Toren, certainly. He turned the mask over in his hands. These thoughts were unworthy of him, he realized. He should be overjoyed that Llyn could be healed.

"I would do the same for you, Father, but you did not lose your sight. You were born without it. It cannot be restored."

"It doesn't matter. I have been blind my whole life. It isn't a hardship. But if Lady Llyn can be healed . . ." His voice disappeared, suddenly.

Elise stepped forward and embraced him again. She kissed him. He could feel how hard it was for her to release him. There was that, at least.

He heard her steps on the gravel.

"Elise!"

The steps stopped. "Yes?"

"You have given up everything to fight this war—" He lost his voice, emotion stealing it away.

"I am the daughter of Carral Wills. How could I have done less?" Her footsteps retreated through the garden, growing more and more distant as though she had passed through a wall and out into the hostile world beyond.

He collapsed onto a low stone bench and wept like a child. *No.* He'd wanted to say. *Your strength came from your mother*, but it was too late, too late to say so many things.

Forty-seven

Dease entered the ballroom. He had not been there since the costume ball that ended the Westbrook Fair—and began so much else. There was furniture in there, now, as there was much of the year. Tapers cast their warm glow over the gathered masses: a crowd of his cousins and aunts and uncles. They were a subdued lot, even somber. Escaping destruction by the Wills and their allies would do that, Dease thought. Almost none of them knew the true story. That would have sobered them for some years.

"Dease! Returned and looking hale," an uncle said, clapping him on the back. And then in a more intimate tone. "Do you have any idea what this is in aid of?"

"I haven't, Uncle. I was sent a message that Toren wanted to see me most urgently."

"Ah. Well, here's Toren. Perhaps he will have the goodness to explain why we are here on this night of all nights."

A hush of expectation fell as Toren entered. He was followed by a scribe and several servants bearing boxes of what appeared to be paper, documents of some sort. Behind them all came Lady Beatrice. The boxes were set on a long trestle table.

"Well, Cousin," someone said, "it is comforting to know that you love us all so well that you have asked us here while leaving so many others uninvited. Yet I can't help but notice that we are the Renné most closely related to you. A coincidence, I'm sure."

"As you suspect, Cousin," Toren said. "It is no coincidence. We all lie in the succession from my father to . . . well, I will get to that." Toren took a few paces across the end of the large room, gathering his thoughts. He was dressed in somber clothes and wore a black velvet ribbon around his arm. He had lost no immediate family member in the battle, though numerous men and women present were not so lucky, and they wore the elaborate black clothing of mourning.

"Let me begin by saying that if anyone realized how close the Renné have just come to utter defeat there would be no celebration going on this night. The feud between Wills and Renné almost brought to ruin more than our own fortunes."

"So why is there a Wills still living in this castle?" someone called out.

"A good question," Toren said. "And the answer is that he is the future of a continuing peace with the Wills."

There was some murmuring among the thirty or so Renné present, but no one would say more. Carral Wills was respected even there, and he was the guest of Lady Beatrice, whose presence prevented any more criticism.

Dease closed his eyes, and felt something inside grow still and cold. Toren was talking about Llyn. *Llyn.*

"You tried to make peace with the Wills before this war broke out, Cousin," a woman said. "We know that it isn't possible."

"I think it is possible," Toren said. "In truth, it is essential."

There was the briefest silence while people absorbed this.

"Carral Wills might be a man of honor," Dease's uncle offered, "and he might uphold a peace between us, but what of his grandchildren? Will they?"

"They will if they're Renné."

This caused a little whispering, some quizzical looks. More than one person glanced at Dease as though he might have an explanation.

"Most of us have heard the rumor that Lord Carral has fallen under the spell of one of the ladies of the castle. No need to name which one. Even if they were to have children, his daughter lies in the succession claimed by her family. And subsequent children would be pushed aside."

"Lady Elise has renounced her family's claims. She is leaving the old kingdom this night, and I don't expect we will see her again for many years."

The Renné were looking one to another, uncomfortable with where this discussion appeared to lead.

"Let us stop being coy," one woman said caustically. "If Lord Carral and Lady Llyn have children, they will be raised among the Wills. Their children will be of that family and forget any allegiance to the Renné. And what has all this to do with us?"

Toren looked up at the crowd then, determination burning in his eyes. Dease had seen this look before many a tournament.

"I am proposing this. No. That is not strong enough. We have only one path to continued survival: the Renné and the Wills must be joined into one family. Lady Llyn must be made the legal heir to Renné aspirations."

The room fell utterly silent. Dease looked around at the stunned faces, his precious relatives staring, slack-jawed, at the madman before them.

Dease took a deep breath. If he had learned one thing in these past weeks it was that he was unworthy of Llyn's favor. He took a step forward. "If that is what the documents are for," Dease said loudly, "I will sign away my claims in the succession." He walked up to the table. "Where is a quill and ink?"

"I won't sign such a document," a lady said firmly, "nor will I stay here and listen to this"—the woman glanced over at Lady Beatrice and decided to choose her words more carefully— "proposal."

"Why?" Dease said, turning on the woman, unable to hide his anger. "Do you think you will one day come to the throne? There is no throne, and you are so far down the list of succession that neither you nor your children will ever sit at the head of the Renné table. Toren is offering a resolution to our dilemma. The child of Llyn and Lord Carral would be the head of both houses. There would be no hatred to fuel our feud."

"Such a child would be a Wills," someone called out angrily.

"No. The child would be a Renné-Wills," Toren said. "The child of both houses."

"But it is said that Lady Llyn loves another," a woman argued. Which caused Lady Beatrice to shift uncomfortably in her chair.

This stopped Toren for a moment, and Dease wondered if he had an answer. "Her heart has changed," he said softly.

"But why not a union between you and Elise Wills?" a woman wondered. "That would make giving up our claims unnecessary."

"Llyn and Lord Carral will bring peace, I believe," Toren said almost sadly. "Lady Elise and I are only suited for war."

Fondor had said nothing until this point, but now he stepped forward. "Only Toren is making a sacrifice, for he is the heir of Renné aspirations. The rest of us are only giving up a dream. I will give up a dream for peace."

"As will I," said Kel. "And if more of you had fought in the recent battles, you would not be hesitating as you are now. In truth you are signing away nothing. Signing away nothing for a chance at lasting peace. I would take that chance in hopes that my sons would not give their lives to a feud they did not make."

"I will sign your papers," one of Toren's cousins said. She was dressed in black, her face a mask of anguish. "I have lost one son this day. I would give up anything to save others this sorrow."

Toren's secretary found the appropriate document. She signed, and Dease acted as first witness, Lady Beatrice as second witness. The woman's hand trembled a little as she wrote her name, but her resolve was firm. Her husband signed after her, though he said nothing and met no one's eye.

Fondor and Kel both signed their documents without hesitation, showing solidarity among the men who had fought. Two others who had fought in the battle came forward, embracing Toren first, then signing away their claims.

Dease felt the whole enterprise balanced on a sword's edge. If one person refused, all would be lost. Toren had shown great insight to gather everyone together in one room. They could see the others committing themselves to this course. Anyone who refused would be remembered as the one who had thwarted a chance for peace, and all subsequent deaths in battle with the Wills would be laid at that person's doorstep.

As each person signed, the pressure on those remaining increased. Dease thought all would be for naught, as in the end a particularly stupid aunt and uncle refused to sign. But the rest of those present surrounded them and bullied them into signing. It wasn't quite the way Dease had hoped it would go, but everyone signed.

Toren signed last—the only one who really signed away any rights—and, though he didn't hesitate, Dease thought his face went a little pale.

"It is done," Toren said as he blotted his signature. "Lady Llyn is now the heir to all Renné claims and effectively head of the family— Llyn and her children after her."

Lady Beatrice came forward and kissed him on both cheeks, her pride unspoken but hidden from no one. Dease found he had to sit down. He beckoned a servant and asked for wine, and when it came he drained his glass in one draught. It didn't help. He had lost everything he once valued, and this night he had lost twice, though neither had been his to possess.

I have given up my hopes, he thought. *Let some good come of it.*

Forty-eight

Lady Beatrice stood with her hand upon the stack of documents, looking a little uncertain. Toren pushed open the shutters, letting the night air spill in over the windowsill.

"Nothing like this has ever been done in the long history of the Renné. Thirty-one people gave up their claim to the throne, all in one night. I fear come morning there will be some who regret this decision."

"Too late. It is done," Toren said. He closed his eyes and let the cool air bathe his face.

"Not quite done. There is one more person who must agree to this course. I expect you'll want me to speak to her?"

"No. I will do this myself, Mother."

"You should have spoken to her before you did this."

"She wouldn't have agreed. But now. . . . I have some leverage." Toren turned away from the window and gazed at his mother standing in the light of a chandelier. Her face seemed flushed in the candles' warm light. "I will tell you honestly, Mother, I would rather face the servants of Death than wound Llyn."

"It is not a wound. It is release. She will be free to give her love to Carral Wills, who loves her with all his open heart. You are all that stops her."

Toren nodded.

"You are giving up a great deal this night, my son," Lady Beatrice said. "First your position in the family, now the adoration of a woman whom I respect more than almost any other. Who will you be in the morning?"

"I will be the champion of Lady Llyn and Carral Wills and of their children—that is if they will let me."

"I think they will consider it an honor."

"Then I have one last task this night." Toren bowed to his mother and turned toward the door.

"Toren?" Lady Beatrice said, stopping him in his tracks. "It will be more difficult than you know, giving up your position. People will still look to you for leadership, for answers."

"I know, but I will not undermine Llyn and Lord Carral. Their authority must be paramount. Too much depends on it."

Llyn was surprised to have a visitor at this hour, let alone Toren saying that it was most urgent. Llyn stood in the garden beneath the shadows of a lace maple, the silhouette of Toren visible above. She thought him beautiful even in this poor light, his bearing noble without being proud. It was one of the things she loved about him.

For a second she glanced down at the golden mask she held in her hands. It was still wet and did not seem to dry. Just the thought of it stole her breath away.

"You are hurt," Lynn said.

"I've sustained greater wounds in tournaments, if truth is told. A few days will see me whole."

"I am glad of that."

Toren fell silent, and Llyn sensed he had some news that he did not want to give. *Someone has died!* she thought suddenly.

"You have something to tell me," she prompted.

"Yes," Toren admitted. "I have come from a council with news." He drew himself up a little. "I have renounced my claims to the mythical throne and will no longer sit at the head of the Renné council table."

"Oh," Llyn said as though she'd been pinched. "I suppose I should not be surprised. Dease, then, has taken up your duties?"

"No, Dease has signed away his own claims, as have several others."

"What in this strange world is going on beyond my garden? Who is the titular head of the Renné now?"

"You, Llyn."

She laughed. "It is late for jokes, Cousin," she chided.

"It is not a joke, Llyn. It's the truth. We have all given up our place in the succession in favor of you."

A cool wind seemed to blow through her. She felt as though she balanced upon a precipitous ledge and dared not look down. "This is not right. No one spoke to me of this."

"You would have refused."

"I do refuse," she said hastily. "I will not accept this responsibility."

"Even if it means the end of our feud with the Wills and peace for our children and their children after them?"

Llyn sat down upon the small bench beneath the tree. "Cousin, please . . ." she pleaded. "You can't ask this of me."

"And I won't, if you insist, but let me ask you this. Do you love Carral Wills?"

She glanced down at the mask she still held in her hands, then up at the obscured silhouette of Toren Renné. Her mouth went dry, and the words evaporated.

She loved them both—Carral and Toren. She also knew why Toren was asking this question. And she knew what answering it would mean.

"Llyn?" Toren said softly. "I love you as a sister, but Lord Carral . . . he loves you as you deserve to be loved." Toren took a quick breath. "Your children will be the heirs of both our houses—Renné and Wills. They will be our hope for peace."

She felt herself nod, and glanced down again at the mask she turned in her hands. *But I will be healed,* she thought. *You will be able to look upon me without pity or revulsion. You might even think me . . . beautiful.*

She knew these thoughts were not worthy of her—but she could not deny her feelings. *Shame.* She had felt shame all her life. Shame that she was a monster. That people couldn't look upon her without horror.

"We are asking a great sacrifice, I know. But peace Llyn. . . . Is it not worth any sacrifice?"

She felt herself nod. "Yes," she whispered, the single word sounding like a final judgment.

"Of course, if you don't love Lord Carral," Toren said, "then you should refuse."

"I do love him," she said, and turned her gaze up. She could just see Toren through the leaves, his perfect frame dark against the light spilling from within. How long had he embodied everything she hoped for? Too long, apparently.

"Then you will accept this?" Toren asked.

"Lord Carral has not asked for my hand."

Toren seemed a bit surprised. "Perhaps he needs to be sure of your feelings for him."

"Perhaps."

"May I tell Lady Beatrice that you have agreed?"

"I will speak with her myself."

Toren nodded. "Llyn . . . ? I owe you thanks. I know how difficult this will be for you."

"No you don't," Llyn whispered to herself.

Toren hesitated a second. "Good night to you, Cousin."

"And you," she answered.

Llyn sat for a while after Toren had gone, feeling more hollow than the mask she turned over and over. All her hopes for so many years had centered on Toren, as foolish as they had been. She had always known that, but her feelings were stronger than her reason. Just a brief moment in his company was all it took to fan them back to flames. And now would the flames go out? She didn't know. She hoped that they would—and that they would not.

Rising, Llyn went inside and found Lord Carral sitting by an open window. Without a word she slipped into his lap and pressed her face against him, her eyes closed.

Neither spoke for some time, then Llyn said; "What is it you do?"

"I am letting the night air wash over me and indulging senti-ment, to be honest. Memories have been finding me this evening. Memories of my wife, but of Elise most of all. With a little effort I can recall any number of moments—much of her life, I suspect."

"She is still alive, Carral. You must remember that."

"But if I'm never with her again, is she not dead to me?"

"You will be with her again. I'm sure of it."

"Why are you so sure?"

"Because she loves you as I do, and I can't bear to go a day without seeing you."

Carral smiled his perfect, unself-conscious smile. "Is it because I'm so handsome?"

"No, it is your charm that I can't resist." She took his hands.

"Your hands are cold," he said.

"It is that mask. It never dries, and it is always cool."

"Have you . . . put it on?"

"No. I'm afraid to."

"Magic is disconcerting. There is no doubt of that."

"True, though I'm not sure that's the reason. Will you come with me? I will tell you a story while we walk."

"Certainly," Carral said, and they both rose. "Where is it we go?"

"To visit someone." She led him through her rooms to the door that opened into Castle Renné. A door she had seldom been through.

"Your grace," her servant said, as Llyn unbolted the door.

"It is all right," Llyn said. "I know where it is I go." She opened the door and led Carral out into the hall. For a moment she could not catch her breath, but then she did.

They passed servants who started at the sight of her, but then bowed and went on their way. Some of her cousins nodded but said nothing.

Carral squeezed her hand tightly. "Llyn," Carral whispered. "You are very brave."

"I'm not going into battle," she said.

"No, but death is not always our worst fear."

She flushed.

"You said you'd tell me a story . . ." Carral said.

"Yes. But first I must ask you a question: do you love me?"

"With all my heart, as I have said a thousand times, though repetition does not seem to have made it more believable."

"Something exceedingly strange has happened this night, and it has to do with you and with me."

They continued down the hall, passing people now and then, Llyn telling her story. Carral clinging tightly to her hand, lest she slip away, as had his wife and daughter before. Clinging like a man to his love, and she like a woman to her husband.

Forty-nine

Toren had last been to A'brgail's small tower with his cousin Arden. He had failed, then, to convince Arden to join the Knights of the Vow, which had surprised him at the time. It was not a mystery, now—Arden had been involved in a plot to take his life. Toren closed his eyes at the memory. His own cousins . . .

Two guards stood outside, their great, two-handed swords held point down to the ground, so that Toren thought they looked like statues in the dim light of dusk. They bowed to him as he dismounted, and one took the reins of his horse. Toren was led into the great hall, hung with ancient banners, lit by torches. Arden had stood there, by the long table. Toren could recall him in perfect detail. Remembered the strange, troubled look on his face—guilt, he realized now. Not long after he'd been dead, killed by one of his own.

A door opened, and A'brgail hurried in, looking very dignified in his gray robe.

"Lord Toren! I apologize for keeping you."

They clasped hands.

"You look much recovered from our ordeal," Toren ventured.

"As do you," A'brgail responded. His look was very solemn.

The truth was that A'brgail looked like a man who had seen too much, or had seen things that forced him to ask difficult questions.

"And what of the others?" A'brgail asked. "Has Lady Elise been lost to us?"

"I have not seen her; nor have I had word. Perhaps she has returned to the river, Gilbert. One might go sit by the bank. . . . Stranger things have happened."

"Sianon sacrificed herself to bring down Caibre," A'brgail said softly. "I became the ally of a nagar—worse—a woman who bore such a monster inside her. It was the avowed purpose of my order to see that these creatures did not return. And I became their ally."

"The world changed, Gilbert. Without Elise Wills and your brother, Hafydd would rule these lands now—Hafydd and the thing that dwelt inside him. You did the right thing."

Toren noticed that the hilt of a massive sword lay on the table. "Slighthand's sword!" he said.

"Yes. Or at least what remains of it. You have seen my guards with their two-handed swords? That is a tradition of my order. Something we have done for centuries in honor one of our founders, Orlem Slighthand."

"It is appropriate that this has come to you," Toren said, running his hand over the hilt. "I still can't believe that I met such a legend. To think that he and Kilydd lived all these centuries."

"Yes. The man who now calls himself Kai is not interested in any of the honors we have offered. He would be welcomed among us, venerated even, but he will have none of it. He has moved on." A'brgail shrugged.

"I would not give up on Kai. He might have a place among you yet." Toren took a rolled paper from his cloak and set it on the table.

"And what is that?" the Knight asked.

"A charter," Toren said. "Signed by myself and Lady Beatrice, sanctioning your order to bring peace and safety to the roads of our lands and those of our closest allies. I know it is a small start,

Gilbert, but once the Knights of the Vow earn the trust of the people, more responsibilities will be granted to you."

A'brgail took up the paper, slipped off the ribbon, and let it unroll. "Don't apologize, Lord Toren, my order has much to prove. Our history is both glorious and shameful. Only by our actions should we be judged." He laid the paper on the table by the remains of Slighthand's sword. "I cannot begin to thank you," he said.

"You don't even need to begin," Toren said. "I will soon be thanking you, I think." Toren smiled, then quickly changed the subject. "Now tell me again of these lost companies of Knights."

"They were led into the hidden lands by Orlem Slighthand to fight alongside Slighthand's people."

Toren shook his head. "A people all the size of Slighthand. We had better not offend them."

"I think they are a peaceful people, Lord Toren. That is why they needed our help."

"Yes," Toren said. "We are not a peaceful people. It is the great tragedy of our race. War is in our blood."

"But there are more noble qualities in our blood as well," A'brgail said. "That is what I leaned from Elise Wills. She struggled against that side of her. Sianon did not conquer her. If Elise Wills can do that, then it gives me hope for the rest of us."

Toren looked up at all the rows of banners of fallen companies. "If only my family could learn that lesson," he said. "But I fear hatred and vengeance will always be so much more alluring. Reason is a thin wall against the storms of passion." He looked over at Gilbert. "Perhaps that will be your part, Gilbert. To be that wall of reason. To stand between the Renné and the Wills, who I fear would sink back into their cycle of murder and revenge at the slightest provocation."

"Justice rather than vengeance?" Gilbert said.

"Yes, in all of its imperfection. Let us try that."

Fifty

They decided to slip away at first light, and very nearly did so unnoticed. Tuath, the vision weaver, stood by the entrance to the Fáel encampment, watching them with her icy pale eyes. She seemed, though, less ghostly that day, as though a little of spring's color showed through the snow.

"I hope you have no visions to darken the road ahead?" Fynnol said.

"I have had no visions at all," she answered. "It is as though we have come to a division of the roads and have gone a wholly new way. All that lies ahead is a mystery to me and might be for some time. Luck to you on your journey. Perhaps I will travel north with my people one spring and come see the Vale of Lakes. It is said that the people there are friends to the Fáel, and make them welcome."

"It is true," Tam said. "Bring Cynddl, if you can."

"And tell him he still owes us horses!" Fynnol laughed.

They rode out of the circle of tents and along the trail beside the Westbrook. They crossed the high, curving bridge, then stopped to wait for Kai. Baore took the opportunity to tighten the ropes on their packhorses, for they were going home laden with gifts. A Fáel cart appeared out of the trees, the great horse lifting its feet high as though on parade. Up on the high bench sat Kai, and beside him Ufrra and the boy named Stillman.

"Kai!" Fynnol called. "Have you brought our map?"

Tam remembered that Fynnol had once laughed at the idea of a map that would lead to hidden lands—but he seemed to have forgotten that now. Tam would have to remind him later.

"I have brought more than that!" Kai said.

Out from behind the cart, on horseback, trotted Alaan, Theason, and Cynddl. They seemed more refreshed and joyful than Tam could remember, and they smiled and laughed to see their friends.

Kai passed a rolled map down from the cart. "That will be the shortest path to the Vale," he assured them.

"Do you see how Kai has risen in the world," Alaan said. "He would not take an estate from the Renné, or a house from Carral Wills, but this cart and all its contents were much to his liking. Better than a barrow, he thought."

"I have not lived in one place or beneath a roof for more years than most can count. A Fáel tent and this cart will suit Ufrra and me." Kai nodded to the boy beside him. "And young Stil seems to have hitched himself to our wagon, as it were, and we are glad of it. Now I can see the lands without feeling that I'm perpetually on my way to a slaughterhouse."

"Where will you go?" Tam asked.

"South when the winter comes. There is seldom snow even this far north, but the winter is more agreeable by the shores of the great sea."

"Come north in spring," Fynnol said. "I know just the place to pitch a tent in the Vale."

"A long journey for a man of advancing years, but perhaps I might manage it. We'll see."

"And you, Alaan?" Tam asked. "Where will you go now?"

"Into the Stillwater, to begin with. There is an enchantment there that needs my attention." He tugged the green jewel out of the collar of his shirt. "And the design for that spell is in here. Theason has agreed to travel with me, so I shall not go alone."

"Beware, good Theason," Kai said, and not entirely in jest. "If you join the company of men who have traveled with Sainth, you might have a long life, but there will be no home for you." He gestured behind him. "You'll be lucky to have this."

The little man did not seem to think this a jest. "Theason would consider himself fortunate indeed to live as the Fáel do, but as you know, good Kai, his great joy is to see new lands. I shall be on the lookout for any plants that might ease your suffering."

Cynddl dismounted and embraced each of the Valemen in turn. "None of us knew where the river would take us when we set out. It was not a journey without loss, but the gains, too, were great." He paused, and looked at each of them, his eyes glistening. For a moment his voice eluded him, but then he spoke. "You three are the friends of my heart—my brothers in arms. You have each saved my life, and more than once, and I believe I have done the same for you. None but we four and the river know what we have been through. The story can be told, but a story is but an artifice. A great complex of emotions, events, thoughts, and deeds, distilled down to a mouthful of words. Like trying to imagine the river by listening to a spring." He clapped Tam on the shoulder. "I will journey north in the spring and visit you. Be well, and hasten north, or the snows will catch you."

Alaan handed Tam a sealed letter. "For you, Tam," he said.

The Valeman glanced at the hand and slipped it into a pocket. Shy Theason stood back while the men embraced, then mounted their fine horses.

"I would tell you to beware of highwaymen," Alaan said, "but it is the highwaymen who should beware of you."

"There will be no highwaymen on the paths I have laid down for them," Kai said.

Reluctantly the Valemen spurred their horses and set off toward the north road. Fynnol turned in his saddle and called out.

"People will never know what you did for them, Alaan!"

"Nor will they know what you three have done," Alaan rejoined, raising a hand. "Fare well. Good speed, my friends. Good speed."

They stopped to let the horses drink from a small stream, and beneath the shade of a tree Tam took out the letter Alaan had given him. His name was written on it with an elegant, almost old-fashioned hand. He took a long breath and broke the seal.

Dear Tam:

Now that I am no longer a lady of property, I go off into the wildlands to take up my new position as nursemaid to children unlike any who have lived before. Who better to do this than a woman who carries a sorceress inside her?

I know it is not proper for me to say I will miss you, as we never arrived at an understanding, but I will miss you, and will not pretend otherwise. Eber tells me that people who have once found their way to Speaking Stone are often able to find it again, so if a desire for adventure should seize you . . . Of course you have likely had enough adventure to last you for some time.

I often wonder what course events might have taken had I not leapt from the bridge that night after the Renné ball. I feel, even now, that I had no choice, yet it is an act I regret above all others. Elise Wills ceased to be that night, and in her place appeared a creature, young and ancient, callous and caring. A woman divided against herself. But without the cold heart of Sianon I should never have managed the things I did. And it seems that heart is not entirely cold, for there is in it a warmth that always kindles when I think of you.

Now that I have broken every rule I was taught as a young lady, I will close. That is a part of me too—Sianon's

disdain for the conventions of polite society. Where shall
such a woman find a home but in the wildlands?

Yours utterly,
Elise

Tam read the letter several times through, as he would every day
during that long journey, extracting from the few words all the
meaning that he possibly could. One phrase echoed in his mind
over and over: *'we never arrived at an understanding'*. He did not
think that any six words would ever cause him such confusion and
regret. It was, he feared, true in every possible way.

Autumn in its copper glory spread across the northern forests,
turning the world crimson and gold. Flights of swans passed south,
stark against the high blue. Three riders leading pack animals came
up the great road, wrapped in warm cloaks against the cool morning air. At the fork to the stone gate the leader stopped.

"Let's ride out onto the bridge," Tam said, and the others nodded, not needing any explanation for this detour so close to home.

In a few moments they were above the narrow gorge where the
broad, calm lakes transformed into a racing river. None of them
spoke. Tam, Baore, and Fynnol sat on their fine horses and gazed
at their surroundings: the rocks where they hid from Hafydd's
guards; the tower by Telanon Bridge rising up out of the crimson
trees; the old battlefield where they had unearthed a whetstone that
had once belonged to a sorceress.

It had all begun there, where the rain streamed down from the
mountains and formed a river to the sea. A river fed by a thousand
springs and streams, that bubbled and whispered among the sunlit
woods.

A silver haze hung over the river, floating the bridge on a thin
cloud, and the sun glanced off the stone railings. It seemed too
peaceful a place to be the wellspring for an adventure.

"Let's go home," Fynnol said, "and see if anyone remembers our handsome faces."

They turned their mounts and rode back toward the stone gate. Over the clatter of horses' hooves Tam thought he heard a flutelike phrase off in the deep wood—a sorcerer thrush singing its way south—and he thought of Alaan, as he often did.

Fifty-one

$\mathbf{S}$pring, borne on a warm breeze, flowed north from the sea, pressing back the snow and spreading a warmth of color across the lands. Not far behind, the black wanderers followed. The trains of horse-drawn carts appeared on the roads of the land between the mountains, the exotic Fáel playing music and singing as they went as though they were the heralds of spring and hope returning.

There was much news to be spread that eventful year. The Duke of Vast had been found starving in a herdsman's hut, and had taken his own life. A great tremor had been felt one night, shaking the earth with a sound like thunder. An act of sorcery, some said, but little ill came of it. Lady Llyn Renné had wed Lord Carral Wills, and she was with child. Though the stories that she had been seen for some time wearing a mask of gold, and that when she removed it, all her burns were healed, were not widely believed.

In early summer a company of Fáel came up the north road and pitched their sculpted tents in the meadow by Telanon Bridge. When this news reached Tam he saddled the horse that had carried him home, took leave of his grandfather, and rode out through the stone gate.

Cynddl greeted him as he entered the encampment, appearing younger than Tam remembered, despite his gray hair and pale complexion.

"Tamlyn!" Cynddl called. "Have you come to travel the river?"

"Maybe one day," Tam answered, "but not today."

Tam jumped down from his horse and embraced the story finder, pounding him on the back.

"You look well," Cynddl said, as they released each other.

"So do you. I think you've grown younger."

Cynddl laughed. "It is the grey hair. No one can ever tell how old I really am. And how are Fynnol and Baore? Well, I hope?"

Tam touched a hand to Cynddl's shoulder. "I sent word to Fynnol, hoping you had come with the Fáel, but Baore . . . Baore died this winter."

Cynddl's hand went to his face. "He survived the swans' war. What could befall him in the Vale?"

"He fell through the ice crossing the lake one night. It was strange, as he knew the lakes better than anyone. But Baore had not done well after we returned. He sank into melancholy, and though Fynnol did everything he could to lift his mood, he slipped farther and farther into darkness."

Cynddl closed his eyes for a moment. "I hope your people honored him as he deserved," the Fáel whispered.

"It was a funeral filled with silence," Tam said. "Baore said little in life and we paid tribute to him in kind. Without a word being spoken, we poured Baore's ashes into the river, and they were borne away like a cloud on the wind."

"I thought we were all safe after Hafydd went on the pyre," Cynddl said softly. "But Baore never recovered after he met the nagar. I would have done anything to save him, but sometimes a man can be drowning in sight and can't be saved." He turned away for a moment, mastering his feelings.

"I'm sorry to bring you this news, Cynddl."

"Don't apologize. Bad news will find its way, my people say. It spoils my own tidings a little."

Tuath appeared across the green then, walking toward them, a winter spirit not yet banished by the change of season. She smiled at Tam and took his hands in the Fáel way. Then she took Cynddl's hand in her own with both pleasure and familiarity.

Cynddl looked very happy and proud. "We wed on New Year's Day—"

"Beneath a canopy, in the snow," Tuath said. "We thought it would be appropriate, somehow."

"Well, congratulations to you both!" Tam said, shaking Cynddl by the hand and kissing Tuath on the cheek. "But will you still go about the world collecting stories?"

"We're Fáel," Tuath said, shrugging. "It is in our nature to go traveling."

A meal was set at the traditional, low table, where they lounged upon cushions. Tam had almost forgotten how exotic Fáel food was. Fynnol had once said that after Fáel cooking, all food in the Vale tasted the same—mutton became indistinguishable from porridge. They ate and drank and talked of people they knew.

"Alaan hasn't been seen since you took your leave of the south, but Theason returned in the spring and reported that they found their way into the Stillwater, where Alaan spent some months studying the great enchantment before he remade the spell. When he finished, there was an earth tremor that was felt all across the south. Theason told us that Death is once again walled inside his kingdom."

"And what of Elise? Has anyone seen her?" Tam asked, hoping his inquiry sounded more casual than it was.

Cynddl shook his head. "No. But it has only been a few months since she went off to Speaking Stone."

Tam looked off to a group of Fáel children playing on the grass, turning cartwheels and climbing trees. "It isn't the best thing for Llya and Sianon to live there in isolation. Children need others of their kind."

"That's true, Tam," Cynddl said, "but there are no others of their kind. I think other children would shun them."

After the meal Tuath excused herself, and Cynddl took Tam for a walk. Out of habit, they both carried bows and swords, though it didn't seem likely that they would be needed there. The afternoon was warm, the new green spreading through the trees, warblers swarming from branch to branch. Among last season's rotting leaves, fiddleheads curled up, and snow blossoms appeared, scattered over the brown.

"Tell me; how fares Fynnol?" Cynddl asked, as they walked.

"I think poor Fynnol has become a man divided, both wanting to stay here, safe in the Vale, and wanting to go back to the courts of the south. When he learns that you're here I think he might decide to travel south with you, back to the old kingdom."

"Tuath and I should be glad of his company." Cynddl fell silent for a moment. "And you, Tam; how fare you after all your travels?"

"Well, I have not fared as poorly as Baore, but I will admit it hasn't been an easy winter. I suffer nightmares, and even in the day my mind strays often into dark paths—fighting the servants of Death in the Stillwater, standing before the final gate. I'm sometimes idle, and care little if I eat or sleep or venture out into the clear air and sunlight."

A look of concern crossed Cynddl's face. "I have found many a warrior's story, Tam, and I can tell you that few returned from battle unchanged. Men of heart and conscience do not pass through that crucible unscathed. But most heal. Perhaps not entirely, but they do find a kind of health again. I have had Tuath and Nann to help me, or I should have suffered more, I'm sure."

"My grandfather said much the same. It's been only a few months, after all. Wounds don't heal overnight."

"Perhaps you should make a journey down the river. New horizons might draw your thoughts away from dark places. I'm sure Eber would welcome you at Speaking Stone, not to mention a certain lady who dwells there."

"I'm not ready to leave the Vale just yet. I have this strange feeling, no doubt baseless, that I need to stay there to protect my people. Only Fynnol and I have fought in a war and understand how cruel outsiders can be."

Cynddl eyed him, weighing his words. "I think the Vale is safe, Tam. A'brgail's Knights have secured the roads of the old kingdom, and north of Willowwand we saw only two families traveling north, probably in search of gold and silver."

"Two families we can find room for," Tam said.

Cynddl seemed to be leading them somewhere, and finally he stopped by a small mound with an angled rock set into the earth at one end.

"Do you see this place, Tam?" Cynddl said. "It is where your father was buried."

"How do you know?"

"I'm a story finder, Tam. His story is here."

Tam felt a strange wash of emotion, as though he stood on the beach and was struck by the surf.

"I can tell you the story of how he died," Cynddl said, "if you wish."

Tam felt his head shake, and he closed his eyes. "I know how he died. He was murdered by brigands."

"There is another story to be found here, Tam; how this man had a wife and son he loved more than life."

Tam felt his eyes grow moist and warm. "Thank you Cynddl, but that story is known to me."

Cynddl nodded, gazing down at the sun-dappled grave, the scent of spring in the air. "Then there is one last thing to be done. I will sit here and tell the father his son's story. How he journeyed down the river and became a man among men of renown. How he gained the friendship of wanderers and noblemen, and traveled hidden roads to battle the servants of a sorcerer." Cynddl sat down on a bit of rock that broke through the soft forest floor.

Tam turned aside and made his way through the birch trees. Once, he glanced back to see the story finder seated among the snow drops and fallen leaves, speaking softly in the sunlight.

As Tam walked, the forest began to blur—a world viewed through rain-streaked glass. The murmur of Cynddl's ancient voice followed him, as though it issued up from the ground like a spring, whispering. Trees murmured their secret tales, and as he drew near Telanon Bridge, these voices flowed into the story of the river where they swirled away, spinning endlessly south toward the speaking sea.